The
Secret Hour

DOUBLEDAY LARGE PRINT HOME LIBRARY EDITION

BANTAM BOOKS

The
Secret Hour

LUANNE RICE

This Large Print Edition, prepared especially for Doubleday Large Print Home Library, contains the complete, unabridged text of the original Publisher's Edition.

THE SECRET HOUR
A Bantam Book

Published by Bantam Dell
A Division of Random House, Inc.
New York, New York

Book design by Virginia Norey

Bantam Books is a registered trademark of Random House, Inc., and the colophon is a trademark of Random House, Inc.

ISBN 0-7394-3196-X

Manufactured in the United States of America

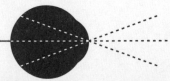

This Large Print Book carries the
Seal of Approval of N.A.V.H.

*For Irwyn Applebaum
and Bruce Springsteen*

acknowledgments

This novel took shape in stages, beginning in my childhood with the story of a murdered girl. Although I didn't know her, I have spent my life captivated by the small details I have learned along the way. I have thought of her always, and I think of her still.

I wish to thank Georgetown University Law Center for allowing me to sit in on classes in 1980. A writer can easily be taken for a law student, so I would find an empty chair and listen to the lectures and consider the ways in which law and fiction intersect. I especially loved evidence classes, where law was often stranger than fiction, but I thank all the professors for that wonderful opportunity to learn.

My gratitude to TGF, for making that experience possible.

My cousins, William J. Keenan Jr. and John T. Scully, both wonderful lawyers, have always been generous with their time—willing to discuss legal issues, baseball, and so much more with me—love and thanks to both (and to their wives and children and to all my other cousins.)

Much gratitude to Charles J. Irving, for all his support, for sharing his knowledge and trial experience, and for reviewing the documents.

Thanks to Mia Onorato for her seriously amazing manga. She is a great animator and storyteller.

Love and thanks to everyone at the Jane Rotrosen Agency and Bantam Books.

Epic gratitude to Karen Covert, Tim Donnelly, Jim Weikart, Jill Rick, Phyllis Mandel, and Trooper Robert J. Derry Jr.

Finally, to Dev Waldron and his house band, for coming over one summer night and putting on a concert to end all concerts, just when I needed it most. Thank you all for the laughter, love, and bar chords, not necessarily in that order.

The Secret Hour

chapter 1

The kitchen was quiet. The kids were trying so hard to help. Sitting at the breakfast table, his back to the cove, John O'Rourke tried to concentrate on the legal brief he'd stayed up last night finishing. Maggie buttered a piece of toast and slid it across the table. He accepted it, nodding thanks. Teddy hunched over the sports section, scowling at the scores, as if all his teams had lost. Brainer, the dog, lay under the table, growling happily as he gnawed an old tennis ball.

"Dad," Maggie said.

"What?"

"Are you finished reading yet?"

"Not quite, Mags."

"Is it about Merrill?"

John didn't respond at first, but his stomach twisted in a knot. He thought about his eleven-year-old daughter knowing about Greg Merrill, his all-time most time-consuming client, the Breakwater Killer, the star of Connecticut's death row and, as such, the talk of barrooms and courtrooms everywhere. John wanted people talking; it was part of his strategy. But he didn't want his daughter knowing.

"It is, honey," he said, lowering the brief.

"Are they going to kill him, Dad?"

"I don't know, Maggie. I'm trying to make it so they don't."

"But he deserves it," Teddy said. "For killing those girls."

"Everyone's innocent till proven guilty," Maggie intoned.

"He admits he's guilty," Teddy said, lowering the sports section. "He confessed." At fourteen, he was tall and strong. His eyes were too serious, his smile a shadow of the grin he used to flash before his mother's death. Sitting across the wide oak table, John reflected that Teddy would make a fine prosecutor.

"He did," John said.

"Because he did those things—murdered girls, ruined families. He deserves what's coming to him. Everyone says he does, Dad."

Outside, the wind blew, and a shower of autumn leaves fell from the trees.

John stared at his brief. He thought about the confession, the sentencing—to death by lethal injection—the months Greg Merrill had already spent on death row; and he thought of his current strategy—to argue before the Connecticut State Supreme Court that Merrill deserved a new sentencing hearing.

"Ruined families?" Maggie asked.

"Yes," Teddy said, glancing at his sister. "But don't worry, Maggie. He's in jail now. He can't hurt anyone anymore. People want to make sure it stays that way, which is why our phone rang ten times in the middle of the night—even though we have an unlisted number. You should hear what people say when we go by. They want you to stop what you're doing, Dad."

"Okay, Teddy," John said softly.

"But it's his job," Maggie said, her eyes

filling. "Why is it his fault, *our* fault, that he's just doing his *job*?"

"It's not your fault, Mags," John said, staring into her deep eyes. "Everyone in this country has rights."

She didn't reply, but nodded.

John took a slow breath in and out. This was his hometown, yet he felt the outrage of his friends and neighbors and strangers alike. Most of all he hated that his children were being made to suffer.

The critical issue in Merrill's case had always been his mental condition at the time of the crimes; John intended to argue that Greg Merrill suffered from a mental illness that made him physically unable to control his actions. His first act upon becoming Merrill's attorney was to engage a top psychiatrist—to examine his client and aid in his defense. John's unpopular work would, he hoped, result in Merrill's being resentenced to multiple life sentences without the possibility of release.

Teddy stared at his father, green eyes dark with gravity and sorrow. Maggie blinked, her blue eyes—the same shade, exactly, as Theresa's— framed by the raggedy bangs John had trimmed the night before. His daughter's bad haircut filled him with shame, and his son's solemn gaze seemed an admonishment of the worst, truest, most deserved kind. Since his mother's sudden death, Teddy had become the self-appointed protector of women everywhere.

"It's your job, right, Dad?" Maggie asked, squinting. "Protecting everyone's rights?"

"You'd better get ready for school," John said.

"I am ready," Maggie said, suddenly stricken.

John surveyed her outfit: green leggings, a blue skirt, one of Teddy's old soccer shirts. "Ah," John said, inwardly cursing the last baby-sitter for quitting, but—even more—himself for being so hard to work for. He'd called the employment agency, and they were supposed to send some new prospects out to interview, but with his track record and late hours, John would probably just work her ragged and blow the whole thing by Halloween. Maybe he should just move the whole family over to his father's house, let Maeve take care of them all.

"Don't I look good?" Maggie asked, frowning, looking down and surveying her ensemble.

"You look great," Teddy said, catching John's eye with a warning. "You'll be the prettiest girl in your class."

"Are you sure? Dad didn't even think I was ready for school—"

"Maggie, you look beautiful," John said, pushing the papers away and tugging her onto his lap.

She melted into his arms, still ready to cuddle at a moment's notice. John closed his eyes, needing the comfort himself. She smelled of milk and sweat, and he felt a pang, knowing he had forgotten to remind her to take a bath after the haircut.

"I'm not beautiful," she whispered into his neck. "Mommy was. I'm a tomboy. Tomboys can't be beautiful. They—"

The peace was shattered by breaking glass. Something flew through the kitchen window, skidding across the table, knocking milk and bowls and cereal all over, smashing into the opposite wall. John covered Maggie's body with his own as squares and triangles and splinters of glass rained down. His daughter squealed in terror, and he heard himself yelling for Teddy to get under the table.

When the glass stopped falling, the first

sound was Brainer barking, running from the broken picture window to the front door and back. A big wave crashed on the rocks outside, down by the beach; the sound, un-muffled by window glass, was startlingly loud. Maggie began to sob—whimpering at first, then with growing hysteria. Teddy crawled out from under the table, kicked glass away, and scuttled across the room.

"It was a brick, Dad," he called.

"Don't touch it," John said, still holding Maggie.

"I know. Fingerprints," Teddy said.

John nodded, realizing there wouldn't be any. People, even noncriminals, had gotten sophisticated about evidence. Even the local hotheads—whose prior worst crime might have been overzealous letters to the editor or loud protests outside court—had absorbed plenty of information about fin-gerprints and hair and fiber from the cop shows they watched and the legal thrillers they read.

Drops of blood splashed on the floor. Fo-cused, John examined his daughter to make sure she hadn't gotten cut. When she looked up into his face, her eyes widened with horror and she shrieked in his ear.

"Dad, you're cut!" she cried. Touching the side of his head, he felt a spot of warm liquid; grabbing a green-and-blue napkin, he held it against the gash. Teddy ran over, pushed Maggie aside, looked at his father's head. John rose and, holding his kids' hands, walked into the bathroom.

"It's not too bad," he said, peering at his reflection in the mirror. "Just superficial—looks a lot worse than it is."

"Oh, Mommy," Maggie cried spontaneously.

John hugged his daughter. His heart ached horribly for her. She missed her mother all the time, but something as traumatic as this was bound to bring thoughts of the accident back. He had brought this on himself. Wanting to salve his own wounds, he had taken on the busiest case in his career—not even two years after his children lost their mother. He was a selfish jerk, and his kids were hurting for it.

As if Teddy felt the same way, he edged John aside and took his sister's hand. Two spots of blood had stained her soccer jersey, and Teddy grabbed a washcloth and began to clean them off.

"I know you're a tomboy, Mags," he said,

"but people will think you got roughed up on the field if we let you go to school like that."

"I don't get roughed up," she sniffled.

"That's right," Teddy said, scrubbing the shirt. "Any roughing that gets done, you're the one doing it, right?"

"Right," she said, tears streaming from her clear blue eyes.

God help me, John thought, backing away. He touched the cut on the side of his head. Maybe it was deeper than he had first thought. It was bleeding more heavily now; he swore inwardly, not wanting to go to the emergency room for stitches. He had meetings scheduled at the office, as well as cases to read and the brief to finish.

The doorbell rang.

Had one of the kids dialed 911? Starting for the door, he stopped in the hallway. What if it was the person who had thrown the brick, one of the shoreline residents angry with him for pursuing Greg Merrill's emotionally charged case to the state supreme court?

Over the years, John O'Rourke had received many threats. His work made people angry. He represented citizens accused of the worst acts a human being could do. Their victims had families and friends, sweet lives and beautiful dreams. People saw John as a champion of monsters. He understood and respected the public's rage.

He knew someone could decide to come after him someday, wanting more than a conversation, but he didn't own a gun. On principle, but also out of healthy respect: As a criminal defense lawyer, he saw every day the damage that guns could do. Right now, remembering Maggie's terror, he hoped he wasn't wrong. Shaking from the attack in his kitchen only moments ago, he put his hand on the front doorknob, paused to gulp air, then yanked it open.

A woman stood on the top step. Dressed in a charcoal gray coat, appropriate for the chilly fall day, she had shoulder-length brown hair and eyes the color of river stones. Freckles dotted her nose. Her smile was fluid, but set—as if, waiting for him to open the door, she had determined to look friendly and pleasant. But upon seeing his face—his expression wild, he imagined, with blood streaming down the side of his head—her jaw dropped.

"Oh," she said, lurching back, then stepping forward. She reached up, as if she wanted to touch his cheek. "Are you okay?"

"Did you see anyone drive away?" he asked, looking up and down the quiet seaside street. Her car was parked in the road—a dark blue sedan.

"No," she said, those deep obsidian eyes peering up at him with marked concern. "I didn't. Shouldn't you sit down?"

John didn't reply. He leaned against the doorjamb. Strangers rarely rang his bell. More often, they called at night, while his family slept. Sometimes they wrote long, impassioned, well-reasoned but hateful letters. They hardly ever showed up, smiling, acting as if they cared.

"What is it?" he asked. "Can I help you?"

She laughed, a liquid trill that sounded so gentle and tender, it made him weak in the knees. He hardened his gaze. After Theresa, the sensation repulsed him, and he refused to let it get him.

"I think it is I who should be helping you . . ." she said, smiling, touching his elbow. Her voice was gentle, vaguely southern, reminiscent of Virginia or the Carolinas.

"Oh," he said, as she attempted to push

him down to sit on the step. She was a professional caregiver—it was written across her face, in her tone of voice, in her plain coat and sensible black leather shoes. She was a nanny, sent by the agency, to take over after the latest Baby-sitter X's defection. "Are you here for the position?"

"Let me help," she said softly as his knees buckled again and stars flashed before his eyes and the siren wailed up the street—brilliant, wonderful children; one of them had called the police—and John O'Rourke sat heavily on his stone steps and took her response as a "yes."

Thaddeus George O'Rourke had called the police, but he ignored their arrival. Maggie was a mess. He had to finish getting her ready for school, then get his own stuff together and make the bus—otherwise his father would have to drive him, and the middle school was out of his way.

"Maggie, you'd better take the shirt off and start over," he said, realizing the blood wouldn't come out.

"No way," she said. "You said I could wear it."

"I know, but those blood splotches make you look like State Exhibit Twenty-four. We'll wash it, and you can wear it tomorrow."

"That means next week—no one ever washes clothes around here," Maggie said. Then, catching Teddy's scowl, she tugged his sleeve. "Sorry," she said quickly. "It's not your fault. Or Dad's. I could learn how . . ."

"You're eleven," Teddy said, frustrated, resuming his efforts to clean the spots. "You're supposed to be playing, not doing laundry."

"Everyone has to pitch in," she said, casting a worried look toward the front hall, where deep voices were beginning to interrogate their father. "Do you think they'll do anything this time?"

"Sure," Teddy said.

"But they won't catch who did it, will they?"

"They might."

Brainer had run out to greet the police officers, and now he came bounding back to see Teddy and his sister. A huge golden retriever, he'd been part of the family since Teddy was nine. He was the best, smartest, coolest dog on the planet, and Teddy had named him himself. His fur used to be as smooth as silk, but that was before; now his coat was tangled, matted with burrs, twigs, and bits of dry seaweed. He nose-bumped Maggie, then leaned against Teddy for some reassuring pets.

"It's okay, boy," Teddy said, crouching down. "Good dog, Brainer."

The dog licked Teddy's face. Closing his eyes, Teddy rubbed the dog's soft fur. Brainer had always been insecure. He was superfriendly to strangers, but he always ran back to the family to get affirmation that he was good and brave enough. Kind of like Teddy himself, he thought. That's how he used to be when his mother was still alive. He'd go act all rough and tough on the soccer field, worrying the whole time that he was blowing the game. But then he'd climb into the car where she'd make him believe he was the best player on the field.

"Brainer could have gotten hurt," Maggie said sadly, scratching the retriever behind the ears. "Don't the brick-throwing people think of that?"

"No, they don't."

"But why? I don't get it. They hate Greg Merrill for hurting those girls, but they throw bricks through our window and don't care about hurting Brainer."

Or us, Teddy thought. He shivered, and he was glad he had his hands buried in the dog's thick fur so Maggie couldn't see them still shaking. Two policemen passed the door, on their way to see the broken window, and he heard them say, "What does he expect?" Teddy's stomach tightened the way it did when he was out with his father and someone stared them down.

Or called his father "Counselor" in a sarcastic way. Or, the worst, the time he and his father had been waiting in line at Paradise Ice Cream and the sweet-looking little old lady had walked over, smiling, to ask, "Do you think Anne-Marie Hicks would like to have a nice ice cream right now?" Anne-Marie Hicks was one of Greg Merrill's victims. The police officers paused, glancing in at Teddy and Maggie. He wouldn't give them the satisfaction of looking up.

"Teddy?" Maggie asked, her voice dropping so the officers wouldn't hear her.

"Yeah."

"How come Dad represents him? *Really?*" she asked, frowning. The age-old question. Teddy had asked it when he was her age, only back then the defendant had been someone else.

"Like you said yourself before, it's his job."

"Why doesn't he represent innocent people instead?"

Teddy laughed, throwing the wadded-up washcloth into the sink. He was giving up on the bloodstains; let Maggie wear the dirty shirt if she wanted. Their father's voice rose, talking to the cops in the front hall. The crisis was over—no one was hurt, and the police were on the case.

"Why are you laughing?" she asked.

"I was just thinking," he said. "Of telling you to ask Dad that question."

"Why? Because you think he should, right? Only represent good people who didn't do it?"

Teddy's spine tingled again, thinking of that old lady at Paradise Ice Cream. After she'd said that, he had gone online and looked up the murdered girls. Anne-Marie Hicks had been seventeen. Her high-school yearbook picture had been posted, showing blond hair that slanted across her eyes, seven earrings in her left ear, four in her right, and a huge smile revealing braces and a little gap between her front teeth.

"Right, Teddy? That's why you think I should ask Dad?"

Teddy felt another pull deep inside, remembering how their mother had sat with their father for hours, rubbing his shoulders while he wrote briefs and studied legal documents, getting ready for the murderers' trials, supporting him no matter what she felt about the cases.

"Tell me, Teddy!"

Smiling into his sister's anxious blue eyes, so innocent and worried, he felt like crying, but laughed again. "Mags, I think you should ask Dad why he represents guilty clients because I'd love to hear the lecture he'd give you."

"Lecture?"

"Yeah. All about 'the miracle at Philadelphia that resulted in the Constitution, the Sixth Amendment, and a defendant's right to counsel. . . .' Yay, team. And then he'll tell you about Oliver Wendell Holmes and how law is 'a magic mirror' . . . where we get to see our own lives reflected. Just ask. You'll get Dad going, and he won't stop till dinner."

"I wish he would," she whispered, burying her face in Brainer's matted fur. "Not stop till dinner. Never leave . . ."

Teddy stopped laughing. He figured it was the same for Maggie as it was for him: Ever since their mother's death, he hadn't wanted to let their father out of his sight. He listened to the voices in the hall. His father was trying to be friendly to the officers—people he grilled mercilessly when he got them on the witness stand—and the police were treating him coolly back. Maggie had heard, too. When she lifted her head, her eyes swam with tears.

"It's okay, Maggie," Teddy said, pulling her into a hug. Her thin body trembled in his arms. Her hair looked terrible, as if their father had taken nail scissors to it. It was dirty—just a few hours away from being greasy—and she smelled funny. She smelled like an under-the-bed mixture of dust and sneakers. She smelled like Brainer, tangled and stuck with dried leaves and seaweed without their mother to lovingly brush him every day.

Teddy wanted Maggie to smell like lemons and lavender, just like their mother had. He wanted her to have clean hair and straight bangs. She cried, missing their mother as much as Teddy did, and he held her closer as the policemen passed by again, whispering into her ear, "Don't cry, okay? You're my girl, Mags. My best girl in the world."

Maggie didn't like the noise. The siren, first of all, but then the police radios squawking like trapped mice. Poor little animals caught inside a speaker box, wanting to get out and run home to their mamas.

She didn't mind the actual police officers. Most of them were nice—to her. They smiled, crouched down to say hi, asked her how was school or was she hoping to be the next Mia Hamm. The soccer jersey, of course. She just acted polite, not bothering to explain that the jersey was her brother Teddy's, that she wore it because it was like taking a little bit of him to school with her.

The reason she was so polite, and the reason all the police officers made her heart hurt, was that they didn't like her father. She thought that maybe if she was very kind, quiet, and well-mannered, the officers would see that her father was a very good man. Didn't they know what it was like for him, raising his children all alone? But the policemen didn't care about that. They were like most of the people around: All they knew about her father was that he was the lawyer for Greg Merrill.

Maggie understood all this. Teddy thought he was shielding her from knowing, but she knew anyway. She'd grown up fast since their mother died. She was eleven, but she felt old. She figured she probably felt twenty. Old and tired inside, wound up like a kid outside. She had come flying out to the porch, just to give Teddy a chance to get ready for school: to let him off the hook from having to take care of her.

Her father sat in a chair, being examined by an EMT. Maggie sidled closer. She wanted to make sure the cut wasn't deep and deadly. Their mother had died in a car accident, and at first the EMT's had thought she would be okay. Her car had hit a deer, then crashed into a tree. She had been on the Shore Road, just past the police station, and help had arrived immediately. The EMT said she had stood up, walked over to the animal to see if it was still alive, and then sat down because she was feeling dizzy.

Maggie could see all this in her mind, even though she hadn't been there. She could see her mother in her blue dress and white sandals. The moon had been full that night. It was July, and her mother had had a sunburny tan that glowed in any light—even moonlight. Her sun-streaked hair would have been windblown, from the car window being open. Her lipstick had been fresh and pink—she had heard her dad say that to Gramps.

Maggie sometimes forgot what she knew and what she had been told. So much about her parents she just *knew*—held deep inside, the way she knew how to breathe, the way she remembered every day how to walk and ride a bike. But some of this story had come from her father, from so long trying to make sense of the fact her mother was no longer here.

Was no longer anywhere.

The part about the EMT's thinking she was fine. They had examined her. She wasn't cut anywhere, but they had taken her blood pressure and listened to her heart, thought she was okay, but told her to stay still anyway. An ambulance was coming. It would take her to the hospital, where doctors would check her out thoroughly.

Her mother had laughed. (Was that the story or something Maggie just knew? It was so there, in Maggie's mind, the image of her mother's blue eyes wide and amused, her throat rippling with soft laughter.) "I'm fine," she had said, concern replacing the amusement. "But what about the deer? Should we call a vet—to put it out of its misery?" And she had gotten up to go see if the deer—a female whitetail—was in any pain.

And she had sat down. Just like that: a sigh, and she had sunk onto the ground, leaning against a tree as if suddenly exhausted. As if the whole thing—being out so late at night, too late to put Maggie to bed and kiss her goodnight, driving home in the moonlight, hitting the whitetail deer, hearing the waves on the rocks like the thump of blood in her ears—as if it all had simply been too much.

Thinking of her mother, Maggie saw her father tilt his head so the EMT could better examine his cut head. The whole time, police officers were talking. "An eye for an eye," one of them was saying. "Seven girls in the ground, a brick through the window, you do the math."

"I have two children," her father shot back. "Watch what you say."

"Seven girls," the policeman said, holding the brick in what looked like a huge Baggie but which Maggie understood to be an evidence bag.

"He's been cut," a woman said. "Take care of him and lose the attitude." Her voice was sharp, with a different accent, and made Maggie look. For some reason, Maggie hadn't noticed her before. She'd been standing at the door, dressed in a dark gray coat with straight brown hair touching her shoulders, but now she moved toward Maggie's father, as if she wanted to protect him. Was she a detective? Or another lawyer? She was pretty and plain at the same time.

"Who are you?" the head officer asked.

"She's from the employment agency," Maggie's father said, prodding the side of his head—no longer bleeding—with two fingers. "She arrived just after the incident, but she didn't see anyone."

"That's right," the woman said, her voice edgy, as if she didn't like the cops being mean to Maggie's father. "I didn't see a soul."

"Pity," the cop said, but Maggie no longer cared about the officers' sarcasm or meanness to her father. Her attention was pulled to the woman. She gazed down at Maggie's father, her expression something between a frown and a look of pure worry. Maggie must have been staring so intensely the woman felt it. Because suddenly she raised her eyes, looked across the room, locked her gaze with Maggie's, and gave her a wonderful smile.

She was their new baby-sitter.

Maggie's heart kicked over. They had had so many. Roberta, Virginia, Dorothy, Beth, and Cathy. None of them were bad, but none of them lasted. The job was too hard. Maggie's father worked such long, intense hours, he needed someone extra responsible to take up the slack. Someone extra smart, extra nice, extra good, someone who cared when their father had a cut on his head and gave Maggie a great, huge smile to let her know everything would be okay.

Let her be our baby-sitter, Maggie thought. She liked the woman's eyes—dark blue-gray, like the Sound at night. But, oh!

Turning her head, now her eyes caught the light and looked deep green, like a river. Her eyes were alive and deep, filled with the kind of mystery that would make her a good storyteller. Maggie didn't care about how the laundry was done, and she didn't care whether eyes were blue or green. She cared about stories.

Mrs. Wilcox, the next-door neighbor, opened her front door and walked down the sidewalk. The police stopped her, asking questions about what she'd seen and heard.

"You need stitches, Counselor," the EMT said, making notes on his pad.

"It's nothing," her father said.

"Hey, you want a scar to make you look tough around the creeps you see in prison, that's your deal. But you're gonna have to sign off on it—acknowledging that you're denying my first-rate medical advice."

Seeing her father reach for the pen, Maggie's heart stopped.

"No," she whispered.

Only she must have screamed, because every single person in the room turned to look at her, and Mrs. Wilcox gasped. Brainer came tearing in from the den, straight to her side.

"Maggie, I'm okay," her father said, smiling to reassure her. Streaks of blood were drying on the side of his face, on his white dress shirt.

"Yeah, he is," the EMT said, trying to set her at ease. "I was just busting him—don't worry."

Her father pushed off with his right hand, standing up, and Maggie felt the sob tear through her lungs, screaming through her skin. "DON'T STAND UP!" she cried. "Let them take care of you! Don't walk, Daddy!"

"Maggie, I'm fine," he said, grabbing for her. "It's not like your mother—it's just a superficial cut—nothing serious at all."

"Sit down, Daddy," Maggie wept, pushing him onto the couch. "Please, please. Let them take care of you! Please, Daddy, please!"

"Maybe she's right," the woman, the baby-sitter, said softly. "Why don't you just do that? Sit down a minute . . . and let them give you the stitches. It would make her feel better."

Maggie cried and shuddered, feeling her father's arms around her, hearing the

woman's quiet voice and somehow suddenly, completely, loving her for it. This
stranger had come out of nowhere that awful, bloody Tuesday morning to take care of
their family. She was saving her father's life.

"What's your name?" Maggie heard her
father ask in that flat, unfriendly way that
made him sound like the lawyer no one
liked, the hard-planed voice designed to
drive everyone away from him, from them,
and leave the O'Rourke family alone with
their private tragedy and dirty clothes.

"Kate," she said. "Kate Harris."

"Fine, Kate Harris," Maggie's father said,
his voice just as flat but even icier than before, a frozen lake of a voice. "I'll have the
stitches, but you'll have to get them off to
school. Maggie and Teddy. Mrs. Wilcox, can
you help her out?"

"Of course, John," Mrs. Wilcox said.

"We'll have to work out the details afterward," Maggie's father said.

"You're on," Kate Harris said, and Maggie
suddenly felt a hand on her head. The fingers were light and cool, and they moved
down to take her hand, gently easing her
away. Maggie didn't even put up a fight.

She drifted out of her father's embrace.

He was watching her, and she felt him wanting to take it back—not get stitches, but walk her to the bus stop and then hurry to his office. Maggie's stomach was in a knot, but Kate Harris crouched down to look her in the eye and melt the knot away.

"He's going to be fine," she said. "He'll be very brave and let them stitch him up. When they're done, they might even give him a lollipop."

"Why?" Maggie asked, her mouth tugging up in a smile.

"To treat him, for doing the right thing even though he doesn't want to do it."

"I don't want a lollipop," her father said, sounding as sullen as Teddy did when he had to do the dishes.

"You might not want one," Kate Harris said, her smile so pretty and gentle it pulled Maggie even closer to her, "but you might need it. A little sweet now and then never hurt anyone. Right, Maggie?"

"Right," Maggie breathed. Her eyes filled with tears, but for the first time in longer than she could remember, from happiness. Kate Harris was her new baby-sitter. She had landed on their doorstep, just like Mary Poppins or a new baby, just like a basket filled with the most beautiful summer flowers imaginable.

"Right," her father said, his voice very edgy and hard, but it didn't matter. Kate Harris had gotten him to sit still and get stitched, taken care of by the proper authorities, so he didn't stand up, sit down, and suddenly die—just like Maggie's mother.

Kate Harris had just saved her father's life, and Maggie loved her for it.

chapter 2

Kate watched the lawyer climb into the back of the ambulance, waving wanly at his children as it pulled away. Stitches were in order; also X rays and perhaps even a CT scan, to determine the extent of the damage. Veins, arteries, blood vessels in the head: wouldn't want to overlook anything.

"Can't we go to the emergency room with him?" Maggie asked.

"Better not," Kate said. "Didn't he say something about school?"

"Yes, he did," the neighbor woman said. Maggie said nothing, watching the street. The ambulance had long since turned the corner, but Maggie stared intently, as if she could see ghosts hovering in the cold October air.

"I'll never be able to concentrate in school," Maggie said. "Till I know how he is."

"Come on, Mags," said her brother—Teddy, older by three years, according to the newspaper clippings—tugging her into the front door. Kate watched them go. She yearned to follow—to stand inside the house, to look around, to feel so close—but the neighbor was standing right there beside her. The dog stood inside, a beautiful golden, his coat matted with mud and burrs. Kate thought of Bonnie romping through thorny seaside fields, felt a pang in her heart.

"So," the woman said, staring at Kate with steady, warm but wary eyes.

"So," Kate said.

"You have no idea what he's been through," the woman said. "All of them, really. We like to think the children are resilient, will bounce back quickly, but how can they, after losing their mother so young? And then, to think of someone attacking them this way—"

"Who do you think did it?"

"Could be anyone," the woman said. "The papers are full of stories, every day. . . . This is a small town, and people know where John lives. They drive by all the time. Some yell horrible things."

"Breach of privacy," Kate murmured, feeling herself redden.

"Yes. Terrible—regardless of how you feel about Merrill. I would give him the dose myself, personally, if they'd let me. What he did . . . but never mind. John's a hometown boy. I've known him his whole life—he followed in his father's footsteps and became a fine lawyer. He's doing what he thinks is right—don't let it get in the way of you taking this job. I'm Ethel Wilcox, by the way."

"Kate Harris," she said, shaking hands, surprised by the strong grip. The woman was in her seventies, and she was dressed like someone who'd spent five decades as a suburban mom: navy blue slacks, navy blue cardigan, small gold watch, brand-new Reeboks, short gray hair.

"You seem like a serious person," Ethel said, giving Kate the once-over. "And I hope you are. Because I can't bear to see these people let down again."

"Let down?"

"By someone who doesn't intend to stay."

Kate took a deep breath. She was in difficult territory. Being interrogated—by a nosy, if caring, neighbor, no less—had not been part of this morning's plan. But Ethel Wilcox was staring at her as if she could read her mind, as if she had summed her up and realized she was all wrong for the O'Rourke family, so Kate stood up taller, her eyes direct and steady.

"I intend to stay," she said, bending the truth.

"Good," Mrs. Wilcox said, her mouth twitching, lifting in a smile that grew stronger. Kate felt a kick in the stomach, but she nodded in something like partnership with the woman next door.

"Well, I'd better get them off to school," Kate said.

"Would you like some help?" Mrs. Wilcox asked. "I'm sure John wouldn't expect you to do it without help the first time, and since he's not here . . ."

"I'm sure I can handle it," Kate said, smiling, looking—she hoped—convincingly relaxed.

Mrs. Wilcox peered into the front door,

saw the two kids rummaging through their book bags. "Well, if I didn't have plans to go to Newport, I'd stay and help you anyway. But if you're sure . . ." The police had finished their work inside, and came out onto the porch. They had a few questions for Mrs. Wilcox; she looked at her gold watch and said she had fifteen minutes before her friend came to pick her up.

Kate nodded, inching away. She put her hand on the doorknob.

She stood at the threshold: not just of the house, but of something more. The children's voices—bickering, rising in volume— came through the screen. The hallway was in shadow, dark and filled with mystery and a weird sort of hope. Turning her head, she saw blue sky, high clouds, her car, the road. She could just climb right in, drive away before anything got started.

"Kate?"

Jumping, she turned to look back inside. The children stood there, holding their book bags, watching her. The dog wagged its tail. Her heart was like a small bird, caught in her chest, trying to get out. She felt it beating against her ribs, her collarbones, her throat.

"Kate?" Maggie asked again. "Aren't you coming in?"

Kate stared down at her feet. The toes of her black loafers touched the threshold. All she had to do was step over. The big yellow dog waited inside, his tongue hanging out in a big grin. And so, looking into Maggie's eyes, smiling, Kate turned the knob.

"Yes, I am," she said, and walked into the house.

"Should we call you Kate? Or Mrs. Harris?" Maggie asked.

The lady laughed. She was pretty, and when she shook her head, her straight brown hair swung around her face from side to side; Teddy O'Rourke watched, mesmerized.

"I'm not 'Mrs.'," she said. "Call me Kate— is that okay?"

"Sure," Maggie said. "We called the other baby-sitters by their first names, right, Teddy?"

"Yes," he said.

"Good," she said. "Now what?"

"Well, school," Teddy said, alert.

"Right. Of course. I knew that. So, what do we do to get you to school?"

"Bus," Teddy said. Was she kidding?

"Do you take the same bus? Or . . ." Assessing their ages, she looked from Teddy to Maggie and back again. "Different ones? There was only one bus for all the kids where my sister and I went to school . . ."

"Different ones," Teddy said.

"Of course. I should have guessed. Okay. And what about . . ." She looked down at Maggie, straight at her wrinkled and now bloody soccer shirt.

"I'm not changing, Kate," Maggie said, hugging the shirt's folds of fabric around her.

"No," Kate said. "Who would? Great shirt."

Maggie's mouth flickered in a smile. Teddy had been stiff, on guard, since the brick came through the window. Having this new baby-sitter show up so suddenly—looking more like an associate at his father's law firm than any child-care person he'd ever seen, and not knowing about school—had made him feel funny, kind of suspicious. But making Maggie smile like this won her many points.

"Five minutes till your bus, Maggie," Teddy said, checking his book bag, pulling their jackets down off the coatrack.

"Hmmm," Maggie said, bending down to nuzzle Brainer.

"Should I walk you to the bus stop?" Kate asked.

"Thisssisssbrrrnnnnrrrrrrrrrrr," Maggie said with her face buried in the thick fur, and as Kate looked confused, Teddy translated.

"She says, 'This is Brainer,' " he said, tugging on his sister's arm.

"Would Brainer like to walk to the bus too?" Petting the dog, Teddy watched Kate's fingers catch in a twig-and-thorn fur tangle. She tried to gently work them out, and Teddy had a quick picture of his mother doing the same thing.

"Imntttttttgooonggggggtossscchoooooolllllll," Maggie said, face pressed into Brainer's back.

"Yes, you are," Teddy said. "Do you want to stay back?"

"What did she say?" Kate asked.

This time Teddy didn't even have to interpret. Because Maggie raised her head, looked Kate straight in the eye, and said, "I'm not going to school." Just then her school bus pulled down the block. Teddy heard it slow down for Maggie, then accelerate and drive away.

Teddy felt panic rise in his chest. Maggie missed too much school. She was always faking a sore throat or stomachache, just to stay home. This time, she wasn't even pretending. Their father would be upset when he got home from work—Teddy knew he'd go straight to the office from the emergency room. The worst part was, Teddy couldn't even stay around to fix it; his own bus would be there in four minutes, and he had to leave.

"Maggie, I'll drive you," Kate said.

"Come on, Maggie, get ready," Teddy said sharply, gathering up her knapsack and holding out her down jacket. "You're going to school."

Maggie sat down hard, arm clenched around Brainer's neck. Her face was red, scrunched up, reminding Teddy of when she'd been a baby. Maggie had cried a lot. She'd always been too sensitive to hot and cold, to being hungry, to needing more sleep. Right now, she was being too sensitive to having their father at the hospital with a cut head. Maggie's tears were huge and clear, the biggest tears Teddy had ever seen.

"I'm . . . not . . . going to school . . ." she sobbed, "until . . . I . . . know . . . Daddy's okay!"

"He's fine," Teddy said, crouching down, feeling the panic again. He had to reassure his sister, so he would believe it himself. "It was just a little cut."

"Mommy wasn't even bleeding," she gasped. "They said she looked perfect . . . there wasn't a bit of blood anywhere . . . but she just sat down and died."

"That was different," Teddy said, feeling ice in the pit of his stomach. "Mommy was in a car accident. She had internal injuries."

Maggie just squeezed her eyes shut, unable to keep those big tears from popping through.

"Come on, Teddy—here comes your bus," Kate said gently. Teddy felt her hand on his shoulder. It felt so small and warm, but so solid, he wished she would hold on forever. He wanted to close his eyes and disappear into the feeling, but Maggie needed him. So he stayed focused, staring at his sister.

"Maggie," he said. "Don't miss school."

"I don't care about school," she wept.

"Teddy," Kate said, insistent. "She'll be okay. I hear your bus."

Crouching on the floor, Teddy felt torn. He was on track for getting high honors this term—his progress report had shown straight A's. He had perfect attendance, the first time since his mother had died. Today they were having elections for the eighth-grade dance committee.

But how could he leave his sister with this stranger? She said she was their baby-sitter, but she'd seemed so vague about school. Teddy was clear about reality: His father was a top defense lawyer, so he knew the world was filled with killers, rapists, thieves, and victims.

Kate didn't seem like any of those, but people said that Greg Merrill had seemed like the boy next door. That he had an open face, a friendly smile; that he'd gone to UConn and worked on the school paper. That he had made money house-sitting and walking people's dogs. People had trusted him to do that.

Outside, Teddy's bus rumbled up the block. He heard it stop at the stop sign. If he stood up now, he'd make it. Kate's hand was still on his shoulder. She squeezed, pulling him to his feet.

They were about the same height: The realization surprised him, giving him a jolt. Although she was an adult and he was only fourteen, Teddy looked straight into her eyes—dark green, shining like clear water. Teddy swallowed, waiting.

"I know, Teddy," she whispered.

Teddy was frozen, captured in the moment with Kate Harris. Her river eyes glistened.

"You know what?" he whispered back.

"About loving your sister . . . about how you'd do anything for her."

"I would," he said, casting a glance down at Maggie, still clutching the dog—poor patient Brainer, his once soft coat studded with dry rockweed, thorns, and probably ticks. The hopelessness welled up inside Teddy, and he forced himself to swallow it down.

"I would do the same for mine," Kate said. "Anything, Teddy. I know just how you feel."

"I can't go to school," Teddy said, his throat so thick he could hardly talk. "If she doesn't."

"Oh, Teddy," Kate said, her cool water eyes warming up, making her smile. "That's where you're wrong. See, you're her big brother. She looks up to you. You have to be an example, to show her how things are done."

He heard the school bus pull out from the stop sign; slowly, it approached the house.

"One day won't matter," Teddy said unsurely, looking down at his sister.

"You can trust me," Kate said. "To take good care of her. That's what this is about, isn't it? You don't want to leave her with me?"

"I don't know you," Teddy said, meeting her eyes. The bus slowed down, gears grinding.

"You're a good brother," Kate said. "You love your sister the way I love mine."

He nodded.

"So go to school. Be strong—for her. No matter how hard it gets, show up. I promise you I'll take care of her. You don't have to worry about that."

The bus stopped outside. Teddy's fingers twitched on his backpack. Maggie huddled with Brainer, face still hidden in his horrible messy fur.

"Get your face out of there," he said, yanking his sister's shoulder. "You want to get a tick bite on your face? Or scratched with goddamned thorns?"

"I don't care if Brainer's messy," Maggie cried out. "So am I. We're the same!"

"That dog needs a bath," Teddy said, his teeth gritted. "I swear, I'm skipping practice tonight to give him one. I'm gonna get rid of every tick, every goddamn tangle."

"Don't do that, Teddy," Kate said softly. "Take care of yourself. I'll take care of Maggie and Brainer."

"Because you took care of your sister?"

Kate nodded. "And her dog."

She stared at Teddy, and suddenly Teddy knew: They were the same. Kate was older, she was a woman and a stranger, but she and Teddy were exactly alike in the way that mattered.

Teddy had no doubt that Kate was telling the truth: She loved her sister.

And she would take care of Maggie—till Teddy got home from school, till their father came home from work. The bus driver blew his horn.

"Okay," Teddy said, making up his mind

as the driver gunned the engine, starting to pull away.

Kate threw open the door. "WAIT!" she called.

The bus stopped. Teddy pulled on his jacket, hoisted his backpack. Maggie refused to look up. Words caught in Teddy's throat. He touched his sister's hair—nearly as grungy as Brainer's—and backed away.

"You're my girl, Mag," he said.

She didn't reply, didn't raise her head. Kate held the door open, and Teddy ran down the steps. He tore across the yard, noticing the driver's open mouth, curious expression—the kitchen window was jagged with broken glass. Jumping up the bus's step, Teddy turned to look back at his house. Yellow leaves rained down from the trees in the yard.

Kate stood in the door.

Cold October sunlight struck her face, her brown hair. Her eyes glinted in the slightest of smiles as she petted Brainer. Teddy stared as he made his way to his seat, remembering all the times his mother had stood in the doorway, waving and smiling as the bus pulled away; Brainer had been silky and golden back then. Maggie chose that moment to peer around from behind Kate and wave.

Kate didn't wave. Neither did Teddy. They were both staring at each other, but he had the feeling they were thinking of other people. Other people they missed, who weren't there anymore.

The bus sped up, rounding the corner where the seawall dropped down to the rocky beach and breakwater, past the dirt road leading to the tall and lonely lighthouse, and Teddy's big white house disappeared from sight.

The ER was a hive of activity. If John O'Rourke were another type of lawyer, he could be drumming up business left and right. In Exam Room 1, an old woman who had slipped and fallen at All-Save, was waiting to have her hip x-rayed; Exam Room 2 contained a child whose inhaler had failed, on oxygen and a heart monitor; Exam Room 4 held a drug addict, thrashing and moaning in withdrawal, waiting for a bed to become available in the detoxification unit. Pain equaled lawsuits.

John, in Exam Room 3, heard everything.

Waiting for the next in a parade of doctors, he tried to read the brief he'd brought from home. His head spun, and he felt sick to his stomach. Lowering the document, he could practically see his desk calendar looming before him and thought of how he didn't have time for this.

Why couldn't he at least have gotten the kids off to school? In the midst of life's total insanity, he calmed himself by knowing he was a good father. Okay, so he gave crummy haircuts. But he had the main bases covered: food, shelter, carpooling. Child care. He hoped Kate Harris would turn out to be the best Baby-sitter X so far.

"Hello, good morning," a technician said, holding a wire mesh basket of vials. "The doctor sent me to get your blood. Roll up your right sleeve."

John complied, staring at the needle. His stomach flipped—he had always hated needles. When his kids got injections, cheering them to be brave, John would feel queasy inside. "Uh," John said, stalling for time, "any idea when I can get out of here?"

The technician chuckled. "What, you've got something more important than your health to worry about?" She glanced at his cut; a doctor smelling of coffee and peanut butter had closed it with cool hands. The local anesthetic was wearing off, and the sutures pulled his skin.

The technician was taking her time. Had she recognized him? Was she going to stick him extra hard because he was Greg Merrill's lawyer? John gritted his teeth, waiting for the sting.

Bang—the needle pricked his skin. He looked down at his blood, flowing through the tiny tube. Whoa—he felt like he was going to faint. Another reason his kids would laugh—to know that their dad hated the sight of blood. He looked away, up at the ceiling, felt immediately better, and then was hit with a memory of Theresa.

They'd brought her here after the accident.

John had been home with the kids. He had gotten the phone call, left Teddy to watch his sister, sped here to the hospital. Walking through the wide doors, into the bright room, running to the desk . . .

John had known even before they told him: His wife was dead.

It was one of those freak things: Although she had walked away from the wreck, hadn't gotten even one cut on the outside of her body, her chest had slammed into the steering wheel. The impact had severed an artery in her heart—cut it right in half—so she'd bled to death by the time the cardiac team even started their work.

His beautiful wife. His golden-haired, blue-eyed Theresa. Such an old-fashioned, sturdy name for such a delicate, porcelain-skinned girl. She had been wearing such bright pink lipstick the night she died. Such shiny, cool, freshly applied lipstick . . . The memory of it jabbed him, unexpectedly, like a knife in the ribs.

"Mr. O'Rourke?" the doctor said now, coming around the curtain with John's chart in his hand.

"Yes?" John asked, dazed, still rocked by the sudden vision of Theresa's lips.

"Your films look fine. There's no sign of concussion, although I'd like you to take it easy for the rest of the day and watch for symptoms. You're going to have a bad bruise—that can't be avoided, and I've called for a consult with a plastic surgeon," the doctor said.

"A what?"

"A plastic surgeon. The cut was deep,

and you're going to have a nasty scar. Might as well get it looked at now so you don't regret it later."

John shook his head, already reaching for his file. "That's okay. I'll live with it," he said, thinking suddenly of the cop's bitter remark about a scar helping him to fit in at the prison.

He signed the necessary release forms. Bending over the desk, he felt some of the staff watching him. When he pushed the papers across the desk and said thank you, he heard one secretary say to the other, "I wonder if he knows that one of the girls died here." "After the killer left her for dead," the other said, in a much louder voice.

John's head began to pound. *It's a hospital,* he told himself. *Many people die here. Theresa . . .* He walked fast, out the wide doors. The autumn day was bright and crisp; the cool air slicing into his central nervous system, shooting his alertness up a notch.

Patting his pockets for car keys, heading for the parking garage, he remembered his ride in the ambulance. Instead, he caught a cab dropping someone off. At first he gave the address of his office, then changed his mind and told the driver to take him home, to change out of his bloody shirt.

Settling back, with nothing to do but be driven, the names came.

Antoinette Moore, he thought. She was the one who had died at Shoreline General. John knew the case, the women, so well; they were inside him now, with him at all times. Antoinette, known as Toni . . . nineteen years old. A sophomore at Bushnell College, a long-distance runner in training for her first marathon. Petite, wiry, with short dark hair. Parents in Akron, Ohio. An older brother, two younger sisters.

A close family, and they had sent her to Connecticut to die.

She hadn't, at first. Merrill's pattern had been to wait until the waves came lapping at his victims' mouths, until they were about to bleed to death or drown, but that day he miscalculated the tide, and Toni became the only one of Greg's victims to live long enough to be rescued.

He had left her, like the others, in a breakwater—in this case, a stone-and-wood jetty on private property, jutting into Stonington Harbor. He had slit her throat, wedged her between the weathered boards at the end of the jetty, and waited for the tide to take her away.

He hadn't counted on her amazing strength, on her marathon-woman determination. Toni had hauled herself out of the wet-wood grave, throat bleeding, to crawl into the air, into plain sight. A lobsterman checking his pots had seen her, his attention caught by the crimson streaming from her body, thinking at first that one of his red buoys had gotten snagged in the jetty.

She had died at Shoreline General, forty-five minutes later, without ever regaining consciousness.

John closed his eyes, picturing Toni's face from the pictures in his file. The floodgates were now open: The other names and faces and facts came flowing through.

Anne-Marie Hicks: seventeen, five foot four inches, curly blond hair, braces on her teeth, disappeared one April afternoon, her body found snagged in fishing lines.

Terry O'Neal: twenty-two, model, pretty, darkly intelligent eyes, never made it to work at her father's insurance agency, body found by two boys crabbing off the Hawthorne Town Dock.

Gayle Litsky: eighteen, long blond hair,

taking time off from college and living back home with her parents, last seen heading to the movies, body found wedged in the rocks of a Black Hall breakwater.

Jacqueline Rey, fourteen, only child and spitting image of her bright-eyed single mother, missing for four nights before being found among the timbers of the Easterly Yacht Club jetty.

Beth Nastos, twenty, bookkeeper at Nastos Seafood, tall and slender with a shy smile, body hidden—more cruelly, perhaps, than any other—in the stone-and-steel breakwater of her family's century-old Mount Hope fishing business.

Patricia McDiarmid, twenty-three, newly married mother of one, murdered in her workout clothes and stashed in a tunnel under Exeter's concrete State Pier.

Never a day went by without John thinking of the victims. At first they had visited him in his dreams, one by one, and he had begged them to tell him what they wanted while he, in turn, had asked them for something in return: forgiveness. He had wanted them to forgive him for defending their killer. This was his town, and he loved the people in it.

Everyone thought defense lawyers were tough and thick-skinned, so intent on obtaining victory for their clients and headlines for their own careers, that they forgot about the victims and their families. John was the son of a judge. He had grown up sitting in the back row of his father's courtroom, watching townsfolk brought before the bench. So many secrets and sorrows went on behind the closed doors of Connecticut's fine homes—John's father had taught him to understand and even love his neighbors for their complicated, not always tidy lives, and he understood that justice and life were more complicated than people wanted to believe.

"This is it," he said to the cabdriver as they pulled up in front of his house. John looked through the window at the big white house, stone walls, and tall, old trees. The sugar maple—Theresa's favorite—had turned brighter red during the cold night, approaching its peak. On the headland a quarter mile away, the lighthouse gleamed white in the cold sunshine. A patrol car cruised slowly by.

We had it all covered, the four musketeers . . . he thought, taking it all in. Thinking of his high school friends, all of whom had remained local, he was unexpectedly flooded by emotion.

John, the son of a judge, had become a lawyer. Billy Manning, son of a cop, had become a cop. And Barkley Jenkins, whose father had been the last lightkeeper, now ran an inn and had a contract to keep the automated lighthouse in working order.

Theresa had been the fourth musketeer: From the day they had started dating in sophomore year, John had never wanted to be without her. Although Billy and Barkley would break away from their girlfriends some nights, deep down John had been afraid to let her out of his sight. The guys would razz him, but John was too in love to care. Had he known even then? That she was too beautiful to stay with him forever?

Hurriedly, John pulled out his wallet and paid the driver.

The broken window gaped in the sunlight, the jagged glass creating an open star. John would call to get it fixed before the kids got home.

Walking up the steps, he looked through the front door and saw Maggie's book bag lying on the hall floor. Had she forgotten to take it to school? John's stomach tightened, thinking that the new baby-sitter was screwing up already. Hand on the doorknob, he instinctively turned around to glance at her blue car.

The car wasn't there.

The door was unlocked.

John's heart beat fast in his throat, like a cluster of moths. He stepped into his own front hall. This was where he and Theresa had stood twice, bringing both kids home from the hospital—why had that memory come to him now? He shook it off, noticing Maggie's lunch on the chair, the brown bag he'd packed himself last night. She'd stayed home from school, that's all. That's what happened.

Maybe a stomachache. Maggie, especially since her mother's death, had been prone to stomachaches. Or maybe it was her patented stubbornness—refusing to go to school till she saw with her own eyes that her dad was okay.

"Maggie!" he called, dropping his briefcase.

No answer. The hall clock ticked loudly. "I'm home, sweetheart. I'm fine."

That should bring her running, he

thought. His good, caring, easily worried girl: She would want to know her father was safe and sound.

But she didn't come running. She didn't even answer.

"Hey, Maggie. Brainer—where's Maggie?"

Palms sweating, John walked through the first floor. Slowly, in control, he glanced through the living room, dining room, kitchen—faster now, starting to run—into the den, the sunporch. *Where's Brainer? The dog's gone too,* he thought.

"Mags!"

His guts thudded, hard and sudden. What was the baby-sitter's name, the woman who had shown up at their door—and what kind of *idiot,* knowing what John knew about what human beings are capable of—would leave his kids with a stranger? Where was Mrs. Wilcox? Hadn't she said she'd stay to help? John heard himself groan, tearing up the stairs two at a time.

"Kate?" he shouted. That was her name—Kate Harris.

Ripping through the bedrooms upstairs, John found himself formulating a usable description of the woman. Five foot six, slim, straight brown hair, odd stone-colored eyes, gray coat, black shoes, something to help the cops find her—his blood turned cold as he realized what he was doing. Knowing himself becoming, in that instant, the father of a missing girl . . .

chapter 3

John felt the chill of cold truth. Searching his own house, the feeling grew stronger: Was he one of them now? One of those parents—loved ones who came home one bright day to find the nightmare starting—those parents he knew so well from witness lists and cross-examination—parents who had lost their children? Was he on the after side of a before-and-after life? The before-Maggie-was-missing and the after-Maggie-was-missing life?

"MAGGIE!" he bellowed.

The house responded in silence.

John thought of the Moores, the Nastoses, the McDiarmids, the Litskys . . . they had gone through this; he had heard them testify to it: "I came home from work, and she wasn't there . . ." or, "We called her on Friday night, but she didn't answer . . ." or, "We searched and searched, but we couldn't find her." They had somehow opened the door to the monsters. . . .

"Maggie! Kate!" he yelled.

Kate Harris! A plain name, a nice, normal-looking woman. John felt the stab—the standard description of a serial killer. "Seemed so *nice,* seemed so *normal* . . ." The boy next door . . . But women killed too, he thought. Women were not exempt from the inner forces that drove people to harm others.

Where had Kate Harris taken his baby girl? His sweet little stubborn little soccer-shirt-wearing bath-forgetting beloved daughter . . . Maggie. Margaret Rose O'Rourke. Maggie Rose. Mags, Magpie, Maguire, Magsamillion, the Magster.

"Maggie!"

Up to the attic. Smells of dust, mothballs, something dead rotting in the walls—the bats were back, John thought. They'd had bats three years ago, and Theresa had called an exterminator. His throat caught, thinking of his wife.

Another before-and-after, he thought. The before-the-accident, the after-the-accident. How best to define the moment his life first fell apart? Too frantic to think, John raced through the musty attic, looking in the old wardrobe, behind the cedar chest, inside Theresa's grandmother's leather-bound trunk.

He let out a sound so inhuman—the relief of not finding his daughter's body mixed with the anguish of not finding his daughter—that it flushed the bats from the rafters and brought them swarming around his head. They surrounded him with dark, translucent violence, scratching his ears and face with something shockingly sharp—claws? Teeth?

John didn't know. He ran down the stairs, wedging himself through the door and slamming it behind him. One or two bats escaped the attic, dispersing into the bright vastness of the colonial house's second floor.

He still had the basement to search: his workshop, the laundry room. The garage, the garden shed, the boathouse. But he didn't have time; minutes were flying by, and he already knew.

This is it, he thought, going for the phone in his bedroom. *This is it, this is the moment. Payback for your career, payback for defending the people you defend.*

Does it mean they're right—you're a demon doing the devil's work, that you're a party to the crimes after the fact, that you should just let the killers fry? Is that what this means?

My daughter's missing, just like those other families.

Now I know what it's like, he thought, starting to dial. *Now I know.*

John sat on the bed. He picked up the receiver. It felt slippery in his hand. Fingers shaking, he went to punch the buttons and hit air instead. Trying again, he dialed the 91 of 911, when he heard the front door open. Brainer barked. Maggie squealed.

"He's home! There's his briefcase— Daddy!"

"Maggie," he yelled.

Running down the stairs, he felt his daughter fly straight against his body. She clamped on in a death-defying hug, as if she were out to win the Olympics of hugging. Usually he had to pry her off, but right now John held on even tighter than she did. Brainer tried to bump between them, getting nowhere.

"We didn't expect you home so soon," Kate Harris said.

John raised his eyes, looked at her over Maggie's head. Kate was smiling. Or at least, she was trying to. Her mouth turned up, dimpling her smooth, freckled cheeks. But her river-stone eyes looked so sad, as if no smile had really touched them in a long, long time. John wasn't in the mood for smile analysis, so he dropped the thoughts and gently eased his daughter away.

"Why isn't Maggie in school?" he asked.

"She wouldn't go," Kate Harris said.

"She goes anyway," John said. "You're supposed to know that."

"I am?"

"You're the adult."

"Hmmm," she said, as if giving that some thought. "Yes, you're right."

"Where were you?" he asked.

"We wanted to take our—Maggie's—mind off worrying about you," she said in that faint southern accent.

"I was worried," Maggie confirmed.

"Mags, will you give me a minute here? Go out to the sunporch. I'll be right there, okay?"

"Dad, don't be mad," Maggie said, looking stricken. John had seen her look stricken so many times in the last two years, it activated an automatic guilt mechanism in his brain. He did what he always did—promised her something to make her feel better.

"I'll play checkers with you," he said, regardless of the work he had waiting for him at the office. "Go set up the board."

"I will," she said, backing away, "but don't be mad at Kate."

"Don't you worry," John said. "Go set up the checkerboard."

They watched Maggie walk down the hall; her shirt, stained and too big, was now also quite wet. But her chopped hair was neatly brushed.

"You heard her," Kate said, perfectly dressed and impeccably groomed—all except for the cuffs of her gray pants, which John noticed, were also sopping wet. "Don't be mad at me."

"She's a kid," John said. "She doesn't know what's going on. Where the hell were you? Do you know how crazy I was? I was just about to call the police—I thought you'd taken her . . ."

Kate's expression changed. From calm, almost playful, she went straight to looking shocked.

"God, I'm sorry."

"You must have realized!"

"Honestly, I thought we'd be home long before you. We just ran down the street to the car wash—"

"You washed your goddamn *car*?" he asked, blood pressure rising, knowing that the previous winner of the Baby-sitter X Bad Judgment Award had just been knocked off her pedestal.

"No, we—" Kate began.

"I don't have time for this conversation," John said, shaking his head, holding his temple. It had swollen up and felt the size of a melon under his hand. "I have to play checkers with Maggie, then take her to the office with me—if you had any idea how much work I have to do!"

"I know—I'd be happy to stay with her."

"No, *thanks*," John said.

"Will you please listen to me for a minute? I'd like to explain—"

"No need, Ms. Harris."

"Honestly, there is. It's very important to me! I've waited—"

"I don't know what explanation you think will suffice for taking my kid without asking, without leaving a note. It's outrageous. It's criminal, if you want to get right down to it. The kidnapping statute is written—"

"You think I'd kidnap Maggie! Please, just listen to me!"

Shaking his head, John jammed his hand into his pocket, came up with a few twenty-dollar bills. "Here, take this to cover your expenses. I'll just tell the agency it didn't work out."

Kate backed away, not touching the money. When John looked into her eyes, he saw a shimmer of amusement. Was she kidding—she thought this was funny?

"Take it," he said. "Unless you want me to pay the agency, let them send you a check."

"That would be much better," she said, her voice cool but her eyes still hot. They flashed, like sunlight striking a blue-green river.

"Your choice," he said, shrugging. He thought about wishing her good luck, but what a joke—although he didn't believe she was a criminal, she had no business in the field of child care. Now, anxious to see Maggie, he walked Kate Harris to the door—for the sole reason of making sure she walked through it, to watch her drive away as he locked up tight behind her. Brainer stood beside him, wagging his tail.

"I had a feeling we might not get to talk today," she said. "I tried . . ."

"Talk?" he asked, confused.

She shook his hand. They looked into each other's eyes. The moment stretched out longer than it should have, and John slowly pulled his hand back. To his surprise, her gaze had made him feel nervous; his palm was cold.

"Good-bye," she said. "Will you please say good-bye to Maggie for me? And Teddy, when he gets home from school?"

"Yes," John said, watching her walk down the steps, carrying her coat. Her posture was erect, her head held high. Sunlight touched her brown hair, picking up glints of copper and gold. Her gray pants were snug, her thighs shapely—he quickly lowered his gaze, noticing again those wet, black cuffs.

"Tell Teddy the tangles are gone."

"The *what*?"

But Kate Harris had climbed into her car, started it up. John waited until she had turned around, started to drive away. Brainer bumped his leg, and instinctively John gave him a pet. The dog's coat felt damp, soft, and smooth. When John looked down, he noticed: Brainer's fur was five shades lighter without the mud and thorns and seaweed.

The dog had had a bath.

Reaching for the door, looking down the street, he saw Kate Harris's car drive past the seawall and out of sight.

Tell Teddy the tangles are gone. . . . John shook his head. What a day—the brick, the hospital, thinking Maggie was missing. Glancing down at the hall table, he saw that Kate had left a card: a small white business card printed with a Washington, D.C., address and one handwritten local phone number. That summed it up for him, and an entire story flashed through his mind: relocation. She'd probably burned her bridges down south, come up here to start over.

"Mags," he called, sliding the card into his shirt pocket. "Ready to play?"

"Bring it on, Dad," she shouted from the sunroom. "And prepare to lose!"

John took a deep breath. He had bats in his attic, a shattered front window, and no baby-sitter—but his daughter was safe, home. Brainer, gleaming in sunlight streaming through the broken picture window, bounded ahead, leading John O'Rourke straight to Maggie.

"She's gone," Maggie whispered as soon as Teddy walked through the door at four-thirty.

He stopped short, standing in the front hall. He was all gross and sweaty from his soccer match, freezing cold because he hadn't worn a warm enough jacket. It was getting dark earlier the closer they got to Halloween, and the house had looked gloomy from the street—not enough lights on. His mother used to always welcome them home with lamps blazing; Teddy flipped on the hall chandelier.

"What do you mean?" he asked.

"She's gone," Maggie whispered, gesturing toward the closed den door. That meant that their father was working at home. "Dad didn't like her."

"Kate?" Teddy asked, feeling the breath knocked out of him.

Maggie nodded. "Because she took me in the car without asking. Dad was here when we got back, and he was *ballistic*."

"Where did she take you?"

"He *fired* her, Teddy," Maggie said, not even hearing the question. "He told me to go set up the checkerboard, and when he came in to play, he said he'd 'let her go.' That's how he put it, but that means *fired*, right?"

"Right," Teddy said, looking at his father's closed door. He wanted to go in and reason with his father, tell him that Kate was good. She understood him—Teddy had known that after ten minutes in her presence. He hated to think of some of the other baby-sitters they had had—some nice, some mean, but not one of them able to understand him. Kate had gotten Maggie *and* Brainer—right away.

"Where do you think she went?" Teddy asked.

"Probably off to the next family," Maggie said miserably. "I tried to tell Dad he had to keep her, but he wouldn't listen. He said she showed poor judgment, and that was the end of it."

"What did she *do*?" Teddy asked, looking at his sister. For the first time, he noticed that her skin looked pink and scrubbed. Her hair was shining in the chandelier light.

Outside, Brainer started barking. He must have finished his afternoon circuit of checking out the beach and marsh. But when Teddy opened the door, he couldn't believe it was really their dog: Although Brainer had a few new brambles stuck to his fur, he glistened and gleamed. Bending down to pet him, Teddy felt that his coat had been brushed through, all the ticks and tangles gotten rid of.

"How'd she do it?" he asked, feeling the world tilt, turning his head to look at Maggie.

"We took him to one of those do-it-yourself car washes," Maggie said. "She put on a raincoat and sprayed him with water, and then we dried him off with about a hundred towels. It was fun."

"Who brushed him?"

"She did. And Brainer let her."

Teddy closed his eyes, feeling the dog's soft fur against his cheek. He had lost in soccer that day. Distracted by something—someone in the stands calling out "Merrill-lover"—he'd let his opponent blow by him, to score a goal. He hadn't let himself think about it till now, but suddenly the overwhelming sense of loss surrounded and filled him.

"I couldn't believe it," Maggie said, kneeling down, her whisper hissing in Teddy's ear. "Brainer just let her do it! He hasn't let anyone brush him since . . ."

"Mom," Teddy said.

"Yeah."

"How about you?" Teddy asked, looking at his sister's hair. "You look like you had a shampoo, too."

"I took a bath myself," Maggie said proudly. "I just felt like it."

"Good job," Teddy said.

"She bought us a pumpkin, too."

"Where is it?"

"Right on the front steps. Didn't you see it when you came in?"

"No," Teddy said, his heart tightening. "Because there weren't any lights on. Not even the porch light." That was the worst part. Seeing their formerly bright and happy house so dark and morguelike was kind of embarrassing—being driven home by other kids' moms, getting dropped off at the grimmest house on the block. But the worst part was not being welcomed: His mother used to leave the outside lantern on until everyone in the family got home.

Now, rising, flipping on the porch light, Teddy peered through the side window and saw the pumpkin. It was squat, fat, and pale orange, with a spooky, curly stem.

"Good for carving," he said.

"Yeah," Maggie said. "That's what she said."

"Maybe if I talked to Dad . . ." Teddy said, looking over at their father's closed door.

"Do it, Teddy," Maggie said excitedly, grabbing his wrist. "Make him get her back!"

Nodding, Teddy rose. He petted Brainer for luck. He and Maggie touched knuckles, like teammates always did, and then Teddy walked toward the door.

The family den became John's office on days like this. He had cleared his grandfather's desk of the framed photos and bird sculptures placed there by Theresa, replaced the collected works of Hawthorne and Melville with a stack of case law, and installed two extra phone lines.

But even the computer, fax machine, and high-speed printer couldn't change the room's basic warmth—rug on the polished wood floor, leather chairs, a Windsor desk chair with the seal of Georgetown—his law school—emblazoned on the back, marble fireplace, a sunrise painting by Hugh Renwick, an undersea watercolor by Dana Underhill, and landscape paintings by other Connecticut Impressionists—Theresa had really known how to put a room together.

John was hunched over his desk, reading doctors' reports. Gregory Merrill had a paraphiliac mental disorder, resulting—according to Dr. Philip Beckwith, the psychiatrist John had hired for his defense—in a compulsion "to perpetrate violent sexual activity in a repetitive way."

The State's own expert psychiatrist had called him a sexual sadist. He had described the obsession of Greg's mind, how he was constantly filled with repetitive thoughts, urges, and fantasies of the degradation, rape, and murder of women. The harder he tried to stop the thoughts, the more compelling they became. The feelings would build, until he felt there was no choice but to act upon them.

John's challenge, with Beckwith's help, was to convince the court that this mental illness should be considered a mitigating factor in overturning the death penalty.

Hearing a knock on the door, John shuffled the papers to hide them and called, "Come in."

"Dad?"

It was Teddy, and John waved him in. Seeing his son standing there in his grass-stained soccer clothes, John let out a big breath. He had missed another of his son's games.

"Whoa, Dad—your face. It's all cut and bruised."

"I know," John said, laughing. "Looks worse than it is. But I'm going to rule at court—even the judges will be giving me wide berth. What's going on?"

"I just wondered about the baby-sitter," Teddy said. "Kate."

"Ah, Kate," John said, leaning back in his chair, arms behind his head.

Teddy didn't reply. Eyes hopeful, he waited for his father to explain.

"She seemed like a smart, competent person," John said. "Unfortunately, only in matters having nothing to do with taking care of my kids. She took your sister out on an errand without my permission, without leaving a note—"

"That was my fault," Teddy said.

"Your fault?"

"That she took Brainer to give him a bath. It was because I said he had tangles. She said her sister had a dog, and—well, never mind. You had to be there. But trust me, Dad, she's good. She's the best so far. Both Maggie and I liked her."

"You hardly knew her, Teddy. She was in your presence for a total of—what? Fifteen minutes?"

Teddy didn't flinch. He was tall and lean, with a serious, dark expression deep in his eyes. He'd lost his little-boyness so long ago, John hardly remembered. Teddy stood before him now, like an adversary at the bar.

"We want her back, Dad."

"Ted, that's not going to happen. She used—"

"I know, I know—you're going to say she used bad judgment. And maybe, if you didn't know the facts, you'd be right to think that. But actually, she used *good* judgment, Dad. Think about it: Maggie was upset, worried about you. Brainer was totally tick-and-flea infested—what if one of those ticks bit Maggie and gave her Lyme disease? Instead, Kate gave him a bath. You shouldn't have fired her, Dad."

"The prosecution rests," John said, chuckling.

"Get her back, Dad," Teddy said. "Before the agency sends one of those bored ladies who does everything right—they use such good judgment it's ridiculous. But they don't laugh at Maggie's jokes, or give Brainer a bath, or buy us pumpkins."

"She bought us a pumpkin?"

"Didn't you see it on the steps?"

"Yeah," John said, picturing it now. "I guess I figured Mrs. Wilcox dropped it off."

"No, it was Kate. Something else, Dad: Those other ladies don't last."

"I know," John said, feeling the twist in his guts. They didn't last because he was a slave driver. "What makes you think Kate will?"

"I can't explain it," Teddy said. "I just know."

John sat back, thinking it over. Tempers

had been running high, that was for sure. Perhaps he *had* overreacted. The Harris woman hadn't meant any harm; in fact, her bathing Brainer had inspired Maggie to give herself a long bubble bath. Two problems solved in one day.

Glancing at his watch, he saw that it was four-fifty-eight. That left him two minutes to call the employment agency. He supposed it would do no harm to at least check Kate Harris's references; besides, he had to make arrangements about sending her check. . . .

"Let me call and ask about her, Dad," Teddy said eagerly. "Come on, okay?"

"Go ahead." John pushed the phone across the desk, proud of his son's sense of responsibility.

Relating the number he by now knew by heart, John watched Teddy call the Sea and Shore Employment Agency.

"Hello?" Teddy said. "This is Thaddeus O'Rourke. We have an account with you. We live at . . . oh, you know us? Good. Well, it's about the lady you sent over here today. Kate . . . um, maybe it's Katherine, or maybe Kathleen . . ."

John fished her card out of his shirt

pocket and read the name: "Katherine," he told Teddy.

"Katherine Harris," Teddy said, nodding silent and solemn thanks. "She came to our house today . . ."

Listening to his son take care of business, John was filled with pride. Teddy had a knack for talking to others. He was direct and efficient, yet respectful and kind. He would make a great lawyer someday—or anything else he decided to do.

"No, she did," Teddy said now, into the receiver. "She arrived first thing this morning. Tall, brown hair, drives a blue car . . ."

John's ears perked up. He sat forward, leaning over his documents, watching the expression on Teddy's face turn to worry. Teddy listened for a while, growing paler by the second. His face drained of color, but his eyes filled with tears. By the time he hung up the phone, he'd gotten every bit of his childishness back from wherever it had gone—and John knew what he was going to say before he said it.

"She doesn't work for them," John said.

"How did you know?" Teddy asked.

"Because," John said quietly, wishing he could pull his son into a hug the way he used to—the way Theresa would have done. He shivered inside, thinking of what might have happened. Whoever the woman was, she had been alone with Maggie for several hours. "I just know."

"She seemed . . ." Teddy said, helplessly.

"So nice," John said, knowing they had somehow just dodged a bullet. "They all do."

chapter 4

Kate Harris stood in the shower that evening, water streaming down her body. It was as hot as her skin could stand, and great clouds of vapor billowed around her, misting the glass. Her sister was a great believer in the healing powers of showers—of any water, really. Even as a little girl, she'd always want to go swimming or take a shower whenever she got upset.

"Water washes troubles away," Willa would say, towel pulled around her body, fresh out of the billowing surf. Her eyes would be shining—they always did, with a light from within, her beautiful spirit bursting forth. "Can't you feel it, Katy? No matter how mad or hurt or terrible you feel, water cleanses everything. . . ."

"You're too young to be so wise," Kate would say, pretending to frown. In fact, she was incredibly proud of her younger sister. Willa was an artist, a spiritual child, her personality the opposite of Kate's type A overdrive. Born and raised in the sea-and-pony territory of Chincoteague, Virginia, the two girls had gone in totally different directions.

"Just try it, Katy—don't hold onto everything so tight. Just let things gently flow away, breathe in and out, let all the bad stuff go. Be like the ponies! Even they go swimming . . . and don't you love the way they just stare out to sea so steadily, breathing in the wind?"

Kate tried it now. Leaning against the inn's tile shower, she thought of Willa's words and wished for it all to wash away. She tried to sing—remembering that Willa had always sung in the shower, from when she was a tiny girl, that exuberant voice drifting through their house on the tidal channel between the island and the mainland—but she couldn't quite manage that.

When Bonnie started barking in the other room, she quickly turned off the faucets and heard knocking at the door. Any calming effect had by the shower drained away faster than the water. Her heart began to race. She wasn't expecting any visitors.

"Just a minute," she called, quickly pulling on the terry-cloth robe hanging behind the bathroom door.

Bonnie, Willa's Scottie, patrolled the door, seriously barking. The inn was small, with just six cozy rooms. Kate had chosen it for its location—by the sea, within range of most of the breakwaters—and because it took pets. Willa had stayed here six months ago, and had sent a postcard saying how nice the place was for Bonnie. The Scottie ran a circuit from bed to chair to window to door to Kate, covering all bases.

"Okay, Bon," Kate said. "Calm down."

The knock sounded again.

Kate stood against the door; the problem with these old inns was that they lacked certain modern amenities, like peepholes. The owners, Barkley and Felicity Jenkins, had named each room after famous paintings by the local artist Hugh Renwick: "High Tide," "Day Lilies," "Red Barn," "Country Fair," "Lighthouse," and, Kate's room, "White Sails."

"Who is it?" she asked.

"John O'Rourke," he said.

Kate leaned against the doorjamb, relief turning her bones to jelly. When had a knock on the door started making her feel terrified?

"Ms. Harris, are you there?" he asked.

"Yes," she said, grabbing a fresh towel. "Just let me get dressed, and I'll be right out. Meet you in the parlor downstairs in a few minutes, okay?"

"Okay," he said.

And as she heard the echo of his footsteps going down the hall, she took a deep breath. *This meeting was what I came here for,* she thought. Maybe it would be the answer to her prayers. Toweling her hair with one hand, pulling on her jeans with the other, she hurried as fast as she could while Bonnie, mistaking the excitement for walk time, came running over, dragging her red leash the way Willa had taught her.

The East Wind Inn stood at the end of a long driveway, on a tall bluff looking out over the Sound, midway between the O'Rourkes' house and Silver Bay Light. The white house had wide porches and a sharply peaked roof, black shutters with cut-out crescent moons. Built over a hundred and fifty years ago, it had once stood beside the lighthouse where, before automation, Barkley Jenkins's father had been the light keeper.

When technology took over, the government sold Barkley the old house and permitted him to move it off the bluff. Barkley had named it the East Wind—the house's name an homage to the constant wind that blew in from the sea. He made his money by operating it as an inn, by serving as the light's caretaker, and by being a jack-of-all-trades around town. John and Theresa had hired him to fix their roof, and that's how the affair had started.

John sat in the front parlor drinking a cup of Earl Grey tea. Felicity Jenkins had brought it to him, barely able to hide her curiosity. Did she know the whole story about her husband and John's wife, or had Barkley managed to keep his secret safe?

"Here, John," Felicity said, proffering a plate of cookies decorated to look like jack-o'-lanterns. "Have one, and take a few home for the kids. Caleb used to love when I made these—it's my Halloween tradition."

"Okay, thanks," John said, taking one just so he didn't hurt her feelings. They had known each other forever, since she and Barkley and he and Theresa double-dated in high school, but now he felt a secret kinship with her that she might not ever understand: Their spouses had had an affair, meeting in secret up and down the shoreline. John's pride made him sit up taller, even though he was burning to be inside Barkley Jenkins's home.

"Go on," she said, rattling the plate lightly. "Take some more for Teddy and Maggie. I saw her on her bike the other day—adorable."

John glanced at his watch. Against Teddy's protests, he had asked Mrs. Wilcox to come over to stay with the kids for an hour. Teddy thought he was old enough to watch out for his sister, but after this morning, John wasn't taking any chances. He had locked the doors behind him—Brainer slipping out for the car ride—and headed over to see Kate Harris.

Felicity stood there, watching John chew. He could feel her eyes on him, sense her wanting to say something more. Perhaps she *did* know. She had the strong body of someone who did lots of physical work, blond hair swept up in a messy bun, and a sharp, direct gaze.

"How's Caleb doing?" John asked, to head her off.

"He's great," Felicity said, and the words began spilling out. "Never been better. He's working on his father's crew—Barkley's got him doing some plasterwork on the light-house. Those storms take their toll, and with winter coming on . . ."

"Great," John said, muscles tensing at the name. "I'm glad to hear it."

"There's never been another problem—not a one—since . . ."

"That's terrific."

"Not that we thought there would be." Felicity laughed. "Boys will be boys, and just because some people can't take a prank . . . I'm so glad that wonderful psychiatrist convinced the jury about his ADD . . ."

But just then, they heard a door close in the hall upstairs. Felicity patted John's arm and smiled. "She's a mysterious one," she said. "Never even been here before, but seems to know everything about the place.

Her sister apparently stayed with us. Client of yours?"

John shook his head, brushing the cookie crumbs from his fingers, and rose from his seat.

"I'll leave you your privacy," Felicity said in a stage whisper, backing out of the room.

Kate Harris came down the front staircase. Very slender, she wore a black wool turtleneck and jeans—somehow managing to make faded jeans look incredibly elegant. She had a small black Scottie dog on a leash, and the dog jumped all over John's legs, tongue hanging out in a friendly smile, as if he were a long-lost friend.

"Great watchdog, Bonnie," Kate said wryly.

"She barked a good game when I knocked on your door."

"How did you find me, anyway?"

"Well, you left your card. I called both numbers, and when Felicity Jenkins answered the second, she said you were staying here."

"So much for high security," Kate said.

"Hello, Kate," said Felicity Jenkins, bearing another china cup. "I thought perhaps you and John would like to have tea here in the parlor. I didn't know you two knew each other! I thought you said you didn't have any friends in town . . ."

John glimpsed annoyance in Kate's eyes, but he felt sad for Felicity. She was threatened by the other woman—perhaps she was worried that Barkley would notice her.

"We'll have tea another time," John said, rising, setting his cup and saucer down on the doily on the small mahogany table beside his chair, bending down to pet the Scottie. "Looks like this beast is ready for a walk."

"How right you are," Kate said. "Would you like to join us?"

"Sure," John said. "Brainer came along— he loves the car. Think your dog would mind some company?"

"Not at all," Kate said. She took a heavy dark green wool jacket down from the brass coatrack and, pulling it on, opened the front door. A gust of cold air swirled up the bluff, into the house. John ran over to his car, opened the door, and let Brainer out. Grateful, the big golden retriever ran in circles, stopping to say hello to Kate and the Scottie.

"Brainer, meet Bonnie, Bonnie, meet Brainer," Kate said.

"Brainer's shiny and clean tonight, thanks to you," John said, watching her.

"Thanks to Teddy," she said, correcting him. "He has a very fine-tuned sense of responsibility. You have a nice son."

"I do," John said.

Cold air swept up the bluff, making John pull his jacket closer. October stars blazed in the clear sky overhead, reflected in the dark waves and Kate's eyes. He stopped, stood still, and held her gaze.

"Who are you?" he asked.

"I told you: Kate Harris. I'm a staff scientist for the National Academy of Science—in Washington. I'm a marine biologist."

"I went to law school in Washington. That's a long way from here."

John listened to the white pines rustling overhead. Waves crashed on the rocks below, dragging loose stones over the moraine as they swept out to sea. The line of breakers glowed, one long white thread stretching along the coast in the darkness, interrupted by breakwaters jutting out from shore, illuminated by the lighthouse beam.

There was clearly plenty here for a marine biologist to be interested in.

"Why did you lie?"

"I didn't lie," she said, chin tilted up as she stared into his face.

"You don't work for the Sea and Shore Employment Agency."

"I never said I did."

"You told me to send your check there—"

"No," she said firmly. "You said you would, and I decided not to correct you. You'd been making assumptions all over the place—all of them wrong. Since you wouldn't give me a chance to explain myself, I figured I should let you run with it."

"You said you were there for the job!"

"No," Kate said, shaking her head vehemently. "I said I would stay with your kids, that's all. When I got to your house, the police were there, you were bleeding from the head, Teddy and Maggie were frantic. You needed help."

"You should have told me you weren't a baby-sitter."

"I realize that now," she said. "But everything was crazy—I really did just want to help. And since *I* know I'm trustworthy, I figured I'd just explain later."

The East Wind and abutting lighthouse property were on about fifteen acres, so Kate dropped Bonnie's leash. The two dogs ran together, sniffing along hedges and circling granite boulders. John heard them scuffling through fallen leaves; he had a memory of autumn Brainer-walks with Theresa, and his heart tightened. "You still haven't told me what you were doing at our house at eight this morning."

"I know," she said, drawing in a sharp breath.

"So?"

Kate crouched down, calling Bonnie by clapping her hands. Brainer responded too, and she rewarded them with treats from the pocket of her wool jacket. Standing above, John saw her face in shadow. Her cheekbones were high and fine, her eyes bright.

"You still haven't told me how you happened to walk straight up to my room and knock on the door," she said.

"I represented the Jenkinses' son last year," he said carefully. "He'd 'borrowed' a neighbor's motorboat, and the neighbor pressed charges. Felicity's grateful; when I called the number on your card and asked if you were there, she told me you were staying in White Sails. I just walked up."

"She must think you're a good lawyer," Kate said.

"I told her she shouldn't be giving your room out to anyone else who calls," John said, ignoring her statement, thinking of how vulnerable women—people, really— were in this world. He leaned toward her, feeling unexpectedly protective and attracted, both at the same time.

"So, are you?" Kate asked. "A good lawyer?"

Standing on the bluff, bundled up against the cold wind, John felt his stomach clench. His heart sank a bit. Was that it? Did Kate need a good defense lawyer? John looked at her small frame, her wide eyes, her freckled nose, and knew that anyone could be guilty of anything.

"I am," he said, his back straighter, his voice harder. "I'm a good lawyer."

"You went to law school in Washington?"

"Georgetown."

She nodded, seeming to take that in.

"Do you want me to represent you?" he asked. "Is that why you came to my house? To ask me?"

Kate didn't reply right away. John watched her carefully. Sometimes people who needed defense lawyers weren't completely forthcoming right away. They were wrongly accused, or they hadn't meant to commit the crime. Or they had meant to, but they hadn't expected to get caught.

Very few people thought of themselves as criminals, even when they'd been caught red-handed. The label never quite fit. No matter what their crime, the end usually justified the means—someone had betrayed, cheated, tricked, or maligned them. It was always something. So John waited, staring at Kate, wondering what her story would be.

"That's not why I wanted to see you," Kate said, her voice suddenly soft. "I don't need you to represent me."

"Then why do you care if I'm a good lawyer or not? Why did you come to my house this morning?"

The night was very dark; stars were everywhere, all the way down to the horizon, the sky enclosing John and Kate like a great inverted bowl. The sea air was salty; it must have stung Kate's eyes, because she suddenly wiped away a tear. More came, filling her eyes. John stared, his heart beating harder.

"I came to see you because you're Greg Merrill's lawyer."

"Merrill? What does he have to do with anything?"

Kate swallowed. The dogs had run back from the thicket along the cliff, begging her for more treats. She seemed not to notice. Bonnie was jumping up, nuzzling her hand, and Brainer sat patiently, waiting for her to offer. Kate just stood there, tears running freely down her cheeks, until she turned to look John straight in the eye. Her face was filled with grief, as if she knew that whatever she was seeking was already lost, but she cleared her throat and spoke anyway.

"I think he killed my sister," she whispered.

chapter 5

Blinded by her own tears, Kate let John O'Rourke lead her to his car. It was a Volvo station wagon, and the minute he opened the door, both dogs bounded inside. Brainer leapt into the backseat, and Bonnie followed behind. They sat together, tongues hanging out, waiting to go for a ride.

John started up the car. Until Kate felt the heat start to pump out, she hadn't realized how cold she was. Thinking about Willa, imagining what might have happened to her, always made Kate cold. Her thoughts were jumbled, but she felt that if her sister couldn't be warm, neither would Kate. The radiator, scarcely cooled off from John's ride over, did its work, and in spite of herself, Kate began to feel the heat right away.

The stereo had been left on; a song by Suzanne Vega drifted out, sweet and sad. Kate remembered how her sister had loved her music. Willa used to listen to it in her bedroom, white curtains blowing in the salty wind. "She sings about loss," Willa had said, explaining it to her older sister, sitting on the edge of her twin bed. "She knows what it's like, just as we do. . . . She's one of us. Thank God I have you, Katy."

"Thank God I have you," Kate had whispered back.

Now, sitting in John O'Rourke's car, she held on to her seat and focused on not crying. Her love of the sea had led her to become a marine biologist, but she was on leave from her job in Washington. How could she oversee the fragile balance of ecosystems and tidal zones when all she could think about was Willa?

"I can't talk to you," John said quietly, facing forward.

Kate didn't trust herself to speak yet. She wished the music would finish, so the memories would stop and her emotions would quiet down. The sad melody opened up all the wounds of the past months, and she felt the pain all through her body.

"Greg Merrill is my client; it's not ethical for me to discuss his case with you, with anyone."

Kate took a deep breath. The last notes played, the last guitar chords finished. She closed her eyes, forcing her voice to be calm. "I wouldn't want you to breach any confidences," she said, floundering as she reached for the right words. "You wouldn't have to tell me anything—just listen to my questions and help me rule him out . . ."

"Discussions with my client are privileged," John said. "And privilege is an all-or-nothing deal. I can't just pick and choose where to apply it."

"I understand."

"Why come to me anyway?" John asked. "You can go to the police. Or to the state prosecutor's office. If you have any suspicions, they can help you."

"I've talked to all of them," Kate said.

"And they couldn't help you?"

She shook her head. A lighthouse beam slashed the sky. She knew, from the chart, that it was Silver Bay Light. The tower sat on a headland overlooking a long breakwater, built of locally quarried gray stone, with a dogleg in the middle. The breakwater protected Silver Bay Harbor.

"He never used that one, did he?" she asked, watching the white beam rake the sky.

"Which one? What are you talking about?"

"Merrill. He never hid a body in the Silver Bay breakwater—and you'd think he would. It must have been perfect—so long, hard to see from shore, with so many apertures between those rocks . . . easy to get to at low tide."

"This conversation is over," John O'Rourke said, opening his car door. Both dogs, sensing that the ride was scrubbed, let out barks of disappointment.

"Please," Kate said, swallowing. She reached for his wrist and held it. Slowly he turned his head to look at her; she saw that his eyes were hard, guarded. She had blown it by bringing up Merrill and the breakwater. *Keep him out of it,* Kate told herself. *Talk only about Willa.*

John had one leg in, one leg out of the car. The lighthouse beam swept the sky again; she watched him follow it with his eyes, then come to rest on the front side of the East Wind Inn. Someone stood just inside the front window. The curtain moved slightly, and a shadow tilted against the light.

"Please," Kate said. "Give me just five minutes of your time."

John didn't answer, but he pulled his leg in and slammed the car door. Still watching the front window, he shifted into reverse, turned around, and then drove down the long driveway. Excited and happy, the dogs ran back and forth, their noses pressed to the windows. As Kate looked over her shoulder, she saw the curtain drawn back, Felicity's face peering out the window.

"Keeping track of every move," Kate said. "Thanks for driving away. I appreciate the privacy."

"Just say what you have to say," John said. "If you bring up my client again, I'll drive you right back."

"Don't worry," Kate said. "I don't want you to violate your code of ethics. I won't ask you anything about Merrill—" She caught herself and bit her lip. "I won't mention him again. Just my sister . . ."

"Teddy told me you spoke of her to him," John said.

Kate smiled, thinking of Teddy O'Rourke. "I saw a lot of myself in Teddy," Kate said. "He loves his little sister."

"Yes, he does."

"I loved—*love,*" she corrected herself, "mine. Willa is twelve years younger than I am. When she was born, I thought my parents had brought her home just for me. She was like having a living, breathing baby doll. . . . I never wanted to put her down. I used to cry because I had to go to school, had to leave her at home for the whole day."

"Teddy used to do that."

Glancing over, Kate saw John nodding. Heartened, she continued. "My mother used to say she'd had two families. My older brother and me . . . and then Willa. Willa was her 'unanticipated treasure.' My mother was forty-five; she hadn't thought she'd ever have another baby. And then Willa came along."

"So, you loved her," John said sharply—hurrying her through the story?

"Yes. And when my parents were killed in a car accident, I took over. Willa used to say I was almost like her mother. I'd moved from

Chincoteague to Washington, D.C., by then—first for school, then for work. Willa stayed with me. . . . We used the insurance money to send her to a private school in Georgetown. Weekends, we'd head home to Chincoteague."

"What about your older brother?"

"Matt. Well, he . . . let's just say he wasn't eager to take on the care of a ten-year-old. That's okay . . . Willa and I never held it against him. He's an oysterman, totally free-wheeling. Pocomoke's about as far as he likes to get away from Chincoteague, but he's always been there if—when—we've needed him."

"What happened, Kate?" John asked.

His tone was sharp, urging her along. He'd hear her out, say he couldn't help her, and drive her back to the East Wind. Kate steeled herself; she would state her case, and get him to help her—privilege or not. She didn't know how yet, but Willa's story was too important for someone—even a hardball lawyer like John O'Rourke—to ig-nore.

"Six months ago, she headed for New England . . ."

"And?" he asked, waiting.

"And she disappeared."

John kept his eyes fixed on the road. When Kate didn't say more right away, he shook his head. "No one 'disappears.' It's impossible."

"Willa did," Kate said as they drove through the small town, the church's white steeple lit up with a spotlight. The light- house beam seemed to follow them as they sped along the main street. Stars burned in the black sky. Everything appeared illumi- nated: a good sign, Kate thought.

"She might wish not to be found," John continued. "Something might have hap- pened to her. But she can't have disap- peared without a trace. Phone records, voice mail, voice prints, DNA, credit card trails, E-mail trails . . . there's always a trace."

"There was," Kate said. "You're right."

"Where did it lead?"

"Right here," Kate said, her voice low and her throat sore.

"Here? To Silver Bay?"

"Yes. Six months ago. Just before . . ." she glanced over, not wanting to say Mer- rill's name; refusing to give John any excuse for stopping their talk.

"Before my client was arrested."

"Yes."

John drove in silence. They'd left the center of town, and now drove out the eastern shore road. It wound past coves and marshes, over small bridges and along a narrow abutment. The car heat had felt good, but now Kate felt herself sweating. Rolling down her window a crack, she smelled the pungent odor of low tide. The tide flats were exposed, all those shellfish and dead marine creatures rotting in the cold air.

She watched John's face carefully. Was he mentally reviewing his files, trying to remember whether Willa's name had come up anywhere, in any part of the investigation? Was he trying to summon up the face of a girl who had looked like Kate, only twelve years younger?

"I don't recall seeing her name in any of the materials . . . if she *was* here then," John said carefully. "Why didn't you contact the police?"

"Because I didn't know she'd been here . . . at that time."

"I don't understand."

"We tracked her to Newport, Rhode Is-

land. She was . . . getting over a bad love
affair." Kate could hardly get the words
out; they rasped at her throat like sandpa-
per, as if they could make her bleed all over
again. "She'd driven up from Washington,
checked into an inn there—a bed-and-
breakfast, really. Very much like the East
Wind."

"One of the old mansions?"

"Yes, on Ocean Drive. Just around the
bend from Breton Point."

"She told you she was going there?"

Kate shook her head. "No. She didn't tell
anyone. But after she'd been missing for a
week, and I hadn't heard from her—"

"A week's not very long to get over a bad
love affair," John shot out.

"No, but it's six days longer than she and
I had ever gone without talking," Kate flung
back. "She had *never* not called me for a
whole week. I was worried after the second
day . . ." She drew a breath, remembering
the terrible circumstances. "And getting
frantic after the fourth. I called Matt, and he
convinced me to wait, to give her space. . . .
We'd had a fight, you see, Willa and I. . . .
That was so rare." Kate's eyes filled with hot

tears, but she brushed them away before John could see.

"How did you find out she'd been to Newport?"

"Like you said, a credit card trail. I called the D.C. police; they found them. And phone records. She'd called the man—her reason for running off in the first place, but she couldn't stay away from him. She called him every day. . . ."

"But not you," John said. His tone was suddenly soft, and by the way he turned his head to look, Kate knew that he understood her pain. The lighthouse beam flashed through the car, illuminating his eyes.

"Not me. She didn't call me once."

John nodded, and she thought she heard him let out a long, low breath. His knuckles were white on the steering wheel—did he know something he wasn't saying? Kate's pulse began to race.

"Then what? After you tracked her to Newport?"

"The police said she'd checked out of Seven Chimneys Inn on Tuesday, April fifth. She made a call to Andrew—her . . . lover— that night, and again the next morning. Then, nothing. No phone calls, almost no credit card activity. On Thursday, her Texaco card was used in Fairhaven, Massachusetts. On Friday, her MasterCard was used at a camping supply store in Providence."

"But nothing on the Connecticut shoreline," John said.

"No."

"No credit card use, no phone calls originating from the area."

"Nothing."

"Then," John said, turning to gaze into Kate's eyes, "what makes you say what you did? That my client killed Willa?"

"Because she was *here,*" Kate whispered, the word "killed" like a knife in the wind. She would never get used to it, "killed" in the same sentence as "Willa." Fumbling in her pocket, she pulled out the postcard. "She sent me this."

Passing it across the seat, she saw John hold it up, braced against the steering wheel. They sped along the Shore Road, and he looked at the picture—of the scene just to their right—the rocks and lighthouse of Silver Bay—and read Willa's writing by the streetlights overhead. Closing her eyes, Kate went over the message she now knew by heart.

Hi, Katy,

I'm okay . . . are you? It's all been too much, and it's gone on for too long. I'm so sorry about everything, and especially, now, about making you worry, making you wait to talk. I hate what I did to you . . . I'll be on my way home soon . . . Bonnie likes it here—there's a long beach, and she runs along the tide line . . . It reminds me of home—of Chincoteague. I wish you could be here—maybe someday, when things are better . . .

I love you.
Willa

"She mailed this on April sixth," John said, turning on the car's inside light to peer at the postmark, noting the date. "Six months ago."

"I know."

"Then why . . . why didn't I hear about her? That was right in the heat . . ."

"Of Merrill being active," Kate said. "I know. But I didn't receive her postcard until last month."

"Why did it take so long? Why didn't you receive it for five months?"

"It went to my old address," Kate said. "Because it was just a postcard, it wasn't forwarded by the post office. It was sitting in a pile of old catalogues and circulars."

"Did you take it to the police?"

"Yes," Kate said, thinking of her visit to local police stations over the last few days. "But they all point to the fact that Willa's credit cards were used in Massachusetts and Rhode Island after the card was sent. Meaning, this wasn't her last stop."

"The police looked at all women reported missing," John said carefully, his tone letting her know he wasn't breaching any ethical code.

"I know, but because we hadn't tracked her to Connecticut, I guess her name never registered in the Merrill investigation . . ."

"What about Bonnie?" John said, glancing into the rearview mirror. The small black dog, tired from her romp along the bluff, lay beside Brainer, chin resting on his golden back.

"Felicity remembered her," Kate said, "as soon as I checked in—but she didn't so much remember Willa. I saw her signature in the guest book, though." Her stomach churned, recalling that moment when she'd seen her sister's handwriting, home address printed neatly on the next line.

"I mean, what happened to Bonnie? If she wasn't with your sister, where did you find her? And when?"

"Five and a half months ago . . . right after I reported Willa missing. Using the credit card information, we checked with animal control departments in those areas. Bonnie was in a dog pound, in a small town south of Providence. Her collar and tags were missing. She'd been found in a rest area off I-95, begging for food." Kate's throat constricted, remembering. "She was so happy to see me."

"So, Bonnie wasn't left in *this* area," John said.

"I know. Leading you to believe that Willa wasn't last here, right?"

John shrugged, frowning at the road.

"Well, I think you're wrong. I have this postcard," Kate said, tapping it on the dashboard, "that makes me think she was."

"Who had it all this time? Sitting in that pile of catalogues for the five months since she sent it?"

"My ex-husband," Kate said.

"Your . . ." John asked, surprise on his face.

"Andrew," Kate said.

"But I thought you said that was the name—"

"Of the man my sister had a bad love affair with," Kate said quietly, looking out the window at the tidal flats, black and shining in the night, at the row of white waves breaking over the sandbar. "My husband, Andrew Wells."

"You . . . your husband had an affair with your sister?"

"Yes."

"I'm so sorry. That must have been terrible for you."

Kate couldn't quite reply.

Silence filled the car as John turned it around. Kate could hear the soft muffled thud of her own heart beating in her ears. Her mother had always been a private person, teaching her children to keep their family secrets hidden. Since April, Kate had become willing to tell it all: anything to get Willa back. But it struck her as strange that John should be focused on the affair itself— not her sister's disappearance.

They drove back the way they had come.

The scenery rushed by; the ride home seemed much shorter than the ride out. Kate's breath was shallow and hurt her chest. She had been heartbroken for so long; sometimes she thought all she really wanted was for her mind to rest, a respite from all the terrible thoughts.

When they had about a mile left to drive, just as the road curved past the pictur- esque, floodlit white church, John turned his head. Their eyes met and held; Kate was so struck by the depth of feeling—the hurt shimmering just below the surface, filling his entire being—that suddenly she knew. She could feel it, as if he had taken her hand and told her the whole story: He knew betrayal, because it had happened to him.

"It *was* terrible for me," she said, finally.

"As . . ." he searched for the right words. "As unbelievably painful as being cheated on is under any circumstances, it must have been much worse, being your sister and your husband."

"I think so. Yes. It wasn't her fault—"

"What do you mean?"

"She was only twenty-two. My husband went after her . . . as, I found out later—or," she paused, correcting herself, "*admitted* to myself later, he'd gone after many others. We live in Washington. There are so many hopeful young women . . . Don't you re- member from being in law school there? . . . it was so easy to seduce them."

"Is he a politician?"

"He works for one. He has power." She closed her eyes, picturing Andrew's easy smile and laughing eyes, his wavy hair, and his forward-leaning way of fooling people into imagining instant intimacy.

"Are you still married?"

"Why? What does that have to do with Willa?"

He paused, taken aback. She looked over, and in the dim light, she saw his eyes staring ahead, as if he were haunted by pri- vate doubts and demons. "I just wonder . . . whether any marriage can survive adultery. Or whether you'd have to end it—by choice."

"By choice?" She laughed nervously. "What other way is there to end a marriage except by . . ." The word was so obvious, and so was the reason he'd been asking: death. The death of his wife . . .

He didn't reply, but just kept staring ahead, toward the lighthouse, as if it might illuminate his life, answer his unanswerable question.

"My divorce just became final. When I went over to clean out the rest of my things, I found the postcard," she said.

His eyes had been clouded with something like sorrow and compassion, but suddenly the mention of the postcard jolted him back to the present. Kate wanted to go back—to hold on to their connection. She had felt it, strong and true.

"What do you want from me?" he asked.

"I'm not sure."

"There must be something; you came a long way . . ."

"I did," Kate said, feeling a homesick flash—not for the alabaster buildings and monuments of the capital, but for the salt hay and oyster beds, the dunes and ponies of Chincoteague. Willa would never willingly stay away from their island home this long.

"So tell me," John persisted. "Why did you come to see me?"

"To ask you," Kate said, barely trusting her voice, "to ask him."

"Him?"

"I know you can't tell me anything now, but please, John—ask your client. Willa fits right into his pattern—she was small, she had brown hair, she was only twenty-two."

Glancing over, she saw that John's jaw was tight. He hit the gas, making the car go faster. They turned off the main road, bouncing down the rutted driveway, between two long rows of tall spruce trees, into the clearing where the East Wind perched on the high bluff. Kate knew he couldn't wait to get her out of the car. She was threatening his code of ethics, and—she knew, from his questions—he had been where she was once. He had been hurt by infidelity.

Reaching into her pocket, she brought out the photo of Willa. She had intended to leave it for him that morning, when she'd been at his house. Whether he'd even look at it or not, she had no idea. With one last glimpse of her sister's easy smile and shining green eyes, feeling her heart kick, Kate passed the photo across the seat.

"Please take it," she said. "Show it to your client. Please?"

"No," John said, both hands on the wheel. He stopped the car at the East Wind's brightly lit front door. The lights were out in the front parlor, but Kate saw Felicity's omnipresent shadow hovering just behind the curtain.

"Thank you for listening to me," Kate said, turning back to John. She made no move to take Willa's picture, and although John didn't pick it up, he didn't push it back either.

"The police are still your best bet," John said, staring straight ahead.

"No, John. You are."

"If that's true, you're in trouble."

"Really?" she asked.

The shifting light caught his face. Although bandaged, his temple was bruised. A track of dry blood ran into his graying brown sideburn. Kate thought of the mayhem she had witnessed at his house that morning; although frustrated, she felt grudging admiration for his devotion to his client.

"Do you ever," she began slowly, thinking about her big office filled with scientific treatises, salinity reports, seismic records, fishing quota information, "just want to chuck the rules and the evidence, and go by your gut?"

"Excuse me?"

She closed her eyes, thinking of her

brother's and island neighbors' wrath, the hate mail she'd received after her office at the National Academy of Sciences had issued their oyster and crab fishery guidelines and quotas last year. If only she could have ignored the facts—a growing shortage, depletion of current stocks—she could have made everyone happy.

"Yeah," John said, a slow and ruminative smile coming to his face, as if he understood exactly what she was talking about. "Like, a hundred times a day. But I'm in the wrong business for that."

"So am I," Kate said, the scientist in her coming out. But then—as it always did—the sister in her won. "I'm going to ask you anyway: Show Merrill the picture."

John just tensed his shoulders and shook his head, as if he'd just gotten stung and hadn't seen it coming.

Not wanting to give him the chance to say anything or force her to take the picture with her, Kate jumped out of the car. She opened the back door, grabbed Bonnie's leash, gave Brainer a good-bye pet, and ran up the East Wind's front steps.

Her heart was pounding. Sitting next to John O'Rourke, she had known that he *knew* her. He had been there. A person he trusted had wounded him in the deepest way possible.

Bonnie barked once, and Kate turned to wave good-bye, but she doubted that John O'Rourke saw: His taillights were already blazing into the twisting allée of spruce trees, driving away from her as fast as he could go.

chapter 6

Judge Patrick O'Rourke had been retired for ten years, but still wore a shirt and tie every day. Even now, taking out the garbage, he was dressed as if he were about to go into court: starched broadcloth shirt, Yale club tie tied in a full Windsor knot, flannel slacks. Everyone in town—with four exceptions—called him "Judge" or "Your Honor"—and not only, he suspected, because of the iron hand with which he had ruled his court, but also for Leila's sculpture that had graced his garden since his first days on the bench, of Lady Justice herself.

School was out for the day, and the bus stopped at the curb, discharging Maggie.

She came flying up the driveway, a tropical storm in sneakers. Arms flying, book bag thumping on her back, she reminded the Judge of her father at that age: filled with purpose and enthusiasm. Dropping the plastic bag into the trash, the Judge opened his arms to hug his granddaughter.

"How's my girl?" he asked.

"Good, Gramps. What're you doing?"

"Just taking out the trash."

"Why isn't Maeve doing that?"

"Well," he said, trying to come up with a good lie. "She fixed you a nice after-school snack, and she was in there washing up the dishes. Couldn't have her doing everything, right?"

Maggie shook her head, looking worried. "We're a lot of extra work, aren't we?"

"You and Teddy?" Justice asked, snorting. He pitched in, taking care of the kids after school when John was working too hard and the latest baby-sitter had quit. The whole family had moved in temporarily—as they had done before—and the Judge was happier than a clam at high tide. "You're not a bit of work."

"Really?" she asked, worried.

"One thing you can always count on,

Margaret Rose," he said. "That's me telling the truth about things that matter. Now, what've you got in your book bag—rocks?"

"No, Gramps." She giggled. "Books."

"Well, they must make 'em extra heavy these days," he said, helping her hoist the heavy knapsack.

"No, I just have a lot of homework. I missed school yesterday because of what happened. The brick coming through our window and hitting Dad . . ." she trailed off, an embarrassed look on her face as if the attack had been her fault.

"Damned hooligans," he said. "Driving around, making trouble. Let's just hope our fine policemen catch them."

"They won't," Maggie said. "They didn't leave any clues."

The Judge had been on the business end of many threats in his day, but to subject his beloved granddaughter to it: That was too much. Good thing the family was here, away from danger. He was just gearing up to reassure Maggie, tell her everything would be okay and she shouldn't worry about her dad, when she ran ahead of him—into the kitchen.

Maeve had set the plate of brownies out

on the counter. Maggie went straight for the milk. She poured a glass, then helped herself to a brownie. The Judge hoped she wouldn't notice the dirty bowl and pan piled in the sink and know he'd lied about Maeve.

"We almost had a good one, Gramps," Maggie said, sitting at the kitchen table.

"A good what?"

"A good baby-sitter. One we liked."

"Really? What happened?" the Judge said, sitting in his place at the table, getting ready to pump his granddaughter for information. Life was circular; as a young man, the Judge had often been too busy to talk to his son. Now Johnny was too busy to tell his father what was going on.

"Well, Dad didn't like her. Or, maybe he did, but he didn't appreciate her taking me in the car without asking. Only, Gramps—how was she supposed to ask, when Dad was at the hospital getting stitches? All she wanted to do was help."

"Help how?"

"By running Brainer through the car wash. It was . . ." Closing her eyes, chomping on her brownie, Maggie sought the perfect word. "Magical," she finished.

"Magical," the Judge scoffed. "That mangy old hound in a *car wash*?"

"Yeah. Kate—that's her name—said all animals thrive on showers. She said that where she comes from, the ponies take baths in the sea, dogs go swimming in the creek—anything for a shower. She said it's true for people, too. That water makes us feel better. And you know what, Gramps?"

"What?" the Judge asked, reaching over to wipe the chocolate crumbs off her mouth.

"It does make people feel better. Me, anyway. I gave myself a bath and a shampoo after she left last night, and I'm gonna give myself another one tonight."

The Judge narrowed his eyes. Was John crazy? The new baby-sitter had washed the dog, gotten *Maggie into the bath* on her own, and he was grousing about technicalities? Although the Judge knew that people—especially parents—couldn't be too careful, he also understood the difficulties of John's life. Good help was hard to find, and unfortunately, both O'Rourke men needed it.

Take Maeve.

That morning she had gone out to the

garden for a heart-to-heart talk with her sister Brigid—and Brigid had been dead for the last fifteen years. Sometimes Maeve talked to her children, too—only, she'd never been married, never, to the Judge's knowledge, had any progeny. She even had names for them: Matthew, Mark, Luke, and John.

The practice alarmed the Judge. Not only because his housekeeper was on the fast track for losing her marbles, but because occasionally—not as often as Maeve, but often enough—he found himself doing similar things.

Twice he'd found himself sitting at his desk, delivering instructions to the jury— only there was no jury. Last week, in the middle of the night, he'd opened his eyes and discovered himself standing in the middle of his bedroom wearing, not his tattered plaid bathrobe, but the judicial robe he had worn on the bench for so many years. As if, by letting him put it on, his subconscious was restoring to him a bit of the dignity and self-respect he felt slipping away by inches.

Same thing for Maeve. A great cook for the twenty years she'd served him, she still went to the kitchen, assembled all the copper and stainless steel pans, and whipped up batches of deliciously seasoned water. People, even in their dotage, gravitated toward what they had always loved, practices that had always told them who they were.

"Where's Daddy?" Maggie asked, refilling her glass of milk. "At his office?"

"I think he said something about a meeting out of town," the Judge said.

"Out of town?" Maggie asked, freezing in place.

The Judge bit his lip, wishing he could lie, say he'd made a mistake. He would, too. Certain lies were useful; he didn't hold by the standard of full disclosure for parents or grandparents. White lies had been critical to his tenure in those roles. Nowadays, parents got all hung up on "openness." Forget that: Keep the children comfortable so they could focus on scholastic excellence and leave the worrying to their elders.

"Gramps?" Maggie pressed, squeezing her second brownie so hard, it crumbled in her fingers. "He's out of town?"

The Judge took a deep breath. What was it about this that panicked her? The idea of her father getting killed on the road, like her mother? Or was she bothered, as John had been at her age, by her defense attorney father's going behind the heavy, reinforced, unyielding steel doors of a maximum-security prison to visit his clients?

"What's in that book bag, young lady?" the Judge asked sternly. "Time to get started on all that homework, if you want to go to Yale. Yale doesn't take just anyone, you know. You must do the time, if you want to wear the blue. Not to mention George-town law; Yale for undergrad, Georgetown for law school. You've got quite a heritage to live up to."

"Gramps, tell me!" Maggie wailed, a veil of despair over her eyes, her face twisted in a painful knot. The Judge had seen this before. She was about ten seconds away from fretting herself into a full-blown tearfest. Having seen John deal with this, paradoxi-cally, by delivering the hard truth—whatever it was—the Judge went against his own best judgment and decided to lay the cards on the table.

"He went up to the prison," the Judge said. "To visit Merrill."

Maggie nodded, the knot relaxing almost instantly—to the Judge's surprise.

"That's okay with you?" he asked.

Maggie shrugged. "I don't know," she said. "I get worried when he drives, and I know that Merrill's a bad man, but I like to know where Daddy is. No matter what."

"Hmmm," the Judge said, reflecting. "When your father was young, before I became a judge, I was a defense lawyer like your father. Don't tell him I told you, but he used to get all in a swivet whenever I'd go to the prison. I think he was afraid those big doors would close behind me, and I'd be locked inside with all those murderers."

"Dad explains it to me," Maggie said, eating her brownie. "So I don't have to think bad things. He could never get locked inside, because the guards are watching out for him all the time. And Merrill gets searched, so he can't carry a weapon to hurt Dad."

"What a smart father you have. He must have learned from my mistakes."

"How come you went from being a lawyer to being a judge?" Maggie asked.

"Because of my stellar courtroom performance and brilliant legal mind."

"When you're a judge, you don't have to visit criminals in jail anymore, right?"

"Right. In fact, you'd be booted off the bench if you did."

"Huh," Maggie said, chewing thoughtfully.

The Judge sat back, watching her. His granddaughter had such a thoughtful face, intelligent eyes. She might make a fine jurist someday. Teddy, too. But he hoped they would choose corporate law or estate planning.

The Judge thought of Greg Merrill. That baby-faced, soft-voiced, unassuming, college-educated serial killer. What he had done to those girls made him a monster—he defied any other definition.

Johnny was with him now. The Judge looked at his gold watch: at this very moment, as time ticked by. Why, after a lifetime of trying cases involving violent crimes, should the Judge be made uneasy by the thought?

His gaze falling upon his granddaughter's innocent face, the Judge tried to smile. How many violent men had he and her father, over the years and with the full weight and imprimatur of the law behind them, released into society? Hundreds?

Thousands?

The Judge sighed. The truth was—in spite of this sunny child, this vision of goodness sitting beside him with brownie crumbs dotting her lips—he knew that a fair trial was their right.

Problem was, the Judge had lost his stomach for the whole thing. A passionate liberal in his youth, he had—in the lingo of Teddy—shape-shifted into a conservative jurist. He had one hundred percent supported Judge Miles Adams, the judge selected to preside over the long, emotional sentencing hearing that sent Gregory Bernard Merrill to the Death House.

"It's because of you," he said out loud. Staring at Maggie, her blue eyes so reminiscent of her ravishing mother's, the Judge knew that the kids were the reason for his conversion to a more conservative way of thought. What's a conservative but a liberal who's had grandchildren?

"What, Gramps?"

"Hmm?" he asked, still watching her face.

"You said 'it's because of you.' What's because of me?"

The Judge felt himself blush. He'd been caught having a Maeve moment. Talking out loud, instead of keeping his thoughts to himself. Get himself in trouble, that way.

"Nothing, my sweet girl. Just enjoy your brownie."

"You said Maeve was doing the dishes," Maggie said, her cool gaze flicking to the overflowing sink. "But she must have been too tired to finish."

"Looks like you're right."

"I'll help her," Maggie said, lifting her glass and plate off the table, starting to run the water. "Washing is good . . . all that warm water flowing, sending everything bad away, down the drain. Kate told me."

"Kate?"

"Our almost baby-sitter," Maggie said wistfully.

"Kate sounds like she has that rare combination of wisdom and practicality."

"Yeah."

"Well, Maeve will certainly appreciate your help," the Judge said calmly, watching Maggie roll up her sleeves and squirt green detergent into the sink.

He had come, over time, to believe that his role in life was to protect Maeve. He didn't want her being sent to some old age home. She had no kids; her sister was dead.

She'd cared for him since Leila had died, and now it was the Judge's turn to give back. The Judge was all she had—and vice versa. To his surprise, in one of life's beautiful mysteries, he'd found himself able to love again.

Judge Patrick O'Rourke's job now was going to be keeping Maeve Connelly safe at home. Everyone needed someone to love. Everyone: without exception. The Judge thought of John, of what he'd gone through with Theresa, and his heart ached. John had been devastated by her betrayal. He wouldn't even consider dating, and the Judge doubted he ever would again. Like everyone, he needed love, but he wouldn't let himself go looking.

Some things just cut too deep.

John O'Rourke walked into Winterham, the state's only super-max prison, where death row was located. Greeted by some guards, ignored by others, he made his way past the razor-wire-topped walls, through a series of metal detectors and automatic-lock doors.

"Here to see Greg Merrill," he said to Rick Carmody, a burly, steroid-ridden guard he saw frequently, who pretended not to know why John was there.

"You gotta wait," the guard said without looking up from his magazine.

John didn't reply, but he felt his blood pressure skyrocketing. As defense counsel for a death row inmate, he got about ten degrees of respect less than a thief; experience had taught him that making waves would just slow everything down more.

Sitting down in the hard brown vinyl chair, he opened his briefcase and began to read his brief. He pictured Kate Harris, thought of what she'd told him about her sister and her husband. He hadn't slept last night. The feelings had kept him up—chills, as if from a fever, racing through his body. Betrayed by two people close to her—how had she gotten through it? Thinking of Theresa and Barkley, John shivered now. When he glanced up, he saw the guard smirking.

"Hey, Counsel," Carmody said, gesturing at John's bandaged head. "You get that in a barroom brawl?"

"You should see the other guy," John

said, taking a deep breath to dispel the memories of Theresa.

"Huh, I bet." The guard chuckled, cracking his fat knuckles one by one. When he had finished, he yawned and gestured for John to step forward. With outward patience, John allowed the guard to wave the metal-detector wand up and down his arms and legs. Inwardly, he longed to clock the keghead: not simply for the ignominy of being so blatantly disrespected, but for the gall with which Carmody leaned forward, examining John's head wound.

"They really got you," the guard said.

" 'They'?" John asked. "You know something about it?"

"No, Counselor, not me," Carmody said, hands up in mock innocence.

"That's good," John said, breathing raggedly, "because my kids were there. You understand? My kids could have gotten hurt by the brick, by the broken glass. They saw it happen, violence in their own home!"

"Hey, whoa! Watch your mouth—you go making accusations you can't back up, I'll get you ejected so fast—"

"My client has the right to counsel."

"And I have discretion over everything

goes on in here. Back off from that garbage about the brick and the window, you hear me?"

"Whoever did it . . ." John began, hardly caring whether he got himself chucked from the room. Until he had come face-to-face with someone who would probably cheer the brick thrower, John hadn't known the full depth of his own rage. His home had been ripped apart once—he wasn't going to let it happen again. ". . . Could have hurt my kids. Hear me? My *kids.* So forgive me if I'm short on good humor right now."

"I don't want trouble here—let's forget it. Your kids okay?"

"Yes."

"That's what matters."

"You're right. Can I see my client?"

Carmody threw the bolt, letting John pass into death row. John's heart was beating fast; from how Kate Harris had stirred up old deadly pain, from Carmody—could he have had something to do with the brick? And from the normal human response of entering death row.

The inmates lived in seven-by-twelve-foot cells, each containing a metal bunk, desk, and combination toilet-sink. Twenty-two hours each day were spent in solitude; from six to eight each night, they were permitted to mingle in the common room—only with each other, never with other prison inmates.

Merrill lived in the "Death Cell." Adjacent to the execution chamber, it faced a desk continuously manned by a guard and afforded no privacy. The guard observed everything Merrill did, from washing his face to going to the bathroom. All activity was logged. Although John had filed briefs citing the inhumanness of the treatment, Merrill remained in the Death Cell. And he'd stay there, John knew, until someone worse came along.

"Hi, John," came Merrill's soft voice, the instant John walked into the consultation room.

"Hi, Greg."

Unrestrained, Merrill sat at a wooden conference table in his orange jumpsuit. He clutched a Bible; he was never without it. A closed-circuit television system monitored the room, allowing guards to observe.

"What happened to your head?"

"Just a bump." John opened his briefcase, removed papers. Was he holding back the truth so Greg wouldn't feel bad about being the proximate cause of his injury? Or because of an atavistic fear of letting the killer anywhere close to the details of his home?

"God bless you, John," Greg said quietly, fingers steepled and head bowed. "I pray for you, you know. That no harm ever befalls you."

"Thanks, Greg," John said, brushing it all off. Finding religion was standard practice in prison; over the years, John had learned not to put too much stock in it. "Okay—here's what we have . . ."

John outlined his brief to the court and his latest motion to have Greg moved to a more private cell.

"It's horrible," Greg said, his voice breaking. "The guards jeer when I go to the toilet. They laugh at me."

"I know. I'm sorry, and I'm working on it."

"You know, John . . . I'm not afraid to die. I have the Lord with me; I know my loving God won't send me to Hell. I *know* that, John. Does it sound crazy when I tell you that I know for sure?"

"I know you believe it, Greg," John said steadily. He looked into his client's cloudy brown eyes. The man had the urge to hurt.

It was part of his makeup, just like his brown eyes and curly hair. Merrill had confessed to having murdered seven women, having assaulted, stalked, and frightened many more.

"*This* is my hell," Greg whispered, his voice becoming a hiss. "This prison— manned by the worst of the worst. At least I admitted what I did. These men lord it over me with such unbelievable hatred, John. I *want* death to come; it's *life* that's so unbearable."

John nodded. Greg talked this way, but he was fighting with all he had for the right to live. And it was John's sworn duty to help him.

"Listen," John said, pulling out another sheaf of documents. "I've reviewed Dr. Beckwith's reports."

"You have?" Greg asked, his eyes a little brighter.

"Yes." John had used Beckwith before— sometimes to testify, sometimes just to examine his client. From simple cases such as the one where his testimony had been invaluable in supporting a medication level-imbalance defense ("My client had been prescribed insufficient medication, became emotionally overloaded, and committed the theft . . .") to determining the state of mind of a real estate lawyer who had killed his unfaithful wife.

"Does he think we have a chance, John?"

"It's possible. He'd like to meet with you again," John said, glancing at the file. Beckwith had interviewed Merrill once a week since joining John's defense team at the beginning.

"I like him, John. He understands me . . . says my paraphilia is like a cancer of the mind. Can people help themselves from having breast cancer, brain cancer? No, they can't. Dr. Beckwith knows it's like that for me . . ."

John nodded, watching his client's eyes. Merrill never got emotional—even now, with his voice rising and falling, there was no affect on his face. John tried not to get too personally engaged or curious. He was a hired gun; his job was to find legal solutions to legal problems. His client had as many rights in that area as anyone.

"I have a broken mind," Greg continued. "It's not my fault I couldn't stop thinking of having sex with those girls, couldn't force myself to stop imagining—Dr. Beckwith knows that. I can't choose what to have on my mind . . . the thoughts just came."

"I know," John said, his gaze falling on the thicker file in his briefcase, the transcript where Greg confessed to his murders and revealed the locations of the bodies.

"He understands that Depo-Provera helps, that I don't get the thoughts any- more . . . I'm not stupid, I'm not dumb—I just have a mental illness. Dr. Beckwith agrees that I'm a genius, that Darla and I are both members of Mensa."

"He knows," John said, still staring at the file. "Darla" was Darla Beal, Greg's girl- friend, one of the many women who had contacted him in prison. The phenomenon amazed John.

Searching the file, he found himself recall- ing the locations where the bodies had been found: Exeter, Hawthorne, Stonington . . . then he ran through a list of places Greg had mentioned off the record, where he had stalked or assaulted women and not gotten caught.

Kate Harris had kept John awake last night. No doubt about it. Not just the story of her marriage—the pain John understood very well—but her suspicions regarding her sister's disappearance. Unable to push the thoughts away, he'd finally thrown off the covers and gone downstairs to page through Merrill's file.

By three A.M., he had satisfied himself that there was no mention of Willa Harris, no discussion of anyone fitting her description in any of the locales Kate had mentioned: Newport, Providence, the Connecticut shoreline.

And then, turning one last page, John had found it: *Fairhaven.*

The place where Kate's sister's Texaco card had last been used. Fairhaven, Massachusetts. A small town just east of New Bedford, filled with boatyards and fishing boats, of prim houses surrounded by rose gardens and white picket fences.

Fairhaven: Greg Merrill had admitted, only to his lawyer, to having stood in the backyard of a Fairhaven house, having climbed onto an overturned dinghy to peer at a thirteen-year-old girl in her bedroom, one hand down his pants as he tried to raise her window with the other.

"Dr. Beckwith thinks there might be a new category for me, doesn't he?" Greg said, suddenly full of life, leaning all the way across the table, knocking his Bible aside.

"I'm not sure," John said carefully. "I just know he wants to examine you again."

"An important man like him," Greg said, eyes glittering. "With all his credentials . . . Director of the Center for Sexual Disorders at Maystone University; a member of the committee for the definitions in the DSM-IV . . . that's it, right?"

"What, Greg?"

"He wants to use me for a new definition . . . I'm a magna cum laude graduate of UConn, but I have—what did he say? 'An extremely primitive personality structure'?" Greg's eyes flashed. "A zombie-maker . . . I leave my victims alive, just barely, in breakwaters on the incoming tide . . . so they'll have time to know what's going to happen. And then there was that girl who survived all those days . . . He thinks I did that on purpose . . ."

John looked up, with some alarm. This was new. Neither he nor Philip Beckwith was getting into this kind of diagnostic discussion with their client yet, and Merrill had seemed content to leave it that way.

"At the same time," Greg continued, "I'm

power-bestowing. I give them a last chance. I give them hope: Because until the tide rises up to their mouths and noses, they're not at all sure they're going to die. That girl who lived ... she had hope until she drowned, then got brought back to life. Zero brain function—a zombie—but alive. Now *there's* hope! A gift, John. I know, because I have it here. I'm in the Death Cell, but until they strap me down, there's hope. People live in hope, John—it's human nature."

"Where did you ... ?" John began to ask as his temple started to throb.

"Dr. Beckwith thinks I have a God complex," Greg said, shaking his head ruefully. "I give, so I can take away. Or give, as I so choose. I gave that girl those last minutes, John. And believe me, it was a gift. I did things to her, and she liked them. So—I killed her mind, but left her body alive."

"The tide," John reminded him, "was in control ... you misjudged the time that day." He knew that Greg always spent the last hour with his victims, slipping away just before the tide rose over the top of the breakwater to drown them.

He didn't want to get his feet wet.

"I kill in those girls what I hate most in myself . . . Dr. Beckwith gets it," Greg said, as if John hadn't even spoken, his flaring nostrils the only sign of internal disturbance.

"I don't think Dr. Beckwith has reached a conclusion yet, Greg," John said evenly. "He hasn't told you that, has he?"

Greg laughed sadly, shaking his head. "That would be counterproductive, wouldn't it? If I know where Dr. Beckwith is going with me, he might suspect me of trying to fake thoughts and symptoms. No, I just know."

"How do you know?"

"It's not really such a mystery, John," Greg said. "I'm in Mensa, remember? My intuition is more finely tuned than lay people know. I've probably read more about cases like mine than any psychiatrist alive. I'm just telling you what I'd say about me if I were the doctor. Don't read too much into it," he continued, leaning forward to grip his Bible again. "The Lord steers my boat; I only row. I speak to whomever you ask me to; I'm humbly grateful for your excellent representation, John. Even though you shouldn't talk about what you don't know. You don't know I lost track of the time, and I don't like you saying it. Okay?"

"Sure, Greg."

Merrill nodded, satisfied. "Anyway, thank you for putting me in touch with Dr. Beckwith. Now, is there anything else?"

"Yes."

John took the file of Greg's testimony from his briefcase and laid it on the table between them. He reached into his pocket and touched the photograph of Willa Harris. Picturing Kate's face, the tears glistening on her freckled cheeks, he closed his eyes. He was gripped by internal conflict: serving his client versus . . . what? Helping a sister find answers? Satisfying his own curiosity? His eyelids flicked open, and he raised his eyes to meet Greg Merrill's.

"Tell me something, Greg."

"Anything, John."

"Fairhaven, Massachusetts," John said, watching for Greg's reaction.

A small smile touched Greg's thin lips. His cheeks dimpled, but his eyes remained flat, without affect. "Ah, yes. Sleeping Beauty."

"Tell me."

"You have it there, in the file. I've told you already, haven't I?"

"Tell me again." Then, softening his tone

because he saw Greg's smile disappear, "Please."

"I'm sensitive, John," Greg said, his chin trembling. "I don't like it when you're harsh with me."

"I know. I'm sorry. Please, tell me again. About Fairhaven."

"Okay." Smile back, forgiving, touching the Bible for luck or comfort. "I was passing through . . ."

He might be speaking about a regular business trip: a traveling salesman, stopping in a seaside town for lunch, John thought.

"I had to go to the bathroom. I pulled into a parking lot, to relieve myself . . . it was behind a Laundromat, I think. In one of those little strip malls, with a convenience store and a card shop. The girl's house was out back, across the lot. I just happened to turn my head . . . I saw her bedroom light go on . . ."

Greg's eyes became misty. He experienced fugue states; John had watched him go in and out. Recounting an event—one of his killings or stalkings—his eyes would glaze over, his mouth might get dry. He'd speak with such bottomless longing, as if he were describing the long-lost love of his life.

"Why then?" Greg asked. "Why that moment? I mean, I was sitting in the car. Had to relieve myself against a brick wall . . . if she hadn't turned on her bedroom light, if there hadn't been a split second before she pulled the curtain. Thin white curtains that didn't quite meet. I looked through the crack."

John listened. He had heard this before, and his heart kicked again: the timing always seemed so capricious. Half a minute one way or the other, and Greg Merrill would have just passed by.

"She was lovely. Thirteen, going on fourteen, I'd say. She didn't know who she was yet. Didn't know the power she had . . . I crossed the parking lot. Scaled the anchor fence—snagged my jeans on a rusty edge. Walked right through her yard . . . someone had put an old rowboat by the house. I pulled it over, climbed up, and watched through the space between the curtains till she went to sleep."

"Did anyone see you? Catch you?" John asked, his hand on Willa's picture.

"No. I was like the night wind—swift,

sure, invisible. I wanted her, though. My mind was going . . . even had the breakwater in mind. The big rocky one in New Bedford. You know—right near the boat that goes to the Vineyard . . ."

"I've seen it."

"But it wasn't to be," Greg said, shaking his head. The film had left his gaze, like the third eyelid rolling back from a cat's eye as he emerged from the trance. "Her window was locked, and her father was home. I could hear his voice from inside . . ."

"That's the only reason?"

"What other one would there be?"

John's fingers brushed the picture and he found himself wondering whether the convenience store had had gas pumps, whether Willa Harris had interrupted Greg and become his second-choice victim.

"I don't know, Greg. You tell me."

Merrill shook his head. "That's all. I wasn't ready to get caught . . . didn't want to get beaten up by some nasty fisherman. That's not how I wanted to come in . . ."

"I know; it's not how you 'came in,' " John agreed. Then looking directly into Greg's eyes, "What time of year was it? You remember?"

Greg closed his eyes, sniffing the air. "Spring," he said. "I can still smell the flowers in her garden. Last spring."

"Spring . . . like April?"

"Maybe," Greg said. "Because it was still cool enough for her to have the windows closed . . . they weren't an air-conditioner family, John. Simple, low-cost. You know? You should have seen that rowboat I stood on. Really old."

"Okay," John said, thinking of Willa's April 6 gas receipt. He packed the papers back into his files, then shoved the files into his brown leather briefcase. The overhead lights hummed. Food smells drifted into the closed room. Greg pushed his chair back; he was fed in his room, meals in a Styrofoam box, three times a day.

"Oh, Greg," John said, his voice casual even though his pulse had taken off, racing as he took hold of the picture in his pocket. "One last thing."

"It's dinnertime," Greg said, apologetically, on his feet.

"I know . . . just this." John held up Willa's picture. "Ever seen her?"

Greg hesitated. John stared hard at his eyes. Greg reached out, to take the picture for a closer look, but for some reason, John wouldn't let him touch it. He wasn't sure why, but an image of Kate's plaintive eyes filled his mind. He held tight to the photo and pulled back slightly.

"Ever seen her?" John repeated.

Greg tilted his head. His flat eyes rarely betrayed any emotion. Even when he was acting the part—voice rising or dropping with great drama, shoulders hunched, head shaking—his eyes remained dead, like a shark's. But right now, looking at Willa Harris's smiling picture, John could swear he saw a flicker.

That was it: just a flash, a small swell, as if a great fish had passed just beneath the water's surface. A rise, and then nothing. The sea was undisturbed, and John was left wondering whether there had been anything there at all.

"No, John," Greg said. "I'm sorry."

John waited. He watched Greg's eyes, hoping to see ripples.

Nothing.

"I've never seen her," Greg said pleasantly.

Called by the smell of his next meal, Greg Merrill turned to go. Reverently holding his

Bible, he departed the small room, left his lawyer holding the picture of a smiling young woman, and padded down the hall in the company of a guard.

John stood to leave. The stitches in his head had really begun to pound. He stared down into Willa Harris's sweet face and felt a ridiculous shock of betrayal. *How could you do it?* he wanted to ask her. *How could you have hurt your sister that way?*

chapter 7

Two and a half days passed; by Thursday, Kate had driven by the O'Rourke house five times. She couldn't help herself. John O'Rourke was the last and only thread connecting her to the hope of learning more about Willa. She understood it was a long shot; he had made it clear that he was forbidden by the Code of Professional Responsibility to speak to her. She also knew that she was behaving badly, like a stalker herself, driving past his house so often. Each time she went by, she'd look for the kids.

How were they? she wondered. Had John found a baby-sitter everyone liked? Had

Brainer run through more brambles, making a mess of his coat again? Was it Kate's imagination, or had Bonnie fallen in love?

Because every time Kate drove past, Bonnie would press her nose to the window and run the length of the car—as if to keep Brainer's house in sight for as long as possible.

"Cool it, Bon," Kate threw over her shoulder. "He doesn't even seem to be home."

None of them did. John's car was never parked in the driveway; she couldn't spy the kids in their yard. Both nights, the same lights were on, as if lit by a timer. Had Kate's request somehow convinced John O'Rourke to leave town, taking his whole family with him?

Even the pumpkin she'd bought with Maggie was gone from the steps.

Finally, on her fifth trip past in two days, she parked the car across the street and stared at the house. She wished it could somehow give up all the answers she'd come to find about Willa.

Sitting back in the seat, Kate saw Teddy's soccer ball on the front lawn, Maggie's rain boots left on the porch. The broken window was boarded up. Flowered curtains hung at another window; Kate felt a pang, thinking of the children's mother. She had died in a car crash—disappeared from the kids' lives as suddenly as Willa and her parents had from her own.

Had she and John been happy? He had reacted so strongly to Kate's story of adultery; she'd been sure he had been through it himself. Kate sat very still, her heart beating hard, staring at the white house. She wondered whether John had seen it coming, seen the clues all along, not wanting to face what they meant.

The late October afternoon was bitter cold, as if winter was bearing down on them. Kate closed her eyes, forcing her curiosity away. What did it matter to her, the truth of John O'Rourke's marriage? Infidelity destroyed love. It had ripped Kate apart, causing her to question everything in her whole life.

Now, her only peace and sanity came from much farther back in time . . . from childhood, the years when she, Matt, and Willa had been each other's only family. Back in Chincoteague, long ago . . . Kate drew the memories of her little sister around her now.

Willa . . .

They had ridden on the fire trucks, swum the wild ponies across the channel on Chincoteague's Pony Penning Day; they'd gone oystering with their brother on his wide wooden boat; they'd planted petunias, their mother's favorite flower, at their parents' graves; they had cut their own Christmas trees, decorated them with old family ornaments, oyster shells, and sand dollars; Kate had taken Willa to the ballet at the Kennedy Center; she had helped her find a favorite place to study at the Library of Congress; she had taken her to Senate hearings on water pollution and the shellfish industry; she had bought her her first set of watercolors.

Life with Willa . . .

When she was small, in third grade at Washington's exclusive St. Chrysogonus School, Willa had had to do a book report. Kate had taken her to the library, where they had found an entire shelf of biographies— orange volumes with the titles *Florence Nightingale, Woman of Medicine; Amelia Earhart, Girl Pilot; George Washington Carver, Boy Scientist.*

"Who are they, Katy?" Willa had asked, trying to decide.

"Read their biographies, and then you'll know."

"But who will I like most?"

"You won't know till you read them."

Willa had laughed, and Kate had smiled. "You know *me,* Katy. Who do *you* think I'll like most?"

"I think . . . Amelia Earhart."

"Because you like her, right?"

"Yes, I do."

"Who was she?"

Kate, opening the little orange book, had flipped through, read one of Amelia's quotes: " 'Courage is the price that life exacts for granting peace.' "

"Tell me, Katy!"

"She was a woman pilot, one of the first. She had a really strong, wonderful spirit, and she proved that women can do anything."

"Like what?"

"Like, read the book, and you'll find out. . . ." Kate had teased.

Willa was riveted to the orange volume, reading it straight through. Fascinated by the little red airplane that had first captivated Amelia, she had also been torn apart by Amelia's loss.

"Wasn't she brave?" Kate had asked, tucking her sister in that night. "Did you like how she challenged all those prejudices people used to have, about women not flying?"

Willa had nodded, huddled under her covers with the book. Kate had sat down on the edge of her bed; she had an ulterior motive for asking. Having finished her master's in molecular biology from Georgetown, she had gotten her first job with the National Maritime Fisheries. Her duties included checking shellfish beds from the Chesapeake to Penobscot Bay, and she'd been thinking about getting a pilot's license to make it easier to get them home to Chincoteague.

"Where did Amelia go?" Willa had asked. "Why can't they find her?"

"She disappeared," Kate had replied. "It's a mystery."

"Her plane crashed?"

"They think so. No one is sure."

"*Someone* must have seen her. . . . *Someone* must know where she went."

"The Pacific is a huge ocean," Kate had said, stroking her sister's silky hair.

"And it swallowed her up?" Willa had asked, captivated and grief-stricken.

"I don't know, Willie. Maybe she landed on an island . . . a beautiful desert island with palm trees and freshwater lagoons . . . filled with oysters for her to eat and pearls for her to wear."

"And pink sand on the beach . . ."

"And rare birds in the trees . . ."

"A magical place," Willa had whispered, her voice breaking.

"Like Narnia or Oz," Kate had whispered back. She had read her sister the books of C. S. Lewis and L. Frank Baum, and she found herself conjuring up the places the authors had created, wanting to soothe Willa.

"I hope so," Willa had said, starting to sob. "Katy, I hope Amelia's on a wonderful, enchanted island with a lagoon."

"She'd be very old, if she were still alive."

"That's okay . . . I want her to be old." Willa had wept. "Everyone should get to be old. . . ."

Had she been thinking of their own parents, taken from them so young? Kate wasn't sure, but she had held her little sister, deciding for the moment not to mention flying lessons. Although she wound up taking them—getting her pilot's license and sharing a chartered plane with several other scientists—that night she just rocked Willa to sleep, mourning with her for the loss of their parents and Amelia.

Death had been so familiar to them; they were orphans, after all. But disappearance had seemed impossible, too horrifying to contemplate. Thinking of Amelia Earhart just falling out of the sky, swallowed up by the sea, had seemed so terrible, that the Harris sisters had had to invent a beautiful island of pink sand and rare birds just to accept her loss.

Willa had started sketching, then painting: panels of color and line, telling the rich, emotional story of Amelia Earhart. She had layered truth and myth, imagination and reality, creating a story and a world of what might have happened, learning to be an artist in the process.

"Willa," Kate said out loud in her car in front of the O'Rourkes' house, holding tight to the steering wheel.

If only her sister could be on a desert island, a magical place; if only there were some explanation for the six months she had been gone; if only she would walk thorough the wardrobe door, or click her heels three times to come home; if only she had ruby slippers; if only she had gone off painting somewhere; if only she weren't missing.

"Willa," Kate said again, but this time the name became a wail. She heard it echoing in the car, her voice reverberating in her ears.

All Kate's praying, wishing, cursing, begging with the forces of the universe, and bargaining with the fates, should have brought her sister back. The many nights of sitting still, staring at the stars, wondering whether she had somehow caused Willa to stay away, to be too afraid of Kate's anger to come home.

And all those nights of hating Andrew— despising her husband for hiring Willa as his intern, for having her work late, for preying on her and getting her to fall in love with him. . . . And—for Kate couldn't, after six months of soul-searching, deny this part— hating Willa.

She had watched her sister grow up. Willa had always been shy and beautiful, more comfortable painting alone on the dunes than being with other people, especially men. When she turned twenty-one, something changed. Her inner grace began to radiate outwards. She wasn't so withdrawn; she began to go out more. Andrew noticed, joking to Kate, "I think we've got a heartbreaker on our hands." And Kate had joked back, "As long as her heart's not the one being broken."

She'd spent so many nights awake, wondering: How had the affair started? Who had initiated it? Where had they gone together? Had Willa pleased Andrew more than Kate did? Kate—she couldn't pretend this part wasn't true—had wanted to attack her sister. Willa's heart hadn't been broken: Kate's had.

Six months, Kate thought, holding the steering wheel. A six-month-long time of darkness and despair.

Her spirit was parched and dry; her bones ached with grief. Her throat was sore, and there were so many unspoken words. *I'm furious with you, why did you do it? I love you more than anyone in the world. I love you like my own child, you broke my heart . . .*

The cold New England winds of October whistled through the car; Kate closed her eyes and pictured the alabaster city of Washington. Great white buildings, illuminated, none taller than the graceful domed Capitol glowing like Oz. The green parks and squares, the Mall, the low bridges across the gentle Potomac.

That's what life was like back home: gentle. Washington was a gracious city, less rushed and not as hard as New York or Boston. And the grasslands and marshes and tidal creeks and dunes of Chincoteague and Assateague were softer than the seashore of New England . . . no rocks or high places, just the gentle cradle of ponies and oysters and motherless girls.

But Willa had run away.

Kate, closing her eyes tight as the car heat pumped and the chill wind stung her fingers anyway, had had six months to think about it all, to try to understand. Willa had rushed away from herself and what she and Andrew had done. Fearing Kate's grief and rage—over finally losing her husband, but perhaps even more, over her sister's betrayal—Willa had fled the jurisdiction.

How had she decided on *here*?

With the whole world to choose from, north-south-east-west, how had she spun the globe and pointed to southern New England?

Now, rocking herself in her car outside John O'Rourke's house, Kate knew. Of course she knew; no one understood Willa better.

The refuge would have had to be by the sea; it would have had to promise the smell of salt air, the sound of the tides as they rose and fell. There would have had to be museums—places of culture, art, and nature. It would have had to be far enough away from Washington and Chincoteague to define "escape," but close enough for Kate to reach quickly when the call came.

The call had been Willa's postcard.

Kate removed it from her pocket, held it in her hand. It showed the view from the East Wind: the rocky coastline, the lighthouse shining in the distance, the crooked stone breakwater jutting out from the beach, Willa's handwriting on the back. Willa's love affair was over; she'd wanted to make things right with her sister so they could get on with their lives.

For years, Kate had known her marriage

was on the rocks. Her husband was an important man, the chief aide to a prominent senator. He knew his way around Washington as well as anyone. His work kept him out late and, often, away from home. Kate, absorbed in her own busy career and in raising Willa, had turned a blind eye to so much.

She had sometimes wondered why she had married him in the first place. . . .

But he was so attractive, and he had made her feel so special. That was one of his great gifts, why he'd been such a successful lobbyist in years gone by: because he could sell a person her own car. He had sought Kate out at a Hill cocktail party, celebrating the senator's bill protecting shellfisheries—Kate had been impressed by Andrew's behind-the-scenes work, by his unfailing commitment to the environment.

"What makes you care about shellfish beds in the Chesapeake?" she asked, impressed and a bit intimidated by his custom-made suit, his elegant manners.

"I'm a country boy from way back," he had said, leaning closer. "I was born and raised in Maine, and I know how fast a little greed can kill a whole lobster population."

She had grinned, sipping her chardonnay. "For me it's blue crabs and oyster beds."

"Your work is personal?" Andrew asked, trying to be heard over the voices and music.

"You can say that—I'm from Chincoteague."

"No kidding! My sisters grew up in love with Misty. So, you obviously love nature. What brought you to the big, bad city?"

"College, then my job. I work for the National Academy of Sciences. How about you?"

"Wanting to do good," he said, rolling his eyes and pretending to hit his head against the wall. "As crazy as that sounds."

"I don't think it sounds crazy," she said, feeling herself sparkle as she smiled into his eyes.

"Got to keep our planet going—for our kids."

"And our little sisters," Kate had said.

At Andrew's friendly, curious smile, she had told him all about Willa: about their parents' deaths, about Matt's life on the water, and about trying to raise a teenaged girl by herself. About being the youngest person chaperoning Willa's high school dances, starting to teach Willa to drive in the Chevy Chase Safeway parking lot, taking her on trips.

"Oh, those shoulders," Andrew had said, stepping forward, touching the base of Kate's neck with his hand, concern in his eyes.

"What about them?" she'd asked, his unexpected touch and kindness sending a jolt down to her toes.

"The weight of the world is on them. You must have been so young when all this fell to you—too young for so much responsibility."

Two senators stood at the bar. There was a presidential aide, a lawyer from the Justice Department, three members of the House of Representatives, several newscasters, and many other players of power. Kate barely noticed. She had eyes only for the kind, understanding Maine country boy as he took her glass from her hand, plunked it on a bookshelf, and led her outside.

The Washington night had been sultry, fragrant with wisteria and lilacs. When the valet had brought his car—an old Porsche—they left the fancy party. By the time they'd reached the Tune Inn for a beer, they were holding hands. And once they'd ended up at his Watergate apartment, Kate's fate was sealed. Little did she know that that was his pattern, not the hallmark of a lasting love.

He had taken the world off her shoulders for one night. In the weeks to come, he had promised her love and security. The fatherless girl in her had needed—grabbed for—it all. Willa had been just fifteen at the time. Kate was so emotionally drained from raising her young sister, she had accepted with gratitude Andrew's seeming desire to take care of them both.

The marriage had lasted seven years. Had he been faithful for any of them? Kate wasn't sure. She didn't think so. He had a weakness for women in need, and there had seemed no shortage: assistants in need of more money, interns in need of more excitement, lobbyists in need of his time and attention, constituents in need of his boss's ear. Andrew, in his generosity, had been willing to give to everyone.

Or, he was a predator for the women who looked to him for help—another way to look at it.

By the time Willa had started working for

him—to make money while she pursued her art—Kate had given up on the marriage. Perhaps she had harbored one last hope; that having her sister at work in his office would keep Andrew in line. She had never dreamed that Willa would become his next conquest. And she felt a sickening combination of guilt and fury for encouraging her sister to take the job.

What if Kate had received the card in time? Sitting in her car now, she reread those words: "I wish you could be here . . ." Would she have gone?

Bonnie whimpered, wanting the car to start moving again, but Kate just stared at the postcard. What if she hadn't moved out of the Watergate apartment she and Andrew had shared, if Willa's card hadn't gotten stuck in a pile of third-class mail for half a year?

If she had received Willa's card, would Kate have been able to save her sister? The answer to that question hung upon the answer to another one: Would she have been able to bury her pride, head north to meet Willa at the East Wind, talk things out?

No.

Kate knew that now—had admitted the

truth to herself during this long dark night of her soul. She hadn't been ready. She had still been too angry. She had *wanted* Willa to disappear, had longed for the red slippers' opposites: *Click your heels three times and go away forever,* had hated her little sister, the person she'd loved and protected most in the world, with a sudden and powerful passion.

Bonnie cried again.

Kate blinked her eyes open. The sea wind rose. With darkness falling, the lighthouse came alive, its beam resuming its journey through the sky.

Time had changed everything.

Six months had bleached the bones of Kate's hatred, had scoured them clean, purified them, left them brittle and crumbling, ready to be washed away by the tide. The only thing left behind was a burning love.

Kate's love for her little sister burned like a star. It glowed in her chest with white heat, where her heart should be. The love filled her blood, and it flowed with everything good: Christmas trees hung with oyster shells and sand dollars; spying on the wild ponies from sea-grass dunes.

Staring at John O'Rourke's house at

dusk, Kate watched the lights come on—
snap!—at six o'clock, and she thought of
John. Had this been a difficult time of night
for him? Had his wife been home where she
was supposed to be, cooking dinner for the
family? Or had she been off . . . who knew
where? Six o'clock had always been the
hardest time for Kate. Because she had
known Andrew had left the office but wasn't
home yet . . .

Kate blinked, forcing herself back to the
present. Where had John taken Teddy and
Maggie? Kate wanted to know—not only
because she hadn't given up, because she
planned to hound the lawyer till he either
begged for mercy or agreed to ask Merrill
about Willa—but because she longed to see
the kids. They had lodged in her heart on
that brief, intense morning she had first
come to this house.

Maggie and Teddy O'Rourke. In a different life, she'd like to be their baby-sitter.
They were sweet kids, loyal to their father,
devoted to each other. They reminded Kate
of herself and Willa when they were young;
she had no doubt that Teddy had helped
Maggie with a book report or two.

The O'Rourkes were siblings without a

mother, and Kate was a woman without her sister. She cared about them. Whether their father decided to help her or not, she needed to know they were okay. Disappearances—even ones that could be explained—were not to be borne.

Heading back to the East Wind, Kate knew that although this was her fifth cruise past the O'Rourkes' house, it wouldn't be her last.

Friday morning, Teddy woke up early. He had a big day ahead of him—a soccer game against Riverdale High. Their archrivals, the Riverdale Cannons, were nicknamed the "Cannibals"—because they killed their opponents and ate their dead. Shoreline Junior Varsity had lost in overtime on their last encounter, and Riverdale had promised to kick their butts again today.

The family was staying in his grandfather's house, with the idea that Gramps and Maeve could pitch in with him and Maggie till a new baby-sitter came along. Although Maggie was homesick for her room, Teddy liked it here, even more than his own house:

The hole left by his mother wasn't as obvious.

Padding barefoot down the hall, he entered the laundry room. Things were different here than at home. For one thing, the clothes got washed. For another, everything was starched and bleached. Maeve came from Ireland, where she'd learned to be a washerwoman. She made the Judge's shirts so white they were almost blue.

Teddy's soccer uniform had never been so clean. The white letters and numbers popped, like 3-D. But the nylon fabric was also stiff as a board with starch: Teddy practically had to crack it, to stuff it into his gym bag. Brainer's tail thumped against his legs, as he followed Teddy down the hall.

Irish oatmeal simmered on the stove. Maeve made the long-cooking kind, and she stood in the avocado green kitchen— all the appliances rounded, old-looking— stirring the oatmeal with a long-handled wooden spoon, when Teddy walked in.

"Morning, Maeve," he said.

"Morning, Luke, darlin'," she said in her soft brogue, smiling and giving him a kiss. She was small and plump, and when she hugged him, it felt soft and safe.

Teddy didn't bother correcting her on the name. She used to know who he and Maggie were, but lately she'd been forgetting. Her hair was white, so thin on top that her pink scalp showed—a lot like Gramps. They seemed like a pair, a married couple growing old together; since Teddy had never known his real grandmother, Leila, he loved Maeve and wondered what would happen to her when she retired.

His father sat at one end of the table, reading the paper. His grandfather sat at the other, doing the crossword puzzle. Eating his oatmeal, Teddy watched the two men drink their coffee—they both had thick white mugs, and they both gripped the handles with tension and might, as if they were going to finish breakfast, try cases, and slay the world.

"Hey, Dad," Teddy said.

His father didn't look up from the paper; it was early, and his father woke up slowly—only after reading all the football scores and drinking two cups of coffee—but did manage to make a sound like "What?"

"I have a game today. Against Riverdale."

"Your big rivals," his grandfather said.

"Yeah," Teddy said, grinning.

"You'd better cream 'em," his grandfather said. "Great rivalries deserve extra effort."

"It's only Junior Varsity—"

"Junior Varsity, nothing! Make no apologies! Great rivalries are all alike in character. Army and Navy, Yale and Harvard . . ."

Teddy laughed. "Riverdale and Shoreline . . ."

" 'Go Shoreline, Beat Riverdale,' " his grandfather chanted, beating his spoon on the table.

"More, dear?" Maeve asked in her pretty brogue, thinking the Judge was demanding more oatmeal.

"No, thank you, Maeve," his grandfather said, suddenly stern. Was he embarrassed because Maeve had called him "dear"? Yes, he was! Teddy saw the red begin just above the knot of his grandfather's tie, spread into his face. Teddy felt himself grinning. Now, to chase away the blush, the old man rattled his son's paper. "Hear that, Johnny? Big game today!"

Teddy's grin wavered. He tried to eat his oatmeal, but he couldn't swallow. He hoped, he hoped . . . *Come on, Dad.*

"I'd be there myself," Gramps said, "but

I've got to get my foot looked after. Got an appointment with the podiatrist. . . ."

Teddy didn't speak. He knew his grandfather was lying; it was Maeve's appointment, not his. Teddy knew, because he'd seen Maeve limping for two days. He'd spied his grandfather sitting beside her on the sofa yesterday, helping her take her sock and heavy shoe off, examining her bare foot with such tenderness Teddy had longed for his mother. And then he'd heard his grandfather call the podiatrist. . . .

"You've got a game this afternoon?" his father asked, lowering his paper.

"Yes," Teddy said.

"Go on, tell him what time, so he can set his clock for it," his grandfather urged.

"Four o'clock. At home."

By the devastated look on his father's face, Teddy could see it wasn't going to happen. His father opened his mouth— probably to explain about a motion hearing or a conference call or a meeting in chambers—but Teddy didn't wait around to hear.

"That's okay, Dad," he said, smiling so his father couldn't see his disappointment, hurrying out of the kitchen—Brainer at his heels—as Maggie walked in, bleary-eyed,

saying she didn't like oatmeal and needed a
Halloween costume for the pageant.

"Teddy, what should I be?" she called,
wheeling to run after him.

"Anything you want, Maggie," he said.

"You don't want to help . . ."

"I'm sorry," he said, seeing the injury in
her eyes. His dad's busy schedule wasn't
her fault, and Teddy felt bad for hurting her
feelings. The thing was, Teddy was hurt inside, too. His dad hadn't been to one game
all month. Teddy had blown one game and
scored two goals in another, and no one
from his family had been there to see.

"Can I go as a soccer player?" Maggie
whispered. "In your old uniform?"

"Mags, you wear it to school," Teddy
said, his throat aching. "The kids have seen
it already. But if you want to, yeah. Sure you
can. . . ."

He grabbed his jacket and gym bag. His
book bag was wedged against the table in
the front hall, and when he bent down to get
it, he knocked against Brainer, who bumped
into the table; a flurry of papers fell to the
door.

Things from his father's pockets: He always emptied them out at night, wherever

he was. Keys, wallet, business cards, scraps of paper picked up through the day. Teddy's mother had called the piles from his father's pocket "archaeology." Meaning that if she sifted through them, she could learn what he'd been doing all day.

Restoring the papers to the table, Teddy noticed a woman's picture. Smiling, head tilted prettily, she reminded him of someone. Wide-open eyes, straight brown hair . . . *Eyes the color of river stones,* Teddy thought, and then he had it: Kate.

Kate, his friend, the woman who had taken care of Maggie and Brainer. This picture was of her—of a younger Kate. Taken years ago? Or could it be someone else . . . her daughter?

Suddenly the truth came to him: her sister. Kate's younger sister, her "Maggie," the person Kate Harris loved most. In the same pile of his father's things, Teddy found a scrap paper with "East Wind Inn" written on it. Teddy just knew—why else would his father care about the East Wind? Kate had to be staying there. He thought of her soft voice, her slightly southern accent, the way she'd helped him.

Although the inn wasn't on his direct

route to school, it wasn't far out of the way. Teddy checked his watch. It was early, just seven-fifteen. He didn't want to wake her up, but he had an idea. He could leave her a note. . . .

Even if his father and grandfather couldn't come to his soccer game, maybe someone could.

chapter 8

The crowd was wild. Parents lined the field, screaming encouragement. Classmates jumped up and down. Girlfriends couldn't look. The coaches yelled. Cheerleaders had dressed in pumpkin heads and witches' hats. Dark clouds raced overhead, threatening rain or snow. The J.V. squads were on fire, and the game was tied, 1–1.

Kate pulled her green wool jacket tighter, watching Teddy race down the field. Sure on his feet, he had the ball, deftly weaving between Riverdale players. Although she didn't know much about the game, she found herself screaming louder than anyone.

"Go, Teddy!" she cried, holding Bonnie's red leash.

The crowd joined in, calling his name.

"You can do it, O'Rourke! Go, go, go!"

Teddy scored, and Shoreline went ahead, 2–1. Kate pumped her fists in the air, shouting with glee. That morning, returning from her walk along the bluff with Bonnie, she'd found a note signed by Teddy, tucked under her windshield wiper and asking her "if she had nothing better to do," to come to the game. She had planned to check out of the inn, head up the coast to Rhode Island, and broaden her search for Willa. But Teddy's request had touched her heart so completely, she'd decided to postpone her departure.

"*Better* to do?" she'd asked Teddy as he'd run by, taking the field. "This is the best offer I've had since coming to Connecticut!"

Now, still cheering his goal, she felt someone tap her arm. Bonnie let out a short, friendly yelp. A woman stood there, slim and blond, wearing a tight ski-suit-looking outfit. Her lips were full, shiny with gloss, her eyes made up in stylish shades of beige and slate. The only blight on her perfect face was her tiny nose, flaming red from the cold.

"Hi, there," the woman said, backing off slightly from the dog.

"Hello," Kate said, smiling. "She's friendly," she added.

"Do I . . . know you?" the woman asked, totally ignoring Bonnie's tail-wagging hello.

"I don't think so," Kate began, but her voice caught: Could this woman have met Willa, mistaken Kate for her sister? "Do I remind you of someone?"

"I'm not sure," the woman said, laughing. "People always remind me of someone else. But I heard you cheering for Teddy O'Rourke."

"Yes, the team hero." Kate smiled.

"How do you know Teddy?"

Kate was taken aback by the woman's directness.

"Well, I sort of know his father."

"Oh, Johnny. We're pals from way back. Are you a personal friend? Or a client?"

"Neither," Kate said, feeling herself close off. The woman was staring at her with a hungry grin, as if she wanted to jump inside her skin and find out what she was doing with John O'Rourke. Although the woman wore several rings, none of them looked like a wedding band. Did she think Kate was intruding on the local single-man territory?

"Well, whatever. I'm Sally Carroll. It's nice you're here for Teddy. Theresa—his mother—was my best friend. She never missed a game. That's my son—number thirty-two. Bert and Teddy have been friends since 'Mommy and Me.' And Theresa and I date back to high school—we were all in the same crowd."

"I'm sorry . . . you lost your friend," Kate said.

Sally nodded. "Yes, it was very unexpected. Well . . . nice talking to you. You know, you really do remind me of someone."

"My sister was in town," Kate said, her pulse quickening. "Maybe you met her? She stayed at the East Wind. . . ."

Sally smiled. "Like I said, everyone looks like someone else to me. . . ."

Kate opened her mouth to say more, but Sally hurried away. Going straight to a cluster of other mothers, she began to talk in a low voice, so Kate couldn't hear. Still, by the way the women looked over, she knew that Sally was spreading the word, that there was a stranger in town watching Teddy O'Rourke play soccer.

When she looked up, to see Teddy passing the ball downfield, she caught sight of a man wearing a Shoreline High windbreaker, watching—not the soccer team, but her. Tall and thin, in his thirties, with dark eyes and short curly hair, he frowned in Kate's direction, as if, like Sally Carroll, he was trying to place her.

At halftime, when the teams gathered round the benches to drink water and strategize, Teddy ran over to Kate.

"Thanks for coming," he said, breathless. Then, bending down to pet the Scottie, "You have a dog?"

"Bonnie. She's my sister's."

"Good dog, Bonnie."

"Great first half, Teddy," she said. "I'm really glad I saw you score."

"Me, too."

Kate wanted to ask where his father was, but she noticed a deep sadness in Teddy's eyes that she recognized from Willa. When her sister was little, no matter how hard Kate had tried to get away from college or work, Willa had sometimes had to go to field hockey, glee club, and art shows on her own.

"He'd be here if he could," Kate heard herself saying.

"I know."

"He's a big-time lawyer," she said. "Even dads with jobs half as important as his have to work during the day."

"My mom used to come," he said.

"I know. Sally Carroll told me."

Teddy's eyes narrowed. He seemed to shiver, looking over at the group of mothers—all watching him and Kate.

"They wonder who you are," he said.

"Well, it's a small town."

"Yeah," Teddy said. Just then, they saw the mothers turn their heads as one, and Kate spotted Teddy's coach coming their way.

"Hey, O'Rourke—better hydrate if you want to have a good second half."

"Okay, Mr. Jenkins," Teddy said.

Jenkins? Wasn't that the name of Kate's hosts, Felicity and Barkley? Kate was about to ask, when the coach crossed his arms across his chest and gave her a cute, crooked smile.

"A new fan," he said.

"Excuse me?"

"I know most of the moms around here. You must be . . . an aunt?"

"No," Kate said, smiling. "Just a friend."

"I'm Hunt Jenkins . . . and you're . . . help me out."

"My name is Kate Harris."

"Well, nice to meet you, Kate. Any friend of Teddy's is a friend of mine."

"Yes," Kate said, flashing a big smile. "Your star player!"

"Yup. Best forward since my cousin Caleb used to play."

"Caleb Jenkins?" she asked, remembering how John had mentioned the name— the client who'd borrowed the motorboat. "Then you must be related to Felicity."

"She's my sister-in-law. How do you know her?"

"I'm staying at the East Wind," Kate said, aware of all the questions she'd answered that day, of how the locals looked after each other. It was the same in Chincoteague, and for a moment she longed for the ease and anonymity of life in the city, of Andrew's world in Washington. She'd be returning home soon . . . just a few more stops in

New England, and then she'd be back in D.C.

"Well, well. Small world."

Suddenly the man with the dark curls and Shoreline windbreaker came walking over. Kate saw Sally wave him over, but he just threw her a smile and kept walking.

"Hi, Hunt," he said. "Who's your friend?"

"I'm Kate Harris," she said.

"Peter Davis. Nice to meet you."

"You, too," she said.

"She's not a mom or an aunt," Hunt explained. "Just a soccer fan and a friend of Teddy O'Rourke's."

"Great . . . listen, Hunt—got a second? I've got a great second half strategy, something from my soccer days at Hotchkiss . . ."

"Any help gladly taken." Hunt grinned. "My job depends on winning!"

"Take care, Kate," Peter said. "Nice to meet you. Maybe you'll wind up at the Witch's Brew later . . . Friday and Saturday nights, there's a band."

"Yes," Hunt Jenkins said. "Save me a dance, Kate."

"I don't think . . ." Kate began, blushing as she felt his eyes on her body.

"Hey, time!" one of the soccer officials yelled, and Hunt and Peter hurried toward the sidelines to confer on game tactics.

Both benches began to empty out, and someone in the crowd squeezed an air horn. The cheerleaders, dressed in their Halloween masks and pointy black hats, began to dance on the sidelines, in antici-pation.

Teddy grinned, reaching his fist out. Willa used to do the same thing, so Kate clinked knuckles with her young friend, and watched him take the field. Hunt Jenkins smiled, walking backward, but she ignored him, and he eventually turned away.

A woman behind Kate was talking to her friend. "Which one's the lawyer's son?" she asked.

"That tall boy—number twenty-two."

"It's not his fault, but still—I wonder if his father sees the unfairness of his children being free to enjoy life while those girls lie buried . . ."

"I know—it's disgusting to me, thinking of Greg Merrill alive and well while Toni Moore is dead. She used to run on that track, right over there. She was such a fine athlete . . ."

"Oh, she was. She made our town proud.

John O'Rourke ought to be ashamed of himself, working on behalf of her killer. Talk about a warped set of priorities . . . no wonder Theresa did what she did. I can't imagine being close to someone who thinks like he does."

The two women clucked, and Kate felt her back stiffen.

"Did you hear about the brick through his window? Look at his son out there—playing soccer, running in the sun. It's almost criminal, when you think of those girls, of the unfairness."

"What's unfair—" Kate snapped, turning around fast, thinking of Willa, thinking of Teddy, her heart in a knot. She felt anger exploding, and she stared straight into the shocked faces of two suburban women. "—And what's *criminal* is taking any of this out on his children. They didn't do anything. They're as innocent as the victims."

"Who are you?" one of the women asked, anger in her eyes.

"Their friend," Kate said, backing away, watching Teddy take the ball down the field. Her heart was racing, as if she were running toward the goal herself. She had seen the broken glass, the blood on John's face, the terror in Maggie's and Teddy's eyes. The whole town was talking about the O'Rourke family, and the kids had to know.

Teddy, at least, was a teenager, and probably heard things about his parents. Kate's stomach clenched. The women behind her continued to whisper, and Kate moved away.

John had heard the expression "move heaven and earth" his whole life, but he'd never actually done it until today. He rushed his associates through reports of their research projects—one in charge of medical testimony, another whose memo on change-of-venue would certainly make its way into the appeal. He spoke with two psychiatrists, arranged interviews the following week, and postponed a visit to the prison.

Swinging by his father's house, he picked up Maggie and Brainer, and made it to the field just as the second half got underway. He parked on the grass, and walked briskly toward the Shoreline side as Maggie and the dog bounded ahead. Teddy had the ball;

he was dribbling fast and furiously, setting up the shot.

"You've got it, Ted," John called. "Shoot!"

"Teddddyyyyyyyyyyyy!" Maggie yelled.

The crowd jumped up and down, and John reeled with pride, knowing the excitement was all for his son. John had played soccer at Shoreline and, later, at Yale, and he knew how great it felt to hear everyone shouting your name. He hoped that Teddy could distinguish his among the voices, and he felt a sharp stab, remembering how few games his own busy lawyer father had made it to.

Teddy passed, his teammate held up as Teddy tore into place. The pass came, Teddy angled it in, and the Shoreline side erupted as their team went up 3–1.

"Hello, John."

John felt her arms around his neck, her lips on his cheek before he saw who it was: Sally Carroll.

"Hi, Sally."

"Quite a chip off the old block. I seem to remember his old man pulling a move just like that—scoring when Shoreline needed it most."

"Long time ago," John said, looking past

her shoulder to the man she'd been standing with. Peter Davis, a friend of Teddy's coach; John knew he had bought a house in Point Heron, and he'd heard that Sally had started dating him during her separation. The whole idea of dating—of trying to connect, trust another person again—gave John such a strong reaction that he felt a shiver go all the way down his spine.

"Yes, well, we do date back . . . old friend," Sally said.

"Accent on the 'old,' " John said.

"Don't let me hear you say that," Sally said, her fingers resting lightly on his arm. "You're just tired, I'm sure, after all you've been through. How are things, by the way?"

Her eyes were liquid, melting. John felt her gaze boring into him, and he looked away. His breath picked up—a sort of natural reaction to Sally's beauty, her sexual intensity . . . but she'd been Theresa's best friend, her divorce wasn't final, Peter Davis was watching them, and he'd never been attracted to her in that way, anyway. John glanced down at her again, wished he could just let his guard down and tell her—really tell her—how things were.

"They're fine," he said.

"Hmmm," she said. "That why you have dark circles under your eyes? Why Jillie Wilcox told me her mother said the glazier truck was back again this week?"

"A brick through the window," John said. "Occupational hazard."

"Well, the crowd is out for blood," Sally said. "See the way they're all watching you?"

"As long as they leave my kids alone, I can take it."

"Who takes care of *you,* Johnny?" Sally asked, touching his arm again. "While you're taking care of two kids, the house, those horrible clients?"

John's jaw tightened. When she put it like that, reduced everything to a few words, his life really did sound grim. He shivered in the penetrating sea wind, focused on watching his son play soccer. Teddy played defense as well as offense, and he stayed on his man, darting in, trying to steal the ball away.

"Who's the mystery woman?" came Sally's voice, breaking into John's concentration.

"What are you talking about, Sally?"

"Plain Jane over there—cheering for your

son as if she was his mother. Your dog seems to know her quite well."

John followed the direction of her finger as she pointed, and gazed straight at Kate Harris. She was staring, bright-eyed, at the field, hands clasped as if in prayer, but probably to keep them warm, appearing rapt and enthralled by the game. She wore the green jacket she'd worn on their walk the other night, and as Brainer romped with Bonnie, she crouched down to kiss his nose.

John smiled in spite of himself—first reaction to seeing her. But his second reaction came fast and hard, a train slamming through a tunnel. What was Kate Harris doing at Teddy's game?

"Excuse me, will you, Sally?"

"Of course," he heard Sally's voice over his shoulder as he strode down the sideline. Brainer tussled with Bonnie, and both dogs broke free to circle him as he approached Kate. The sky was steel gray, the trees were covered with bright yellow and orange leaves, and her eyes, as she turned to watch him, were filled with warmth and hope.

"Brainer remembers me," she said.

"Seems to," John replied, his jaw unbelievably tense and hurting.

"Or maybe it's Bonnie," she said. "I think they're true friends. Actually, I think they're mad about each other. Have you noticed how—"

"What are you doing here?"

"Hmm," she said, lowering her eyes.

The freight train tore through his chest. It crashed along his veins, through his blood vessels. It hurt like hell, smashing tissue and bone. This woman, this small, pretty, open—and she wasn't a "plain Jane" at all; it was just that women like Sally, like Theresa, would never get her quiet beauty—this woman was here at Teddy's game, and she didn't belong.

"That's not an answer," he snapped. "Tell me what the hell you're doing here."

"Watching Teddy play," she said.

"How the— Don't lie to me, okay? You knew I'd come, and you want something from me. You think I forgot our last meeting?"

"I didn't know you'd come," she said softly.

"Come on! What other reason—"

"I don't think even *Teddy* knew you'd

come," she said. Now, raising her eyes and smiling out at the field, connecting with Teddy's gaze—as John looked over, he saw his son, beaming from ear to ear, his cheeks bright red, so intent on catching John's attention that he missed a pass.

"Get it back, Teddy," John shouted as the Riverdale left wing intercepted the ball and wheeled around toward the goal.

"Go, Teddy!" Kate called, waving her fist.

"He lost it," John said, as the wing passed the ball to Riverdale's center. The shot was set up, and the big kid scored for Riverdale and the opposing side went crazy.

"They're still up three–two," Kate said helpfully.

"You're implying that goal was my fault? That Teddy was so distracted by seeing me here? Is that what you're saying?"

"Actually," Kate said, her voice cool but her eyes still warm, "that's what *you're* saying. I'm sure you know your son better than I do."

"So," John said, his blood on fire, a harbor covered with burning oil, flames licking all the bulkheads, docks, piers . . . all the tissue in his body boiling over with fury and frustration, "Teddy screwed up because I *came*? Is that what you mean?"

"First of all, he didn't screw up," Kate said. "That Riverdale guy *stole* the ball from him—it was a blatant case of *offsides,* or whatever it's called . . ."

"He wasn't offsides," John said. "The Riverdale guy just happened to be standing there when Teddy let the ball go through his legs. You don't know anything about soccer."

"That's true," Kate said. "But never say I'm not willing to learn something new. I'm loving this game." She jumped up and down again, eyes on the field, pointing as Teddy received the pass, took the ball masterfully down the field ahead of his team, and got into place for a goal.

"Go, Teddy! Kick it in! Take the shot!" John heard himself saying. He wasn't a parent who shouted out instructions, but he was with Teddy all the way.

"You can do it," Kate called. "Go!"

"C'mon, O'Rourke," the voices roared. If John closed his eyes, he might have believed it was him they were cheering for, but he didn't want to shut his eyes, not even for a second. He stared at his son, hand raised, calling the play, passing the ball—score!

The crowd exploded.

John leapt into the air. He shouted till his lungs hurt. Kate jumped up and down beside him, dancing in place, and he could feel her heat, her excitement. His arms wanted to grab her, hug her out of joy, out of triumph for Teddy—and out of relief for having been here for a big moment.

"You have a great son," Kate said, breathless.

"I know."

"You were here for it, too. That's great."

"Yeah," John said, his throat tight as he pictured Teddy's face five minutes ago—the look of shock and rapture at seeing his dad here, actually at the field, not at the office—for his game.

"You have a lot to be proud of."

John knew he did. His heart swelled. He thought, for just a second, of Theresa; he imagined how happy she would be for Teddy, how pumped and proud . . . that image of his wife sent his joy and all shreds of trust flying, brought him straight back down to earth, and he cleared his throat and stared right into Kate's smiling eyes.

"Enough," he said, feeling all the old pain and betrayal come flooding back. "I want to know right now: What's your business here?"

"I told you—"

"You're not a soccer fan, you don't have a kid on either team—so tell me, Kate. What do you want?" Now he watched her reach into her coat pocket. She pulled out a small piece of paper, hesitating as if trying to decide whether now was the time, whether she should show him or not. His blood began to sizzle again: She had to be kidding! "What's it this time? Another picture of your sister? A different postcard? A note she wrote? Well, give it to the goddamn police, not me. Okay? *I can't help you!*" In spite of himself, he grabbed the note from her hand.

There was Teddy's own handwriting on a small scrap of paper; reading it, John's hand began to tremble:

> *Hi, Kate,*
> *I have a soccer game today. If you don't have anything better to do, maybe you could come. It's at Shoreline Field, four o'clock. Hope you can make it.*
> *Thaddeus G. O'Rourke (Teddy)*

"How'd he get this to you?" John asked harshly.

"He left it under my windshield wiper," Kate said.

"How did he know where to find you?" He couldn't help himself; he thought of old scenarios, of notes left by Barkley for Theresa, of hang-ups on the answering machine, of nighttime whisperings, of secrets and surprises.

"I'm not sure."

"Did you call him? Have you been in touch with him or Maggie?"

"Of course not."

"Then how'd he find you?" John repeated.

"I haven't been able to ask him, because he's been playing this whole time."

"He's been in all game?" John asked, glancing up from the note, unable to block the pride gushing through him.

Kate nodded.

John's chest hurt. He felt confused, off center. Humanity hadn't proved itself to be very kind, helpful, or trustworthy in recent years. The temperature was dropping; he watched her pull her coat tighter. A storm was forecast for later that night, high winds and freezing rain driving off the Atlantic.

Brainer and Bonnie had taken off on a circuit around the field, and now they came galloping back to John and Kate. Was it John's imagination, or was every person at the field watching him? He stood taller, made his expression tough. Maggie ran over, drinking a cup of bug juice she'd snagged from the team cooler.

"Dad, Teddy's coach gave me some Gatorade . . . Teddy passed the winning shot, did you see . . . and check out Brainer and his cute little buddy—whose dog is it, and what do you think—" Catching sight of Kate, she gasped and rushed forward, stopping just short of giving the woman an embrace. "Hi!" she exclaimed, her voice full of rapture.

"Hi, Maggie."

"Is this your dog?"

"Yep. Her name's Bonnie."

"She's so cute!"

"A Scottie," Kate said.

Just then the horn sounded, signifying the game's end. The teams lined up, shaking hands, saying, "Good game, good game." John watched Teddy acknowledge his opponents, speak to his coach, then run through the crowd of parents and players.

"Did you see me, Dad?"

"I did, Teddy—you were great."

"I blew that one shot—"

"Yeah, we all do once in a while. The important thing is, you kept your focus, didn't let it throw you off, and set up Kevin to score the next goal."

"Yeah, we won."

"Congratulations," John said as Maggie pumped her brother's hand.

"And two of the goals were yours," Kate said.

Teddy glowed, nodding.

John's chest tightened again. He'd missed one of Teddy's goals? "You scored twice?"

Teddy nodded, and Kate said, "He did. He's the star."

"You are," Maggie said, staring up at her brother with pure adoration. "Of the whole team."

"Thanks, Mags."

Now John really felt low. He'd been so proud of himself, being here for the great pass, but he'd really blown it by missing a goal. He had to make it up to the kids somehow. He had planned to run into Billy Manning, his old friend and a detective on Connecticut's Major Crime Squad. Not a formal meeting—Billy hung around the Witch's Brew on Friday nights, and John had thought he might drop in for a beer, just to ask a few questions about Willa Harris. But Manning would have to wait.

"We have to celebrate," John said. "Shoreline's victory, Teddy's goals and assist. Where do you want to have dinner, Ted?"

"Vesuvio's Pizza!" he exclaimed.

"You got it."

"Should we invite Gramps and Maeve?" Maggie asked. "We're staying at his house," she explained to Kate. "Gramps would be proud."

"Yeah, we got 'em back for last time," Teddy said. "But Gramps said he had a late doctor's appointment."

"It has to be a party," Maggie said, her eyes shining. "We need more than just *us,* so we should invite . . ." Her eyes drifted over—past John, straight to Kate, her gaze really telling the whole story—but Teddy finished her sentence for her.

"Kate. Kate and Bonnie."

"Yes," Maggie said. "You have to come. Definitely. Vesuvio's has the best pizza in the world. You'll love it—won't she, Dad?"

John didn't reply, aware of both kids watching him, expectation filling their eyes, wanting him to do the gracious thing.

Kate beat him to it. "I wish I could," she said. "But I have other plans."

"No!" Maggie burst out. "You have to come. Please? Not just because of the pizza, but because I need to ask you about Halloween costumes. You're a girl, I mean a woman, and maybe you know more about what I can be than Dad and Teddy . . ."

"Oh, Maggie," Kate said.

"Come on, Kate. Cancel your other plans and come with us," Teddy said.

Kate smiled, biting her lip as if considering doing that. She didn't want to let the kids down, John could see. His heart was still raging—for some reason, the freight-train effect hadn't ceased one bit—and he was half tempted to see whether she'd change her mind and say yes. He spoke up, destroying the suspense.

"She said no, Mags," John said. "We have to respect that."

"Your father's right," Kate said. Her tone was mild, her expression sweet.

"Oh, rats," Maggie said.

"You're missing out," Teddy teased. "The pizza's really great, and we'll probably have ice cream on the way home. Paradise, have you ever had it?" Just then, out of the corner of his eye, John spotted Sally and Bert Carroll coming their way.

"No," Kate said, picking up Bonnie's leash and backing away. "Maybe another time."

"Hi, everyone!" Sally said. "Where's the party? Peter's busy till later, so Bert and I are inviting ourselves along."

"Vesuvio's," Teddy said, and Bert replied, "Awesome!"

"Bye, Kate," Maggie said, and John heard sadness in her voice.

"Bye, Maggie."

Kate walked a few steps away, as Sally murmured in John's ear, "Something I said?" John shook his head, just as Kate turned toward Maggie again.

"Amelia Earhart!" she said.

"What?" Maggie asked.

"That's who you should go as," Kate said. "Amelia Earhart . . ."

"For Halloween?"

"Yes. All you need is a white scarf . . . a long, white scarf. And maybe some aviator glasses. And, of course . . ."

"What?" Maggie asked, clutching her hands in front of her heart, listening as if Kate Harris had just offered her the Holy Grail. "What else do I need?"

"Courage," Kate said, smiling, winking as she walked away with Bonnie. "My sister used to say that Amelia was the bravest woman in the world."

"Oh, yes," Maggie said, nodding, gazing up into the cold October sky, as if the earth had just fallen away, as if John and Teddy and Sally and Bert had disappeared from sight, as if she might spread her wings and go flying bravely into the future, in search of her own destiny.

chapter 9

The Witch's Brew was packed and lively, the Friday night crowd jammed shoulder to shoulder, three deep at the bar. Cigarette smoke was thick, and music blared from speakers everywhere. The room was dark, the crowd was dressed up, and the place was too loud to hear anything Billy Manning would feel like saying. John cursed himself for thinking this was a good idea.

Edging his way along the long, chrome bar, John met the eyes of at least twenty people he knew. Hanging out in bars wasn't his M.O., and he could sense the surprise. He could also feel the ripple of pure animal tension. This was the mating game, no doubt about it, and his body reacted.

He found Billy in the back room, where it was marginally quieter, but no less crowded. The cops who went to Henry's after work on weeknights came here on Fridays. Located half a block from the courthouse, the Witch's Brew used to be called the Gavel, and it had attracted a law-and-order crowd. Looking to improve business, the owner had revamped the premises, started hiring bands on the weekends, and changed the name to something more overtly that of a pickup joint. The cops and lawyers had stayed loyal.

"Hey, Johnny," Billy Manning called, waving him over.

"How's it going, Billy? Hi, T.J., Dave."

"Hi, John," the cops said. Everyone shook hands, with "no hard feelings" looks on their faces. Over the years John had gotten them on the witness stand, cross-examining the hearts out of them. He'd come as close as he legally could to calling them liars, eviscerating them as if for sport.

"How's it going?" Dave Trout asked.

"Great," John replied to the thin, white-haired detective. "And you?"

"Damn fine. At least I can sleep at night."

"Yeah, well, you need it." John grinned. "You're older than I am."

"Puttin' 'em away keeps me young," Dave said. "Knowing I'm on the side of right, keeping the streets safe for our daughters."

"Well, I thank you for that, Dave. Let me buy you a beer for them."

"You're on," Dave said. "At least you didn't hit me with—what's his usual line?" He looked around at the other cops.

"Protecting our children's constitutional rights," T.J. chuckled. "Their rights to legal representation, et cetera, et cetera."

"Raise 'em right, they won't need legal representation," Dave said.

"Tell yourselves that," John said, signaling the waitress. "A whole lot of good parents in this town have."

"Like the Jenkinses," Billy said, his voice pitched low, gesturing over at the back bar. "Bark and Felicity—who'd have thought they'd raise one like that? There's their little darling, Caleb. He's one of yours, isn't he, John?"

"You should know," John said, watching Caleb Jenkins huddle over the bar with his uncle Hunter, Teddy's soccer coach. "You arrested him."

"Right. For that little prank involving a fifty-thousand-dollar sportfishing boat. I'd still like to know what he was doing, heading back from North Rock. That's about half a mile outside the three-mile limit, and if I had to guess, it was either drugs, smuggling, or destroying evidence."

"You left out white slavery," T.J. said.

"Play nice, guys," John said.

"We're stepping on the sacred ground of privilege," Billy laughed. "Better back off now. So, what brings you down to the Witch's Brew, John? Haven't seen you out drinking for a while. How's life going for you?"

"Someone threw a brick through our window the other night, the last baby-sitter quit—saying that my hours made working for me 'cruel and unusual punishment'—we have bats in the attic, and we're staying at my father's. Celebrated Teddy's soccer game with a pizza tonight, then decided to come out for a beer."

The waitress brought everyone a round, John paid, and they all drank.

"Heard about the brick," Billy said. "The town cops reported in."

"Merrill backlash?" Dave asked.

"I think so," John said.

"They ought to leave your home alone," T.J. said. "Your kids there?"

John nodded, sipping his beer.

"Nice. Really nice. Not that I don't agree on principle—Merrill really needs to die for what he did, but—"

This was a conversation John didn't want—or need—to have. He backed off, just slightly, and T.J. turned to Dave, getting the message, and going back to whatever they'd been talking about before John's arrival. Now Billy turned to John, and their eyes connected. They had been best friends in high school, and they had a relationship that usually transcended the careers they'd each chosen.

"What's up?" Billy asked, knowing that John had something on his mind.

"Take a walk with me."

Billy nodded. The two men put their mugs down on the scarred wood table, walked out through the crowd. The Witch's Brew was in its glory, the day before Halloween. People drifted in from parties, dressed in costumes. A black cauldron bubbled over, misting with dry ice. The band was called "Goth," and the music was discordant—making it hard for the generally middle-aged crowd to dance.

Sally Carroll spied him from the bar, said something to Peter Davis, and started over. John waved, moving faster. He'd mentioned it at the pizza place, the fact that he was stopping by the Witch's Brew to talk to Billy later. Was she a regular here? Or had she come just to see him? He noticed her black witch's outfit—a low-cut black dress, revealing full, pushed-up breasts, the edge of a purple lace bra showing.

"There's Sal," Billy said as they passed by.

"Yeah."

"Why you two don't get together is beyond me. Ever since she booted Todd out . . . she and Pete Davis are just passing the time together. At least comfort each other, man. She's always been hot for you, and I think she'd really like to offer you succor and warmth. Know what I mean?"

"Yeah, I know what you mean. How about shutting up about it?"

John scowled, shouldering through the

throng at the door. The smell of smoke and perfume was sickly sweet, and bursting out into the fresh air—past two couples wearing masks—felt good.

"I haven't been able to say anything right to you since . . ." Billy began, trailing off.

John shot him a look, just to make sure he didn't continue. He knew Billy was about to mention Theresa. One night after the funeral, Billy had stopped by the house and the two friends had had a few beers on the porch. As darkness fell and the beers took hold, John's tongue was loosened, and he told Billy everything about Theresa. How she'd been having an affair. How John had suspected for a long time, had wondered about the hang-ups and her mysterious errands.

Billy had leaned forward, set his beer down, and looked John in the eye.

"All you had to do was ask me," he'd said.

"What do you mean?" John had asked. "Because you're a cop? You could have tracked her? Or showed me how to do it? Surveillance on my own wife?"

"No, John. Because I knew. Everyone did."

"Everyone?"

"Theresa and Barkley."

"Jesus, Billy!"

"They weren't very discreet—I saw them at the Drawbridge Bar. And I saw them pulling out of the beach parking lot one night. And I saw—"

John had stood up. He had taken the empties into the kitchen. When Billy had followed him in, John hadn't offered him another. He'd stood at the sink, rinsing out the bottles, not looking up. He wanted Billy's words to disappear. He wanted Billy not to have known about Theresa, or, at least, not to have told him. *Everyone knew.* That's what Billy had said. "I'm sorry, John," Billy had said. After a few minutes, he had left.

Now, walking out behind the Witch's Brew, John had the feeling Billy wanted to say something about that night. They'd never talked about it—just acted as if the conversation had never happened. Cars drove past on Main Street. Some turned into the parking lot. John's heart was beating hard.

He thought back even further. They had all been so close: John and Theresa, Billy and Jennifer, Barkley and Felicity, Sally and Todd. John and Theresa married the summer before his third year of law school.

John remembered graduation from GULC—Georgetown University Law Center. He and Theresa had bought an old Volvo 122 and driven up from Washington. He felt so idealistic—wanting to go out and change the world. John couldn't wait to pass the bar, get started at work. But first the Judge threw him a graduation party, and everyone had come, newly married themselves.

It had been a beautiful summer night, a full moon rising over Silver Bay. The women had worn sleeveless dresses, the men had worn blue blazers. Theresa had made the canapés; Sally had brought a casserole. After so many proms and dances and bonfires together over the years, this was their first gathering as adults.

The Judge had hired a band, and people were dancing. John had looked around: The party was for him, and he loved everyone there. He was a lawyer now, or would be as soon as he passed the bar exam in July. Real life was about to begin. He felt Billy grab his arm, and he pulled Theresa.

The inner core—Billy, Barkley, John, and

Theresa—slipped away, behind the privet hedge alongside the garage.

"We should get Jen and Felicity," Theresa said. "The other wives . . ."

"In a minute," Billy said, producing a bottle of champagne. "This is just for us—the four musketeers."

"Three," Theresa said, smiling, trying to back away. "I don't belong."

"Always did and always will," Billy said. "Johnny made sure of that."

"You're the fourth musketeer, Theresa," Barkley said. "Even Jen and Felicity know that."

"I'm honored," Theresa said, smiling. John had felt so proud to be married to her. She looked radiant in her summer dress, tan and slim. Her eyes were glowing, as if she knew the secret of life, that it was a wild adventure, that she knew that these were her companions for the ride.

"This is it," Billy said, preparing to pop the cork. "Here's to John O'Rourke, Silver Bay's latest lawyer."

"And Billy Manning," John said. "Silver Bay's latest cop."

"I've been on the force three years now."

Billy laughed. "Got a head start on you—I bust them and you'll try to get them off."

"I'll represent them," John said.

"Call it whatever you want, Johnny," Billy said, holding the bottle. "For the first time in our lives, we're about to be on opposite sides. I'll kick your ass, too—don't think I won't."

"I'll kick yours back, Officer Manning," John joked.

"Just read everyone their rights, Billy," Barkley said, "so John can't get them off on technicalities."

"I don't care what happens as long as we stay friends through it all. Here's to that, okay? This toast is to you—"

"And you." John nodded.

"Don't leave out Barkley Jenkins, keeper of the light," Theresa said with a laugh.

"And Theresa O'Rourke," John said, holding her close. "Love of my life."

"Cheers," Billy said, the cork shooting into the side of the garage, the impact sounding like a pistol shot. The four of them laughed, passing the bottle of Mumms Cordon Rouge around. John and Billy's eyes met, silently acknowledging this crossroads in their friendship.

John had kissed champagne from Theresa's lips; he could almost taste it still. He and his friend Billy had survived life's changes; he and his wife had not. . . .

Now, standing in the Witch's Brew parking lot, the music was still audible through the bar's thick walls. John's ears rang, and his clothes smelled like smoke.

"Spill it, O'Rourke," Billy said now, staring at him.

"It's not that simple."

"Nothing ever is. You think you'll get disbarred for talking to me? Well, fuck it. We both know that's not gonna happen." Billy laughed, reminding John that they were friends first, cop and lawyer second. He was tall and dark, his face rough and angular, his nose still crooked from when he'd gotten hit with a beer bottle in eleventh grade; when he'd decided to join the state police, all their friends had teased him that he looked more like the bad guy than a cop.

"Off the record . . ." John said.

"What do you mean?"

"I mean, what I'm about to ask you is delicate."

"Delicate for who?"

"Me. My client."

"Ah." Billy smiled. "Greg Merrill raises his ugly head."

"I didn't say that."

"You don't have to. You're running yourself so ragged working on his case, you got no room on your calendar for any other scumbag. What's his problem?"

John hesitated. More cars drove into the parking lot. Although the two men were standing in back, far from the bright lights, John had the fleeting thought that a reporter could make plenty of a back-alley conversation between Merrill's lawyer and his arresting officer.

"Don't worry, John. Ask me. It won't come back to bite you in the ass."

"I don't want to give anything up . . ."

"Hey, I'm half in the bag. I probably won't even remember this conversation tomorrow. I'm an excellent forgetter of conversations, and you know it. Shoot."

"Willa Harris," John said, ignoring the dig. His heart beating in his throat, he watched Billy's eyes. They didn't react, didn't even blink.

"What's a Willa Harris? That a boy or a girl?"

"Girl. Missing person."

"Huh. Doesn't ring a bell," Billy said, frowning. "Round when?"

"She went missing six months ago."

"Right at the peak of Greggie's run. Where'd you hear about her?"

"From Kate Harris, her older sister. She came to see me a few days ago."

"Willa's still missing?"

"Yes."

"How'd her big sister trace her here?"

"A postcard of the East Wind," John said. "Mailed from Silver Bay last April, but not received until recently. The sister's divorced; apparently Willa and Kate's husband had a thing going, and Willa needed to get away to think about it."

"Maybe Kate got jealous and—"

"Doesn't strike me that way," John said quickly.

"Maybe the husband got worried. Willa threatened to tell, Kate was breathing down his neck." Billy exhaled, shaking his head. "Wouldn't want to be there myself—the ham in a sister sandwich. Sounds dangerous."

John nodded. "Kate says she reported her sister missing back then, that the word went out."

"FBI?"

"No. No suspicion of kidnapping."

"Huh. Well, you know how that works. I might have gotten notice, but if there wasn't reason to think she'd been in our area, I'd have passed right over the sheet. Maybe it was a different East Wind . . ."

John shook his head. "Nope. I saw the card."

"And the trail stopped here?" Billy asked, frowning.

"No—it went on to Fairhaven, Massachusetts, Newport, Providence . . ."

"There you go!" Billy said, shrugging. "Why's the sister bothering you—as if I didn't know?"

"Merrill."

"Obviously. He's the most famous serial killer in New England, the time frame works, why shouldn't he have been the one? Did you tell her he's but one of many such cuties plying their trade, that her sister's probably—"

"No," John said, for some reason cutting Billy off, not wanting to think of all the other predators out there, or of Kate's sister's fate.

"You know, if the general public knew

what we know ... Ever think of that, Johnny?"

"Not when I can help it."

"It's like that thing with sharks ... You know from fishing, right?"

"Know what?"

"How people would be horrified to know what's swimming around them every time they go in the water. There's that old saw about most shark attacks occurring within ten feet of shore, in three feet of water ... and everyone thinks that's be-cause it's where all the swimmers swim."

John was silent, watching the beam of Silver Bay Light cross the sky, reflecting off the low, black clouds. There wasn't a star in the sky.

"When, in fact, it's that sharks are *every-where,*" Billy said.

"I know."

"It's the same with freaking killers. Every-one loves it when someone like Merrill gets caught. That gives them their explanation for all the free-floating evil in the world. You serve up the Breakwater Killer and everyone breathes a sigh of relief. They vote for the death penalty, and they think they're safe from another monster."

"Careful—your liberal colors are show-ing."

"Bullshit. They can't juice him fast enough to suit me. I'm just saying, he's just another shark in the cove. Plenty more where he came from—they just haven't been classi-fied yet."

"I know. So—nothing on Willa Harris?"

Billy shook his head. "No. Tell me, though—are you asking on Merrill's ac-count? Or the big sister's?"

"I'm not sure," John said honestly. He shook Billy's hand, ignoring the concern in his friend's eyes. The first freezing raindrops began to fall. They stung like ice, like tiny ra-zors on the skin. He started toward his car, then half turned. "Ever been to Fairhaven?"

Billy nodded. "Mass? Sure. I've bought fishing gear there. A great little store just east of the boatyards. Why?"

"You know where the Texaco station is?" For some reason, asking the question made John's heart speed up. He swallowed hard, past the ache in his throat. He hoped Billy wouldn't say, *At a convenience store, in a strip mall with a Laundromat . . .*

"I don't know, man," Billy said. "You're on

your own, there. You want me to call Fairhaven P.D.?"

"Nah," John said. "I can always call Information."

Billy waved, heading back into the Witch's Brew. The door opened, letting out loud music and voices. John caught a glimpse of people, of all those women at the bar. He had a picture of people having fun, trying to make a connection. He thought of Sally, and then of Theresa. Their girls'-nights-out had occasionally included the Witch's Brew on a Friday night.

Then John thought of Kate Harris. He wondered what she was doing tonight. Was she, perhaps, inside right now?

Something made him think she wasn't. He imagined the East Wind, perched on the high bluff overlooking the sea. It would be blustery out there with sleet driving in off the Atlantic, the lighthouse illuminating the low storm clouds and the building white waves. His fingers brushed her sister's picture, still in his pocket.

His chest felt frozen. He thought of Kate Harris, a stranger who'd told him her story so easily—as if she'd needed someone to trust and talk to, as if John was that person—the second time they'd met. When Billy had gotten too close, trying to talk about what Theresa had done, John had pushed him away.

Maybe it was only possible to talk about it with someone who had gone through the same thing. It was a very intimate thing, adultery. Between the married couple, one of the most private things there was. Making love, planning a wedding, conceiving a child, cooking your first holiday meal, going to your first PTA meeting: all things that bound a couple closer and closer, events that only they could share and know, memories they would take to their graves.

Adultery could be part of that list. The shadow of all those shining times; the flip side of the bright coin of marriage. For infidelity to cut as sharply as Theresa's, there had had to be so many things in place: trust, hope, longevity, family, and love. If those hadn't been present, what difference would her cheating have made?

John had loved her so much. He remembered back to law school; they had lived in a big, old Victorian house on Macarthur Boulevard, and John had ridden his bike to classes at the law center on Capitol Hill.

She would rub his shoulders while he studied, he would bring her breakfast in bed on weekends. They had been so inseparable that she'd sometimes come to class with him, listening to Irving Younger's tapes on evidence, sitting through hours of contracts and torts.

John never would have believed they could grow apart. It had happened slowly, without his even noticing. Anniversaries and birthdays, if not actually missed, then neglected. He had taken her for granted. And it worked both ways—sometimes he had felt more like a wallet with legs than a man. She bought, he paid. She adored the kids and raised them well; she made it possible for him to work late, to attend conferences, to not be there as often as he wanted to.

Their sex life. He'd thought it was good. Better than the average small-town married-a-long-time sex life. They'd heard their friends, at parties, joking about spicing things up with dirty movies, massage oil, weekends at a motel with heart-shaped tubs. John and Theresa had laughed, slightly embarrassed that their friends had needed things like that. Wasn't what they had *good*? Maybe not frequent enough—

someone was always falling asleep before they had the chance—but when it happened, worlds were rocked.

At least for John they were. He had always been excited by Theresa. When she was young and thin, after she'd had the kids and gained some weight: It didn't matter. He loved her smooth skin, her beautiful face, her strong tennis-playing arms, her familiar scent. He'd climb into bed at the end of the day, and he'd take her in his arms and think his heart might break through his rib cage. She'd make his blood pound in his veins, and he'd kiss her lips.

A man who made his living with words: memos, briefs, opening and closing arguments, direct and cross-examination, conference calls, interviews, depositions . . . with Theresa, he had tried to speak with his body. He had tried to show her, the best he could, how much he loved her with his hands, his mouth.

There was a saying he remembered from Latin: *Cor ad cor loquitor.* Heart speaks to heart. That's how it had been for John, and how he thought it had been for Theresa. He hadn't known how she felt; sometimes it seemed he hadn't known her at all.

Standing in the parking lot of the Witch's Brew, watching all the smiling, laughing, costumed people go inside, John couldn't help wondering whether there were husbands, wives, left behind somewhere this festive night. Sitting at home, waiting by the phone, trying not to watch the clock.

He knew that those weeks, when Theresa was cheating on him, he had felt bound to her as never before. Because he had felt her slipping away, and she'd become even more precious to him than she'd been since the night he had proposed to her. He had reached for her, trying to pull her back, but it was like trying to hold a handful of sand: it kept running out of his fingers, back to the beach. By the night of her death, Theresa was already long gone.

He had found notes in her datebook, to call Melody Starr, a divorce lawyer in Hawthorne. Had she? John didn't know, and he wouldn't ask. When he saw Melody in the hall at court, he said hello and tried to discern whether she was looking at him strangely, with sympathy or loathing. Had Theresa told her their deepest secrets?

John didn't know, and he believed it didn't matter. Divorce lawyers were like the third parties: They were beside the point. The marriage—blissfully happy or falling apart—was between two people. It could break up only if one of the two wanted it to—if he or she had already started leaving. And Theresa's leaving had begun before the start of her affair.

John wondered whether it had been like that for Kate. Whether her husband had already left before the affair with her sister. Once more, he looked at the photo of Willa Harris. Such a pretty, friendly, innocent smile. Hard to believe a woman like this would have an affair with her sister's husband. But, as John had learned the hard way, she was just the third party, and the third party was beside the point.

He wanted to help Kate Harris find her sister. He wasn't sure why it felt so important to him, driving him to the Witch's Brew this cold Friday night when he'd rather be home with his kids, but it was. It had to do with answering questions, finding peace. Doing the right thing. Strange, how they shared a connection with Washington, and now with Silver Bay.

He took a deep breath, climbed into his car and out of the freezing rain, and drove slowly over the slick, black roads toward his father's house. If there was any peace in the world for John O'Rourke tonight, it was there, with Maggie and Teddy.

chapter 10

Before leaving the East Wind on Saturday morning, Kate took pictures from her bedroom windows. She wanted to remember the view Willa had had, so she snapped photos of the rocky coastline, the breakwater, and the lighthouse—all contours softened by ghostly fog. Her time here had been bittersweet. Although she hadn't found out anything more about Willa, she had met the O'Rourkes.

Forehead against the glass, hoping for a glimpse of Maggie or Teddy, she tried to see their house. It looked so quiet: no sign of Brainer running through the fields. She hoped they'd had fun having pizza last night, celebrating Teddy's victory. A memory of Willa playing field hockey—in the prim playing fields near Rock Creek Park, behind the gothic spires of St. Chrysogonus's School—filled her mind.

Willa in her dark green uniform, waving her hockey stick over her head, thrilled because they'd won, wanting Kate and Andrew to be proud. Feeling like parents, they had taken Willa and her teammates to the Chicago Pizzeria. Everyone sitting at one big table, digging into deep-dish pizza, toasting with frosty mugs of soda.

Willa had been sixteen.

That night, Andrew had held Kate close in bed, making slow love to her with extra tenderness, whispering that when they had a baby of their own, they'd be ahead of the game, practiced in the care and raising of teenagers. He had told her he loved Willa like his own kid, that he was so blessed to have married into a ready-made family. Kate had glowed, unable to believe she'd found someone so special.

Someone who loved her the way she was, took her the way she came: with a shy, beautiful, needy teenaged sister. For Willa had been just like a wild pony—cautious, hesitant, slow to trust, more suited to the dunes of Chincoteague than the brick sidewalks of Georgetown, happier with a paintbrush than a field-hockey stick.

Andrew had won Willa over. He had worked out with her, doing drills on the field, encouraging her till she believed she was as good an athlete as anyone else. He had also praised her painting, insisting that one of her watercolors hang in his office. It was a small portrait Willa had done of Kate, sitting on the dunes one chilly day, her arms wrapped around her knees.

The years had passed. . . . Willa grew up, became an adult.

They—Andrew and Kate—had taken Willa to the National Gallery's East Wing for her twenty-first birthday. Together they had wandered through the small French paintings exhibit, past Monet's "Water Lilies." They had admired the Hassams, the Metcalfs, the Renwicks. At lunch, in the small restaurant upstairs, Andrew had commissioned Willa to do a painting.

"Of me and Kate," he'd said, handing Willa the check.

"Andrew, this is huge!" she'd said, looking at the amount.

"Well, it'll be worth it. Me and the most beautiful girl in the world. To hang on my walls, for all to see."

Willa had beamed. Kate had been unable to smile. Her heart had felt so heavy that day. Andrew had been late the last few nights; she'd been unable to reach him on his cell phone. Although he had claimed to be working late, lining up a new job after the senator's inevitable loss in November, Kate hadn't believed him. His words said one thing; her gut said another.

"Kate, he's so romantic," Willa had said, leaning across the table to give her brother-in-law a kiss.

"I know," Kate had said.

"You guys are so lucky. I hope that when I fall in love it's with someone who loves me half as much as he loves you!"

"Hear that, Kate?" Andrew had asked, trying to hug her toward him. But Kate's body wouldn't yield, and she'd sat up straighter in her chair.

"Would you want that for her?" Kate had asked, her voice cold.

"Katy . . ." Andrew had taken her hand, clasped fingers.

"Sure he would!" Willa had exclaimed,

staring at the check. "Why wouldn't he? Andrew's my self-esteem coach! I swear, I wouldn't have made it through St. Chrys's without him. All those field-hockey-crazy, preppie congresspeople's daughters . . . and now he's giving me my first commission."

Under the table, Andrew had squeezed her hand. She could almost hear him: *Come on, Katy. Loosen up, will you? I love you, only you . . . I married you, no one else.* She had heard him say those words before. And because she so badly wanted them to be true, she always let herself try to believe them.

"I already have your portrait of Kate," Andrew said. "The airplane one. But that's of her alone. This one has to show us together, and don't leave out my absolute adoration." He'd struck a lovesick pose, staring at Kate with huge eyes, making Willa laugh and Kate smile. She was starting to soften; she always did. After all, he'd never stopped denying her accusations. Maybe she was wrong—being suspicious for no reason.

"You're crazy," Willa had said, shaking her head.

"Mad is more like it," Andrew had said,

dropping his hand to Kate's knee under the table, starting to make lazy circles on her skin. "Madly in love with your sister."

"I love you both," Willa had said, smiling at them with sheer joy, like a child who knows her parents love each other, that her home is secure. "I'd do the picture for free."

"Take the check," Kate had said, smiling back. "If Andrew wants to pay you for it, I think you should let him."

"Listen to your sister, kid." Andrew had laughed. "She knows what she's talking about: I always get what I want!"

Now, staring out the window at the O'Rourkes' house, Kate remembered feeling happy about at least one thing that day—that Andrew cared so much about Willa. Art was a hard field—much more mysterious and difficult to earn money in than marine biology—and she was all in favor of bolstering Willa's confidence.

Andrew had always been so good at that. . . .

Sighing, stepping away from the window, she picked up her bags. The old memories had made her hands shake. Her love of Willa collided with her feelings of betrayal. Why hadn't Willa seen Andrew for what he was? How could she have succumbed to whatever line he had offered her, told her?

The portrait had never gotten done. Willa hadn't been able to get them together long enough to sit for it. She had started a job in Andrew's office on Capitol Hill. Filing, answering telephones, stuffing envelopes: easy stuff that wouldn't get in the way of her art.

"Oh, Willa," Kate murmured, still feeling the pain. That moment when she had come upon them . . .

Carrying her luggage downstairs, she settled up her bill.

"I would have come up to get your bags," Barkley Jenkins said, smiling. "At least let me carry them out to the car."

"That's okay—they're light."

"We're a little surprised you're leaving so soon," Felicity said. "You'd reserved the room for another week."

"I know, but I'd like to see a little more of New England before I head back home."

"Understandable," Felicity said quickly. Kate was taken aback, a little surprised. She had expected a protest about her sudden decision to leave, perhaps an argument about getting her deposit back. But instead, Felicity put through the paperwork, refunding the seventy-five dollars to Kate's credit card. Watching, Kate thought Felicity looked haggard, with sallow skin and swollen eyes, as if she hadn't been sleeping well.

"Hope we didn't drive you away," Barkley said.

"No, it's been very pleasant. Even Bonnie enjoyed it."

"She's a cute dog," Barkley said, petting Bonnie and letting her lick his fingers. "I swear, she remembers me from before."

Kate's stomach dropped, and she thought she heard Felicity gasp. "Barkley," she said warningly.

"That's okay," Kate said. She had confided her reasons for being there to Felicity on arrival, wanting to learn everything the family might know. Felicity had said she remembered Bonnie—or a Scottie just like her—but not her owner. "Some people come for just one night," she had explained. "They're here, and then they go. . . . we hardly get to see them."

"You remember Bonnie, too?" Kate asked now, staring at Barkley. He was tall and rangy, with graying blond hair and a big blond mustache. He had good-time eyes— easy to smile, and bloodshot from last night's drinks. She recognized the signs from the Washington cocktail party circuit.

"No," he said, shaking his head. "Wish I could say I did, Kate. But Felicity told me you were here looking for your sister, that Bonnie's her dog. Really hope you find her. . . ."

"So do I," Kate said.

The owners smiled, and Felicity handed her the bill stapled to the credit card receipt. Barkley, in spite of her protestations, carried her luggage to the car. There was one package she carried herself, not letting it out of her grasp. Standing in the driveway, letting him load the bags into her trunk, she heard hammering. Each bang sounded loud and close, amplified by the fog.

She gazed around the grounds, following the sound, and her eyes came to light on a barn just north of the path leading to the beach, the breakwater, and the distant headland where the lighthouse stood.

The barn was weathered and old. Its roof, missing shingles, sagged in the middle. A young man stood on the very top of a tall ladder, hammering under the barn's eaves.

His slim silhouette was dark in the luminous fog. Suddenly he stopped banging, turning to look at Kate from a hundred yards away. He waved, a friendly salute, and Kate waved back.

"It looks like he's going to fall," she said.

"Not Caleb," Barkley said, shaking his head.

"Your son?"

"Yes. He works with me on my crew, doing construction all week, and he's got some kind of gift—hangs from the rafters; carries hundred-pound bales of shingles up ladders, one on each shoulder; climbs to the top of the lighthouse to repair the mortar in those walls . . ."

"He's good at what he does," Kate said, wondering why she hadn't met him once during the whole time she'd been there.

"The best. He's working overtime, giving up his Saturday, to get that old barn into shape. We're expanding bit by bit. I turned over the lighthouse to him—we come from a long line of light keepers."

"What do you have to do?"

He chuckled. "Since you asked . . . she's a brick and iron tower. Lots of upkeep there, fighting the sea and the salt air. My father used to work twenty-four/seven, maintaining the property, monitoring the fog and light signals. The system became automated twenty years ago, and it got a lot easier. Now we rely on sensors—light-sensitive relays to operate the light."

"Machines do everything?" Kate asked, thinking of how sad that was, how much more romantic was the notion of a light keeper, watching over the coastline and its passing ships, of a family whose work it was to keep seafarers safe, prevent ships from being wrecked on the rocky shores.

"Well, they run the light . . . but we have to replace the materials. A one-thousand-watt tungsten-halogen lamp in the fourth order lens . . . a backup lamp kicks in if the first ever fails. Even the fog signal has a sensor—measures the moisture in the air. When I was a kid, we had a reed horn. Broke down constantly, and I had to sit there . . . while John was away at Yale, and then Georgetown, I was sitting there making sure the horn gave off two-second blasts every thirty seconds. Caleb doesn't know how easy he has it."

"What a great family tradition," Kate said.

"We think so. Okay, then," Barkley said,

slamming her trunk closed. "Good journey . . . If you find yourself in a boat, look for our light. Silver Bay tower lets out a white flash of light every six seconds, with a red sector covering two nearby shoals."

"Thanks—I'll stay off the shoals," Kate said, letting Bonnie jump into the backseat. Smiling, she said good-bye, placing the package she held right beside her on the seat, and climbed into the car.

She had one last stop before leaving Silver Bay. Although she didn't have directions, she had the address. She had looked it up in the phone book—surprised that a retired judge would have a listed number. On her way through town, she turned up the car's heat, trying to chase the chill in her bones.

The Judge's house was surprisingly easy to find. In a quiet, prosperous section of the village, it overlooked the green, the town hall, and two churches. Gray-blue, it had white shutters and a slate mansard roof. A wrought-iron fence surrounded the tidy yard. Shaggy white and golden chrysanthemums bloomed in straight beds. Kate recognized the pumpkin she had bought for Maggie on the front steps.

Brainer barked when she parked in the driveway. He stood at the window, crying, eager to get outside to see her and Bonnie. Kate half hoped he would attract his owners, so she could hand the package to Maggie herself.

No one responded. It was ten o'clock in the morning, and there were no cars in the driveway. Perhaps John was working, or maybe he had taken the kids out to breakfast or another soccer game.

Kate felt a lump in her throat to think of the family. The kids were great. She was so glad they had each other. In a different scenario, she would have liked to get closer to them. But she pictured John's eyes last night, when the kids had invited her for pizza, and knew that that would never happen. She had recognized the steel plating: He told himself he wasn't getting close to someone who wanted information about his client. But Kate knew the real truth.

He wasn't getting close to anyone.

Kate put John O'Rourke out of her mind and walked up the stone steps. She opened the screen door and crouched, to leave the package inside, when the heavy door flew open.

An old woman stood there. She was small and stooped, with snow-white hair drawn up in a bun. Her face was soft and pale, a field of wrinkles, but her eyes were startlingly blue. She wore a black dress and white apron, and she smiled with great curiosity and warmth of spirit.

"Who has come to call?" she asked with an Irish brogue, smiling broadly at Kate standing one step down.

"Oh—Kate Harris," Kate replied, standing up. "But not to call—just to leave this package for Maggie."

"Miss Margaret?"

"Yes—Miss Margaret."

"Aye, ye're her mother," the old woman said, nodding knowingly as she accepted the parcel.

"No," Kate said, confused. "Her mother's—"

"With the angels," the old woman said, clutching Kate's package to her chest. "I know. Not *that* mother . . ."

Kate was speechless.

"Do you know the angels?" the woman asked, tilting her head.

Kate shook her head, stunned, almost in a trance.

"Oh, but you do. Of course you do. The good girls who have gone before us, who were stolen away. Our sisters, dear lady. Are they not angels?"

"Willa? Are you talking about my sister Willa?"

"Aye," the woman said, lifting her bright eyes to the cloudy sky, crossing herself, and then gazing back at Kate. "Ye're Mary, are ye not? Blessed Mother . . ."

"Mary? No, I'm—" Kate stopped, suddenly getting it. The old woman had Alzheimer's, or something like it; she thought Kate was the Virgin Mary. Brainer came around the woman's legs, and Kate hugged him with relief.

"Will you look after them, dear Mother? My sons? And our sisters? And all the lost girls? The hurt girls? And all the wicked boys . . ." The woman's eyes glittered with fervent love, and she reached out to clutch Kate's wrist with one warm hand while hugging the brown parcel to her bosom with the other.

Kate wasn't sure what to say or do. She was a scientist, and religious visions were beyond her domain. But Willa used to say that on a good day, Kate was compassionate all the way down to her toes; summoning up her sister's good opinion of her, Kate was suddenly clear. She smiled into the old woman's eyes, then leaned forward and kissed her forehead. The smell of rose-scented talcum powder filled the air.

"I will," she whispered, her throat aching as she thought of all the hurt girls.

And, petting Brainer one last time, Kate ran down the steps. The smell of roses had transferred to her hands, making her feel light-headed. She didn't go to church, never prayed, and she hoped she wouldn't be struck down for impersonating the Virgin Mary. She had the clearest sense, instead, of having just been blessed.

Waving at the old woman, she backed out of the driveway. She hoped the woman would remember to give the package to Maggie. And, as Bonnie stood in the backseat, barking farewell to Brainer, Kate Harris took the back roads to the highway, pointing east, toward Newport, Rhode Island, in search of her lost girl.

The day was a disaster.

Maggie had begged her father to spend

the day with her, but she'd imagined the mall and a movie—or maybe a hike through Foxtail State Park. Not, repeat *not,* a morning at the office.

Some days his office was fun. Maggie loved the secretaries and paralegals. Many of them were young women, and they'd let Maggie sit at their desks, typing on their computers or drawing pictures on firm letterhead.

But today was Saturday, Halloween, and the only secretaries there looked grumpy and overworked, trying to finish projects for their busy bosses. Dad's own secretary, Damaris, was just about the nicest person alive, but this morning even *she* barely gave Maggie the time of day.

"Can we go to the copy room?" Maggie cajoled, hoping Damaris would allow her, as she sometimes did, to copy her hands on the big Series 5 color copier.

"Can't right now, sweetie pie. Your daddy's counting on me to finish this typing so he can get done early and have a nice afternoon with you and your brother."

"My brother's at his friend's," Maggie explained. "He'll be home for dinner, but tonight he's going to a Halloween dance."

"Just you, then," Damaris said, never breaking stride, just typing like mad. "That's enough."

"I'm going to be Amelia Earhart for the Halloween pageant tonight," Maggie confided.

"Superb choice," Damaris said, but she was concentrating so hard on her typing, Maggie had the feeling she could have said she was dressing up as the postmistress, Elaine of Elaine's Clip and Cut, or Damaris herself, and gotten the same response.

Shrugging it off, Maggie roamed the law firm's halls. Saturdays were quieter than weekdays, but by no means deserted. Lawyers huddled over their desks, shirtsleeves rolled up, reading, reading, reading.

The library was a popular spot. More reading in the carrels, long tables, and computer stations. Most of the people here were associates—the younger lawyers, not long out of law school, who did the grunt work for partners like her father.

As she walked around, Maggie realized she was scouring the firm for things to wear with her costume. The costume itself would have to wait; when her dad was finished today, he'd promised to take her shopping.

But Maggie was resourceful, and she could look for emblems right now.

She had long known who Amelia Earhart was, but last night she had looked her up on the Internet and found pictures of a pretty girl, dressed in a leather jacket with a white scarf and small cap. Kate had said Amelia had courage, but the photos had revealed that she also had happiness, curiosity, and excitement: all things that Maggie wanted for herself.

Each characteristic needed an emblem.

For happiness, Maggie was going to wear her mother's gold hummingbird pin. Her father had given it to her after five years of marriage, to commemorate her mother's speed, efficiency, and love of red flowers. The pin had emerald eyes, and when Maggie received it after her mother's death, it became her most prized possession.

For curiosity, Maggie planned to borrow a firm library access card. It symbolized reading, research, searching for the answers. Hadn't Amelia been doing that on her flight across the Pacific?

For excitement, Maggie would tuck a photo of herself and Teddy at the top of Wild Expedition's tallest roller coaster—

taken by their dad, just before their car had tumbled over the precipice. Maggie's stomach still roiled when she recalled that ten-story drop.

But for courage . . .

That emblem took a little more effort.

Maggie wasn't known for her courage. In fact, she was the biggest coward she knew. She couldn't stand the sight of blood—her own or anyone else's. She hated when her father went over the speed limit, even though he was a great driver. Most kids loved Bambi, but since her mother's accident, the sight of deer terrified her. She jumped out of her seat at any loud noise. And, if she could have stopped that Wild Expedition roller coaster from climbing to the top, she would have—halfway up.

So, making her way through the law firm, Maggie kept her eyes open for something that would prove her courage.

Many things were off-limits: She understood and respected the rules. Her father had explained that people's lives and rights were at stake; to him, they were the same thing. He had told her that he trusted her and Teddy implicitly, but that they had to promise that anything they saw or heard stayed "at home."

They had both promised.

The law firm made her feel safe and secure. It was in a stately old brick building designed by Stanford White—one of the best architects of the 1800s, her father had told her. Tall windows overlooked the granite courthouse with its fluted columns. The firm was quiet, but Maggie could feel that it was also important. Her father and his partners believed completely in what they did, and this gave an aura of might and righteousness to the very air.

Maggie wandered past walnut desks and overflowing bookshelves, past oil paintings of the Connecticut shoreline—many of them of local lighthouses done by the most important landscape artists of the last two centuries—that looked as if they belonged in museums. She trailed her fingers over soft leather chairs and highly polished conference tables, dreaming of her Halloween costume, trying to find an emblem of courage.

She found it.

Her father was in his office, working on the Merrill file. He had zillions of documents spread everywhere: interviews with witnesses, with psychiatrists, with the coroner. Blue-bound transcripts of testimony were stacked on the cherry table. Redwelds lined the floor. A manila folder—so innocent looking from the outside—was shoved under a pile of books. Just seeing it made Maggie's heart begin to pound.

Her father, wearing his tortoiseshell half-glasses, was writing furiously, copying out of a book. Maggie took a deep breath, walking closer.

"Daddy?" she asked.

"Hi, Mags," he said, not looking up.

"What're you doing?" she asked, staring at the folder.

"You know . . ."

"How much longer?"

"Not much."

"You said we could go to the mall."

"We can. Just give me till lunch."

"What are we going to eat?"

"Whatever you want."

"I'm hungry."

"Hang in there, Mags. I won't be much longer."

"I mean *really* hungry, Dad."

Her father let out a long exhalation, just

short of a whistle. He slid his glasses off, pinched the bridge of his nose. When he looked up, smiling, Maggie smiled back.

"You realize I'm right in the middle of something," he said.

"Just a coffee break, Dad."

"Yeah?" he asked, rising to stretch. He wore jeans and a blue chamois shirt; his shirt had come untucked, and Maggie laughed at the sight of his bare stomach. "At the cafeteria downstairs?"

Maggie nodded. "Bring me a cinnamon bun? With extra icing? And a milk?"

Her father looked surprised. "Don't you want to come?"

Maggie shrugged. Her cheeks felt hot and her nose felt cold—even before she told the lie. The fact that it was a harmless white lie made things better, but not much. "That'll take too long," she said. "If we have it here in your office, you can keep working."

"I get it." Her father laughed. "That way we get to the mall sooner."

"You're a genius, Dad." Maggie grinned.

She sat very still, in his swiveling desk chair, until the sound of his footsteps grew fainter in the hall. Listening carefully, she heard Damaris's fingers clicking over the computer keys in the cubicle just outside the office door.

Gazing at the manila envelope, Maggie began to sweat. She knew what was inside; Teddy had looked once, and told her. Her father sometimes brought it home, but he never let it leave his desk. He guarded it carefully, as if it contained poison or explosives, things that might harm his children if left untended.

Teddy had waited till Dad had had to go to the bathroom once. Darting into the office, he had flipped open the folder to look. . . . What he had seen was so terrible, he had refused to tell Maggie even one detail. No matter how much she begged or cajoled, he wouldn't spill.

"C'mon, Teddy. What's in there?"

"Don't ask me, Maggie."

"If you don't tell me, I'll look."

"Please, Maggie—don't do that. I know you. You'd never fall asleep again."

"They're really bad?"

"Worse than really bad."

"Terrible?"

"Yeah, Mags. Terrible."

"Just tell me one thing—one little thing,

so I won't have to look. Knowing nothing is so much worse than knowing something, because my imagination is torturing me!"

Teddy had cringed at the word "torturing," and then he had capitulated and told Maggie the one thing that had stolen her sleep for the next two weeks:

"They're cut . . . in ribbons," he said, stopping himself.

"Ribbons?" she'd asked, focusing on the pretty word used in such a horrifying way. "What do you mean?"

"I can't tell you, Maggie," her brother had said, his face white with horror and, probably, the shame of disobeying their father to look at the forbidden forensic photographs of Greg Merrill's victims. "I won't. I don't want you to have the pictures in your head. Okay, Mags? Don't ask me . . . and don't ever look yourself."

"I won't," she had whispered, worried because her brother looked so upset.

Now, about to break her promise, she pushed herself out of her father's desk chair. Her pulse raced; she felt it fluttering in her throat. She was a good girl, very careful, and she never liked to go against her father's rules or wishes. But this was Halloween, the season of pranks, and she really needed to get some courage so she could be Amelia Earhart. . . .

Touching the smooth cream-colored folder, her fingertips felt cool and steady. How bad could it be? The folder itself looked totally innocuous, with a typed label on the flap: GM23–49. That referred to evidence numbers, and Maggie knew, just from hanging around lawyers her whole life, that there would be twenty-three photos inside.

She drew in a deep breath and started to flip the folder open.

"MAGGIE!" her father's voice yelled in her ear, and she felt herself pushed aside as he grabbed the file. Her father hadn't touched her hard, but Maggie had been standing on one foot, and she felt herself teeter, lose her balance, and fall over.

"Oh," she heard herself say. "Oh, oh . . ."

Trying to catch her, her father dropped the photos. Unable to decide what to do—to catch Maggie or cover up the pictures—he tried to do both.

"Don't look, honey," he said. "Close your eyes!"

Maggie did, but not before glimpsing one

picture: a lady with her face powdery white
and her eyes open, like a doll's. Somehow
Maggie knew she was dead—the picture
wouldn't have been scary otherwise. Instantly she slammed her eyelids shut because she knew she never, never wanted to
see those other pictures.

"Teddy was right," she whispered, starting to cry. "I never should have looked . . .
I'm sorry, Daddy. I'm so sorry I disobeyed!"

"It's okay, honey . . ."

"Oh, Teddy!" Maggie sobbed.

John drove slowly, holding his daughter's
hand across the Volvo seat. Damaris had
been all for carrying Maggie to the lounge,
putting a cool cloth on her head, and giving
her a cup of soup to soothe her, but John
knew he had to handle this by himself.

Maggie was buckled into her seat. She
gulped over and over, swallowing sobs.
Every noise she made was a nail in John's
brain, driving home the guilt. She was his
sweetheart, his baby. She needed her
mother and father, and lately she'd had neither.

"You okay, Maggie?"

"Uh," gulp, "huh," gulp.

"You sure?"

No reply.

John held her hand tighter as they drove along the shoreline. She had seen one picture for two seconds, called her brother's name, and started sobbing her heart out. By the time Damaris came back from fetching the cinnamon buns, coffee, and milk, John was sitting on the floor, rocking his weeping child in her arms.

"Let me take her home," Damaris had said softly. She was a mother herself, with four kids of her own.

"I'll do that," John had whispered, regardless of his schedule, holding Maggie against his chest. He had felt her thin body, wracked with sobs, her breath rasping in and out. Hidden beneath the jacket he'd thrown over them where they'd fallen were pictures of girls not much older than her: Anne-Marie, Patricia, Terry, Gayle, Jackie, Beth . . .

John had once warned Teddy that forensic photos were harmful to people not trained to view them, that they could be as destructive as "poison and explosives." He remembered the phrase from his own father, from a time thirty years ago when John had sneaked into his father's office to look at similar pictures of a victim back then.

Ironically, her body had been discovered in the well by the old cider mill, two miles from the first breakwater Merrill had used. John had avoided going near that cider mill his entire life, just as he knew Teddy had been steering clear of the breakwaters—places he had loved to fish and crab when he was younger—since seeing the terrible pictures.

Photos were vivid; they made death real. Lately, immersed in the Merrill case, he'd started feeling disgusted with his job. Sometimes he wished he didn't know so much—like Billy had said, predators were everywhere. John thought of himself as a moral man, but he had to face the truth: He was working for killers. He had pictures of their handiwork in his home. He felt sick.

Now, holding his daughter's hand, he felt the heat just starting to come back to her skin. He squeezed once, waiting for her to squeeze back. She didn't.

"Hey, Mags," he said. "We're forgetting something."

"What?"

"The mall."

She nodded, but when he looked more closely, he saw the color draining from her neck again. "Not right now, okay, Dad? I want to go home and wait for Teddy."

"Teddy?"

Maggie nodded, huge tears forming in the corners of her eyes. They balled up, spilled over, and coursed down her cheeks. She licked them away, her voice croaking as she whispered, "I want my brother."

"Okay, honey," John said, feeling a knife in his gut.

He started toward the coast road, then remembered that they were still staying at his father's. Angry at himself for being too busy to interview new baby-sitters—and feeling furious at the memory of the brick through their window—he turned down his dad's street.

Parking in the driveway, he turned to Maggie, but she was already out of the car, running as fast as she could up the stone walk, scrambling up the steps as if trying to escape a monster.

Following her inside, he spotted Maeve sleeping on the living room sofa, covered with an afghan and snoring loudly. His father was out at his weekly "Judicial Session," where half the retired judges from Superior Court got together to play poker and kick around the old days. Teddy wasn't home yet.

Suddenly he heard Maggie squeal, "It's for me!"

"What is?" he asked.

"This package!"

Maeve must have brought it inside. John moved closer, to examine it. Wrapped in brown paper, tied in a blue ribbon, the parcel had Maggie's name on it. John had recently seen the handwriting—become almost familiar with it—from notes on the back of her sister's picture.

Nodding that it was okay for Maggie to open it, he watched his daughter tear in. She pulled off the ribbon and paper, pulling out a long, fringed white silk scarf and a pair of aviator glasses. An envelope fell into the floor. Picking it up to hand to Maggie, John saw the East Wind logo printed on the flap. Maggie read aloud:

Dear Maggie,
I want you to have my flying scarf and

sunglasses. I wear them sometimes, but not very often. They would do much better on you, helping you become Amelia.

Amelia Earhart used to inspire us, my sister and me, and I hope she will inspire you. I think you're a natural: you're smart and brave. I could tell the minute I met you. You kept a clear head that day. . . .

I'm leaving today. The East Wind was a fine place to stay, but right now I feel the wind blowing me to a new destination. Like Amelia, I have a journey to make. We all do! As you make yours, I hope you'll believe in yourself. I believe in you!

Your friend,
Kate Harris

P.S. Please say good-bye to Teddy, your father, and Brainer for me.

"She left, Dad," Maggie said, sounding grief-stricken and breathless.

"We didn't even know her very well, Mags," John said chidingly.

"But I liked her . . . and she liked me! She gave me her scarf and glasses!"

"She shouldn't have. I'd've taken you to the mall."

"This is better," Maggie whispered. "She said I'm brave. . . . How did she know?"

"Like she said—you behaved that way the day she met you."

"If I'd known that, I wouldn't have gone looking for courage today," Maggie said, her chin wobbling again. "Didn't have to look at those pictures . . ."

"That's what you were after?" John asked, pulling her onto his lap in that same wing chair he'd sat in so many years ago.

"Yes," she said, starting to cry again, clutching Kate's white scarf to her face. "I wish I hadn't seen that girl. . . ."

"Me, too, Mags."

John kissed his daughter's head. He found himself thinking of Willa Harris, hoping that she wasn't one of them, one of those girls, one who hadn't been found yet. He hoped Kate would never have to look at pictures like Maggie had just seen.

"We have to tell Teddy she said good-bye." Maggie sniffled. "He'll be sad."

John didn't reply. Somehow he knew that, too. There were nice people in the world; his job didn't always bring him in contact with them, but there were. He found himself touching her scarf with his fingers.

What did it mean, that he had come after Teddy but before Brainer in her list of good-byes? He felt surprisingly, absurdly grateful that she'd mentioned him at all. He wondered where her journey would take her next.

He wondered, and he couldn't let it go.

chapter 11

The Seven Chimneys Inn, the sprawling stone mansion just east of Breton Point in Newport, on Rhode Island's craggy coastline, had once belonged to Rufus Macomber, the railroad magnate. He had built a fireplace in the bedroom of each of his seven daughters, and although the house had five more chimneys besides, he had intended the name to honor his girls.

Kate checked in, and then drove straight to the Newport Police Station. She parked at a meter on the square, walked up the hill to the brick building behind the courthouse, and asked to see Detective Joseph Viera.

"Hi," she said, when the compact, muscular detective came out of an inner office, rolling down his shirtsleeves and straightening his tie. "I'm Kate Harris—we've spoken on the phone before."

"Yes, of course. Come on in."

"It's nice to meet you after all this time," Kate said, preceding him through the door of a small office. "You know, to put a face to the voice. Thanks for all the work you've done on my sister's case."

"You're welcome. Still no word about her?" Detective Viera asked, gesturing at a chair across the cluttered desk.

Kate shook her head. The floor seemed to move slightly beneath her, as it did whenever she realized that her sister had been gone six months, and that no one knew where Willa was.

"You realize, there's nothing much new I can tell you," he said. "I've spoken with— what's his name"—searching his notes— "here it is, Detective Abraham O'Neill, in Washington, D.C."

"Yes, he's overseeing the case. . . . I called the Washington police first," Kate said. "When she didn't come home."

"That's appropriate, Washington being her hometown. The investigation focused on Newport, I seem to remember, because it was the last place she was seen . . ."

She tried to smile at his helpfulness, nodding. "Yes," she said, hearing also the word he hadn't said: "alive."

"What brings you up here now, Miss Harris?"

Oh, that question. It brought tears to her eyes faster than anything. She had to purse her lips, sit very still for a long moment, staring at the big clock on the wall, watching twenty seconds tick by before she could trust herself to answer.

"I have to know . . ."

Detective Joseph Viera waited. He knew she wasn't done, and he probably knew what was happening in her gut right now. She surely wasn't the first sister of a missing person he had met; perhaps Kate's reaction was just a predictable symptom of a horrible condition: Missing Sister Syndrome. There had to be such a thing, she thought. Something as devastating as how she felt had to have a name.

"Sorry," she said, feeling a tremor go through her bones.

"Take your time."

"So much time has gone by . . . I never

stop hoping for the phone to ring, thinking someone will call to say they've found her . . ."

The detective nodded, but the jaded look in his eyes let her know how impossible he thought it was.

"I know the Washington police have done a good job—they've coordinated all kinds of police reports from three states and the District. But I guess I felt it was my responsibility, as her sister, to come up north and do this for her. To *be* here . . . to walk where she walked."

"I understand."

Kate paused, knowing he didn't; not really. The detective didn't know the details—the awful, hurtful details that had led to Willa's going away. He knew about the affair; all the police did. They had questioned Andrew, questioned Kate herself. But he didn't know about Kate's guilt—for encouraging Willa to work for Andrew, and for saying, in a high, piercing voice, that she would never forgive her.

"I think about Greg Merrill a lot," Kate said, watching Viera's eyes.

"The Breakwater Killer?"

Kate nodded.

"He did most of his killing in Connecticut," Viera said. "In fact, if I'm not mistaken, all of it."

"All the ones they know about," Kate said.

"Well, she fits his profile, from what I know of it," Viera said, eyes cast downward at the pile of papers, "but I'm looking at her file here, and plenty of other things jump out. It's possible, Miss Harris, and I'm sure Detective O'Neill would say the same thing, that your sister just doesn't want . . ."

"To be found," Kate said.

"Sounds like an unhappy love affair all around. For everyone. Maybe she thought the best thing to do was just . . . quietly go away. Shame is a powerful motivator."

"That's not possible," Kate said stubbornly. "Willa would never do that to me."

"Okay, well, you know your sister," Viera said. Kate could see his face shut down: The eyes were suddenly guarded, the jaw set. She regretted her outburst. Now he'd be talking to her like an emotional family member, censoring anything he really thought.

He remained polite, even friendly. He reviewed Willa's file, sharing with Kate the details they had come up with.

There was the record of O'Neill's original phone call, back in April. He had sent a unit to Willa's Adams Morgan apartment, found notes on a phone pad indicating an imminent trip to New England—chambers of commerce, reservation services, the elaborately doodled word "Newport."

Credit card records had confirmed her destination, narrowed the search to Newport. The file contained Newport Police interviews with the Seven Chimneys Inn's owners, chambermaids, and other guests; statements given by a bartender at the Candy Store and a waitress at the Pier. Records of Kate's follow-up calls, at least one a month, followed.

"That's really about it," Viera said. "All we have."

"Are you sure?" Kate asked. "No one else saw her, talked to her?"

"Not that we found. I have indications from O'Neill's office that she went on from here . . . something about Massachusetts."

"She was in Connecticut, too."

"Ahh. Well . . ."

"I know; I have to contact them. I've already been to Connecticut."

"Merrill's stomping grounds. They have him, you know. Maybe you could talk to someone there."

"I have," Kate said, picturing John O'Rourke's hard eyes.

"Sorry I couldn't be of more help," Joe Viera said, standing to shake her hand.

Numb, Kate walked out into the cold afternoon. She hadn't learned anything new, and discouragement flooded her body. What was she doing here? She had taken a leave of absence from work, searching for something she might never find: one tiny thread, one unturned stone, one vague hint of what had happened to her sister.

The interview had done one thing: brought back family memories.

When they were children, their parents had driven them north, so they could compare the beaches of Chincoteague with those of Rhode Island. They had stayed at the Sheraton Islander, visited the Breakers, Rosecliff, and Mrs. Astor's Beechwood. Walking the cliff walk, they had watched yachts racing offshore, and they had seen a man land a record-breaking striped bass on the rocks in front of Doris Duke's house.

But one of Kate's happiest memories was of dinner at the Pier. They had ordered oysters and lobster bisque, sole stuffed with huge pieces of lobster, and baked stuffed lobster. Their father had pronounced the oysters as good as Chincoteague's, and Kate and Willa had eaten lobster till they were both too full to move. The salad dressing had had tiny mustard seeds in it, and their mother had been delighted.

"Mustard seeds mean faith," she had said. "All you need is the tiniest bit for it to sprout and grow. And you can do anything with faith. . . ."

Kate went to the Pier in search of a little faith and a sense that Willa had once been there.

The hostess led her to a table by the window. She sat by herself, scanning the tables, wishing she knew where her sister had sat. The police had told her what Willa had eaten that night, so Kate ordered the same things: salad, oysters, stuffed sole. It was all delicious, and the view of the harbor and the soaring Newport Bridge was dramatic; fortified, closing her eyes, Kate could almost feel her sister's hand on her shoulder, hear her whisper, "Keep looking, Katy. I need you to find me!"

"I will," Kate said out loud.

She was sitting alone, and people at nearby tables turned to see whom she was talking to. They probably thought she was crazy. Kate had started thinking that herself, lately. Before taking her leave of absence, unable to concentrate at work, she would close her eyes and talk to Willa.

Or, riding the Metro from her town house on Capitol Hill to her office in Foggy Bottom—just blocks up from her old Watergate apartment—she would imagine Willa sitting beside her. She dreamed of the conversations they would finally have: Willa explaining what had happened between her and Andrew, Kate listening, telling her sister that she forgave her; Kate longed for that opportunity. Because her heart had been so rock-hard and angry when Willa had left.

"I'm crazy," Kate said out loud, sitting alone at the Pier, proving that she really was.

Her life was on hold; there was no doubt about it. Once the top staff scientist on the Academy's marine environment team, she had turned her files over to a colleague, until she could find out about her sister. She knew the work she was capable of, and she was far from doing it.

"Come back, Willa," she said, staring through the reflections in the big windows, straight out to the Newport Bridge. "Come back and let me forgive you. . . ."

She stopped herself. Did that mean that she had started to believe Detective Viera, that she thought Willa had a choice? Could it be possible her sister was hiding somewhere, too ashamed to return home?

No, Kate thought, staring at the dark harbor. No, it was not. The bridge's lights ran between the two tall towers, graceful strands of illuminated pearls. Willa had crossed that bridge, but where had she gone? Kate had checked Connecticut and Rhode Island, which left only one place.

Massachusetts.

Fairhaven wasn't far away; just thirty or so miles north and a little east. Kate had to keep looking for Willa. She thought of the full moon, high and serene, exerting pull over the tides: No one could see it. As children, she, Matt, and Willa had all found it magical and mysterious. Kate's need to find

Willa was like that: a powerful force deep inside. Who knew what unturned stone might be there for only Kate—Willa's sister—to see?

Kate could make the ride to Fairhaven in about an hour. After that, she knew she had to return to Washington, to try to put her life back together.

Besides, she had already gotten through the hard part, hadn't she? Storming the bastions of Greg Merrill's defense, confronting John O'Rourke and demanding he tell her what he knew . . . the fact that he hadn't responded with any measurable degree of human compassion and hadn't seemed to care that Willa—a woman who perfectly fit the profile of his client's victims—was still missing.

If it was true that defense lawyers were all heartless bastards, then John O'Rourke was certainly a prime example. The thing was, Kate saw right through his façade. She knew hurt when she saw it. She wished she could have softened his heart—gotten him to tell her something that might have helped Willa, maybe helped himself in the process. She had the strong feeling that they were kindred spirits.

And he had wonderful kids. His love for them shined right through his hard shell. Kate hoped Maggie had gotten the scarf and glasses, that she would go out on this Halloween night, having the time of her life, feeling the aviator spirit in her own heart.

The waitress brought the check. Kate put her credit card down on the tray, then took a last sip of coffee to fortify her for the ride to Massachusetts. Pushing back her chair, she left the restaurant of family memories for the next stage of her journey.

The miles felt long and tedious. Bonnie kept her company, curled in the passenger seat. The radio was playing, a local station that favored jazz. Perhaps Kate should have waited for morning, when she could actually see something. But her heart was in command of this odyssey, inner compulsions driving her northward to find the places her sister had been. She stopped at a Maxi-Mart for more coffee, and sipped it as she drove, to keep herself awake and alert.

Heading northeast, she crossed the Tiverton Bridge, cut through the mill city of Fall River. Streetlights lit her way, flashing through the car as she passed beneath. Lizzie Borden had killed her parents here a century ago, and Kate felt the chill of murder in the air still. Famous killers, forgotten victims. Fascinated by Lizzie, who even knew her parents' names?

It was like that with Greg Merrill, Kate thought. Who were his victims? Anne-Marie Hicks, Jacqueline Somebody, Beth or Betsy . . . Seven women altogether, and Kate could only remember three. Was it a psychological trick she was playing on herself: to not remember his known victims so she wouldn't have to imagine Willa's name joining the list?

She had read articles about Merrill, seen his face on the news, dreamed of him in her sleep. He had gotten into her mind and imagination. Why had he been so fixated on breakwaters? Why had every victim been found wedged in a stone structure meant to hold back the forces of nature, meant to stem the ocean tides from destroying beach and property—from destroying life?

Greg Merrill. She said the name out loud: it sounded solid, then liquid. Greg: hard. Merrillll: flowing water. Like rock and water—like breakwaters.

Lizzie Borden. A child's name. A cute,

friendly name for a woman who had used an ax from her family's own garage to hack her parents to bits.

Who were these people, and how did they do what they were accused of doing? Lizzie's cold spirit filled the car, following Kate through the Fall River streets, where signs of Halloween mischief were everywhere: smashed pumpkins, toilet-papered trees, shaving-creamed parked cars.

Merging onto Route 195, Kate headed east. Jazz played softly over the radio; on the half-hour, news broke in, local and late-breaking, delivered by a soothing, reassuring, silver-tongued reader. This stretch of highway was unlit, running through dark, flat countryside, the black water of inland marshes flowing seaward on the right side.

At New Bedford, the city lights lit the sky with an eerie orange glow. Kate saw billboards for flights and ferries to Martha's Vineyard and Nantucket. A huge black whale dominated one sign, exhorting passersby to visit the Whaling Museum.

Staring at the black whale, Kate felt a shiver of excitement.

A clue? Could it be?

Had Willa come up here to see the museum? Since she was a very young child, she had been fascinated with marine mammals. Their brother had taken them offshore in his boat twice every year—spring and fall—for the great whale migrations north and south along the Atlantic Seaboard.

Kate remembered holding her baby sister on her lap, Matt throttling the boat down, keeping a respectful distance . . .

"What IS it?" Willa had asked, clutching Kate's neck, her voice filled with awe and delight.

"A mother humpback and her baby," Kate had said.

"See the white fins?" Matt had flung back, ever-present cigarette dangling from his lower lip, cap pulled low to block the sun. "That's how you know she's a humpback."

"Hump-back," Willa had pronounced.

"Good girl!" Kate had said, and Matt had squinted over with pride.

"What's she doing now?" Matt asked as the mother swam in a big circle, creating huge bubbles on the wave tops.

"Feeding!" Willa had exclaimed, laughing.

"Damn right, peanut," Matt had said. "Her

breath is one big depth charge, exploding all the little fish to the surface."

"She must be hungry!"

"Yep," Matt had said, grinning. "You could say that. Hungry like an army."

"You're a smart one," Kate had said, tousling Willa's sun-bleached golden brown hair. "You'll make a good oceanographer some day."

"Don't listen to her, peanut," Matt had laughed, lighting a new cigarette from the stub of the last one, chucking the butt into the sea. "You're gonna oyster with me. We'll be Harris and Harris, and we'll snag all the oysters from Chincoteague to Ocean City till we find the King Pearl."

"Queen Pearl," Kate had said. "If you drag her into the oyster business, you'd better at least open your mind, slack off on the sexism."

"Lighten up, Katy-pie."

"You know, throwing that butt into the sea might ruin your take next year?"

"Yeah? How d'you figure?"

"Say a bluefish eats it, thinking it's a nice tasty minnow. The filter clogs the fish's digestive tract . . . the fish dies. One broken link on the food chain. That bluefish isn't alive to eat the menhaden that eat the eels that fall in chewed-up bits to the bottom of the sea to feed your precious oysters . . ."

"Hey, I'm a litterbug. What do you want to do—sue me?"

"Not a bad idea."

"You grew up with watermen," Matt had said. "You know more about the sea than any of those fancy professors teaching you biology and chemistry and whatever the hell else you're going into debt studyin'. You could teach *them,* Katy."

"Yeah, well, it won't get me a job."

Half scowling, half smiling, Matt had dragged on his cigarette, shaking his head.

"More whales," Willa had said, ignoring her siblings, staring avidly across the waves.

At an age when most little kids were learning their ABC's, Willa Harris was dazzling her oysterman brother and almost-scientist sister with her knowledge of cetaceans. Matt had circled the area, and the three Harris siblings had watched the whales breach and feed for forty minutes, until they had finally sounded for good.

Passing the museum billboard, the huge cut-out whale silhouette remained visible in her rearview mirror. Kate stared at it for another moment—wondering whether Willa had seen the exhibit during her time up north—then took the turnoff for Fairhaven.

She cracked the windows. The air smelled like the sea. Bonnie stood on her hind legs, nose to the opening. New Bedford was still a busy port, and ghostly spars lined the skyline. Fishing boats, sailboats, vessels in drydock were everywhere. Kate thought, with a stab, that Matt would love it here. Memories of him were painful; Willa's disappearance had killed something in their brother.

Always prone toward isolation, Matt had become a true recluse. The sea was his only friend. People said he talked to himself, steering in and out of the channel. He was often seen at the whaling grounds—where humpbacks still made their twice-yearly passage—smoking one cigarette after another as he watched the whales go by.

Matt lived in his tiny, sagging oyster shack, surrounded by mountains of shucked white shells. Kate's personal legend had it that he still looked for the Queen Pearl, believing that finding it would somehow make his sister come home. Bearded and gaunt, Matt was known as "the hermit" to the kids of Chincoteague.

Kate shivered and sighed, pushing the picture from her mind. One sibling at a time, she thought. Tonight was all about Willa. . . .

Connected by a small bridge to New Bedford, Fairhaven was smaller and quainter, but just as salty. Kate reached into the bag beside her, removing the sheet of paper given her by Detective Abraham O'Neill.

It listed the name and address of the Texaco station where Willa's credit card had been used. Peering at the address, Kate shook open the map she'd printed out from the Internet and looked up 412 Spouter Street.

Straight 0.6 miles, left 1.1 miles, immediate right at the traffic light.

Kate followed the directions through boatyards, past an office complex, into a neighborhood of three-family houses. At the intersection, she stopped at a red light and looked right: a strip mall with a Texaco sign at the street.

Catering to the residents, the stores were somewhat . . . humble, Kate thought.

A Laundromat, a recycling center, and a

convenience store with several gas pumps. *Willa was here,* Kate thought, the chills coming back to make her tremble. *It's not a theory, it's evidence.* Her credit card was used to pump seven gallons—ten dollars and fifty cents' worth—of gas. Kate held the sheet of paper, her hand shaking.

Parking her car in front, telling Bonnie she'd be right back, she left the radio playing and walked beneath the brightly lit canopy over to the pumps. A sign indicated that a credit card could be inserted into the pump itself, the gas type and octane level selected, and the transaction completed without a signature.

Kate's heart fell. Although she knew this, the fact that whoever had used Willa's card could have done so without signing—Willa herself, or someone else—she had wished it was otherwise.

She walked into the store. A man sat at the counter, reading a magazine.

"Excuse me," she said.

"Yes?" he asked, looking up.

"Are you the owner?"

The man laughed. "No," he said, as if it was a joke.

"Have you worked here long?"

He smiled. "Three years," he said, making Kate's skin tingle.

"Do you . . ." she began, her throat choking up, pulling the photo from her handbag, "know this woman?"

The man stared at Willa's picture.

To see better, he raised it to his face. Kate found herself staring at his hands. They were clean, soft-looking. Service station employees never pumped gas or fixed cars anymore. But what if those hands had touched Willa? What if she had come here, to fill her tank, and encountered this man alone with his magazine? What if he had wanted something from her that she'd been unwilling to give?

What if he had dragged her into a dark, private place, hurt her, made it so she couldn't return home to Kate and Matt?

The man looked up, a kind expression in his dark eyes.

"No. I was not here the night she came. I know of her, of course. The police questioned us. No one saw her; she—or someone—just swiped her card. You are . . . her sister?"

"How can you tell?" Kate asked, her eyes wet with tears.

"You look alike," he said, looking at the picture again.

"Do you know anything? Anything at all that can help me?"

The man shook his head. At the sight of tears now falling freely down her cheeks—another dead end, another disappointment—he handed her a small napkin from the pile beside the coffeepot.

Kate knew. He wasn't the one.

"I'm sorry. The police checked security tapes, of course. If anything was found, we do not know. They did not tell us. I am sorry."

"It's okay," Kate said. Taking Willa's picture from his hand, she bowed her head and walked away. Her chest rumbled—an earthquake of emotions was locked inside her body. Her organs shook. Her bones reverberated, the connecting tissue strung tighter than guitar strings. Her skin screamed, holding it all together.

Running to her car, Kate felt the howl building.

It was a hurricane; it would shake the world.

She started up the engine. Bonnie couldn't help, although she tried. Licking

Kate's hand, she whimpered for attention. Kate hardly felt or heard the dog. Willa's credit card had been used right here, in this very place; it might have been yesterday, today, this instant, for the feeling of immediacy pounding in Kate's brain. Her fingers ached, wanting to hold her sister's hand, stroke her face.

She felt like screaming; her heart was being crushed by it. Bonnie nuzzled her, alarmed by Kate's mood. Kate wanted to just put her head down on the steering wheel and cry. So, instead of driving away, she ignored Bonnie's yelps and pulled around back—into the darker, more deserted parking lot behind the strip mall.

The lights were very dim back here.

A few cars were scattered at the back entrances to the stores and businesses. An anchor fence ran around the lot's perimeter, separating the pavement from the yards of several houses on the next street.

The houses looked small and tidy, brightly lit. Silhouetted in light from their windows, Kate spotted a station wagon parked by the chain-link fence. She saw the shadow of a man—standing by the Dumpster, perhaps throwing something away. Music played softly on the radio, then crackled into a wailing sax solo.

The tears pressed against Kate's throat, the roof of her mouth. The not knowing about Willa—building up all this trip, during all Kate's investigations in Silver Bay and Newport and now Fairhaven—crashed through her like a wave.

Kate cried so loud, Bonnie jumped into the backseat. She cried for Willa on her lap watching whales, Willa painting pictures at her easel, Willa and Matt hanging sand dollars on the Christmas tree, Matt still searching for Queen Pearl, Matt the Hermit, Willa in bed with Andrew, Willa gone all this time . . .

Kate cried, and then she howled. The radio music was still playing, but the sax had given way to a piano and bass.

Kate's tears were violent; her heart thumped like a bass. Her crying felt like company, made her feel she wasn't alone. And suddenly, she wasn't; terrified, she heard scratching at her window. Kate gasped, but Bonnie let out a bark of recognition.

Brainer stood at the car door, front paws scrabbling at the window glass. Just behind him, striding toward her from across the dark parking lot, was John O'Rourke.

Kate was too upset, too bewildered to know what he was doing there. Maybe his motives were suspicious, bad, evil, but Kate didn't think so. At least her heart—or the part of her brain that was in control of her wildly soaring emotions—told her the opposite.

So, throwing her car door open, letting Brainer bound in to see Bonnie as Kate stumbled out, she blindly threw herself into John's arms and let herself sob against his chest.

chapter 12

What was he doing, standing in a Fairhaven parking lot with wisps of fog and blasts of North Atlantic air and this woman in his arms and his heart banging as if he'd run a marathon? John wondered.

Her hair smelled like lemons. Her breath came in warm, impassioned gasps, blowing straight through the shoulder of his wool sweater. Her chest heaved with emotion as sobs shook her body. John, accustomed to holding Maggie while she cried herself out, just stood very still, disregarding his own intense feelings, until Kate began to calm down.

"You okay?" he asked.

"Whaddaelllrrruudoonggrrr?" she asked, her voice muffled by tears and his sweater.

"Once more, this time so I can hear you," he suggested.

Pulling back from his chest, she looked up with big, worried eyes. "What the hell are you doing here?" she repeated.

"Funny you should ask," he said.

"Why?"

"Because I was about to ask you the same thing. How 'bout you invite me out of the cold and into your car?" he asked, partly stalling for time before answering and partly to hide how surprised and—shocking itself—happy he was to see her in this godforsaken parking lot so far from both their homes.

When they climbed in, John gave her the same once-over he'd give a client suspected of the most heinous crime imaginable. Could he trust what she was about to tell him? Was she going to tell the whole truth or a half-truth? Or lies? Was she going to sugarcoat some nasty, unsavory fact about her sister's case?

He swallowed, looking away. Trust had been in very short supply lately. She was so pretty and vulnerable. Holding her in his arms, he'd wanted to keep her right there for a long time, protecting her from whatever she feared most. He had come here to help her, and here she was. Now, slowly glancing across the seat, he saw her wiping her eyes. He thought of Theresa, of Willa. His heart tugged, and he knew that his deepest wish was that Kate Harris was exactly who she seemed to be.

"What are you staring at?" she asked, wiping her eyes.

"Just . . . nothing," John said, embarrassed, caught in the act of trying to trust her.

"Tell me—what are you doing here?"

"You first. Last I heard, you were hightailing it home."

"Who told you that?"

"Maggie. She thanks you for the scarf and glasses, by the way. She made an excellent Earhart. The note you left said you were leaving—to say good-bye to me, Teddy, and the mutt."

"Hear that, Brainer?" Kate asked, glancing into the backseat. "That's the sort of esteem your owner holds you in . . . and I'm supposed to answer for my movements?" Now, turning back to John, she blinked steadily, her eyes clear in the parking lot light. "I never said I was hightailing it home. I said I had a journey to make."

"I just assumed you'd headed back to Washington."

"Clearly," Kate said, "a wrong assumption."

"My mistake. So—why are you here?"

She didn't reply; he saw her pulse beating in her throat, the pearly white skin flickering as if she'd just run up a hill.

"Why did you scream? I thought someone was hurting you."

"Someone is," she whispered. "The man who took my sister."

John's stomach clenched. He closed his eyes for a minute. So far, his trip to Fairhaven hadn't proved anything. Maybe it was all just a story. Merrill had been playing him along, giving him a detail that wasn't true.

A house, a first-floor window, with a young girl undressing.

Well, it was bedtime now, right? John had never practiced voyeurism before, even in service to a client's case, but all it had yielded through those house windows tonight were glimpses of old women saying their rosaries, a man brushing his teeth, and a family watching TV.

"Why are you here, Kate?" he asked.

"Same reason you are, I suspect."

"I don't think so . . ." he said, unwilling to give up anything Merrill had told him.

"Oh, I do," she said softly, sadly.

John looked out the car window. His gaze went straight to the house across the parking lot. It was the back of the house—the front faced the street a block away.

There was the fence Merrill had admitted climbing; the first-floor windows had all been dark, but suddenly one was illuminated, the view inside blocked by white curtains. Very consciously, as if Kate Harris might follow his eyes and read his mind, he panned across the lot to other houses.

"You know I'm right, don't you?" she asked. "I mentioned Fairhaven to you, and you checked it out. . . . Merrill was here, right?"

"Can't talk about my client."

"He was *here*—right in this very parking lot. Or you wouldn't be! Was it the same night as my sister? You have to tell me," Kate said.

John's eyes flicked back to the window. It

was the right house—it had to be. His heart began to pound. Someone had just walked into the downstairs room, turned on the light.

A person was moving around. Close to the window, away from the window . . . impossible to identify age or gender.

Then another lamp turned on—brighter, toward the back of the room.

A young girl's shadow passed by the light. John's blood began to race. He could see the shape of hips and breasts—a flash through the curtain's opening of skin, of a nightgown being pulled over her head.

How old was she? Fourteen?

Six months ago . . . she would have been thirteen, fourteen at most. Certainly she would have attracted him out of his car, across the glass-littered pavement, across the jagged-topped fence. Her nearness would have triggered that chemical in his brain—that bizarre mixture of hormones and nerves—that made it all happen, set him on his way.

"John? Be fair to me! I'm Willa's sister. If you know something . . ." Kate asked now, her voice imploring.

Without responding, John got out of the

car. He heard the dogs bark behind him, but he just walked faster. Broken glass crunched under his feet. Kids probably parked back here to drink and hang out and have sex in cars—no streetlights, no prying parental eyes.

The girl was in her room. Couldn't someone tell her, warn her father, that perverts could just sit back here and get an eyeful? John thought of some stranger staring at Maggie while she got dressed, made a vow to buy blinds and heavy draperies for her bedroom window. There was so much to protect them against, the people he loved. He had an insider's view of the worst that could happen, and right now it was tearing him up inside.

Running footsteps sounded behind him, but he kept on walking.

"Who is she?" Kate's voice asked, breathless, catching up to him.

"No one," John said, the hole in his stomach as deep and empty as an abandoned well.

"Why are you watching her?"

"I'm not the only one," John said. The words just came out; he couldn't help how she would take them. Gazing left and right, trying to figure out where her house sat, he knew that he would find her street address and get a message to her father—telling him to protect his daughter better.

"What do you mean by that?"

"Nothing."

"Merrill watched her, didn't he?" Kate asked, her voice raised and strained. "That's why you're here—it has to have to do with him. . . ."

"Kate, leave it alone." John hadn't planned for her to be here. He had to investigate, had to satisfy his own need to know, to decide how best to proceed. The last thing he needed was the sister of another potential victim observing him uncovering more evidence of his client's guilt.

"John—he's already on death row," Kate said, yanking his arm. "How much worse can it get for him?"

"That's not the issue!"

"You want to know how it is for me and my brother?" she asked, still pulling his arm. "It's like this: My brother won't see me, won't talk to me—he thinks it's my fault. He thinks if one sister is gone, the other one just might disappear, too. Why get close to someone if this can happen? Why love them your whole life if one day they can just fall off the face of the earth? It's so much better to just stay alone . . . to stop caring."

John stood still, the biting wind numbing his cheeks and chin. He thought of Theresa. He remembered how he had started suspecting the affair. How he had resisted the truth—tried to fool himself into believing he was wrong. When he couldn't—when he'd heard her whispering into the phone, when he'd checked her cell phone bills and found all those calls to Barkley, when he'd found the notes—how he had shut down.

How he had stopped caring. What could she do to him then? Nothing—nothing she did mattered, if John no longer cared. He had his kids, he had his work: Let Theresa try to live with herself for destroying their marriage. That was her responsibility, not his. He didn't want a divorce: He wanted to work things out. She'd come around—she had to. But till she did, John was shut down.

Then the reality of Theresa's death surrounded him with frigid clarity. Time to work things out? What a joke. Death had ruined all that. No one had to ask anyone for a divorce; John would never have to deal with that reality. And so he'd shut down a little more. Stop caring? Maybe he knew a little of how Kate's brother felt.

"I'm sorry," he said quietly.

"Not just for me, but for my brother," she pleaded.

"Don't stop caring," he said suddenly, turning to face her again. "Like your brother."

"I already have," she whispered.

"No," he said. "I saw that package you left for Maggie. It made her day . . . made her year."

"It did?"

"Yes," John said. "It's what she wishes her mother could do for her."

"Theresa."

"Yes," John said, cringing as she said the name. Did she know? Had people in Silver Bay told her what had happened?

"I'm sorry Maggie and Teddy lost their mother. And you lost your wife."

"I lost her before she died," he whispered. He couldn't believe how the words came out, almost by themselves. He leaned closer to her. Suddenly he wanted to tell her—wanted her to know everything. Kate would understand him. She'd completely get it, know what it had been like, trying to

love a person who didn't want his love . . .
The feelings pressed in on his heart, and
God—all he wanted was to let them out.

"You did?"

"She left me . . . she was still living at
home, but she was gone. Her heart was
gone . . ."

"I'm so sorry," Kate whispered. Her voice
tore and trailed off. She looked away, as if
John's eyes were a mirror, and she couldn't
stand to see herself in them.

John raised his gaze, suddenly remembering the girl in her room. In just a few
years, Maggie would be that age.

"He watched her, didn't he?" Kate asked,
now looking over. Was she imagining Willa
as a young teenager? Strangers standing in
a back lot, watching her undress?

"Let me handle it, okay?" he asked. His
tone was soft. He had started to bare his
soul to her; he wanted her to know she
could trust him, that he would follow every
clue and do his best to handle her sister's
disappearance. "I'll tell you when I can."

"I have to know!" she said, her voice rising, ragged.

"You will—I promise," John said, reaching
for her wrist.

Kate's eyes were wild, mad. She stared at the girl. "We can't just let her do that," Kate said. "She has to know that people can look in."

"I know," John said.

Suddenly, Kate ran over to the fence. Like a trapped dog, she raced up and down the length till she found a break in the wire. John watched as she tore through a neighbor's yard. She slipped on a patch of concrete—her leather shoes sliding, soles scraping across the rough surface. Falling to the ground, catching herself with one hand, running through the yard.

John had no choice but to follow her. He watched as she raced through the side yard—past an overturned boat—the one Merrill had mentioned, now moved to a new spot?—and a garden choked with dead tomato plants and grapevines. He followed her past an empty birdbath to the front steps, heard her bang on the door—knocking so loudly that a dog down the street began to bark.

"What is it?" a man said, coming to the door.

"Your daughter," Kate said, out of breath.

"What about her?"

"People can see her undressing—through her bedroom window."

"What the fuck?"

The man was tall, dark, overbearing. He raised his arm—as if to strike Kate, for her words, or for what she had seen. John bounded up the steps, stood between him and Kate.

"Don't touch her," John said loudly.

"What the FUCK?" the man repeated, his muscular, tattooed arm still in the air.

"She's warning you," John said. "Trying to help your daughter."

"What the hell you know about my daughter?"

John heard Kate's breath in his ear. The man's eyes were hooded, menacing—as if he'd just been threatened in the most primal way. Two women—his wife and his mother?—stood behind him, the older one dressed in black from head to toe. And the girl—lovely, fourteen, fear in her green eyes—peeked around the corner, the white strap of her nightgown showing on her bare shoulder.

"Nothing," John said, meeting the girl's eyes. Wanting to reassure yet warn and protect her. "We know nothing about her. Your

windows face out on the back parking lot—
that's all. Just take care."

"Belle, c'mere," the father said, his eyes
still wild. "You doing what they say? Putting
on a show?"

"No!" she yelped, running down the hall.

"She lying?" the man asked his wife,
and the woman disappeared after their
daughter.

"Don't give her a hard time," Kate said.
"It's not her fault."

"Don't go minding my family's business,"
the man warned. "Meddling bitch."

John tasted metal in his mouth. He felt
blood pouring through his veins into his
nervous system; he felt as if he had just
stepped into a domestic with a guy who
didn't like answering to women. He hoped
Kate hadn't just made the girl's life hell. He
hoped he wouldn't throw the first punch
and land in jail before the guy.

"Listen to me, sir," John said clearly, in his
best courtroom voice, his face two inches
from the dark and surly homeowner's. "It
can't feel good, having strangers come to
your door, saying they saw your daughter
through a crack in her curtains. Her *closed*

curtains—you hear me? This IS NOT her fault."

The man flinched, as if John had him by the throat.

"But I can't have you calling my friend 'bitch.' Hear me? She's trying to help your daughter . . . help you. There are monsters in the world, you know? People who could see an angel and want . . . to hurt her."

"My daughter's an angel," the man said, the fight releasing from him. "You got that right."

"See?" John said. "Then maybe we helped."

"That fucking parking lot," the man said, shaking his head. "Kids park there every Saturday night. I been afraid of boys climbing the fence since she turned fourteen. Fourteen going on thirty."

You should have been worried at eight, John thought. *Nine, eleven, twelve . . . there's no magic number.*

"Protect her," Kate said, her throat husky, and John knew she was talking about Willa.

"Yeah," the man said. "I will."

He closed the door in their faces. Kate stood very still, looking into her cupped hands. Stepping forward, John leaned down for a better look. The heel of her right hand was scraped badly, bleeding and raw.

"I cut it when I fell," she said. "In the backyard."

"Looks like it hurts," John said, holding her wrist loosely. If it was Maggie's hand, he would bend down to kiss it. He touched the skin, wanting to.

Kate nodded, but she didn't speak. She started to pull her hand back, step away from John, start back to their cars. But she stopped short because John couldn't seem to let her go. He held her wrist, and he stroked the soft skin, and then he took real hold of her hurt hand.

Standing on the steps of a stranger, John looked into Kate Harris's gray-green eyes. Her hands felt warm and thin, and he suddenly wished she would touch his face. His breath was deep and ragged.

"I'm a defense lawyer," he said.

Kate nodded. "I know," she said.

John weaved on the steps, as if a strong wind had started to blow, as if the tide had just changed and was pulling him out to sea. The current was strong, like a riptide. When he was a boy, he and his friends had skipped school and gone to Misquamicut for the day. John had gotten caught in the undertow, swept into a riptide. No matter how hard he fought it, the tide was stronger than he was.

"Swim parallel to shore," his father had always taught him—wise instructions for a boy who lived by the sea, who was bound at some point in his life to encounter a rip. In his panic, John had forgotten for a few minutes and, following instinct, had tried swimming straight back to the beach. Getting nowhere, tiring quickly, he had felt himself being tugged out to sea.

"I'm in an ethical dilemma," he said now, still holding Kate's hands. His voice was so low, he wasn't sure she'd heard him.

"What?" she asked.

"There's what I have to do as a lawyer," he said, "and what I want to do as a man . . ."

Tilting her head, her stone-gray eyes caught the light. They were deep and somehow warm, filled with unfathomable secrets and sorrow and mysteriously, at the same time, laughter and joy. Staring down, still holding her hands, John O'Rourke was almost overcome with the desire to kiss her.

"What's the difference?" Kate asked. "Are the two parts so distinct?"

An interesting question, John thought. Usually, until right now, perhaps not. He had become a defense lawyer because he was a good man, because he believed in every person's right to a fair trial, because he believed in the law. But this minute, John was at war with himself. He was Jacob wrestling the angel—only the angel was John's own heart and soul.

"Yes, they're so distinct," John said.

"Then tell me what they are . . ."

Gripping Kate's hand, John led her down the house steps, along the street—he wasn't going to walk her through the backyards again.

The night was so cold, they could see their own breath. October ended with Halloween; at midnight, it would be November, the beginning of All Souls or All Saints—in spite of his Irish Catholic upbringing, John had never known one from the other. He had been a heathen in recent years. A stone church stood down the block—*Spiritus Santi* in Portuguese. Holy Ghost . . .

In local custom, the congregants filed out in a silent, solemn procession, holding candles to welcome the spirits of their dead, to greet their lost beloveds . . .

"Do you believe in anything?" John asked Kate as the people filed into the small cemetery.

"Yes," she said quietly. "I do."

"Can you tell me what it is?" he asked, then laughed. He was trying to make a joke, but she wasn't even smiling.

When they circled around the block to the parking lot, they both looked at the house and saw the father hanging a blanket over the girl's window. Five seconds later, not a crack of light was visible. The two of them stood very still, holding hands, watching to make sure they couldn't see the girl's shadow pass.

Kate lifted up ever so gracefully on her toes, and now John knew exactly what to do. He wrapped Kate in a tight embrace, gave her a long, lingering kiss. He would have kissed her all night; the second she broke away, he was already yearning for more.

"Kate," he whispered.

"She's safe now."

"No one's ever safe," John said, stopping dead and taking her face in his hands.

"Don't say that . . ." Kate said, her eyes filling with tears.

He wanted to kiss her again, but he wanted to tell the truth more. Lies had nearly killed his family. He was putting his entire career on the line right now, and he wasn't going to mix it up with soft-pedaling the truth.

"I know it for a fact," John said.

Kate shook her head, but he wouldn't let her go.

"You know it too," he said, his voice breaking. "Or you wouldn't be here."

"What do you mean?"

"Your sister would be home . . . safe at home. She'd be in her nice warm house; you'd be in yours . . . the last six months wouldn't have happened. She wouldn't have come into contact with my client."

"What are you saying?"

"You know . . ."

"Say it," she said, the words tearing out as she grabbed the front of his sweater. Her hand was bleeding, and the blood smeared across the green wool.

"Your sister was here," John said, holding Kate tight, so she couldn't pull away. "And so was my client . . ."

"Merrill?"

"Yes," John said. "He came into this back parking lot, to look at that young girl—" he gestured at the small house, the window now dark. "And he got frustrated. I think . . ."

"Willa was buying gas," Kate whispered, her eyes wild with fire.

"Yes, I think she was."

"And he came upon her . . ."

"He forced her into her own car," John said, not sure, not positive of anything, but using his knowledge of his client's psychological profile and his methods of operation, to try to answer Kate's questions.

"And made her drive away?"

"Yes."

"How do you know?" she asked with horror.

"Because that is what he does."

"Did he tell you?"

"Yes."

"About WILLA?" she asked, nearly screaming.

"No—not about Willa. But about the others. About watching the girl in that window." There—he had done it—breached lawyer-client confidentiality. One call to the court by Kate Harris, and John O'Rourke's career was over. Maybe it was anyway. How could he come back from this?

"Oh, no, oh, no," Kate was saying, shaking her head.

"Sit down," John said, leading her to her car. Pushing her down, so she could lean on the hood, holding her still with both hands on her shoulders.

There were lines in life that good people never crossed. To John they had always been completely clear. They weren't like sins—lying, stealing. They were bigger; they had to do with vows, with the promises a good man made and had to keep in order to stay a good man.

A good man didn't kill. Or cheat on his wife. And, if he were a lawyer, he didn't break his client's confidence. It didn't matter whether the client was a thief, a rapist, a murderer, or all three. The crime was beside the point because the principle was larger than anyone, or anything.

The principle—the ethics of a lawyer keeping his client's confidence, of making sure the client received a fair trial—was something that John had lived by his entire life. He had learned it from his father.

And his father's word and lessons were worth everything to John O'Rourke. He hoped to pass them on, through the generations, to his son and his daughter, and to their sons and daughters.

"What do I do now?" Kate asked, beginning to shake.

"You go home," John said. "You stop searching."

"But Willa . . ."

"Let the nightmare be over," John said.

"How can you say that? It feels as if it's just begun . . ." Her voice rising, Kate reached out with her scraped hand. She needed to touch John—he understood. She had just come face-to-face with the monster he encountered every day.

"Kate," he said. He knew he should leave now. He had given her what she'd asked for; holding her would only make it worse. But he wanted her so badly; he wanted to touch a human being who would touch him back, who would need contact as much as he did, a woman with river eyes and a loving gaze, who had been cheated on, who still cared enough about her sister to come all this long, long way.

"I still have to find her," she whispered, her hand held out. "Willa . . ."

John shook, wanting to embrace her. He took her hand instead. "You have her, Kate. Where it matters most."

"Where?" she asked, the word scraping from her throat.

"There," he said, pointing at her heart. "Inside. Take her home to your brother . . . let this go. Just let it go."

Sobbing softly, she bowed her head. John opened the car door. Brainer wanted to stay inside with Bonnie, but John grabbed his collar and urged him out. He stared down at Kate; if she looked up, if she reached for him again, he'd take her into his arms and never be able to leave. He almost wished she would; he wanted her to hold him, so he'd know he was still good.

Instead, as Kate Harris cried alone, keening for her sister, John strode across the parking lot. Brainer kept pace, and he leapt into the backseat when John unlocked the wagon door.

The girl's window was curtained and dark. John checked his cell phone—no message lights blinking. That meant Maggie and Teddy were at home with the Judge and Maeve. Merrill was locked up on death row. Everything was for now, if not safe, at least okay.

Now, headlights on, John drove over to Kate. Sitting in his car, he watched until she raised her tear-streaked face and stared into the lights. His stomach flipped: How many of Merrill's, of other killers', victims had looked into headlights like his?

Waiting, not rolling down his window—afraid that speaking to her would keep him from driving away—he watched as she wearily straightened. As if sleepwalking, she moved around her car, opened her door, climbed in. Bonnie's face peered over the dashboard, incongruously friendly and cute. Brainer barked.

The streetlights illuminated Kate's face. She stared at him for a long moment. Then, raising her hand, she waved him away. John didn't wave back, just sat there waiting—not wanting to leave her alone in that lot. Finally, she put her car in reverse, backed away, and pulled out. Glancing in his rearview mirror, he watched her head west.

He hung back a moment.

Rolling down his window, he felt a blast of cold sea air. Congregants' voices rose, singing a hymn in Portuguese at the advent of All Souls. John thought he smelled the candle smoke. Turning his head, he saw them flickering in the distance, among the graves.

As he always did, whenever he passed a church or thought of it, he said—by way of a prayer for the women his client had killed—their names. "Anne-Marie, Terry, Gayle, Jacqueline, Beth, Patricia, Antoinette . . ." Tonight he added a new one.

"Willa," he said out loud.

Kate's red taillights disappeared around the corner, and John's heart began to pound harder. He'd just delivered the worst news a sister could ever hear. He wished he could make it easier for her, but he knew he couldn't.

He had kissed her. That was something, wasn't it? Proved he wasn't totally dead inside, that he was still capable of some kind of connection? That Kate was, too? That betrayal hadn't killed them both? But her sister was gone, and the fact he had kissed her was nothing compared to that.

John was sure she'd already forgotten it.

chapter 13

The flight to Washington filled Kate with memories of flying with Willa, of taking her up in the small Cessna, banking over the Potomac and flying east over estuaries of endless green to the sands of Chincoteague. The images were so shimmering and happy that, when she closed her eyes, she smelled tidal waters and salt hay. She remembered John's arms around her, felt his kiss . . . the happiness of touching someone again.

Followed by the terrible reality of what he'd told her about Willa intersecting with Merrill . . .

So, touching down at Reagan Airport, she

didn't even bother to go home. She and Bonnie just walked out of the terminal, straight over to the private aviation hangar; Kate slid her Amex card across the counter and chartered the only four-seater available—the same old yellow Cessna she and Willa had flown a hundred times.

The plane's interior felt like home. The cracked leather seats, the small blue plastic visor, the old-style control panel. Bonnie, aware of the takeoff about to come, curled up in back. Kate ran through her checklist, waved the wing flaps, and took off into the wild blue yonder from which she had just landed. Instinctively touching her neck, she reached for her white scarf.

Of course, she had given it to Maggie. The scarf, a gift from Willa—purchased lovingly, with money from her savings account, from a Paris boutique—had been one of Kate's most prized possessions. Its thick, creamy silk had felt so soft around her neck, the fringe so jaunty and brave.

"Every aviatrix should have one!" Willa had said.

How true that was; and that was why Kate had given it to Maggie. There was something about that little girl—so vulnera-

ble and courageous—that had pierced
Kate, had reminded her of her own sister at
that age. She thought of Maggie, her
brother, and her father, wondered what they
were doing at that moment. . . . Their families were connected now, in some deep and
mysterious way, that had only a little to do
with the kiss, with kissing John in the parking lot where Willa had disappeared, where
his client had probably killed her . . . that
kiss that Kate felt still, that told her body—
her nerves and skin and heart—that she
was still alive.

Isn't it strange, she thought, *that my sister
isn't here anymore? But I am? How can that
be?* The truth hadn't sunk in yet. The reality
was buzzing in her brain, but it hadn't made
it down to her heart, her guts, her toes.
Strangely and somehow upsettingly, John's
kiss felt more real than anything. Her lips
still felt it—the excitement, the warmth, the
gentle touch of another human being.

Heading east, the plane's roar comforted
her. She loved airplane engine sounds, even
the surges and hums that had sometimes
made Willa jump. Flying home to her Atlantic barrier island home, Kate could almost believe her sister was right beside her.

The truth was so hard to accept, she pushed it away. Concentrating on flying the plane, she passed over the Chesapeake Bay, the Eastern Shore of Maryland, then took a hard right and flew down the Virginia coast to the grass strip she knew and loved so well: Wild Ponies Airfield.

The small yellow plane bounded down the flat and wide-open rutted ground of dry brown grass. Kate had called ahead, and she was met by Doris Marley, driver of the Bumblebee Taxi. Doris drove Kate to her brother's cabin without one second of silence, filling Kate in on every aspect of island life: gossip, deaths, one marriage, one custody battle, the need for a new roof on the feed and grain store, Doris's own difficulties with her mortgage, her septic tank, and her son's education—the typical hard-luck story all island cab drivers delivered to every big-city fare.

The words ran together: "Another hard winter coming; gotta get my teeth fixed one of these days . . . lost another molar; Joe, Jr., wants to go to college, trying to scrape the money together for tuition, but it ain't easy when the septic tank gave out, had to have a new one put in . . ."

"Thanks, Doris," Kate said when they'd driven down the narrow road—drifted with blowing sand—into the pine barrens at the island's south end. She pulled out a twenty, told Doris to keep the change, and arranged for a pickup an hour later.

"Thanksgiving's coming," Doris had called after her. "Tell your brother he's welcome at our table . . . you, too, if you're home from Washington for the holiday!"

Kate hardly heard, although she did notice that Doris hadn't mentioned Willa. Their sister's disappearance, though not officially explained, had made it into the island consciousness—and no one knew what to say.

Matt's cabin was as weathered as the trees that surrounded it. Nestled among scrub pines, in a hollow of sand and dirt and pine needles, it blended in with all of nature. Brown owls made their nests in the holes of dead trees; Kate heard their great wingbeats at the sound of her approach. Bonnie, spooked, stayed close to Kate's ankles.

Her brother's rusty red pickup sat out back. Blue plastic barrels, reeking with oyster brine, were piled in its bed. Mountains of oyster shells, as high as the rooftop, glistened in the wan November sunlight. Kate's throat caught; her brother was still searching for Queen Pearl.

She knocked on the door. No answer, so she knocked again. Pressing her ear against the dry and cracked wood, she listened for life. No sounds. She sniffed, smelling that omnipresent odor of cigarette smoke.

"I know you're in there," she called out. "So you'd better open up."

No human reply, but a seagull landed on the mound of oyster shells, creating a small, scuttling avalanche. More seagulls arrived—perhaps, seeing life, hoping for food. An animal moved through the brush; when Kate turned her head, she saw that she was being watched by a scruffy pair of wild ponies. Bonnie growled, very low, flattening her body to the ground.

Finally the door was yanked open.

"Hi, Matt," Kate said.

"Hi, Katy."

He was tall and bone thin, stooped over like an old man. His hair had grown to his shoulders, and it was matted and tangled, like the bed of brown pine needles that blanketed the sandy ground. Crouching down, he tickled Bonnie behind the ears, and she shimmied with love for Matt. His cloudy blue eyes looked across her head at the ponies. Kate watched as he took in their whiskery faces, their huge watchful eyes, their dirty white-and-brown coats.

"They're hungry," he said. "Winter's coming."

"I know."

Matt went to his truck and took out a closed container of slops from one of the island restaurants. Kate's stomach clenched—he'd gotten in trouble before, rooting through garbage, taking food for himself and the ponies. She watched as he pried open the lid, scattered the wilted salad and carrots and cole slaw over the sand, as the ponies stepped forward to eat.

Matt's beard was long, almost all gray. The sight of her brother broke Kate's heart all over again.

"Aren't you going to invite me in?"

He stepped aside without a word, let her pass through the door.

His cabin was its usual mess. He had insulated it since she was last there—pink fiberglass bales covered the rough-board walls, uncovered by beaverboard or any kind of wall material. Dirty dishes overflowed from the sink, onto the counter and formica table. A cigarette burned in a heaping ashtray, stale acrid smoke filling the air. Bonnie investigated the room, then curled up by the smoldering wood stove.

By the room's single armchair were a wide table and an oyster knife. A bucket of discarded shells sat half-filled by the chair's side. A second bucket, bound for the market, was filled with glossy, shimmering oysters, ready to go into his refrigeration unit out back. On the table, a small dish of pearls caught the light.

"Still looking?" Kate asked, smiling in spite of herself.

"Yeah," Matt said, scowling, picking up his cigarette and taking a long drag. His fingers and the beard around his mouth were stained yellow with nicotine. He wanted to look away, anywhere but at Kate, but she pulled his gaze to her, and his eyes began, reluctantly, to smile.

"Still searching for Queen Pearl," he said, the smile moving to his lips. Passing the bowl to his sister, he watched as Kate let the white, cream, pale pink, silver, and near-black pearls trickle through her fingers. Some were perfectly round, others were misshapen. All came from the sea, from

Matt's beloved waters, soft layers of nacre made by the oysters he brought home in his boat.

"They're beautiful," she said.

"Hard to believe, isn't it? That such beauty can come from terrible pain? You know that's how it works, right Katy? Sand gets into the oyster, irritating it so badly . . . the oyster tries to expel it, and makes a pearl instead."

"Beauty from pain," Kate whispered, closing her eyes, hearing the pine boughs brush the tin roof, hearing the ponies whinny as they galloped down the beach.

"Gotta find Queen Pearl for Willa," Matt said. "So I can hand it to her when she gets home. . . ."

"Matt," Kate said. Her eyes flew open, and she took her brother's hand. She tried to lead him to his chair, but he wouldn't budge.

"Tell me here," he said, his eyes burning, his teeth gritted. "I don't have to sit down."

"Willa's gone, Matt."

"Gone? Gone how?"

"That killer I told you about? The one who killed those girls in Connecticut? I talked to his lawyer. They were at the same place—at the same time. The exact spot—they were both there."

"And what?"

"The killer took her, Matt."

Matt stood still for thirty seconds, breathing neither in nor out. He was a statue, frozen in place. But Kate could see his mind working—his eyes on fire, flicking back and forth. He shook his head. "I don't believe it."

"What other explanation could there be? Why wouldn't she come home? Why would she put us through this?"

"She had an affair with your asshole husband," Matt said. "She's ashamed of herself."

"We were getting past it, Matt, Willa and I. She knew I'd forgive her," Kate said, although the words hurt, reminding her of the breach that had existed between her and her sister.

"Maybe she didn't forgive herself—you ever think of that?"

"She wrote me a letter, a postcard. I know she was coming home! We were in touch . . . she wanted us to talk. She wanted us to meet, and so did I. We were on our way to working it out!"

"Self-loathing," Matt said, "is a powerful

thing." He spoke quietly, as if all the worry and intensity had drained out of him, and lit a fresh cigarette, taking a long hard drag.

Kate's mouth dropped open. She was speechless and furious. She'd always known her brother was weird, antisocial, probably mentally ill in his own right—but couldn't he, just once, take an explanation offered him and not turn it into some warped version of his own view of the world?

"You're crazy," Kate said.

"Yup," he said. "Probably so."

"You had to be there," she said. "In this godforsaken parking lot in the middle of Nowhere, Massachusetts—in fact, the town was so full of rusty fishing gear and rust-bucket boats I thought of you, thought you'd probably *love* it there—after dinner, me investigating Willa's gas purchase, and out of the dark comes Greg Merrill's lawyer—tracking down, I swear Matt, the same thing!"

"So what?"

"It's too much of a coincidence . . . and he told me, Matt. Told me that Merrill had confessed to being there."

"Confessed to who?"

"To him—his lawyer! He'd have no reason to lie."

"Did he confess to taking Willa?"

"No, but—"

"Did he confess to hurting her?"

"No! But listen, Matt—"

"YOU LISTEN!" he roared, stepping back with such force he knocked over his pail of oyster shells and the dish of pearls. They scattered, rolling, all over the floor, like pellets in a pinball game—caroming off the chair leg, the table leg, a pile of books, the refrigerator, down the crooked floorboards to the east wall.

Kate, shocked by her brother's outburst, froze.

"She's not dead, okay? She can't be dead," Matt said, the cigarette dangling from his cracked lip as he talked, as he rubbed his chapped and callused hands together over and over, as if trying to wash them of the truth.

"Matt . . ."

"She wouldn't die," he said, his eyes flashing. "She's my baby sister. I go first, then you, *then* Willa. We raised her, Katy. We were like her parents . . ."

"I know," Kate said, tears pooling in her eyes.

"She was our baby girl; she made me so happy. It's because of her I look for pearls, lookin' every day for the big one, the prettiest pearl of all. . . . It's for her, Katy. You—you've got everything you need. The fancy degrees, the ritzy job, that town house you got on Capitol Hill . . ."

Kate listened, crying softly, thinking of how much she had and how little Matt did.

"That's why she went for Mr. Hotshit," Matt continued. "She wanted a little of the big time, a little of what her big sister had . . . she went with your husband so she could be you for a little while . . ."

"Stop, Matt!"

"Don't say he loved her—I won't believe that. He already had you, the stupid idiot. He had one pearl—why go diving for another? He's the one, Katy—you want to go BLAMING SOMEONE . . ." Matt's voice rose in rage and anguish, "BLAME YOUR HUSBAND!"

"Matt!"

"Your big, stupid, power-hungry selfish husband. He drove Willa away, Kate. Wherever the fuck she lies today, that's on him.

On Andrew. Don't give me any of that Greg Merrill garbage—Andrew did it."

"Oh, Matt," Kate said. *I know,* she wanted to say. *I think that, too.* But she wouldn't speak the words, tried not to even think them. What did the reasons for Willa's going away matter? For months, all that counted was that Willa come back. And now, all that mattered was that she wasn't going to.

"He did it, Katy."

"Andrew didn't kill her," Kate said woodenly.

"He might as well have. He corrupted her, and she put herself in exile—from you, from us. Her family."

"You're right," Kate whispered. "She did."

"I'd like to kill him myself," Matt snarled. "My brother-in-law . . ."

"Don't," Kate begged. "Then I'd lose you, too."

At her words, or perhaps at the heartbroken tone of her voice, Matt stopped raging. He fell to his knees, gathering up all the pearls he could find. He held them, cupped in one hand, as ashes sprinkled down from the cigarette in his mouth.

"Could you go now, Katy?" he asked, his voice cracking. With his head facing down,

she couldn't see his eyes, but she knew—
from his gasping breath, from the storms
she had seen before, that he was crying.

"I don't want to leave you," she said,
touching his back.

He leaned into her fingertips for a few
seconds, then shook them off, crawling to
the next pearl.

"Life hurts sometimes, Matt. But we can
face the truth together. We've done it for so
long . . ."

"She's fine, you're fine, I'm fine. Hear me?
I'm facing all the truth I need!"

"By shutting yourself off like this? Living
like a hermit? Not listening to what I *know* to
be true, because I flew north to check it
out?"

"You don't like my way? Leave!"

"Matt, please . . ."

"Go," he said. And then, the volume
building, "*Go,* GO!"

Kate took a deep breath. Dizzy and sick
from the smoke, she backed to the door
and walked out. The air was fresh, salty,
and cold. It seared her lungs, dried her lips
and nose. Seagulls circled overhead, crying
loudly. The thud of hooves sounded down

the beach, the ponies moving from one dell to the next.

Kate longed for the yellow plane.

She knew she could wait for the Bumblebee to come back, but instead she began to walk; she trudged down the sandy roads of her youth, the magical roads of oysters, gulls, ponies, Matt, and Willa.

Faster she walked, Bonnie keeping up beside her, and then she started to run. She couldn't wait to start the engine, get the propeller turning, take off into the sky. She thought of her white silk scarf, a piece of herself, of Willa, left behind in the north, with Maggie.

Life and truth. That's what the O'Rourkes represented to Kate. She had just left a den of death and lies: Matt was killing himself slowly, smoking himself to death, lying his way through life about anything that hurt.

Pearls and oysters and ponies, she thought. Those were Matt's family now. Running along, Kate cried to think of her life, of what was real and what was lost, and the fact that she missed—more than she could understand or dream possible—a family that she had met for just a brief time.

A white scarf, a single kiss: The salty

Chincoteague wind took them both, swirled them together, took them spinning over the pines and dunes, the white sands and silver waves . . . curling, Kate imagined, all the way north to Connecticut, to Silver Bay, to the O'Rourkes.

chapter 14

Maggie hated writing thank-you notes.

They usually took up too much time, kept her from playing and reading, and sounded stupid when she was done. Stilted, kind of phony, no matter how sincere she was when she wrote them.

But this note was different.

Sitting in her bedroom upstairs at Gramps's house—still no sitter had come to fill the position, making Maggie think that she and Teddy must be baby-sitter poison; other kids, all her friends who didn't have moms at home, had baby-sitters that stayed and stayed—Maggie leaned over her desk and wrote like mad.

Dear Kate,

I love the scarf. I know it was supposed to just be for my Halloween costume, which was great because I went as Amelia Earhart and even though people couldn't guess at first because it wasn't as obvious as people who went as Britney Spears or vampires or samurai warriors, once I told them who I was, everyone thought it was cool.

But even though it was supposed to be just for my costume, actually I wear the scarf all the time. I have it on now, wrapped around my neck, even though I'm in my PJ's. Getting ready for bed— finished my homework, yeah. All of it! Give the girl an A for effort, right? (Ha, ha.)

I wish. School isn't my best subject. (Ha, ha again.) I'm not like Teddy who everything he touches turns to an A. Not just for effort, either. Teddy's a genius, like our dad. And like Gramps. He'll probably be a "brilliant legal scholar" too. Ho, hum. Get tired of hearing that phrase around here, because there are so many of them running around!

Me, I'm more like my mother. Except she liked to shop and I don't, except for stuffed animals and books, and that I'm a tomboy and she was a beautiful model-type. She was, really. I'm not just saying that. Open any magazine, and the models you'll see aren't as pretty as my mom. Even the gorgeous-est ones.

I have new curtains.

Red-and-blue plaid ones. To make the room private so people can't spy in from outside, to "protect my privacy"— like anyone would want to check out MY dumb bod! But Dad's overprotec-tive, and we love him for it, so no use fighting city hall! And this is only at Gramps's—by the time we move back home, after some fairy godmother baby-sitter flits down from her pink cloud to grace us with before-and-after-school care, I'll have new curtains there, too.

Dad seems very hepped up on this— probably 'cuz of the "slime" he de-fends. And the ugly tricks those bad guys play to get into all our living rooms. Ever have a dad who's a well-

*known defense attorney? Try it some-
time!*

*Well, got to go brush my teeth.
Teddy says hi. Dad does, too. I have to
get your address from him, so when I
mentioned it, he told me to tell you
about the curtains, and to tell you to
make sure you have some of your own
down there in Washington. Do you
know the president? Senators? Etc.?
Must be cool; the ninth grade got to go
down for spring vacation last year.*

*Maybe when I'm in ninth grade, I'll
get to visit you! Only a few years to wait
. . . (boo-hoo.) Miss you, Kate. Wish
you lived here—wish you were our fairy
godmother baby-sitter instead of what
Dad says you are, a marine conserva-
tion scientist. Although that sounds
neat, too.*

Thanks again for my scarf!

Love, Maggie O'Rourke

**footnote: I don't call his clients
"slime," but half the world does! My
friend Carlie's mother says it every time
I go to her house. Which is why I
stopped going . . . Are you surprised
I'm only twelve and use footnotes?*

Another thing about growing up with lawyers everywhere!

When Maggie asked Teddy if he'd drop the letter to Kate off at their father's office to be addressed and mailed, he asked if he could add a P.S. Maggie said sure, as long as he didn't read her part of the letter. Ever since Dad had hung those new curtains in her room, she'd become very into privacy— a fact that Teddy found endearing and hilarious. But writing to Kate, he made a point of covering up Maggie's words.

Dear Kate, (Teddy wrote)
How are you? How was your trip—or, as you said in your note to Maggie— your journey?
A journey sounds like something I would like to take. Planes, trains, boats . . . just to get on something and go away. Not that I don't like my home—I do. Or that I don't love my family—I do. But I think it's important to go other places, too.
With that said, do you think I could visit you in Washington sometime?
I know we don't know each other too

well, but we had that talk about our sisters, and then you gave Brainer that bath. I knew you were special. Hope you don't mind me saying that. . . .

Anyway, I want to come to Washington someday, so I can visit the Supreme Court and my dad's law school. No rush, but sometime when you're not busy, maybe I could take the train down.

Kind of a start to a journey, right?

Anyway, hope you're doing well. Say hi to Bonnie for me; Brainer needs another bath, and Maggie and I are going to take him to the car wash, like you did! Soccer's done for the year. We finished second in our division, just ahead of Riverdale. Thanks for coming to that game.

Take care, Kate.

> *Your friend,*
> *Teddy O'Rourke*

Sitting in his office, John pulled Kate Harris's card from his wallet. Regarding it, he wrote her office address on Maggie's envelope. Then he placed the letter in his out box, for Damaris to stamp and send.

The sight of Kate's name did something to John's insides. He knew there was a large degree of guilt-induced paranoia involved: When would he get the call from the Connecticut State Police Major Crime Squad, that a woman had called with the news that John had implicated his client in her sister's long disappearance?

But the feeling contained other elements—not linked to guilt of any kind—as well. John couldn't get her kiss out of his mind. He was absorbed and obsessed with it, like a teenage boy who'd held a girl for the first time. The picture filled his mind twenty times a day: the dark parking lot, the light in Kate's eyes, the knowledge they had just helped a family protect their child, the lightning bolt of lust that had overtaken him . . .

It was mad, and he couldn't get rid of it.

Yesterday, sitting across from Merrill and Phil Beckwith, John had drifted off—to Kate and the kiss. Merrill said something, repeated it once, then again. With a smile in his voice, he'd then said,

"You've got it, haven't you, John?"

"What, Greg?"

"A touch of the curse . . . or the gift . . ."

"What curse? What gift?"

"The obsession . . . you've met a girl! Go on, tell me, John. Share with me, as I've shared with you: You're in love! I see it in your eyes."

"Just tired, Greg," John had said, lowering his glasses to rub the bridge of his nose, attempting to hide the jolt of alarm that coursed through him, knowing that Merrill could discern anything about him, that he would think he could relate to John's feelings about Kate. "Overworked."

Merrill had shaken his head, undeterred, the smile widening. He had tapped the table, to get the psychiatrist's attention. "Obsession, Doctor: Am I right? Can you see it in his eyes?"

"You're my subject today, Mr. Merrill," Dr. Beckwith had said dryly without even a glance at John. "Not your attorney."

"God is good!" Merrill had said, head thrown back in absurd joy. "He shows us the way, whether we ask or not. . . . God is using me to show John, and using John to show me: We're all the same under the skin. Our hearts beat alike, Dr. Beckwith. Obsession, by any other name, is just love."

"Let's get on with this," John had interjected, his neck hot, his stomach upset, thinking that what Greg said was actually true—he couldn't chase Kate's kiss from his mind even here in Winterham Prison.

"Yes, Mr. Merrill," Dr. Beckwith had said, unflappable and urbane as he leaned forward to smile. "Are you ready to do some good work here today?"

"Yes. I'm ready . . ."

"Let's begin, shall we, with . . ." the doctor checked his notes, "Anne- Marie Hicks. Tell me, if you would, how you came to meet . . . and what happened next . . ."

John had risen to leave, to allow his client time alone with the eminent expert and their best hope for a mental disorder defense. Beckwith had worked miracles on other cases for John—but Merrill was really custom-made for his area of expertise.

Now, a day later, staring at Maggie's letter in his out box, he was no further away from thinking about Kate's lips on his.

"Good afternoon, Counselor," came the gruff voice from the door to his office.

"Hey, Dad," John said, rising to shake his father's hand. "Come on in. What brings you downtown?"

"Had to stop by the pharmacy, get some

medicine for Mae—*my*—bunions. Hurting like hell, they are."

"Come on, Dad," John said, grinning. "You're shopping for Maeve. I know, so quit trying to hide it. What's going on between you two, anyway? You can tell me."

"Mind your own business, you whippersnapper," his father said, trying to look stern but unable to keep from smiling.

"Okay, have it your way."

His father nodded, glad that was settled. "I went to the courthouse, but there's nothing going on today. Time was, not a day went by without some lawyer or another arguing a case. First me and my colleagues, later, others coming before me to be heard . . ."

"Those were the days, right, Dad?"

"Right, John. What about you? You still hung up with Merrill?"

"I wouldn't say 'hung up.' We're making progress."

"How do your partners feel? Their star defense man tying up all his time on such thankless work?"

"In all honesty, they're divided," John said. Gesturing for his father to sit down in the Windsor armchair—bearing the seal of

Georgetown in gold across the back—John leaned back in his desk chair. "Pretty much right down party lines. Those who oppose capital punishment are supportive, those who don't are getting impatient."

His father chuckled. "I can imagine. You're a young buck, well known in the community, supposed to be bringing honor on the firm. Instead, you're pissing off the whole state, trying to save a man no one wants to see saved."

"I know."

"They're judging him for his crimes, missing the main point: He's still a human being. He has the right to the best defense possible under law."

"Try to get the brick throwers to see it that way."

"I know, I know. It's unfortunate you had to hang your hat on such a loathsome example. People round here all know someone who knows someone who knew one of those girls . . ."

John nodded, thinking of Kate. He thought of kissing her, and then he thought of what he'd told her. He felt himself redden, and his father caught him at it. Now he had the old man's attention. His father stared, peering, waiting for John to speak.

"I did something . . . questionable," John said.

"Yeah?"

John nodded slowly. Standing up, he walked across his office and gently closed the door tight. "I'm glad you're here, Dad. I've needed to talk to you about something. Something important."

His father tilted his head, just waiting.

John took a deep breath. His gaze took in all his diplomas and certificates, his gallery of family photos—from his parents' wedding picture to his and Theresa's, to Teddy's first-grade photo, Maggie with her first tennis racket, both kids on their bikes at Paradise Ice Cream . . .

"I breached lawyer-client confidentiality," John said.

His father's eyes widened with surprise. The Judge puffed out his cheeks, nodded gravely, said, "Go on."

"It wasn't someone from court, no one previously connected with the case . . ."

"Merrill's case?"

"Yes."

John gazed into his father's eyes, needing

guidance, fearing disapproval. It was worth it to him to swallow his pride, get this off his chest and hear what his dad had to say. Another man might ask whether the indiscretion might come back to haunt him, but not John's father. The issue of true—inner, spiritual, moral—culpability was much greater to the Judge than the possibility of being caught and punished—as it was to John himself. Still, he found himself answering as if his dad had asked the question.

"I don't think she'll tell . . . something makes me believe she'll shield me."

"A woman?"

John nodded. "The sister of a woman who's missing. Been missing for six months . . ."

"A long time," his father said with sorrow in his voice. "A very long time to be wondering."

"Yeah," John said. "That's what I thought."

"So, what'd you do?"

"We met," John said. "In Fairhaven, Massachusetts—by accident. A huge coincidence. She had given me a tip that made me ask Greg Merrill about a place he'd been that wasn't in the record—a story he'd never publicly told. I went there to check it out . . ."

"And so did she."

"Right. Her sister had been there, too, around the same time, it seems." John closed his eyes and saw the girl's window, the candle-lit procession, and Kate's river eyes. He felt the kiss again—he couldn't help it. The feeling filled him, making him wish she was here right now, that he could do it again. He physically flinched, and he knew his father had seen. "I had to tell her," he said. "I couldn't let her go on wondering."

"You did the humanitarian thing," his father said.

"Really? You think so?"

"Yes, but you're not off the hook. The *larger* humanitarian act is always to represent your client—adequately. No, better than adequately. To the best of your ability. Without even the suggestion of impropriety."

"What I did was improper." A statement, not a question.

"Absolutely."

"What do I do, Dad?"

His father stroked his chin, pondering the question. "Don't know."

"Did you ever talk to Mom about cases?" John heard himself ask.

His father started, as if shocked. "Yes, of course I did. Spousal privilege supercedes all others in my book. Did you ever talk to Theresa about them?"

John's shoulders tensed slightly, and he forced himself to keep his face neutral. His marriage was something he never talked about—couldn't bear to discuss since her death—even with his dad. The pain never went away—and neither did the shame. "Not really," he said.

"Then why the question? Is this woman someone you confide in regularly?"

"No," John answered, staring at Maggie's letter.

"Who is she?"

"No one, Dad," John said, his heart racing as he stared at Kate's name, remembered how she'd felt in his arms. "She's no one important. What do I do?"

"Well, you never repeat the behavior, for starters."

"I won't. I already know I won't."

"Good. You check your motives—which,

from what you told me, were good. You consider turning yourself in to the Bar Association, throwing yourself on the mercy of their Grievance Committee."

"Of which I'm a member," John said, feeling disgusted with himself.

"Yes."

"After due consideration, much soul-searching, you weigh your options and decide against ruining your career. You—and this is the critical factor—decide against leaving Maggie and Teddy without the financial means to go to college and law school. You then give yourself a swift kick in the ass, call yourself terrible names, and vow never to do it again."

"Thanks, Dad," John said, feeling a weight lift from his shoulders, a grin spread across his face.

"This woman's sister—Merrill killed her?"

"I don't know."

"How're you going to find out?"

"I'm working on that."

"You'd better cover other bases as well. The missing woman's sister—she got a husband? A lover? A brother?"

"At least two out of three," John said,

thinking of Kate's ex-husband and her brother. He hoped there wasn't a lover.

"Check 'em out. Run police checks on them—call Billy Manning. Where did the missing woman live?"

"Not around here," John said. "She was from down south, in New England on a visit."

"Where'd she stay?"

"Some inn in Newport; the East Wind locally."

"I'm sure Felicity took good care of her. No trouble there . . ."

John kept his gaze steady, noting he made no mention of Barkley. It hung between them, the fact his father knew that John's wife had had an affair with one of his best friends.

"Get Billy on it."

"I think Greg Merrill took her, Dad. Pretty sure, anyway. The time and place work with both parties, and she fits his profile."

"He's only admitted *publicly* to killing the seven women he's been convicted of," the Judge said.

"Right," John said.

"A lot of us judges figure that's just the tip of the iceberg," his father said. "You don't have to say—I wouldn't want you to. But a predator like that . . ."

John nodded. He had wondered himself. Greg had only admitted to killing seven; he'd been caught because those women had had families, husbands, people who cared about them. What about the women who had no one? Prostitutes, runaways . . . even Willa Harris had fallen through the cracks because she'd been semiestranged from her sister at the time of her disappearance.

"Don't tell me—I'm not asking you to divulge anything. Just questions to ponder. How about his signature? She fit that too?"

Every serial killer had a private, personal stamped signature, and John had told no one—not even his father—of Merrill's. "Her body's never been found," he said. "So I don't know."

"God," his father said, shaking his head again. "I hope she turns up. It's hell on the families to not know. To have to imagine the terrible things that *might* have happened. To not have a grave to visit."

Again John pictured the procession of Portuguese fishermen and their families, carrying candles, singing hymns in the dark cold night, honoring their dead in the little neighborhood graveyard. The scene had been harrowing, yet somehow beautiful.

It had led John to kiss Kate.

And here it came again, starting up: the thoughts, the feelings, the longing. Sitting in his own office, his father right across the wide desk, speaking of professional infractions and killers' signatures, all John could think of was Kate Harris. Of where she was right now, how she had felt in his arms.

John hoped she didn't have a lover. He wished he could take her pain away, all of it. He knew what she must have gone through with her husband. He wished he could wipe all that away, and he wished he could spare her the grief of knowing/not knowing what had happened to her sister. Of what Merrill had probably done to Willa. Of everything, John most wished he could spare Kate that.

chapter 15

That night, John had scheduled a telephone meeting at home—or, to be more precise, at his father's house. He hadn't spent enough time with Maggie and Teddy lately, and although he had to consult with Dr. Beckwith, he wasn't going to work late another night at the office.

The irony was, he was the only one there. Teddy had some after-school sports stuff going on, Maggie had left a message she'd gone for a bike ride, and—John was amused to read the note—his father had taken Maeve out for a night off from cooking, to the Clam Shanty for some chowder.

John decided to make beef stew. This—

along with chili—was his specialty. He had learned the recipe from a soccer teammate in college, and the recipe called for lots of beef, very few vegetables, and beer. When he made it for the kids, he cut the beer in half. They loved it.

As it got darker, he began to—not quite worry, but feel concerned. The sun was still up, but it was that thin November light that made his mind jump around. Where could Maggie and Teddy be? Standing at the kitchen window, he kept glancing up the street. Here came a car—no, a truck—slowing down, turning into the driveway. Teddy got out, and as John craned his neck to see the driver, he recognized Hunt Jenkins, the soccer coach.

The side door slammed, Teddy dropped his book bag on the floor, and he came into the kitchen.

"Dad!" he said, sounding happily surprised to see his father so early.

"Hi, Ted."

"What're you doing home? It's not even dinnertime yet!"

"Notice who's cooking dinner?"

"Yeah! Beef stew?"

"Yep."

"Where's Maggie?"

"She left a note about taking a bike ride," John said. He wasn't worried, but he'd definitely started to feel concerned. Teddy's question made him look out the window, but then he decided he was being paranoid. "You got a ride home from Mr. Jenkins?"

Teddy nodded, opening the refrigerator. He reached inside, pulled out the milk bottle, untwisted the lid, started to lift it to his lips, locked eyes with his father and thought better of it. Filling a glass, he said, "I was at the gym, signing up for an indoor winter league. Mr. Jenkins is running it with the Riverdale coach, Mr. Phelan, and their friend, Mr. Davis. It was late, and he was driving this way, so he gave me a ride." Glass halfway to his mouth, he looked over. "Is it okay I signed up?"

"Sure," John said. "It's a good thing."

"Maybe I'll get good enough to win a soccer scholarship."

"That would be great."

"Mr. Jenkins says I'm on track. He wants me to start working out with weights, though. To build myself up."

"Yeah?" John asked, stirring the stew.

Teddy nodded, downing his milk. "He

said he'd train me himself. He has weights and stuff at this gym he belongs to. Mr. Phelan and Mr. Davis go there, too. I guess it's a gym for jocks."

"What's wrong with the school gym?"

"Nothing. It's okay. I just thought, maybe working out with them would help me with the scholarship . . ."

John jabbed a cube of beef with a fork, testing it. His stomach tightened, drawing all the way into his backbone. Didn't two grown men have anything better to do than training a high school boy with weights?

"Know what I mean, Dad?" Teddy asked. "I don't think it costs that much, but I could ask."

The stew bubbled on the heat; the meat was done. John let out a long exhalation. His work was getting to him. Too much time spent with guys like Merrill, with doctors like Beckwith trying to explain the ins and outs of aberrant minds. If Teddy's soccer coach wanted to teach him to lift weights, how screwed up was John to assume there was some bizarre motive behind it?

"Sure, Ted. Go for it. Just don't turn into the Rock, okay?"

"Don't worry, Dad—I won't go steroid on you."

They both laughed. The phone rang; when John saw Sally Carroll's name on the caller ID, he hesitated before answering. It was probably Bert, calling for Teddy. But since he was closer, he picked up.

"Hello?"

"Johnny, it's Sally . . ."

"Hey, Sal. How's it going?"

"Delightful. Just fabulous. Lost out on a house sale—the buyer bought in Black Hall instead. I said to myself, 'Sally, you need a drink, and you need a very old dear friend to have it with.' My new boyfriend seems to have dropped off the face of the earth for the night. Naturally, I thought of you."

"Sorry, Sally. I'm fixing dinner for the kids, and then I have a phone conference. Maybe another time."

"Well, okay," she grumbled. "You know, I almost didn't find you . . . I knew you'd been staying at your father's, because Teddy told Bert. But I just saw Maggie riding her bike up your driveway—"

"Our driveway? You mean at home?" John asked, walking back to the window, looking outside.

"Yes. She might have been cutting through from the Nature Sanctuary, or the lighthouse road. I'm not sure. But I thought you might like to know. It's getting dark, and I don't like to see her on her bike at this hour. . . . I know Theresa would want me to tell you . . ."

"Thanks, Sal," John said. Hanging up the receiver, he returned to the window. Long shadows fell across the street and yard. The streetlights flickered on, shuddering like candle flames, then shining steady and bright. The hour of dusk had come, and Maggie wasn't home, and his heart began to pound.

John leaned his forehead against the cold pane. He stared down the street, in the direction she'd be riding from. Almost unconsciously, he reached for his car keys. He had a sick feeling in his stomach, and his hand was on the kitchen door when he heard her wheels crunching on the gravel outside.

"I'm home," she called, coming in the front.

Teddy looked up, smiling, as she walked into the room. John leaned against the door, glad she couldn't see his heart pounding against his ribs.

"Hi, Dad," she said, her cheeks and nose bright red, running across the room to give him a hug.

"Hi, Mags."

At his tone—which he couldn't control; even to his own ears it sounded cold and angry—she looked, up frowning. She stuck her hands into her pockets.

"What's the matter?" she asked.

"Were you just at our house?" he asked.

Her jaw dropped open, and he could see in her eyes the shock of being found out by her father.

"You were, weren't you?"

She nodded, gazing at him. "Not exactly our house," she said. "But the dirt roads in the Nature Sanctuary—"

"Maggie," he exploded. "What did I tell you? Did you cross Lambert Road on your bike?"

"Yes, Dad, but—"

"There's no but about it! A truck could kill you, crossing that road—you know how fast they drive there? And it goes straight under I-95 . . ." He bit his tongue, turning away from her.

The interstate was a corridor for all sorts of criminals. Drug dealers up from Florida, corporate smugglers transporting goods in eighteen-wheelers, pedophiles trolling for unsuspecting kids . . . Client after client had named I-95 in their stories; the highway itself might as well have been an accomplice, an accessory before and after the fact.

"I'm sorry, Dad!"

"Sorry isn't good enough, Maggie," he said. "You're grounded."

"Daddy!"

"Hey, Dad—she didn't mean anything," Teddy interjected. "We both miss the house, the beach . . . I've gone back there a few times, too."

"You want to be grounded, too?" John asked. "Keep it up." His head ached. The kids were being pulled—another compulsion, this one not too mysterious—to their home. The employment agency hadn't called, so John had gotten complacent about not having a baby-sitter. It was so much easier, safer, to stay here with his father and Maeve—a built-in family. He thought of Theresa and felt twin waves of rage and grief wash over him.

"Daddy," Maggie said, starting to cry. He

thought she was upset because he'd grounded her, but that wasn't it. "I don't want you to be mad . . . I don't want to disappoint you . . . please give me another chance. I'm sorry!"

"I can be mad and still love you," John said, clutching his daughter. "I love you, Mags. I don't want anything bad to happen to you!"

"It won't," she sobbed, touching the fringe on the white scarf Kate had given her. "I'm brave—I can take care of myself."

"I know," John said, his fingers brushing the scarf. "But you're still grounded anyway."

Maggie seemed about to say something more, but then she just turned and ran up the stairs, into her room. It was dark out now; when she turned on the lamp, John hoped she'd remember to pull her curtains.

He stood very still, his heart pounding. A memory of standing in that back parking lot with Kate surfaced. Kissing her had felt so right. As if they needed each other somehow, had been brought together for more than just that moment in time. He stood in a house that didn't belong to him, with two kids who wanted only to go home, and he closed his eyes and thought of Kate.

Kate had returned to her office to pick up some things; after what had happened to Willa's postcard, she had become hyper-conscientious about checking her mail. Although her assistant had promised to forward everything, promising-looking or not, Kate occasionally had to stop in and see for herself. Her office was empty, waiting for her to return to work. Although she'd taken an open-ended leave, being back whetted her appetite to return for good.

She sat in her office, staring at all the reports and queries that had come in during her absence. Quota reports from various shellfish commissions up and down the Eastern Seaboard, requests for the Academy's pollution studies from two towns in Maryland. Her work had always been vital to her, but she hadn't been able to concentrate in months.

She knew she couldn't still; not yet. Looking through the stack of mail, satisfying herself there was nothing from Willa, her attention was immediately caught by a postmark:

SILVER BAY CT. Feeling excited, she decided to wait to get home to read it. Saying good-bye to the other staff members, she took the elevator down.

The National Academy of Sciences was located in a large, modern building at the corner of Twenty-first Street and Pennsylvania Avenue. Walking outside, Kate pulled her green coat tighter. Some nights she loved to walk all the way home: past the White House, down to Constitution and the bare-branched cherry trees, along the Mall with the huge, friendly Smithsonian buildings—tourists strolling along in any weather, the Capitol dome lit up, glowing, lighting her way home.

But tonight, feeling the need for immediate shelter and wanting to read the letter, Kate walked to the taxi stand and got into a cab.

Her town house was located on Capitol Hill, just off Massachusetts Avenue. Since her trip to Fairhaven, the street name itself was a thorn—it caused her pain just to look at the sign. The cab driver dropped her in front, and she ran up the tall steps, unlocked her heavy black door, and walked into the cozy brick building.

Bonnie was overjoyed to see her. Kate dropped her satchel, then walked around turning on lights. After moving out of the house she had shared with Andrew, she had refused to take anything from their days together and had furnished her new place with her own taste: furniture from second-hand shops on the Eastern Shore, her grandmother's braided rug from Chincoteague, beautiful watercolors of dunes and bays.

Sinking into her chair, she pulled the small blue envelope from her satchel. Her name was printed in large, childish letters, the rest of the address filled out in sharp adult handwriting.

Just looking at the postmark, SILVER BAY CT, her shoulders relaxed. Energy seemed to flow from the paper into her fingertips, as she opened the letter and began to read.

It was a thank-you note from Maggie, for the white scarf. Teddy had added some words of his own. Kate read the letter through twice. Although John hadn't included a message, she found herself staring at his handwriting on the envelope. Maggie must have asked him to address it for her.

Holding the letter in one hand, the envelope in the other, Kate closed her eyes. She thought of her sister's secret escape to New England, of her brother, alone in his oyster shack in the pines woods of Chincoteague. Family could be so elusive. Her own family seemed lost, but this strange, strong sense of connection was coming from a place she never would have expected. . . .

"Brainer says hello," she said out loud, to Bonnie.

As if that had just made her the happiest dog in Washington, the Scottie jumped up into the chair beside Kate and began to lick her paws. The two of them sat together, dreaming of the north, listening to the wood snap and burn. Kate felt the warmth of her little dog and remembered John holding her.

She wondered what he'd thought, addressing the envelope.

Did he remember their kiss? Did he wish they could do it again?

Kate closed her eyes, holding the envelope to her chest. She had never felt quite this way, and it upset her. She hardly knew John O'Rourke. He was on the "other side," the lawyer for the person she suspected of viciously taking her sister away.

But he was more than that. He was a single father who had lost his wife in the worst way possible. She had died suddenly, on a lonely road, possibly on her way home from being with someone else. Kate understood the strong emotional twist that must have caused John. Love, betrayal, and then disappearance altogether: It seemed impossible to bear. At least, Kate couldn't begin to.

chapter 16

Because Dr. Beckwith hadn't called John at home—one of his patients had had a crisis—the two men met in Providence the next day. John, curious to see the latest in the doctor's expanding operation, drove up to his clinic.

"Surprised you find time to testify," John said. Looking around the office, he had Willa Harris on his mind. Where had she gone? Did their mutual client have something to do with her disappearance? How was Kate surviving, back in Washington, still not knowing the fate of her sister?

"I know," Beckwith replied ruefully. "So many people, so much need. As you know,

I work primarily with sex offenders. Society would like to just lock them in a dungeon, but they're people, too. Call me crazy, but I think I can help."

John nodded, and the doctor laughed.

"Clearly I'm preaching to the converted; we're on the same team. I know you're very busy, so let's start out with a tour of the latest. Funding has been up lately, so there are additions since your last visit. When was that, anyway?"

John frowned, thinking.

"Must have been three years ago now. When you worked on the Caleb Jenkins case."

"Rudimentary, compared to what you'll see today. How is Caleb, by the way?"

"His mother says he's doing well, working for his father."

The doctor nodded with satisfaction. "That's great. Makes me feel good about my testimony, to know we helped a boy avoid jail time for, essentially, pulling a prank. Now he can get on with his life. If only it was that simple for some of my other patients . . ."

John nodded.

"Let me show you the basics of what I do

here now. And, from the start, let me say that I believe our client to be beyond the help I offer other men less 'entrenched' in their obsessions . . . over the months, I've gotten to know him quite well."

"I know. I appreciate your involvement."

"My pleasure," Beckwith said. "It's not every day I get to work with someone like him."

For some reason, John couldn't reply. The words wouldn't come, and he felt slightly sick.

The Beckwith Study's offices were located in the university's only high-rise building. The foundation, federally and privately funded, occupied the entire twentieth floor, overlooking the colonial brick buildings of College Hill, the candy-colored houses of fishing families on Fox Point, and Narragansett Bay shimmering down to the Atlantic.

In contrast to the glorious views outside, the study's offices looked inward at unimaginable worlds of violence, fantasy, and paraphilia. The doctor showed John video rooms, role-playing rooms, a machine designed to measure sexual arousal, and a lab filled with the stench of rotting fish.

"What's that?" John asked.

"Oh, one of my negative feedback methods." The doctor grimaced. "I teach my patients to associate vile smells with their violent fantasies. Hook them up to a monitor, start them talking about their rapes . . . measure their arousal. When it peaks, I bring out the dead fish, and the smell breaks the erotic feelings."

"That works?"

"Takes years, but yes—sometimes. The patient no longer gets an erection from the fantasies."

"Really . . ."

"These people—mostly men—are sent to me as a last chance. They've served prison time; most of them are court-ordered for treatment, and none of them believe it will help. Teachers who molested students, dentists who touched patients, men convicted of rape . . ."

"My clients," John said dryly as they toured the floor. "And this is how you 'help.' "

"Yes, by reworking their fantasies. I try to deprogram them, then start over. See, sex is a mysterious thing. People spend very little time actually *having* it. Their thoughts, their fantasies, are where the trouble begins. Each of us—every human being on the planet—is born with a powerful sex drive. If we weren't, the species would have died out long ago."

"I don't think our clients are overly concerned with propagation of the species," John said. Another wave of queasiness passed over him. He knew the feeling was emotional; it had been building for some time now, ambivalence for the work he did, the people he represented. He wanted to turn and run, take the elevator downstairs, get out of here. But he forced himself to stay.

"No. And when their desire gets linked to inappropriate people or behaviors, it still needs to be satisfied. And they hurt others, hurt themselves, get arrested, wind up here. I'm a behaviorist. I try to link their bad desires with unpleasant consequences—like the smell of dead, putrid, rotting fish."

"Hmmm . . . ," John said, remembering Psychology 101, how Ivan Pavlov had rung bells at feeding time, training his dogs to salivate and grow hungry at the sound—training them to expect pleasure. Concentrating on scholastic memories pushed his own conflicts from his mind.

"Exactly," Dr. Beckwith said. "Society wants retribution. They want these sexual offenders to serve long prison terms, and then, since Megan's Law, they want to keep track of them. All fine, but not solving the problem. Locked up in prison, they spend years refining the same deviant fantasy that got them locked up in the first place. Your client is a prime example."

"In what ways?"

"Shall we go into my office and discuss his case?" Dr. Beckwith asked, leading John into a large suite facing west over the brick-and-granite city—surprisingly not the better, million-dollar view of the bay. A young woman with short brown hair and grad-student-style clothes sat at an outer desk, typing on a computer.

Closing the door behind him, Beckwith gestured for John to take a seat across the wide desk. He pushed some consent forms across, and John read them, noting that Greg Merrill had granted permission for Dr. Beckwith to discuss his case.

"We both know that Merrill is where he

belongs," Dr. Beckwith said. "Behind bars, locked up, for the rest of his life."

"However long that might be."

"Exactly. He fits the formulaic criteria of state law; he's a violent predator who has offended repeatedly. The question is: Does he have a mental disorder that makes him commit his terrible crimes? Again, I think we both know that he does."

"The State doesn't, though. When the prosecutor delivered his argument at the sentencing hearing, he said, 'You've heard a lot about extreme emotional disturbance, but that's just an excuse for a man who likes to kill teenaged girls.'"

"I know, I've read the transcripts."

"I have to tell you," John said. "I have a daughter. When I think of Merrill from the perspective of a father, I want him to stay right where he is, on death row. But as his counsel . . ."

"You've done the right thing, coming to me," Beckwith said, leaning forward, hands folded on his desk. He was an elegant man, with neat white hair and patrician features.

John was silent, waiting for him to go on.

"Greg Merrill is, in many ways, a typical serial killer. Extremely bright, quite personable, an innocent demeanor—permitting him to attract his victims."

John was silent, listening, thinking of Willa Harris.

"But inside, something quite different. Your client is off the charts on a scale of psychological disorders. He can't subdue his fantasies. They haunt him constantly, even today, through the medication. He fits all the DSM-IV criteria for paraphilia, with more added. He not only wants to rape, and eventually kill his victims . . ."

John looked away.

"He wants to possess their souls. His fantasy includes keeping them alive in the breakwaters for one hour after he's stabbed them. He sits with them as the tide rises, until the last possible minute for him to walk away and not get wet. Always just out of sight of the beach, of boats passing by."

"Why?" John asked, focusing on the doctor's eyes.

"So the women can feel how close they are to death—and, at the same time, to help and rescue."

John waited while the doctor continued.

"He feels the primal pull of the tides . . . the sea, to Merrill, is female. An all-giving, all-taking-away mother. She nurtures, then she consumes. His particular pathology includes hatred for his own mother. She was very controlling and possessive, but she worked long hours at her job to take care of her boy. Merrill thinks if he can keep his victim alive for that time, as the water rises around them both and they share that primal experience, then she will belong to him forever."

"He *really* believes that?" John asked. "It's not just a metaphor . . . he's not just gaslighting us?"

"No patient," Dr. Beckwith said with an amused smile, "gaslights me."

"Sorry," John said. "I should have just spoken for myself. I've been manipulated by the best in the business. Believed a client's story totally, then found out he'd been lying the whole time."

Beckwith shook his head. "Merrill can't lie about this. It's too important. His need for control over the girls is paramount, and I see it in the way he abducts them, holds them prisoner in his van, tapes their mouths, hurts them repeatedly, kills them slowly."

"Keeps them alive for that last hour, letting the tide rise . . ." John said, aching with the thought of Willa gasping for air, waiting . . . God, the image was horrendous, and he dreaded to think of Kate hearing this.

"Yes. In a way, he considers the sea—his mother—his accomplice. Although he denies this vehemently, he needs 'her' permission. He allows her to complete the act."

"He's very intuitive," John said, shaking himself out of thinking about Kate's pain. "He already knows that you want to create a new category for him. He says you think of him as a 'zombie-maker.' "

The doctor smiled sadly at the black humor. "Sorry to disappoint our mutual client; he wouldn't be the first. Dahmer had a fantasy of creating a zombie of one of his victims. No, what makes Gregory Merrill distinctive is his need to dominate women while, in fact, being submissive to one."

"The sea," John said, wondering whether Willa Harris's body was hidden in a breakwater somewhere. "The rising tide."

"Precisely."

John checked his watch. He had a busy afternoon, and then he planned to unground

Maggie and take a bike ride with her. "So, we have a sexual disorder–mental illness defense to take to his next hearing."

"Most certainly."

"Thank you, Doctor," John said. Shaking his hand, he walked out of the inner office. Standing in the vestibule, he waited while Beckwith's assistant made copies of the consent forms.

He thanked her and the doctor, and then he took the elevator down. Returning to his car, parked on Thayer Street, he bought a coffee for the drive home to Connecticut and thought about what he and Beckwith did. The doctor wanted to help people, to understand them better.

John wanted to do that for Kate.

Since hearing her grief, locked in her car in that Fairhaven parking lot, he had felt something unlock and release in his own body. He was a defense lawyer in an untenable position.

Hearing Beckwith talk about his clients, John had felt even greater disgust and hatred building inside. Since taking on Merrill's case, he had spent time getting to know the victims, understanding them—to the best of his ability—as young women with hopes, dreams, families who had loved them.

He knew their names and recited the list. But regardless of his desire to humanize them, he had never met any of them before. He had never held one of their sisters, kissed her in the cold, November wind.

John's work was no longer just theory: not just a psychiatric defense. Not just family members sitting across the courtroom, hating him for defending their loved one's murderer. This family member had a name, a face, eyes that looked right into his soul: Kate.

Regardless of whether her sister had met up with Greg Merrill, John knew that he was defending the sort of evil that had destroyed her family's life. Teddy always badgered him about it: "Merrill did what they say he did— murdered girls, ruined families. He deserves what's coming to him. Everyone says he does, Dad."

He reached into his pocket to pull out Kate's card. He would call her, ask if she'd gotten the kids' letter. He'd ask how she was doing, whether she had gained any relief since returning home, tell her he hoped she was okay.

But just as he flipped open his cell phone to dial her number, it rang in his hand.

"Hello?" he asked. His heart was pounding, as if it might be Kate Harris, as if their Fairhaven magic was working again, and they'd found themselves in the same place at the same time.

"Johnny? It's Billy." Billy Manning, his voice deep and filled with excitement. "Just breaking every rule in the book to give you a heads-up. You'd better get down to Point Heron right away—the breakwater."

"What are you talking about?"

"We have a copycat working—"

"A body?" John asked, blood rushing into his head.

"Yeah. Jammed into the breakwater."

"Recently?" John asked, his voice a croak, thinking that if it was Willa, if Greg had killed her, she would have to be all bones by now, praying that Billy hadn't found bones . . .

"Very recently," Billy said. "She was under for no longer than one tide cycle. He left her there before dawn, for the incoming tide. Just like Merrill, John. And the new guy knows the signature."

"Good," John said quietly.

"Good?" Billy asked. "Are you crazy? Get down here, why don't you, before you miss the chance to see what we have. And don't tell anyone who called you."

"On my way," John said, starting to drive. Point Heron was about forty-five minutes from Providence, just east of Silver Bay.

Good. His comment had had nothing to do with the copycat knowing Greg's signature.

Good, because no bones meant that it wasn't a body six months dead, that it wasn't Willa Harris; *good* that Kate wouldn't have to face that horror. Nothing else: there was nothing else *good* about what Billy had called to tell him.

Nothing at all.

A crowd had gathered to watch the police activity.

Vans from the State Police's Major Crime Squad blocked the sandy parking lot. Yellow crime scene tape had already been stretched out across the rocky promontory. Low black clouds scudded across the sky, making the afternoon seem like night. Camera flashes illuminated the scene; approaching white headlights and departing red taillights were reflected in the flat silver wash of each retreating wave.

John parked his car, walked over to the yellow tape, and looked for Billy Manning.

"Hey, what are you doing here?" one of the other cops asked. "You ambulance-chasin' another one?"

"Drop it," John said wearily, watching his friend walk in from the breakwater, his leather shoes slipping on the wet rocks.

"You lawyers got an uncanny sense for where your next meal's coming from," the cop said. "There's got to be a better way than getting rich on death."

John ignored him, but the words made his chest hurt. He could see the crowd gathered out at the end of the breakwater. Detectives, the medical examiner, a cop videotaping. It was getting darker; the tide was coming in. A young officer, dispatched for the black body bag, grabbed it from the back of the coroner's van.

Peering out the breakwater, when the crowd broke up for a moment, John saw in a flash the woman's arm—crooked, raking the sky, fingers splayed. The arm looked thin and hard, like a stick of driftwood bleached by the elements. The water rose higher, and the team set about removing her before she was covered by waves.

Staring, John didn't even hear the person come to stand beside him.

"Dad?"

It was Teddy, dressed in jeans and a jacket, wearing sandy sneakers, holding a soccer ball. He stared up at his father, eyes shadowed with worry and pain.

"What are you doing here, Ted?" John asked.

"I saw her, Dad," Teddy said. "Bert, Gris, and I were playing soccer on the beach. Some lady was walking her dog, and the dog went scrambling over the rocks. Next thing, we heard the lady screaming . . ."

"Did you go out there?"

Teddy shook his head, his face pale. "No. We wanted to help, but the lady said the girl was dead—for sure. The cops came, and then you came . . ."

"I'm glad you didn't, Teddy," John said, giving his son a hug. It was sheer impulse, and he almost immediately pulled back, realizing how embarrassed Teddy must feel. But Teddy actually hugged his father harder, not letting go right away. The feeling choked

John up. He closed his eyes, wondering how far he would have to go to take his family away from all the horrors of the world.

"What're you playing here for," he asked, "instead of at the field?"

"We were supposed to practice at Riverdale today, for the indoor soccer league. But Mr. Jenkins said Mr. Phelan— the Riverdale coach—couldn't get the gym for some reason. Basketball practice, I guess. We're going to do it tomorrow, but Bert and I wanted to get started. So we came to the beach."

"Why Point Heron instead of Silver Bay?"

" 'Cause Bert's mom drove us here. She has a new boyfriend . . . he lives in that glass house," Teddy said, gesturing at the new, modern house perched above the beach. An old 1930s cottage had been bull-dozed to make room for the starter castle; turning to look, John saw Sally Carroll and a man standing on the deck. Sally was watch-ing him with binoculars.

When John waved, she swept the glasses out to the action on the breakwater instead, pretending not to see him. John and the man stared at each other, and suddenly

John recognized him. He'd been at Teddy's soccer game, the one Kate had gone to.

"Peter Davis, right?" John asked.

"Yes. I think he went to Hotchkiss with Mr. Phelan, and he's friends with him and Mr. Jenkins. It's his gym we all went to, to work out with weights. Who's the dead lady, Dad? The victim."

"I don't know, Teddy," John said.

"Is it true, what the cop was saying when I walked over? That you're here because you want to represent the killer?"

John shook his head, watching as they moved the woman's body out of the rocks, into the heavy black bag. Her skin looked so dull and pale in the fading light. Her brown hair hung lank, like a bunch of rockweed. John watched until she was secured on the stretcher, and then looked into his son's eyes.

"That's not the reason I'm here," John said. He could have explained about conflict of interest, how he couldn't be the lawyer for a criminal copying Greg Merrill, how he wouldn't even if he could.

"Then why, Dad?" Teddy asked.

John watched the team slowly bear the woman's body the length of the slippery breakwater, waves of the rising tide licking their feet, splashing their ankles. He thought of Kate, and he thought of Willa, and he refused to take his eyes off the thick black bag.

"For a friend," John answered finally, aware of his son's eyes on him. "I came because of a friend."

chapter 17

Kate had heard through the grapevine that Andrew Wells had masterminded Senator Gordon's trip to China by way of increasing his national profile, enhancing his reputation as a foreign policy expert. It was looking more and more like his latest boss, Senator Gordon, would challenge the President in the next election.

It was Monday, Thanksgiving week. Knowing that the delegation had returned that morning, she knew exactly where to find the senator's jet-lagged chief of staff. At her old home, in the Watergate.

Walking through the neighborhood of Foggy Bottom from her office, she barely felt anything. Darkness had fallen, and dampness was in the air, surrounding the streetlamps with globes of soft silver haze. This had been her beloved route just over six months ago. She had loved the small brick houses, the feeling of a village, the proximity of the Kennedy Center . . . both she and Andrew had been mad about opera, had had season tickets.

She used to walk home from work every day. She would buy tulips at the flower shop, to put on the hall table, a symbol of how she wanted her life to be. On November nights like this, feeling the Potomac chill, she would hurry past the shops and cafés, eager to be home. Hoping Andrew would be home for dinner that night.

But now she numbed herself to all the sights and emotions.

The signs had been everywhere, about a year and a half before Willa had worked for Andrew; as soon as Kate had started noticing them, she'd begun feeling off—worried, doubting herself. Kate would swear he'd been faithful till then; she couldn't believe he'd been fooling her all that time.

Gradually something between them shifted, and the signs were everywhere: his late hours, the business trips when she called his hotel room and he wasn't there. One time she even found lipstick on his collar. When she confronted him with it, she was trembling. He had put his arms around her, danced with her by their window to soothe her.

"Katy, you know I'm never in my room. I'm out working the crowd, the last one in bed . . . I got your message, but it was so late, I didn't want to call and wake you."

"But lipstick, Andrew . . ."

A teasing laugh. "What *color* lipstick? If it was red, it must have been Jean Snizort's . . . or if it was pink, it had to be Vicky McMahon's . . . you know they can't keep their hands off me when they're dogging me to get the senator to pass their bills! It's just a game."

"Love's not a game . . ."

"I don't love them—I love *you*."

Kate had felt his arms around her, wanting to believe him. Because she loved him, because trust was better than doubt. She'd been raised that way on Chincoteague: with a positive, trusting attitude, believing the best about people—and she wanted to believe her seven-year-old marriage was a good one.

But after a while, believing his stories began to take too much effort. Kate would get a stomachache as soon as he started to talk—as if her body was willing to know the truth before her mind. A young woman staffer would call the house, and she would have to fight the urge to throw the phone through the picture window into the Potomac River. One day came when Kate smelled perfume on his shirt, and couldn't even bear to ask.

Walking into the Watergate complex now, she took a deep breath and said hello to Frank, the doorman. He hesitated, before asking whom she wanted to see. She knew it must be uncomfortable for him, after so many years of greeting her as a resident, to now stop her at the door, treat her as a visitor.

"I'm here to see Mr. Wells. Don't worry, Frank," she said, smiling sadly. "I don't live here anymore; I know you have to call up."

"I wish you were still here, Ms. Harris," he said, shaking his head. "We miss you here. We all do."

"Thanks, Frank." Her smile faltered; his

words meant so much, and she knew they were genuine.

Andrew must have given the green light, because Frank let her into the elevator. She hadn't known what to expect; hadn't called ahead, because she hadn't wanted to be told she couldn't come. Stopping at the eleventh floor, she walked down the hallway and into the open door.

Andrew stood just inside, wearing jeans and a blue cashmere sweater. His blond hair was messy, rumpled from sleep; there were pillow wrinkles on the left side of his face. Kate knew all his habits. She remembered that, upon returning from an overseas trip, he drank a quart of orange juice to quench his thirst and replenish his vitamin C. She knew he showered and crawled into bed as soon as he got home. He would pull the quilt up high, over his head, to block out all light and sound.

She knew all these things, and although she stared into his hazel eyes and couldn't quite look away, her heart felt nothing. Her emotions were dull, as if they'd been smashed to bits by the man who stood before her, and never reawakened.

"Hi, Katy," he said.

"Andrew . . ."

"What brings you h—" He stopped himself, shook his head, and smiled. "I nearly said 'home.' Isn't that funny? I *must* be jet-lagged. This hasn't been your home in six months."

"Nearly seven," she said softly. "Since I caught you in bed with my sister."

"And you started the divorce the next day. . . ."

She nodded, staring at him as if he'd just stated the obvious.

"We could have worked it out, Katy."

Kate sighed, gazing into his marsh-colored eyes. There was a time she had wished—with all her heart—that that was true. But she didn't believe it.

"You know," he said pleasantly, sounding more like a politician than ever, "your wrath was totally deserved—but do we have to keep going through it? Who wanted the divorce, after all? Who couldn't forgive me, who wouldn't go to counseling?"

"Me," she said.

"Fastest divorce in District history. Bang, bang—my friends are all asking how it happened. They've been tied up in depositions and interrogatories for years."

"Ours wasn't hard."

"Because you didn't ask for anything. We'd been married long enough. You could have gotten half the assets."

"I didn't want your money," she said.

"Didn't want me, either," he said, never taking his eyes off her. "I would have tried to change."

"When you love someone, you're not supposed to want to change them. My mother always said that. You accept them as they are. But I couldn't accept what you were doing."

"But you love me?"

"Loved, Andrew."

"I could have changed . . ."

Kate glanced away. She didn't believe that was possible. Her view of marriage had been so different from his. One man, one woman, loving each other forever. She couldn't comprehend the idea of cheating, even once—never mind all those times with all those women. Including Kate's own sister.

She stood, looking around the room. It was beautiful, with a view of the Potomac. The bridges were lit up, the Lee Mansion illuminated across the river in Arlington. The graceful leather sofa, the white chairs and ottomans, the sand-and-gold checked rug, were still there. The Dutch landscape paintings were spot-lit from above.

"So, you've come back to berate me a little more?"

"No, Andrew. That's not why."

He invited her to sit down, and she did. She looked at the piano, raising her gaze. Only then, for the first time, did she feel the first deep stirring of emotion.

The painting Willa had done of Kate flying a plane still hung there. It was a beautiful portrait, catching details Kate never saw in herself: a gentle humor, a warmth in her eyes, a childlike concentration—lips parted slightly, white scarf flying out behind as she flew the plane. When she had left this house seven months ago, Kate had been too angry at Willa to take the portrait with her.

"You still have that painting up," she said.

"It's a lovely piece of work."

"I thought you would have taken it down by now . . ."

"I love beautiful things," Andrew said.

Kate's stomach tightened. He had loved Kate, and then he had loved her younger sister— Tearing her gaze away, she tried to catch her breath. *Beautiful things . . .* Artist and subject.

"You can have the painting," Andrew said. "If you want it."

"Thank you. I'll take it when I go. But first . . . I wanted to ask you . . ."

"What, Kate? I've told you everything I can. What good is rehashing what happened? Do other couples have to go through this? One of them makes a hugely stupid mistake, gets divorced, and has to go on answering for it the rest of his life? How many of our friends were idiots with secretaries or Senate interns or someone they met in a bar? Do you think they're still paying for it?"

"Willa wasn't a Senate intern," Kate said, her heart beating hard in her throat. "She was my sister. She was twenty-two years old. And she's missing."

Andrew exhaled. He looked more and more jet-lagged by the moment. His eyes looked old and tired, and Kate noticed he'd gotten more, deeper lines around his eyes than she had first seen.

"She's hiding somewhere, I'm telling you," he said. "Remember how we used to call her 'Will-o'-the-wisp'? She's an artist . . . bohemian as they come . . . offbeat, off-center . . ."

"Is that what you liked about her?" Kate asked. "How bohemian she was compared to me?"

"Don't start, Kate! You're a biologist, and you know how much I respect you. It was a fling. A goddamn stupid, midlife-crisis, idiotic mistake. This is Washington—temptation everywhere. I'd made mistakes before, and we always got through them. I knew you knew—I hated myself for hurting you, swore I'd never do it again. . . ."

"But you always did."

"I know. I felt you slipping away—I knew you were getting tired of it. Of me. And then Willa came to work—I know I shouldn't have. I never would have planned it. . . . She reminded me of you. It's sick, I know, but it felt like going back in time, back to when we were young."

Kate clenched her fists. "It's no less horrible," she said, "hearing it now, than it was hearing it the first time. You slept with my younger sister to recapture the passion you used to feel for me. . . ."

"Katy . . . please."

"She was only twenty-two—we raised her. You preyed on her."

"Don't say that," he said, covering his eyes. "I can't stand to hear you say that."

Kate stared at him, seeing the misery in his whole bearing. She had loved Andrew for the way he'd treated Willa when she was young. She had never imagined anything like this could happen, and, she had to believe, neither could Andrew. Their divorce was final. After this visit, they didn't have to be in each other's lives anymore.

"You're tired, I'm upset. Let's not fight anymore, okay?" she said.

"Yeah. Okay. Why don't you tell me what you came here for?"

Looking up, she knew her eyes were blank again. She'd felt the emotions spinning out of her, as if he had just pulled a plug and set them all free. Andrew's face was so familiar. His voice was very kind; he worked for a senator known for his liberal views and compassionate stands on human rights and environmental issues—Senator Gordon had chosen Andrew for his like views, his open heart. Because Andrew, for all his personal faults, was a good man.

Kate stared into her ex-husband's eyes.

"Because I need to feel close to her," she whispered.

"What?"

"Willa . . . I miss her so much, Andrew. I tried to talk to Matt, but he wouldn't hear it. See, I went up to Connecticut. Then to Massachusetts—the gas station where her card was last used."

"Why, Kate?"

"To understand," Kate said, choking on the word. "To figure it all out. Where she went; why she went. If only I had gotten that postcard sooner . . ."

"I'm sorry," he said, staring at his bare feet. "That was my fault. I couldn't bear to see your name on address labels back then. You'd started the divorce; I'd just throw the magazines into a basket; the postcard was among them. Must've gotten stuck, or caught in the pages."

"If only we'd seen it sooner . . ."

"You think we could have stopped something?"

Kate nodded, her eyes sweeping back to the portrait. Willa's fine eye was apparent in the pale color palette, the sure brush-strokes, the emotion in her subject's face, the soft yet bold white of the scarf.

"What could we have stopped?"

"I'm not sure," Kate whispered.

"I know you were afraid at first, when she was first missing," Andrew said, his face twisted as if the words caused him shame. "That she wanted to hurt herself."

"For hurting me," Kate said. "Yes . . . I was afraid she couldn't live with that."

"I can understand why you were afraid— the way you reacted, when you first saw us . . ." Andrew's hazel eyes flicked, involuntarily, toward the door to the hall leading to their bedroom.

Kate's chest ached, remembering how she had come home early with a bad cold. She had opened the bedroom door, planning to hang her jacket up in the closet and then just collapse on the bed. Andrew and Willa were there—both naked, lying together, touching each other's faces in the most intimate way imaginable.

First, Kate had been in shock.

She had stared, disbelieving her eyes. Andrew and Willa . . . This couldn't be happening. She had felt the room spinning, heard herself cry out, and run out of the apartment.

"She left here so fast," Andrew said hollowly. "I doubt she could imagine facing you again. I couldn't . . . when you came back that night, went into the study to lie down."

"You came in to see me," Kate said. "You got me a glass of cold water, put a cool washcloth in my hand . . ."

"And you broke the glass against the wall, tore the washcloth into shreds."

"Willa didn't see that."

"No, she was long gone by then," Andrew said. "And you left the next day. No second chance for me; for us. But we've been through that . . ."

"What we'd had was broken."

"Maybe your sister thought you felt that for her, too. No second chance . . ."

Kate stared at the portrait. What if he was right? Kate needed to believe she could put the pain behind her, return to loving her sister as much as before.

"She's my sister," Kate said. "We're bound by blood."

"We were bound by vows," Andrew reminded her, his voice low. He stared out the window toward the Virginia side of the Potomac, a hard cast to his eyes.

Kate's hands shook, unsure of what she was after. Maybe Andrew was right; if Willa had never left, Kate would never have learned how much she loved her. She might hate her sister still, unable to relinquish the hurt.

"Did you think I could help you feel closer to her?" Andrew asked, sounding weary. "Is that why you came?"

"I hoped you could," Kate said, bowing her head.

"Sorry . . ."

"We all spent so much happy time here," Kate said. "You were so generous to her; like a father, in many ways. She was so young when we got married."

"Look what I did to wreck it," Andrew said, shaking his head bitterly.

"Oh, Andrew," Kate breathed. Watching him, seeing the toll it had all taken on him, she actually felt a little sorry for him. For the first time, she felt a wave of true forgiveness wash through her. To her surprise, she didn't hurt with quite the same intensity.

"If you were hoping to find something else," Andrew said, "look around. You don't get much mail here anymore, not even junk mail. And what does come, since the thing with the postcard, I look through pretty carefully."

"No," Kate said, rising. "I just had to come . . . to see you. And talk about Willa. There's a lawyer in Connecticut . . ." She swallowed hard, thinking of John O'Rourke. "He represents a serial killer—Gregory Merrill. I went to see him because I think his client took Willa . . ."

"What does the lawyer think?"

Kate was silent, remembering the words John had spoken in Fairhaven, the way he had held and kissed her. She knew that if she told Andrew about the secret, he would know that John had broken his client's trust. . . .

"I don't know," Kate said, suddenly wishing she hadn't brought it up. Just speaking about John to Andrew seemed like a breach of something that she wanted to stay private. "It doesn't matter."

Andrew stared at her, as if waiting to see what she would do next. This must have been strange for him—just home from China, having a visit from the ex-wife he hadn't seen in months. She walked to the piano, leaned on the bench, and removed the portrait from the wall.

"I hope you're happy," she said.

"Same to you," he said.

They stood still, in their old living room, staring into each other's eyes. Kate, unsure of why she had come, suddenly knew: to get Willa's portrait of her, to release Andrew forever.

They gazed at each other for a long moment. Kate could almost feel Andrew wondering whether he should kiss her good-bye; she took a small step back, so he would know that he shouldn't.

Then, nodding, she walked out the door. As she waited for the elevator, she heard it close softly behind her. She took a deep breath, amazed by the growing realization: She hadn't come here only to connect with Willa. She had come to say good-bye to Andrew. Her feelings for him belonged in the past.

She thought of Connecticut. Of the dark blue Long Island Sound, of the golden river marshes. She thought of two children and a dog with briars in his fur. She thought of her sister, searching northward for the answers in her own soul. And she thought of a man, somehow connected to all of it—to all of the luminous and ordinary things that had come to matter most to Kate.

chapter 18

Teddy glanced out the window, worried about Maggie. There was too much danger in the world, and she was so small, pretty, and vulnerable. He had seen Amanda Martin's picture in the newspaper—the latest victim. She'd looked so nice and pretty—just like a girl he might see at school, or around town. A lot like Maggie. And if terrible things could happen to girls like Amanda, couldn't they also happen to Maggie?

Now, checking his watch, he decided to give Maggie ten minutes before he went out looking for her. Ten minutes. It was three-oh-five; he'd give her till three-fifteen. His stomach rippled with anxiety. Usually she was home before he was—he'd walk in the front door, and there she would be, waiting and wanting to play or talk or tell him a joke.

Lately, his life had kept him really busy, and he liked it that way. He didn't have to worry about Maggie when he was working out, which he found himself doing a lot—either before or after practice for the indoor league—wanting to make varsity next year.

Besides, playing so much soccer and doing so much schoolwork kept him from getting really homesick. Gramps and Maeve were in the kitchen right now, baking pies, wanting to make everything nice for Thanksgiving. In spite of how much he preferred being at his grandfather's house, right now Teddy missed his own home. He checked his watch: three-oh-seven.

It was Monday, and Thanksgiving was just four days away. He remembered how his mother would cook for the family, getting up really early to put the turkey in the oven. The house would smell so good. Everyone would go to the field, to watch the annual Shoreline-Riverside football game. Even the soccer fans would show up to cheer their schools on, and his mother would tease his soccer-loving father about how much bigger and stronger the football players were.

Every set of push-ups, of free weights, Teddy did made him stronger. Made him better able to protect his sister from all the harm out there in the world. Plus, his mother would be proud, if she could see him. She would think maybe the difference between football and soccer players wasn't so great after all.

What was it like for the girls in their town, knowing that a new person was out there, wanting to hurt them? Teddy's stomach knotted up, thinking about it, thinking about Maggie: three-ten. While Gramps and Maeve were busy in the kitchen, Teddy wandered into the downstairs study.

Gramps's law books lined the walls, but Teddy's father's papers covered the desk. Volumes of testimony, police reports, lab tests, DNA results. Teddy admired his father for the amount of knowledge he needed just to do his work. Lawyers had to be proficient in psychology, biology, and chemistry—but mainly in the law itself: evidence, criminal procedure, domestic relations, contracts, torts . . .

Teddy used to think he wanted to be a lawyer, just like his father and grandfather. But he hated the things he heard people say: that lawyers were in it for the money, that his father was raking in bucks to defend Gregory Merrill.

None of these things were new: Teddy had been hearing them for a long time. His father would always warn him that criminal cases drew emotional responses, and that Teddy shouldn't engage with people who lashed out about it. Their family had weathered obscene phone calls, hate mail, and most recently, a brick through the window.

Silver Bay was a small town where everyone knew each other. It was the kind of New England town that made it onto calendars: fields of goldenrod, scarlet-tipped trees, white lighthouse on the headland. Teddy's father and grandfather had done legal work for so many families; yet now Teddy felt that friends had turned into enemies.

It was bad enough that they attacked his father for his work. What made everything worse was the gossip about his parents' marriage. He had heard Mrs. Carroll whispering to her friend about his mother—that she had been having an affair. He couldn't stand to believe it, but somehow he knew it was true; he remembered how his mother had stayed out late a few nights before she died, how Teddy had been unable to sleep, waiting to hear her key in the door.

Maybe that was the reason he felt so strange right now: Waiting made him feel worried. He remembered the night his mother hadn't come home.

Teddy felt confused by life. He had a lot weighing on his mind—concern for his sister and the other girls in town, knowing he had to defend his parents. Something had happened yesterday, and he couldn't get it out of his mind.

Getting a ride home from his coach, Teddy had seen Maggie walking along the side of the road.

"Hey, there's my sister!" he'd called from the backseat, and the coach had pulled over to ask if she wanted a ride. Teddy would never forget that instant of terror— just a blink, before she saw her brother, before she recognized Mr. Jenkins. Maggie had thought, for just a second, that the killer was coming after her.

Teddy could always handle the ignorant comments at school, even from guys like

Bert and Gris, as in, "So—did your dad invite Greg Merrill to your house for Thanksgiving dinner?"

What had cut him so badly yesterday were the thoughts expressed by his coaches. Mr. Jenkins and Mr. Phelan were nice guys. They weren't intellectual like his dad, but they were smart. They both had college degrees—Mr. Jenkins from UConn, Mr. Phelan from Notre Dame.

Teddy loved playing soccer, and they were helping him to get really good at the sport. They worked his ass off at practice, drilling him up and down the field, forcing him to "get down and give me fifty." Or sixty, or, today, a hundred push-ups. While Teddy's father was busy at the office, his coaches were working with him, praising him, telling him he could play for Yale-Harvard-Dartmouth, wherever he wanted.

Mr. Phelan kept his car radio tuned to some call-in show, with a loud, friendly-sounding host who was always talking about what was wrong with the country. Mr. Phelan would listen, pitching in when the topics had to do with country-club prisons and guys released from jail to offend again.

"It's the system," Mr. Phelan said yesterday, not directly criticizing Teddy's father. "Cops are so concerned about criminals' rights, they aren't given the power they need to catch the bad guys—or make the convictions stick, or give out the sentences these people deserve."

"And God forbid you stick a killer on death row," Mr. Jenkins said. "Some people think the killer has more right to live than the girls he kills!"

Teddy had cringed at that; the coaches were too polite to say his father's name, but Teddy could feel them wanting to.

"C'mon, Hunt." Mr. Phelan had laughed. "Merrill's a moron. He was stupid, he got caught, he left the cops a roadmap to catch him—he definitely needs all the help he can get."

"Yeah, the guy's definitely not playing with a full deck. Insanity, diminished mental capacity, whatever: Give it to him."

Teddy hated the coaches for saying those things about his father—because Teddy had known what they were really talking about. It hurt to live in such a small town, and to be right in the middle of controversy.

Maybe the worst part—and it hurt to admit it, even to himself—was that he was really angry with both his parents. His mother for whatever she'd been doing, his father for working all the time. Because, whether they meant to or not, they had made it so Teddy and Maggie were alone too much. They needed some adults around them, and the only ones Teddy could find were saying bad things about his dad.

Teddy wished Kate were still here. She'd only gone to one of his games, but he'd had the feeling she would have liked to go to lots more. He had loved looking over at the sidelines, seeing her jump up and down and call his name. Maybe she didn't know, but he'd been able to hear her voice above all the others. And she understood him better than any other adult he knew.

Brainer came padding over now, wanting to be petted. Teddy kneeled by the window, watching for his sister to come home from school. Stroking the dog's coat, Teddy realized that the mats and ticks were back. It had been almost a month since Kate had washed and brushed him.

Teddy longed for a normal family. He didn't want it all to be so *odd*. Living with his retired grandfather and Maeve, having to hold up his father's honor to kids and coaches alike, being the only one at the door to greet his sister when she came home from school.

And if she wasn't here in twenty seconds or less, Teddy would call Dad to tell him she wasn't home, and then Teddy would jump on his bike to start the search. He could see Amanda's newspaper picture, her arm sticking out of the breakwater.

And just then, he heard Maggie's wheels on the driveway. Relief flooded through him in a huge rush. He couldn't believe how hard his heart was pounding as he heard the thump of her bicycle as it hit the ground. Her feet on the stairs, the click of the latch, and her breathless entrance. Teddy pictured Amanda in the breakwater again and couldn't stop the flood of tears scalding his eyes.

"Teddy," Maggie shouted, bursting in. "You're home before I am! If I'd known you didn't have practice today, I'd have taken the bus instead of riding my bike this morning!"

Teddy slid his sleeve across his eyes, so she wouldn't see him crying. He watched her fly across the room, thrilled to see him.

"Hey, Mags," Teddy said, giving her a big

grin, taking the knapsack of books from her arms, welcoming her home and not letting on how worried he'd been. "How's my best girl?"

When Kate got home from seeing Andrew at eight-thirty Monday night, the phone was ringing. Bonnie was barking, and the town house was freezing cold—in her abstracted state these days, Kate had turned the heat off before leaving the house that morning. She placed Willa's painting on a kitchen chair and grabbed for the phone.

"Hello?" she said, frowning, hand on the thermostat as she cranked it up to seventy.

"Kate? It's John O'Rourke."

"Oh," Kate said, gripping the receiver with both hands. Why was he calling? Hearing his voice made her feel warmer already. Back against the wall, she slid all the way down, till she was sitting on the floor, Bonnie climbing right onto her lap. "Hello."

"Hello."

"Are you calling to see whether I got the kids' letters? I did. And I've already started to write back to them . . . I miss them. No one like Maggie down here, and no one like

Teddy, sweet enough to care that his dog has mats in his coat . . ."

"Um, that's not why I'm calling," John said.

"Then . . . what?" she asked.

The line was silent. All the pleasure and warmth suddenly drained out of her body, and Kate put her head down. There could only be one reason he'd be phoning her; she'd been foolish to think it was personal.

"It's your client, right?" she asked, her heart stopping. "He's told you something?"

"No, Kate. Something else. Did you see the papers?"

"Yes—why?"

"You don't know . . . it must not have made the Washington papers. Another body was found up here. In a breakwater."

"John," she said, hands shaking.

"It's not Willa," he said.

Her eyes flooded with tears. She stared at the painting her sister had done of her. The gentleness, the love came pouring out, as if Willa were in the room with her. "How do you know?" she heard herself ask.

"Because the police identified her— Amanda Martin."

"Who is she?"

"She's a young woman from Hawthorne. Her parents own a boatyard, and she worked there part-time. Nineteen, went to the UConn branch at Avery Point."

"Merrill," Kate said. "He didn't get out, did he? Escape, or—"

"No," John said quickly. "He's still in Winterham, still on death row . . . It wasn't him."

"But the style, leaving her in a breakwater . . ."

"Yes, it's very similar."

"What else do they know? Are there others?"

"Not that anyone has found."

"My sister's still missing; what if it wasn't Merrill who found her, but someone else? This one . . ."

"I'll keep close track of the case and stay in touch with you."

"I can't believe it . . ."

"I know," John said, his voice quiet and steady. "I'm sorry to tell you about it, to stir everything up. But I wanted you to know, in case you'd heard another body had been found in a breakwater, that it wasn't Willa."

"You're really kind to call, John."

Her words hung in the air; she could hear him breathing through the line.

"Not many people accuse me of kindness," he said. "I'm a little surprised you would."

"I can't understand why," she said, a smile coming into her voice. "You showed your true colors in Fairhaven."

"In what way?"

"You proved you have a big heart."

"For a lawyer, you mean?"

"For anyone," she said.

"I'm an only child," John said. "But seeing you suffer over your sister made me think of Maggie and Teddy. I can't imagine either of them being without each other for any length of time."

"It's hard," she whispered, her eyes fixed on Willa's brushstrokes. "It's unbelievably hard."

"Be brave, Kate. Maggie would tell you that herself. If you want the scarf, we'll send it back to you."

"I want Maggie to keep it," she said, staring at the picture, at the white scarf blowing in the wind. "Tell her to be careful . . ."

"I know. I have."

"Because of what just happened, and because of everything," Kate said, her mind swimming with the knowledge that shocking things happen every day; that you could walk home after work with an armful of tulips and find your world falling apart. That you could be too angry to say good-bye one day and never see your sister again.

"Good things happen, too, Kate," John said. "Remember that."

"You, too, John."

"Next time we talk," he said, letting out a laugh, "will you remind me of what they are?"

"I'll try," Kate said, saying good-bye.

Sitting on her kitchen floor, she held tight to the phone. Her sister's dog lay in her lap; she heard the wall clock ticking and felt the heat beginning to come up through the vents. The house was warming up—or maybe it was just her heart beating so fast.

The white scarf in the picture shimmered across the room. Kate took it as a message.

The scarf was Maggie's now, connecting their two households. If John were still on the phone, she would tell him two good things: Maggie and Teddy. Brainer and Bonnie, too. Kate's sister Willa. And John himself. Six good things.

Her eyes filled with tears as she realized what a struggle it had been to come home without knowing what had happened. There was so much unfinished business. Was it true that Kate had never really forgiven her sister? She would never know, she now believed, until Willa was found. She had tried to make peace with her sister's mystery, told herself it was time to get back to her life.

But now that she was here, in Washington, it felt as if she was moving in the wrong direction. Her life—or, at least, her mind and her heart—were in Connecticut. The answers to Willa's disappearance were there, and so, Kate realized as she sat on the floor, holding the phone, were the people she cared about most.

Kate glanced at Bonnie and raised her eyebrows. She had the feeling the dog could read her mind.

"We have to do it, don't we, Bon?"

The Scottie wagged her tail.

Kate nodded, petting her back.

chapter 19

Billy Manning called to tell John he wanted to question Greg Merrill, to hear what he might have to say about Amanda Martin's murder. Although he obviously wasn't a suspect, he might have some insights into the crime; his cooperation would be noted for the record, and it might help at his next sentencing hearing.

John and Billy met at Winterham. The two men waited together in the prison conference room, while the guard joked with Billy about hanging out with the Merrill defense squad enemy, and Billy set him straight.

"Hey, John's all right," the detective said.

"We go back to high school together—we're teammates."

"Huh," the guard replied. "Looks like he's on the *wrong* team, now. Or at least a goddamn different one."

"Watch it, buddy. O'Rourke's a good guy," Billy said, as the guard left the room.

Waiting for Greg Merrill to be led in, Billy threw John a narrow glance. "Hear all that? You treat me right when Greg comes out, okay? Let me ask what I need to ask. Who covers you, buddy?"

"What makes you think I need covering?"

"Ahh, you're a white-shoe guy. You should've bucked your old man and joined the cops with me. We have the real fun—solving the crimes instead of undoing the investigations. Next thing, you'll be on the bench like your old man, wearing the black robes."

"Just like you and your old man, Billy, wearing the badge."

"Like father, like son. When's Teddy gonna join the family firm?"

John got quiet suddenly; Teddy hadn't said much lately. While Maggie danced around, begging to go home before Thanksgiving, Teddy had kept to himself, practicing soccer moves in the backyard after dark, doing push-ups in the upstairs hall. John felt the invisible wall between them, and he knew he had to do something to break it down.

Just then the door swung open, and two guards led Greg into the room. Shackled and cuffed, with a close-shorn prison hair-cut, his weight gain was particularly apparent today—his soft body stuffed into an orange jumpsuit one size too small. He gazed from John to Billy and back again. His time in jail had changed his looks completely; he had lost the appearance of the attractive, trustworthy young man who had lured all those young women into his van.

"Hello, Greg," John said.

"What's he doing here?" Greg asked, staring at Billy. "Haven't I answered all their questions?"

"We meet again, Mr. Merrill," Billy said, leaning back in his chair.

"What does he want, John?" Greg asked.

"He's here to question you," John said.

"Tell me about Amanda Martin, Greg," Billy said. "You must have heard the news that someone's walking in your footsteps."

"I had nothing to do with it, as you must

know. As for what I think of it—that's another story."

"Direct him to answer my question, Counselor," Billy said.

John was silent, waiting for Greg to speak. He caught Billy's impatient expression. Although old friends and former teammates, the guard had had it right before: John was on a different team now. John stared at his client, noticing the disturbance in his eyes, the way he stretched his neck like a turtle trying to escape his shell.

"You seem upset," Billy said to Greg, leaning forward. "Want to tell me about that?"

"Why would I be upset? I didn't do anything."

"Maybe you're jealous. That someone else can."

"Hah," Greg said, his face turning red. "I'm not jealous of *him*."

" 'Him'? You say that like you know who did it."

"I have no idea. None at all . . ."

Billy stared, as if he didn't believe him. Even John wasn't sure. He could tell that Greg was uneasy about something, eyes darting all around the small room as if he wished he could escape.

"Did you know Amanda Martin?" Billy asked. "Is there any reason to think of that her killer would have chosen the Point Heron breakwater? Was the time significant in any way you can think of?"

Greg leaned back, closing his eyes. Billy sat still, elbow cocked on the back of his chair. He looked casual, but his gaze was sharp as a hawk on the hunt. Silence expanded, and John found himself thinking of last night.

Kate's voice on the phone, when he'd told her about the latest victim . . . shocked, then bereft. John had lived around murder and its consequences for most of his life. He had tried so many cases, facing the victim's families in court, bringing out facts no parent or spouse or child or sister should ever have to hear; nothing had ever brought the devastation home to him like Kate and her sister.

He had sat at his desk until late the night before—long after he'd called Kate. Papers spread out in front of him, he had spent time thinking about the new case. A breakwater, the stone structure at Point Heron; he stared at the photo in the late paper. A beautiful, lonely place of rock and water. Hard and soft, pain and peace.

Minutes passed, and Greg refused to speak. He just kept looking around the room. After a few minutes, John put his hands on the table and stopped the interview.

"Let me have a minute with my client," he said.

"Jesus," Billy said. "He's so proud of his whole Mensa thing—you'd think he'd want to help us catch this copycat guy . . ."

"You don't understand anything," Greg said.

"No, I'm just a peon. Enlighten me."

"You don't even have a basis for focusing on those questions: time, the breakwater. You're just asking them because you think you should—not from any intuition. . . ."

"Heh." Billy laughed. "If I don't have intuition, I must not need it. I caught you."

"I let you," Merrill answered softly.

"You're the man, Greg," Billy said. "You know it and I know it—that's why I'm here. Come on—tell me who this new guy is."

"I'm presuming you don't mean his name. You want me to tell you who he is inside . . . what moves him."

"Right. What makes him tick."

"I'm not going to tell you anything. I'll talk only to my lawyer."

"You heard him, Detective," John said.

Greg just sat there, his lips getting thinner and thinner, till Billy left. John knew he'd call him later. Greg watched the door swing shut behind him, then looked up at John with fury in his eyes.

"Did he have one iota of comprehension of what he was *doing*?" Merrill asked.

"Detective Manning?"

"No! The person who did *that*—left that girl . . . I'll tell you straight out: no. No, he did not. It was a hateful act."

"Killing Amanda?"

"Because it was meaningless to him. No doubt he lacks the understanding . . . the vision of what the breakwater symbolizes, what the rising tides mean. To him, a garbage dump would have sufficed."

"He was copying you."

Merrill exhaled impatiently, shaking his head. "That means nothing, because he doesn't *get* it. Dreams reveal everything, isn't that right?"

"I'm not a psychologist."

"Try reading Freud's beautiful work about dreams, about the symbols and meanings and power. One flows into another, and no night is long enough to contain them all. Dreams are the wings, the sinews, the muscles, holding our minds together . . . and connecting mind, body, and spirit."

John listened, knowing that his client was a madman. Greg Merrill's internal logic made perfect sense to him alone, but John needed to tap in and understand—even without Billy here—anything that might help him find out about other victims. About Willa . . .

"What do dreams have to do with Amanda Martin's death, Greg?"

"No one—as clever as he tried to be—can understand my dream of the breakwater, my vision of the sea. Freud, perhaps. Jung, almost certainly. But others? Not even the wisest, most gifted psychiatrist could truly comprehend. Not truly. Not with the clarity and compassion of real understanding."

"No?"

"Certainly not the pretender, the poser, the other. Homage? Thank you anyway."

"Tell me about Willa Harris."

Greg looked up, surprised.

"Who?"

John stared at him. He had known his client for nearly six months, since right after the police caught him. And he would swear that Greg really didn't know. Reaching into his jacket pocket, John again removed Willa's picture and placed it on the table. Greg held it, looking closely.

"You've already shown me her picture. I told you, I don't know."

"Are you sure?" John asked, his pulse thudding.

Greg nodded, a small smile touching his lips, a sad look filling his eyes. "I'm sure," he said. "I wish I could help you, though. She must be very important to you, or you wouldn't keep asking me. Right?"

John didn't reply. He just took Willa's picture from Greg Merrill's hands and stared him down.

"Does it bother you at all? That another girl is missing? And another girl is dead? You're on your medication . . . is it working? Does this latest killing bother you?" John said, feeling out of control, his own blood pumping hard through his veins at Greg's coldness.

"John, are you all right?"

John's hands felt clammy. He had lost it— shouted at his own client, here in the inter- view room at Winterham. He was so sick of representing people without feelings or con- sciences.

Greg's smile widened slightly. "Of course it bothers me, John. How can you even ask that?"

"I don't know, Greg," John said, his shoulders aching, feeling weary as he stood from the table.

"I need some stamps, John," Greg said. "I've put in several requests, and they just won't—"

John didn't stay to listen. Suddenly he had a headache. His stomach was twisted in a knot. His children lived in this world, and Kate Harris's sister was still missing, and his client needed stamps. He had to see the sky, had to breathe some fresh air.

John O'Rourke was having an anxiety at- tack. Without saying good-bye to his client Greg Merrill or any of the guards, he walked steadily out of Winterham Prison without looking back.

The Judge knew something was up.

It was Tuesday afternoon, and John had come home early, dropped his briefcase at the door, and gone upstairs to lie down. Perhaps an hour had passed—long enough for him to get started on a good nap—when someone rang the doorbell. Answering, the Judge came face-to-face with a lovely young woman.

"May I help you?" he asked.

"Yes . . . I'm here to see John O'Rourke. I should have called, but I just got to town, and I was coming past the green and saw your street . . ."

"So you stopped by instead. How delightful of you," the Judge said with admiration. She had fine skin with a light sprinkling of freckles across her nose, high cheekbones, and sensitive eyes the color of stone. They were beautiful eyes, and the longer he looked at them, the more he wanted to know the story behind them.

"Is John home?" she asked.

"It's a work day," the Judge smiled. He was a poker player, never one to give something away.

"Yes, but I called his office. . . . They said he was out."

"Hmm," the Judge said, narrowing his eyes. It was moments like this that he wished Maeve were still able to handle the door. She used to turn people away before they even knew what hit them. But she was down in the basement, polishing silver for the Thanksgiving dinner, having a conversation with her sister and a few saints.

"Please?" the woman asked, smiling.

And then it hit the Judge: She was an applicant for the baby-sitting job! He hesitated, unsure of how he felt about this. Over the last few weeks, he had gotten very used to having the kids around. All three of them—Maggie, Teddy, and the biggest kid of all, his son John.

"Time marches on, doesn't it?" he asked the young woman.

"Excuse me?"

"For everything, there's a season. You're here for the job, right?"

"What job?"

"The baby-sitter position."

A soft smile lit first her eyes, then her mouth. She looked amused and delighted, and she tilted her head. "It's still not filled?"

"Nope."

"I got myself in quite a lot of trouble once before," she said. "By not being completely forthright about it. So, no—I'm not here for the position. I'm just a . . . friend of John's."

Although she had hesitated before saying "friend," the Judge could see that she had searched for a word and that was the best she could come up with. He approved of her choice.

"I'll see if he's in. Who shall I say is calling?"

"Kate Harris," she said.

"Ah," he said, having to act as if he had no idea of who she was—when, of course, he had already guessed.

The Judge made his way up the stairs slowly, hoping that John had heard her voice and would come down on his own. But that didn't happen. The hallway was dark and silent. When the Judge got to John's room, he called through the closed door:

"John: You have a visitor."

No reply. A soft knock, a louder knock.

"Kate Harris is here."

Not a word.

"Perhaps you didn't hear me. KATE HARRIS."

The Judge stood in the hallway, stymied. He hadn't walked into his son's bedroom when the door was closed since he was eight years old and in the middle of a temper tantrum having to do with a botched science project. He wasn't going to start up again now.

Brainer, inside the bedroom with his owner, whimpered softly, nose snuffing the space under the door. The Judge shook his head—John wasn't exactly setting the world on fire in the dating department, and the Judge thought Kate Harris would be a good person to start with.

But try to tell kids anything these days. Sometimes he felt like Maeve, lecturing her four sons Matthew, Mark, Luke, and John. They never listened, either.

"I'm sorry, Ms. Harris," he said, hand on the banister as he descended the stairs. Reaching the vestibule, he gave her a half-smile. "My son is otherwise disposed."

"Oh," she said, sounding disappointed. "Will you tell him I was here?"

At the sound of her voice, Brainer—now that he had IDed her via acute canine sensory perception, let out a friendly bark from upstairs.

"Is that Brainer?" she asked.

"The very same."

"Please give him my regards—and Bonnie's. Say hi to Maggie and Teddy, too. And Maeve. I have this note for Maggie . . ."

"Fine," the Judge said, shaking her hand, accepting the note and placing it on the hall table, where Maggie would see it. "Where can I tell John to find you?"

"My home away from home," she said. "The East Wind Inn."

The Judge watched her walk down the steps to her car—obviously a rental; his legal mind was like a steel trap that had rusted only partially shut, and he kept a store of interesting facts, such as rental cars having lot stickers on the bumper and license plates beginning with the letters "CJ."

She waved as she backed out of the driveway. The Judge waved back.

He had seen many human beings in all

stages of life during his years on the bench. He had learned to recognize the acute and subtle signs of desperation, grief, sorrow, and . . . and this was the word that came to mind when he gazed into the lovely unusual gray-blue eyes of Kate Harris . . . hope.

The girl was flowing with hope.

And she'd come to see his son.

"Goddamn it, you picked a lulu of an afternoon to catch up on your shut-eye," he said, looking up at the ceiling.

The Judge was used to people taking naps. Maeve, for example, would sleep the day away if he'd let her. The Judge himself liked to loosen his tie and put his feet up for an hour now and then. But his son—another story entirely.

John never sat still. Never. The boy was always trying cases, driving kids to some sport or other, seeing clients, interviewing witnesses, plotting trial strategy. John Xavier O'Rourke never sat still long enough to see the color of his eyes.

The Judge, having gazed into them upon John's entry into this world, knew very well that they were light brown, the color of root beer. And he was damned well going to see them right now, if he had to pry them open himself.

She was here.

John had heard her voice. First elated, hearing her ask for him, then paralyzed by it all.

His father had come upstairs; John had lain still, pretending to be asleep. The irony was, drifting off earlier, he had started to dream of her. The eyes that looked straight into his soul . . .

What had she been trying to tell him in the dream? There had been no words, just a sort of understanding John had never experienced in his life.

Kate Harris is here, his father had said.

John knew it, but he couldn't move.

What could he do for her, after all? Dreams were one thing, but life was another.

chapter 20

For the second time in half an hour, creaking up the stairs, the Judge rapped softly, then loudly, on John's bedroom door. Receiving no answer, he finally turned the knob.

Lying on his back, a pillow over his eyes, John pretended to be asleep. The Judge had watched this fellow fake sleep many a time. As a boy, John had put up a constant fight about bedtimes. He always wanted to finish reading a book—or at least a chapter. Or he wanted to stay up till midnight, to see a meteor shower. Or till three, when the hurricane was scheduled to hit. Or four, when

Santa was slated to come down their chimney.

"You're not fooling anyone," the Judge said now.

John didn't reply. His faking days had added up, and he really knew how to look asleep. Of course, the Judge knew, pretending—with John—didn't stop with sleep. He'd been pretending his way through life for quite some time. Pretending to be happy, that everything was "fine," "okay," "great." That last year with Theresa had been the most difficult to watch, but the Judge had no one to blame but himself: He hadn't exactly been a role model for sharing feelings or opening his heart.

"Hey, there—Counselor," the Judge said to his son, wiggling the bare toes of his right foot.

John rolled over, pillow pulled tighter over his face. As he moved, the pillow slid away, revealing tear tracks in the sun lines around John's eyes, down his cheekbones.

"Leave me alone, Dad," John whispered.

"She's damn pretty," the Judge said.

When John didn't reply, the Judge breathed out, exasperated. "I'm talking about Kate Harris. Maybe you should go see what she wants."

"I know what she wants," John said dully. "To know about her missing sister. And I can't help her with that."

"Maybe it's not your job to. The police can help her with her sister. Maybe you can just be her friend. Seems like that's why she came here—she was looking pretty friendly to me."

"She wants to know—never mind. But my work puts me in conflict with her," John said.

"Puts you in conflict with half the town, if you're doing your job!" the Judge chuckled. "But that doesn't mean you don't deserve a life and a friend . . ."

"Stop, Dad," John said, rolling over. He shoved his face into the pillow again, as if he'd suddenly become too exhausted to stay awake. The Judge stared at him for a few long moments, then sighed. Because he knew what his son was going through.

"They have a name for this. Battle fatigue," he said. "Or burnout—take your pick."

John didn't answer, didn't even seem to hear, so the Judge went on.

"I used to get it myself. I don't know many lawyers who don't. And how could we not? We're dealing with people's lives, son. It's not just a job where we go home at night and close the door. We have to live with the life-and-death aspect of what we do—and what others do."

Although John didn't reply, the Judge could see he had his attention: The pillow had slipped slightly, revealing his right ear.

"Before I became a judge," he said, "I did what you do. Defended people. Some innocent, many not. Once I had a case—you might remember it. Jack Carsey. A man who kidnapped and murdered a girl in town. You saw the forensic photos, and you couldn't sleep for a week."

"I remember," John said, his mouth in the pillow.

"Your mother was furious with me. Not just because you were so upset, or even for the fact that people hated me for it . . . but because I was defending a *bad man*. That's what she said to me, and—I don't know if you can remember your mother's voice . . ."

"I can," John said.

The Judge nodded. Leila had been an old-fashioned woman; like many in her day, in spite of her brains and talents, she had elected to stay home and be a wife and mother. But when she spoke, her voice had the resonance of Louis Brandeis addressing the court. "She said to me, 'Patty . . .' " he coughed, trailing off. "And she was the only person in the world who could get away with calling me 'Patty.' "

"I know," John said, taking the pillow completely away from his face, looking up.

" 'Patty, I want you to stop defending Jack Carsey.' That's what she said."

"Yeah," John said. "I heard her."

"She told me she wanted me to drop the case. Suggested I think about my life—our lives—and evaluate what was important to me. Reminded me of my Catholic upbring-ing, my sense of right and wrong. Told me—"

"To check your moral compass," John said.

"Yes," his father said, hearing Leila's words. "And then she told me—are you ready? She said, 'Patty—you're helping this man get away with murder.' "

As the Judge spoke, he saw his son close his eyes. A wave passed over his face, something like seasickness mixed with despair of the soul.

"That ring a bell, son?" the Judge asked.

"It's what we do," John said. "Teddy says the same thing."

"What do you say?"

"I tell myself I'm defending an individual's Constitutional rights, that this is what Washington had in mind at Philadelphia . . . I tell myself it was Greg Merrill's right to a fair hearing . . . and that it's his right to counsel now . . ."

". . . And?" the Judge asked.

"And then I see Amanda Martin's hand. It was so white, Dad. Scratching at the sky . . . as if she was reaching for a lifeline."

The Judge listened.

"And Kate Harris . . . that woman who came by?" John asked.

"Yes?"

"Her sister Willa's missing. Kate's the woman I met in Fairhaven. The one I breached lawyer-client privilege with."

"I figured."

John looked clearly at his father. Although still lying flat on his back, the spark was there in his eyes. "How?"

"She's lovely," the Judge said mildly. "I'd've breached it for her, too."

"It's a big thing to do," John said. "I could be disbarred for it. But the thing is . . ."

"You'd do it again," the Judge said.

"How do you know?"

The Judge sighed. From the bedroom window, looking into the garden, he could just see Leila's sculpture of Lady Justice. There she stood, eyes blindfolded, holding the scales high in her hand. Maeve had a habit of putting birdseed in the scales; sparrows and cardinals set upon them, eating the seed. Although the principle of Justice was one of dignity and grace, the human reality could be quite messy.

"Because you're not made of stone," the Judge said, staring at the statue. "You have a heart."

"I have to recuse myself as Merrill's attorney."

"You think someone else would do a better job? Take on the case pro bono, weather the slings and arrows of friends and neighbors, face the difficult moral questions?"

"I can't speak for them," John said. "Only for myself."

"You're serious about this," the Judge

said, feeling stunned. His son was honestly pondering the issue of quitting as Merrill's counsel.

"Yes. I have a meeting scheduled with Dr. Beckwith today, and I'm going to cancel. We're supposed to meet with Merrill, go over Beckwith's findings, come up with a strategy for this mental disorder defense. I can't do it."

"Because you don't believe in it?"

"Because it makes me sick. Because I don't want to live in Greg Merrill's head anymore."

The Judge sat down on the bed, by his son's feet. The dog, lying on the floor, circled once and laid his head on the Judge's knee, dirty gold fur sticking to the fine gabardine.

"I've seen this happen before," the Judge mused. "And, as I said before, experienced it myself. Burnout—that moment of nowhere to run, nowhere to hide, right?"

"Yeah," John said. "I can't push the pictures of Merrill's crimes out of my mind anymore. I know how he thinks, I know what his fantasies are. . . . I know that Phil Beckwith thinks he's a prize case, a pervert who almost deserves a category all his own. I want to just block the whole thing out."

"Dive under the covers . . ."

"Or get rip-roaring obliterated."

"It's why we have so many drunks in our profession. Nothing like a little medicinal single-malt scotch after a long stretch at the courthouse to forget what we're doing. . . . Actually, sounds good," the Judge said, chuckling. "What do you say?"

"It's the middle of the day," John replied. But even so, he hiked himself up on his elbow and swung his legs off the bed.

"Better than sleeping," the Judge said. "Save that till later, for when you're retired."

The two men went downstairs, into the Judge's den. Brainer followed them, stopping by the tall windows facing the street, looking outside—as if to see if Kate Harris was still there. The Judge caught John looking too, and he hid a smile.

Going to the mahogany sideboard, the Judge removed two heavy crystal glasses and a hand-cut Waterford decanter. Removing the stopper, he smelled the whiskey with close-eyed appreciation.

"Don't need ice with this," he said, pouring.

"What is it?"

"Twenty-year-old Talisker."

The Judge handed one glass to his son, and the two men clinked glasses.

"Here's to lawyers," the Judge said.

John hesitated, but then he drank. So did his father. They drained their glasses as if they were drinking shots. The Judge poured again.

"Careful," his father said, replacing the stopper. "This is how fine lawyers become alkies."

"I know," John said, sipping. "When I was young, and I used to see those soused old guys floating around the courthouse . . . usually Irishmen like Brady and O'Neill . . . I used to have such contempt for them. Red-faced, bloodshot eyes, stinking of booze . . ."

The Judge nodded.

"Now I understand them."

"How's that, son?"

"It was the profession," John said, sipping again. "They had their own Merrills to represent . . ."

Again, the Judge nodded, just listening.

"They were too sensitive to handle it. What did Mom used to say about Ireland?

That it was 'a vale of tears.' That Irish lawyers were actually poets who'd gotten locked in the courthouse. . . . She used to say that about you," John said, raising his eyes to meet his father's.

The Judge nodded, remembering, but his throat was too choked up to respond quite yet, so he topped off his glass. He could still hear Leila's beautiful, gravelly voice, rich with heart, soul, and cigarettes . . .

"She'd probably say it about me now," her son said.

"That she would."

"She'd say I'm helping a bad man get away with murder."

"But you didn't, John. Merrill's on death row. If you succeed in your efforts, the best he can hope for is life without parole. You and the good doctor will see to that. Regardless of what happens, Merrill's away for good."

"He inspired someone to kill Amanda Martin."

"I know."

"And Willa Harris is still missing."

"I know that, too. I know something else . . ."

"What?"

"Don't go romanticizing the Irish-poet sensitive-lawyer drinking thing. Those guys drank because they wanted to—this cold hard world just gave them an excuse to do it. They caused more damage in their own families than you'll ever know."

"You know, though?"

The Judge nodded gravely. "Yep. I do."

"So," John said, putting his glass down without finishing the scotch, walking over to the window and looking out. "What do I do, Dad?"

"Your job, Johnny. You put one foot in front of the other, and you carry out the mandate set down by James Madison. You represent your client to the best of your ability. You practice 'principles before personalities' . . ."

"Where'd you hear that?" John asked, as if he liked the saying.

"A.A.," his father said.

"How do you know what they say in A.A.?" John asked.

The Judge shrugged, and his smile faltered. "Way back when, one of those drunken Irish lawyers around the courthouse was your father. This stuff gets to me, too, Johnny. I was hitting the bottle a little too hard, and your mother dragged me to a few meetings."

"I never knew."

"Well, it didn't last. I cleaned up my act. Saw what I was doing to your mother . . . and I'd seen how those other lawyers' drinking wound up hurting their children. Jimmy Brady stood before my bench as often as any kid in this town. Anyway, I learned how to put the principles of law before specific clients, victims, families."

"Hard to practice."

"Yes," the Judge said, staring out at Lady Justice, a starling perched on her head, several juncos pecking at seed in the scales. "But vitally important."

"Yeah, I know," John said. He looked at his watch—perhaps gauging whether he had enough time to drive back to Winterham Prison, meet up with his client and the psychiatrist.

Brainer, wanting affection, walked from father to son. The Judge watched John pet the loyal dog's head, catch his fingers in tangles around the neck. Distracted at first, John seemed not to notice. But gradually, working his fingers through the mats, pulling out a briar and some twigs, the Judge watched John shake his head.

"This dog needs a bath," John said, sounding mystified, frowning as he worked out a burr.

The Judge let the statement hang in the air. John looked to the window, as if a lightbulb had just gone on over his head, as if Kate Harris herself stood on the front porch.

One of the hallmarks of a great trial lawyer is the ability to ask questions with the cutting skill of a surgeon. Don't go where you shouldn't go, or you might kill your case; don't ask any question you don't know the answer to. With that in mind, watching his son extricate dead leaf bits from Brainer's fur, the Judge cleared his throat.

"What," the Judge asked, his tone stentorian, "are you going to do about it?"

chapter 21

Kate had unpacked everything and settled into her room at the East Wind Inn. Bonnie stood on a chair, the better to look out the window. She had been so patient, waiting for her walk, but seeing Kate take the leash down from the bureau, she let out a sharp, happy bark.

Pulling on her dark green wool coat and a cream-colored beret, Kate let the Scottie tug her downstairs. Thanksgiving was two days away, and the smell of baking pies filled the inn.

"Apple and pumpkin," Felicity said as Kate emerged in the front hall. "Hope you'll join us for dinner Thursday."

"Thanks," Kate said. "I'm not sure what my plans will be."

Although what did she *think* they'd be? She reddened at the thought. Perhaps she'd been harboring hopes of being invited to the O'Rourkes'. She imagined their big table, groaning under turkey and stuffing and mashed potatoes and creamed onions; a centerpiece of dried flowers picked by Maggie; laughter and conversation.

"Well, when you decide, you're welcome."

"You're open for dinner to the public that day?"

"No," Felicity said, shaking her head. "Just family . . . Us, Caleb of course, my brother-in-law Hunt . . . if I can tear them away from their jobs, that is."

"Hard workers," Kate said, fighting Bonnie, who was straining at her leash. In the distance she heard the sound of hammering. "Is Caleb still fixing your barn?"

"What?" Felicity asked, tilting her head.

"That sound . . ." Kate said, pausing, so Felicity would hear. "Nails being hammered." It was far-off, but the sound was metallic and steady. Perhaps Felicity, living here, was so used to it she'd stopped hearing. "Last time I was here . . . remember? Caleb was working on the barn."

"Oh, yes," Felicity said, laughing. "The endless project. We're planning to add more guest rooms by next summer, but he's been so busy at work with his father—on things off-property. Well, I don't want to keep you from your walk. Looks like Bonnie's dying to get out there . . . scare up some rabbits, or something. Better get back to my pies."

"Thanks," Kate said, but Felicity was already gone.

She opened the front door and was greeted by a blast of cold sea air as she followed Bonnie down the sandy lane. They walked through the dark allée of white pines and crossed the small brook that trickled through the apple orchard. The O'Rourkes' house, unoccupied, sat on the headland jutting out into the Sound. Up ahead, the lighthouse stood, gleaming white against the cold November sky.

Waves crashed, sweeping the rocky shore. Kate tried to breathe deeply, but her chest was constricted. Here she was, back again—so soon, with no more answers than she'd had before. Her sister was still gone; Kate felt haunted by the things her brother and Andrew had said, the question of whether her anger had driven Willa away forever.

Gazing down the coast, she saw several breakwaters reaching out from shore. Which one of them was Point Heron? She shivered, thinking of the girl they had just found. The newspapers had run stories about her, about her lifelong love of boats, of how she had worked at her parents' boatyard every summer vacation.

Walking toward the bluff with Bonnie, Kate thought of Willa, of the wonderful vacations they had taken together. . . .

On many summer breaks, Kate had taken Willa on what they'd called their "Search for Amelia." Over the years, they had visited many spots of importance in Amelia Earhart's life: Atchison, Kansas, where she'd been born in her grandparents' house; Des Moines, where she'd seen her first airplane at the Iowa State Fair; and their biggest, most ambitious trip, to French Polynesia, where Amelia's plane was believed to have crashed. Andrew had wanted to go too, but Kate had talked him out of it, claiming the mission for the Harris sisters alone.

They had taken a boat across the clear, turquoise water. Mysterious and haunting, the atolls had risen, shimmering under the surface, beds of coral and rock. The water was so clean, they could see a hundred feet down. Fish swimming around the reefs, giant clams; it had seemed possible that they would look down and see Amelia's plane.

"It's so beautiful here," Willa had said.

"I know," Kate had said, not wanting her sister to know that her throat hurt too much to talk, that she was thinking of the pilot following her dream to the South Pacific, having her bright life end in this paradise.

The captain of their boat had been a native of French Polynesia. He had taken them on a tour, one spot more magical than the next, until the sun had set and the sky had turned to fire—purple, red, pink, colors Willa had never seen in nature or on a canvas before.

"I have to paint that!" she had exclaimed.

"When you do, will you dedicate it to me?" the captain had asked.

"You'd want a painting of mine?" Willa had asked. She was seventeen, beautiful, barely aware of her effect on men. Kate had watched protectively, amused at Willa's naïveté.

"Of course I do. You must promise," the captain had said, standing at the wheel, an insouciant grin on his tanned face. "And when the painting is done, send it to me at the marina."

"If you tell me your name," Willa had said helpfully. "I will."

"Hervé Tourneau," the man had said in a French accent. "Aboard Yacht *Chrysalis,* eh? It will get to me, don't worry . . ."

Willa had laughed, delighted and flattered; Kate had just leaned against the rail, watching the sun break into bits of flame, twinkling cinders across the South Pacific, a trail of fire leading to an endless horizon, loving her sister, grateful for their togetherness.

Kate gazed across the moors, at the sea grasses blowing in the wind, the apple trees dark against the slate sky, the tall white lighthouse a beacon even in this thin November daylight. She heard the rhythmic wash of the breaking waves.

As she neared the lighthouse, she saw a chain across the road, then two sandy paths, one leading to the right, the other leading to the left. Kate hesitated, not sure which way to go. Bonnie scuffled ahead, low to the ground, the skirts of her coat picking up grass and bits of seaweed blown up from the beach. Calling her over, Kate pulled a bramble from her coat, hugging her close for a moment of comfort.

"Oh, Bonnie," she said. "Good dog."

Bonnie licked her face, and Kate noticed that her black fur was covered with white dust. Not quite sand, more like plaster, or chalk. Looking down, Kate noticed that the ground—especially on the path leading right—was covered with it.

Perhaps it was some material used to repair the lighthouse. She glanced up. The edifice was thick and sturdy, white brick and mortar constructed to withstand the strongest gales. Could it be limestone? Knowing that lime wasn't good for dogs, she did her best to brush the powder off.

Then, clipping Bonnie's leash back on, she began to pull her in the opposite direction, away from the lighthouse. As she walked, feeling the cold air sear her lungs, one thing became clear.

She had come north for Thanksgiving.

Here in Silver Bay, she was closest to

Willa. Wherever Willa might have gone, Kate felt her presence right here. Walking along the headland, Kate knew exactly why her sister had been drawn here: the crashing waves, the golden grasses, the prim lighthouse. Kate didn't want her sister to be alone.

Teddy would understand. Maggie, too.

She found herself wishing, as she walked east along the rocky promontory, that their father had had siblings. That John could somehow know the incredible, piercing, ineffable bond of having been born of the same parents, of having grown up in the same place.

When she had stopped by his house and spoken to his father, she had gotten the idea that something was wrong. John was home, but he couldn't come to the door. Or maybe he'd decided he shouldn't talk to Kate anymore—he had called her in Washington to give her the news about the girl's death, but he had ethical obligations, and now he had to back away.

The thought of it made her feel colder, made her pull her coat a little tighter as she walked into the wind. She hadn't realized how much she'd been hoping to see him till he hadn't answered the door. Head down to keep the cold from stinging her eyes, she felt the wind pick up. A burst came across the water, and the sound's smooth surface skittered into a flurry of small choppy waves.

In the next moment, Bonnie began to bark. She tugged on her leash hard, yanking Kate's shoulder; Kate looked up, startled, and what she saw made her take in a deep breath. Watching Bonnie race across the field, she began to smile, and the smile grew wider.

On his way to the East Wind Inn, John beeped the psychiatrist and left a message that he would be late getting to the prison. Then he took the lighthouse road and saw two figures walking the path along the bluff. One was tall and one was very short, low to the ground. Kate and Bonnie.

Parking in the sandy turnaround, where in summer and early fall the fishermen parked their trucks to clamber over the dunes and try their luck at bluefish and striped bass, he let Brainer out of the car, and it was all over.

The dogs said it all. Barking madly, running toward each other, tumbling through the tall brown grass. If John could have translated, he would have said, "Joy."

Strange, but seeing Kate Harris made him feel the same thing. They walked toward each other through the knee-high salt hay, and John felt himself smiling as he hadn't in days or weeks. When they came together, he saw that her cheeks were windburned, her eyes bright and shining. Amazing to him was her smile: She looked as happy to greet him as he was to see her.

"Hi," she said.

"I found you."

"Was it hard?"

"Well, I was on my way to the East Wind. Dad said you're staying there again."

"I am. I had to come up from Washington."

He nodded. She had to see about the case; he understood. It often happened this way; family members connected to one crime could be retraumatized by another similar in nature.

"Because of Amanda Martin?"

"Yes," she said. "I bought a local paper and read about her . . . the girl who loved boats."

"Yes, that's what they say," John said, watching her eyes.

"Has there been any other news?" she asked.

He hesitated, peering down the coast. The cold wind stung his eyes. He thought of the case's latest details, his last meeting with Merrill, the glimmer in his client's eyes when he had first looked at Willa's picture. Looking past the lighthouse, he saw the Point Heron breakwater—just a thin black line from here. News of the case . . . it filled his head, but he blinked and pushed it away. He heard his father's parting words and knew they were about Kate: "What are you going to do about it?"

"Yes," he said, his father's voice echoing in his head.

"Tell me."

"Brainer's a mess again," he said.

"Really?"

"Yes. Bad tangles. Lots of burrs and sticks."

"Time for another bath?" she asked, a slow smile coming to her face, as if she was relieved by the sudden lightness.

"Yep."

"Funny, so could Bonnie. She's got white

stuff all over her paws and skirts . . . looks like lime or plaster dust, and I know that's not good for her. Are they building something up there?"

John glanced down at Bonnie, and then smiled reassuringly. "Oh, were you just up at the lighthouse?"

"Close to it."

"Then that's nothing to worry about. There's been some repair work up there recently, so it could be plaster dust, but I have a feeling it's something else: ground-up clamshells."

"Really?"

"Yes. A long time ago, when the lighthouse was manned, the road used to get pretty muddy. The Coast Guard had a whole truckload of stones and shells delivered, dumped on the road, to give their vehicles some traction."

"Clam shell dust," Kate said, smiling, thinking of the mountain of oyster shells at her brother's, of all the dust their broken pieces made. Feeling at home. "I should have known."

"So—our dogs need a bath," he said.

"The car wash?" Kate asked.

John paused. His heart was racing, and

he felt like a teenage boy. This morning, lying on his bed, he had felt depression closing in. Right now, he felt like he could fly. What was happening to him, anyway? Kate smiled up, making the answer very clear, but he didn't feel like analyzing it.

"Our house is right over there," he said, nodding at the headland, at the white saltbox that he and his family had left unoccupied this last month.

"You have a big bathtub?" she asked. "Because Brainer's a big dog."

"Yes," he said. "He is. And we do."

"Then let's go," Kate said, whistling for Bonnie.

He felt his cheeks stretch into a wide smile, and then he felt himself take Kate Harris's hand. It was small and cold, and he rubbed it a bit to warm it up. His hand must have been just as cold, because he noticed her doing the same thing.

Hearing the waves and the pounding of his own heart, he held Kate's hand and led her toward his house. When they got to the orchard, he jumped over the stream, turning to offer his hand. Smiling, she shook her head and leapt across on her own. He began walking along, when he realized that she had stopped.

Turning around, he saw her staring at the water. The brook was a thin trickle right now, frozen a bit along the sides.

"You should see it in the spring," he said. "Then the streambed is really full."

"The brook runs west," she said, unable to look away. The dogs stopped to drink from the stream, getting their paws muddy.

John nodded. He had noticed that many years ago, but had forgotten along the way. "I guess it does."

"A west-running brook is very rare," she said. "Water always wants to run east, to the sea."

"We have a rare brook," he said, surprisingly happy that she would notice.

"I wonder if Willa saw it," Kate said, staring. "We had one in Chincoteague . . . I loved it more than either of them did, Willa or Matt. When things got too much for me, after our parents died, sometimes I'd slip out of the house and go down to the brook."

"By yourself?"

Kate nodded. "Just to get away. There was a big rock; I'd climb up on it. From there, I could see the sea, across the dunes.

The waves were so powerful, I could hear them crashing on the beach. It sounded so loud . . . but the brook was quiet and peaceful."

"A different kind of energy," John said, and suddenly they stopped talking, to listen to the brook. Kate closed her eyes, and he could almost see her back home on her island, listening to the soft music of water playing over the stones. This was where she'd gotten the color of her eyes, he thought. That incredible gray, green, blue: the color of a west-running brook.

"It was my secret hour," she said quietly.

"Your time alone," he said.

She nodded, smiling.

"I feel like I'm having one right now," John said, staring into her beautiful eyes. Kate seemed to feel the connection, took a step closer to him. "A secret hour. This is as peaceful as I've felt in . . . a long time."

"Me, too," she said.

John felt suddenly, amazingly, happy. He could have stayed there forever, but he took her hand again, reluctantly leading her away. Their dogs splashed through the water, then tore across the last stretch of field.

The white house was right there. . . . They were almost home.

When Maggie got to Gramps's after school, she walked into the front hall and took off her coat. She left the white scarf on, though, because she liked to wear it all the time. It made her feel better somehow, and Maggie needed all the help feeling better she could get. Teddy was going to help her. . . .

"Teddy," she called out. "You home yet?"

They were going to make place cards for the Thanksgiving table. It was Maggie's idea, because she liked to draw and because she thought everyone needed something to cheer them up. They'd take some of their father's thick stationery, fold it into squares that stood up, and draw pictures of pilgrims, Indians, and turkeys.

Walking through the house, Maggie looked for her brother. She knew it was a little early—he had said he wasn't sure how long practice would be, that she should just be patient and wait till he got home. But she hoped he was here already.

She smelled silver polish. Thanksgiving

was just two days away. She felt sadness in her heart, missing her mother and their own house. All the big holidays made her feel this way—as if she had a huge hole in her soul that could never be filled.

Okay, Teddy wasn't there. Maggie felt upset and frustrated. She wanted to start on their project right away. Even more, she wanted to be home. At their house, not Gramps's. She wanted to polish her parents' wedding silver—the big turkey platter, the gravy boat with their initials entwined together in a swirling monogram. She wanted to wash the crystal glasses in water with a few drops of ammonia in it, and then dry them with newspaper—the best way to make them sparkle.

She wanted her own room. She wanted her own things—all her stuffed animals, her books, and her posters. She liked the smell of her house; it was different, somehow, from anywhere else. The salt air came in, bringing with it scents of seaweed, clamshells, and beach grass. Gramps's house was just enough inland that they didn't get it.

Standing in the hall, she suddenly noticed

the envelope on the table. It had her name on it. With a surge of excitement, Maggie tore it open and found a note from Kate.

Dear Maggie, (she read)

Thank you for your letter. It meant a lot to me. I'm so glad you like the white scarf. It's almost Thanksgiving . . . one of my favorite holidays! Is it one of yours? I used to tell my sister, when she was your age, that being thankful was the best way to be—all the time, not just in November. We used to make lists of things we were grateful for . . . some of the things I remember were clouds, birds, the sea, books, the ponies, our brother (he made it onto the list most of the time, but not always!), and each other. One of our Thanksgiving traditions was going out onto the dunes, picking dried grasses and flowers for a centerpiece. Beach grasses are so beautiful in November; have you ever noticed? Golden, brown, silver . . . something else to be grateful for! Say hi to your family for me.

Best, Kate Harris

Maggie read the note twice. She had been feeling so sad when she'd first walked into the house, then so disappointed about Teddy not being there, but now she felt excited. Kate had given her an idea: She could go out to their house, walk down the path to the dunes, and pick a beautiful arrangement of dried grasses—it would look great on the table, and it might make Maggie feel a little closer to Kate.

She liked Kate so much. Thinking she was going to be their baby-sitter had made Maggie happier than she'd been since her mother died. Kate had seemed so real and fun and practical and a little sad. That was important. Maggie needed a friend who knew how it was to lose someone, what that was like.

Looking at the envelope a second time, Maggie was thrilled to see that it didn't have a stamp. Did that mean Kate was here, in Silver Bay?

She bit her lip. Gramps was downstairs in the basement with Maeve. She could hear their voices coming up the stairs with the smell of silver polish. If she asked him, he might start fixing her an after-school snack, wanting to hear about her school day. He might keep her from leaving . . . Teddy *definitely* would.

Maggie was grounded.

But maybe—just maybe—"grounded" didn't really apply to what she had in mind. Dad was just being overprotective. Ever since that new lady had been killed, everyone was being cautious. Maggie understood; she felt the same way, and she would never go someplace unfamiliar, NEVER get into a car with a stranger.

He had expressly forbidden her to go to their own house alone. But she wasn't exactly going to the *house*. She was going to the fields *around* the house, near the lighthouse . . . the grasses there were perfect.

If she just rode her bike out there, very fast, and filled her basket with dried grasses, she could be back before anyone even noticed she was gone. Teddy wasn't home yet, but he'd be there any minute.

No, she was pretty sure that any second he'd get dropped off by his coach or Mrs. Carroll. He'd come to Maggie's room, ask her how school was. Since their mother's death, and with their father always working so hard, Teddy tried to act like her parent. That was why he said he'd make place cards with her. Her big, strong, soccer-playing brother, coming home to draw with Maggie.

It made her heart ache, to think of her brother loving her so much. Did he know how much she loved him, too? Holding Kate's note, Maggie closed her eyes and put Teddy right at the top of things to be thankful for. She would make her family, especially Teddy, the most beautiful center-piece imaginable.

She wouldn't stop with dry grasses.

She'd pick bayberry and bittersweet, vines of woodbine and ivy. Beach grass, goldenrod, rose hips, dry lavender, wild thyme . . . and she'd go down on the sand to pick up scallop, ladyslipper, and clam shells to scatter around the table.

Running upstairs, to place Kate's note in her special drawer, she grabbed her Swiss Army knife for cutting tough stems. She stuck it into her pocket like a good tomboy.

And then she headed out on her Thanks-giving mission.

chapter 22

The house was as nice as Kate remembered it—although she had only been inside for a little while, the morning of the brick. Late afternoon light streamed in, through the new plate-glass window, making squares of sunlight on the Oriental rug.

Kate took in the seascapes on the wall, the family photos on the piano. Her gaze traveled to a picture of Sally Carroll with another woman—very trim, pretty, with bright blue eyes. The two friends, grinning, wore white tennis dresses and held a gold trophy between them. That same trophy stood on the mantel, engraved with the names and date: Theresa O'Rourke and

Sally Carroll, Club Champions, September 15, 1999.

Kate glanced at John, but he was already shepherding the dogs upstairs. She followed behind and, laughing, they filled the big upstairs bathtub with water. The enterprise seemed hilarious, and the more they thought about it, the harder they laughed. John undid his tie. Kate tossed off her beret. Both rolled up their sleeves. The dogs, as if sensing what was about to befall them, hid under the bed in John's room.

"What're they doing?" John asked, on his knees and peering under the skirt of the big bed.

"Making themselves as flat as pancakes, hoping you won't notice them there," Kate called from the other side, trying to lure Bonnie out with a dog treat she'd carried for the walk.

"He's pretty obvious under there . . . big yellow dog," John said, peering under the bed, catching Kate's eye on the other side.

"Not Bonnie," Kate laughed. "Look at her, all curled up in a ball, doing her best imitation of a stuffed animal."

They finally got Brainer out first, threw him into the tub, and soaped him up. He sat very still, sad eyes beseeching them to stop, leave him his dignity, as soap clung to his beard and eyebrows and made Kate and John laugh even harder.

"Think we're hurting his feelings?" John asked.

"No way," Kate said. "He's about to become the handsomest hound in Silver Bay."

"Yeah? You sure?"

"Haven't you ever given your dog a bath before?"

"I have to confess—no."

"Well, wait till we're done. He'll be so happy and proud, you won't believe it."

"He was the last time," John said. "And the best part was, you made Teddy really happy by doing it. Teddy worries about Brainer."

"Willa used to worry about Bonnie," Kate said.

"How?"

"Oh, that she'd get Lyme disease or heartworm . . . or that she'd slip her collar and get lost somewhere." Kate laughed. "She was so concerned, she nearly got Bonnie tattooed. They do that in France, she'd heard. Tattoo license numbers inside animals' ears, as a way of identifying them."

"France?"

"Yes. She became a Francophile on one of our trips. We used to take these vacations . . . anyway, she loves France and everything French. We sometimes used to speak French together."

"Say something in French."

Kate smiled, suddenly shy.

"Go ahead," John said, forearms submerged in dirty water, the smell of wet dog rising around him, soap suds on his cheek.

"D'accord," Kate said. *"Ce chien est très beau."*

"Okay, translate."

" 'This dog is very handsome.' And now," Kate said, because she felt embarrassed by the amused delight she saw in John's eyes, "it's Bonnie's turn . . ."

They drained the bathtub and filled it again, drying Brainer off with a dozen clean towels. He raced through the big house, rolling on the carpets, shaking himself off. John laughed in amazement. "It's wild—I wish the kids could be here to see this. Their mother would never in a million years have given Brainer a bath in our bathroom . . ."

Kate waited.

"She always filled a washbin outside."

The conversation stopped. As if realizing that he had just crossed into territory where he didn't want to be, John turned stern. He went back into the room, waited while Kate caught Bonnie and plunked her into the warm tub.

"You can tell me," Kate said, quietly, rubbing shampoo into Bonnie's black fur. "You've let me talk about missing Willa. It's your turn to talk about missing Theresa."

He didn't speak for a minute. "That's one way of putting it," he said.

Kate looked up.

"We were very happy for a long time," he said. "Very much in love."

Kate nodded. Why did the words feel so sharp? She thought of herself and Andrew, of how it used to feel to be happy together, what it was like to have it all drain away. As John spoke, he rinsed the soap through Bonnie's brindle coat, combing out twigs. Kate stared at his hands, listening.

"High school sweethearts," he said. "Inseparable. We made it through college, got married during law school, and came back here. We had a great pack of old friends— did everything as a pack. Us, Sally and her husband, Billy and Jen Manning, and the Jenkinses."

"Felicity and Barkley?"

John nodded, his eyes narrowing.

"I'm so sorry you lost her," Kate said. "It must have ripped everything apart."

"Her accident?" John asked.

Kate knew from her own experience that there were layers and layers in a marriage, so many things to be pulled away before the final tear. She stared at John, wondering whether she should be polite and pretend she didn't know what he was going to tell her. Kate couldn't fake it—it would have been like trying to hide a scar.

"I know, John," she said. "I could tell from the questions you've asked me. About me and Andrew and Willa . . ."

He leaned on the bathtub, looking into her eyes. "I thought you might have guessed," he said. "I wasn't sure, but I thought you'd understand. You're right—everything was ripped apart before her accident. See, Theresa was on her way home from a date that night. A *tryst*."

Kate just watched him, listened to the way he said the word: tryst. Such a pretty word for such a horrible thing.

"She was having an affair, Kate," he said, his eyes bruised and his voice suddenly hoarse, as if telling her had hurt his throat. "With Barkley Jenkins."

"I'm sorry," Kate said, tears suddenly filling her eyes. An old friend: someone John had trusted. Water ran down her arm, soaking her shirt. She couldn't move, thinking of John finding out, of the pain of knowing the person you love wants someone else.

"She was on her way home from being with him," John said. "The night of the accident."

"I'm so sorry," she said.

"She was very pretty, like the girl next door, but with something more . . . her eyes were full of secrets, and that made her, somehow, gorgeous. Exotic, in a black-Irish way. She'd look at you as if she knew you inside out, your deepest darkest secrets, before you'd even said a word. Men were always drawn to her."

Kate waited, listening, holding her breath.

"I got so I hated secrets," John said.

As he looked down, Kate saw him try to hide the pain in his eyes.

"Because that was her great gift. She'd make men feel there was nothing they

couldn't tell her. She'd take in their secrets—I'd see her huddled in the corner
with someone at a cocktail party, and I'd
know she was drawing it out of him . . . the
one thing he'd never told anyone before. . . .
Everyone has a gift. Painting, acting, soccer, the law . . . Theresa's was listening."

"She must have listened to *you*," Kate
said. "Heard all of *your* secrets . . ."

John shook his head. "I couldn't tell her
mine," he said. "She was my wife, but
knowing that she listened to everyone else
made me hold back."

"That must have hurt," Kate said quietly.

John nodded, his face hard. He scrubbed
the dog, and Kate noticed that, in contrast
to his expression, his hands were moving so
tenderly over Bonnie's back. He touched
the Scottie as if he knew she was small and
delicate, and he didn't want to scare or hurt
her.

"John," she said softly, dropping her
hands into the water, covering his on the
dog's back.

"You know," he whispered. "I knew, as
soon as you told me about your husband,
that I could tell you about Theresa's affair.
My secret."

"I guess I could feel that," Kate said. "I just knew, by your questions."

"So much for secrets," he said, trying to laugh.

"Finding out about Andrew and Willa hurt more than anything I've ever felt in my life," she said. "You think you won't survive. You think you'll fall off the face of the earth, that it will just keep turning and turning and no one will ever notice you're not there anymore."

"I'd notice, Kate," John said, pulling her close to him, their hands all wet and not even caring. "I'd notice if you weren't here."

"You, too," she said, touching his face.

They kissed, hungry for each other, soaking wet from the tub. Kate felt herself melting inside, holding onto John. He was here, in her arms, solid and real. His kiss was fire, and Kate knew he wanted her the same way she wanted him. His fingers brushed, then interlocked with hers.

Bonnie whimpered; Kate came back to earth.

Breathless, breaking apart, she looked into John's eyes. Brown flecked with gold, they held her gaze. She felt her heart beating in her throat. She slowly pulled her hand away from his, reluctantly, looking down, turning back to Bonnie.

"Can I help you?" he asked.

Blushing, she nodded as he helped her lift the Scottie from the tub. John held out fresh towels, and they dried her off.

"I wanted you to come back," he said as she put Bonnie down. The second the dog's short legs hit the tile floor, she went flying off in search of Brainer.

"You did?" she asked, clearing her throat, still feeling overwhelmed.

He nodded. "And not just to kiss you," he said. "When I told my dad about you, about breaching Merrill's confidence to you, he asked if I talked to you a lot; confided in you often. Something like that . . . it got me to thinking. I wish I could tell you more."

"I thought the same thing," Kate said. As she looked into his eyes, desire flowed into something else: a feeling of connection deep in her heart. "So many times after I got back to Washington, I'd think of you, and I'd wish I could ask you how things were going, how Maggie and Teddy were."

John kissed her again, more insistently than before. If their first kiss had been a surprise, and their second one had been filled with passion, then this one was a zero-to-sixty blood-rush neither of them had felt in years, and they both knew that in ten more seconds they'd be unable to stop.

"Whoa, John," Kate breathed, clutching his arms.

"Kate . . ." he said, smiling widely, swaying with her, pulling her body against his.

He laughed. Taking her hand, he led her from the marble bathroom into the master bedroom. It was getting dark out; the waves crashed, drawing her to the window. Branches scratched against the pane, stirred up by the building wind. Kate gazed down the coastline, seeing the waves break on the sandbar, her Chincoteague storm sense kicking in.

"We're in for a nor'easter," she said.

"What?" John asked, standing behind her, kissing the back of her neck, as if weather was the last thing on his mind.

Just then, John's phone rang; he reached for it. "I was out of the office all day, and just in case . . ." he explained apologetically to Kate.

"Answer it," she urged, smiling, still feeling the tingle on her neck.

"Hello?" John said. Then, "Dad—what's wrong?"

Kate froze, watching John's face twist.

"Teddy?" John asked. "Is he all right? Is he home? Put him on the phone—"

But Teddy couldn't, or wouldn't, come to the phone. Kate watched John's eyes as he listened to his father for another minute, and then he disconnected.

"I have to go home," he said. "Teddy needs me."

"Of course. I understand. Go—I'll head back to the inn."

"I want you to come with me, Kate," he said urgently. "Please?"

"Of course," Kate said, taking his hand, looking deep into his eyes. "Of course, I'll come, John."

Hand-in-hand, damp dogs at their heels, John and Kate had raced together back to John's car in the turnaround. When they got to the Judge's house, they found Teddy wild with worry.

"She's not here," he kept saying, rushing around the house. "Maggie's supposed to be home, and I can't find her!"

"Teddy," John said, grabbing his son by the shoulders. "Slow down—tell me what's wrong!"

"Let me go, Dad!" Teddy said, trying to wrench himself away, suddenly noticing Kate. "I have to find Maggie!" he said, facing her.

"Of course, Teddy," she said, instantly feeling his anguish.

"Did something happen?" John asked.

Teddy let out a cry. Kate watched the boy smash himself out of his father's grip, then run upstairs. John's eyes were wide, shocked, full of hurt. Maeve sat in a chair in the living room, murmuring softly as she fingered rosary beads dangling from her hand. The Judge, dressed in jacket and tie as before, shook his head with dismay.

"I called you, John, because he's been like this since he got home."

"Where was he?"

"At practice. He said he and Maggie had made plans to do something . . . draw pictures. He said she'd been looking forward to it, that she'd never miss it. He's completely beside himself—nothing I said would calm him down."

John didn't wait to hear any more. He

followed Teddy upstairs, and Kate heard his voice drifting down, trying to talk to his son. The tone was calm but insistent, but it was met with a roaring sob. The boy's pain tugged her so hard, she didn't even hesitate, but ran up the stairs where she hadn't been invited.

"Nothing happened, Dad," Teddy shouted, "but that's the point—I don't want something to happen to Maggie. Enough's happened already."

"I know."

"You *don't* know," Teddy cried. "Always talking about people's rights—but the rights of *bad* guys. Guys who *hurt* people. What about innocent people, Dad? Like those girls in the breakwaters? Maggie's not home, and she's supposed to be."

"She's grounded," John said. "She's a good girl. She wouldn't go anywhere."

"Then where is she, Dad?"

"Teddy," John began, color rushing into his face, stepping closer to his son.

But Teddy just tore into what had to be Maggie's room. A yellow nightgown was folded on the pillow, a blue robe with white lace cuffs hung on the bedpost. Kate and

John exchanged glances as Teddy began to rifle Maggie's desk, her bedside table.

"She came home from school, right?" John asked, panic building in his voice, as if Teddy's words had triggered real fear.

"I don't know!" Teddy cried over his shoulder. "She wasn't here when I came in. Her bike's not in the yard."

"She's been here," Kate said quietly, wanting to be calm.

"How do you know?" John asked.

Kate pointed. There, in the drawer, was the yellow envelope she'd left on the hall table just hours earlier. Addressed to Maggie, it had been opened. She saw the ragged tear marks left by a little girl eager to read the card.

"You left this for her?" Teddy asked, picking it up, looking at Kate.

She nodded. "I did."

"It must've meant a lot to her," he said, his voice raw and eyes red. "This is her special drawer. She has one at home, too, where she keeps the things that matter to her. Except the scarf. She never takes the white scarf off."

"I'm glad she likes it," Kate said quietly,

meeting Teddy's gaze, feeling the primal power of the love he had for his sister.

"She does. . . ."

"Are you okay, Teddy?" she asked softly, some instinct making her careful not to touch him.

He shrugged, shoulders heaving in silent sobs. Swallowing them back, when he could speak, he looked directly at Kate, excluding his father. "I can't be okay," Teddy said, "till I know Maggie is."

"I'll go out and look for her," John said.

"Me, too," Teddy said. "I'm coming too."

"I want you to stay here," John said, hands on Teddy's shoulders. "Okay, Ted? Just wait here, and call me if your sister gets home before I find her."

"Where would she be?" Teddy asked, frowning. "Where are you going to look for her?"

"Maybe the library," John said. "Our old house—even though I told her not to go there . . ."

Teddy touched Kate's note. "Maybe the East Wind," he said. "Maggie knows Kate stayed there. Maybe she went over—to look for Kate."

"Good idea. I'll start there," John said.

Then, raising his eyes, he looked at Kate. "Will you stay with him?"

Kate nodded. Suddenly her instinct took over, and she knew exactly what to do next: She put her arm around Teddy's shoulders—like an older sister, like a baby-sitter, like a mother—and gave him a strong squeeze. He felt big and strong, as if he had grown since she'd last been there, but he leaned, just like a little boy, into the curve of her embrace.

"There's nothing else I'd rather do," she said.

White scarf flying out behind, Maggie rode her bike from Gramps's house to the Beach Road. Late in the day, after school, the day's last light gleamed pewter gray, flat and hard. A few lines of orange blazed in the storm clouds. She rode harder, leaving the main road at the East Wind Inn, cutting through the apple orchard, over the small brook that bordered her own yard and the Nature Sanctuary, and onto the dirt road.

Along the way, she stopped to pick dried flowers and grasses—her bike basket nearly overflowed with them. The storm clouds darkened, and the wind picked up; involuntarily, Maggie glanced up at the lighthouse. It stood about a hundred yards away, gleaming white against the sky.

That was the best place to find salt hay: at the top of the bluff, where it had the best chance of being bleached by the sun, wind, and spray. Kate had made everything about Chincoteague Sound so beautiful and salty; Maggie felt the same way about Silver Bay, and she wanted her bouquet to show it.

Zooming over the bumpy road, feeling the storm coming, Maggie felt a great need building in her chest. Sometimes, since her mother's death, she thought her heart had hardened—grown tight and small, like a walnut. Her shoulders had caved in, as if they could grow together in front, forming a protective cage. Was it just this way in girls, or did Teddy feel it, too?

Now, riding her bike down the dirt road, Maggie thought of her dad. The cold wind made her eyes and nose stream. She imagined her dad, making a long voyage across a vast and stormy sea, with two motherless children by his side.

The more she pictured her father, the wetter her face became. He tried very hard. He was so protective. Remembering the way he had rocked her the day she had glimpsed that evil photo filled Maggie with such emotion she had to pull off to the side of the dirt road and catch her breath.

With his hands, he had stroked her hair. She had felt his mouth against her cheek and ear, and she had heard him whisper, "You're my little girl, Maggie. I'll always take care of you . . ."

Maggie held her handlebars tight, as if they could keep her from blowing away. Her father had known how afraid the picture had made her; he was trying to reassure her that nothing so terrible would ever happen to her. She had the feeling that the new curtains at her bedroom window had something to do with that.

That single photo had made Maggie more afraid than she had ever been in her life. Maybe that's why it meant so much, that Kate had given her the white scarf. Wearing it now, the white silk wrapped around her neck, gave Maggie the feeling of courage.

The sandy clay road had a few fresh tire tracks, probably from the lighthouse's caretaker. There were always things to repair in buildings close to the sea. The road diverged, just past a heavy chain strung across it. One spur went inland, to a small dump. The other veered right, straight to the lighthouse. Maggie wheeled her bike around the stanchion, then climbed back on.

Choosing the right lane, Maggie saw the white tower rising above her. The road was dusty with tire tracks, but there were no cars or vans in sight. It was just as well. Even though she knew Caleb and Mr. Jenkins, a shiver tickled her spine as she remembered what her father always said: "Stay away from men in vans, Maggie. People in *any* car, for that matter. If anyone ever tries to pull you in, scream as loud as you can and run away."

Her dad knew what he was talking about, considering his criminal defense work.

But . . . the Jenkinses were friends, and this was practically home. Couldn't she see her own house, just across the field, on the other side of that shallow cove? Turning to look, she located her own bedroom window in the big white house half a mile away and felt reassured. Nothing bad could happen here—this was her own backyard!

Gazing up at the lighthouse, she noticed

how sturdy it looked. White brick walls that could withstand a hurricane! Maggie counted the windows: six vertical ones, and twelve around the top. Perhaps Rapunzel dwelled in there. She could let down her golden hair . . .

The image made Maggie stop. A strong shiver went all through her body, as if the wind had started blowing colder, or as if she was getting a cold, a fever. That image of Rapunzel: a girl trapped in a tower, unable to escape.

Maggie thought of the girl in that picture. Her face white, her eyes staring . . . So many girls, hurt by her father's client, left in breakwaters. How could a person do such terrible things to another person? Maggie didn't get it. She thought everyone should help each other—not hurt.

Even strangers, like Kate. Riding into town, showing up at their house when she was most needed, taking care of Maggie, giving Brainer a bath. And then, later, helping Maggie come up with the best Halloween costume at school.

Trembling now, Maggie decided she'd picked enough hay. Turning toward her bike, she glimpsed dog tracks in the dirt.

She felt relieved; maybe Brainer had been out here. Or even Bonnie. There were people tracks, too. Big footprints, like her father's or some other man's, and smaller ones . . . like Kate's! Wouldn't it be great if Kate was out here now, walking Bonnie with Maggie's father!

But a chill went though Maggie's bones that had nothing to do with Kate or her father. It came from somewhere very scary, and it was telling Maggie to get away from there, *now*.

She wheeled around, glancing once more at the tracks, when she spotted something buried in the dirt. Bits of stone and broken clam and mussel shells had been ground into the dirt, and among them was a tiny piece of gold.

Crouching down, Maggie brushed it off with her fingers. It was a charm—with a loop at the top, as if it had once dangled from a chain, or a charm bracelet—of a little plane. The wings were less than an inch long, and they had real propellers that spun when Maggie touched them.

Her heart almost stopped. How had the charm gotten here?

Maybe Kate had been here after, or before, leaving the note at Maggie's house. Kate had come back to be their baby-sitter, and she had dropped this charm while walking Bonnie on the bluff.

Suddenly Maggie heard a scratching noise that made her jump. Looking around, she saw a privet bush blown by the strong wind, its bare branches scraping the lighthouse door. The wind whined, sounding almost like someone crying, like one of those girls in the breakwaters. Telling her that something terrible had happened here.

Jumping on her bike, shoving the little gold plane into her pocket, Maggie began to pedal as fast as she could. Dirt blew into her eyes, flying everywhere as she sped down the sand road, just then remembering that Teddy would be waiting for her, worried out of his mind.

chapter 23

John drove back the way he and Kate had just come, from his father's house toward his own house and the inn beyond. When he hit the Shore Road, instead of turning left, toward home, he went right, toward the East Wind Inn and the lighthouse. Teddy's agitation had been contagious, and John's mind was filled with fears about Maggie. Where could she be?

The sky was getting dark. Although it was just late afternoon, the days were getting shorter, and a storm at sea was making the waves build, pushing low, purple clouds in from the east. John pressed on the gas.

The lighthouse blinked on the headland,

just a quarter mile beyond the inn. The beam flashed beneath the dark nimbus clouds, looking like man-made lightning. John's heart was in his throat. Teddy hadn't said much, but he hadn't had to: He was frantic with worry for his sister.

And John felt growing panic.

He hit the gas again, driving faster. He had reasons to dislike—even hate—Barkley Jenkins, for breaking up what was left of his and Theresa's marriage. Could that old resentment be stirring him up right now, as he drove toward the East Wind Inn to look for his daughter?

He had no reason to suspect anyone in the Jenkins family of violence, anything having to do with the copycat killing, but his shoulders and jaws were as tense as they'd ever been. He thought of Caleb, his young client. He had committed a criminal act, no doubt about that.

He thought of Hunter Jenkins, Caleb's uncle, Barkley's brother, a man John had always appreciated for his coaching of the kids. That thing about the gym last week— having Teddy go lift weights at a private club instead of school—had rubbed John the wrong way, but he couldn't have said why, and he had dismissed it out of hand.

Driving toward the inn, John felt a vague but powerful fear building. He had no specific reasons to believe anyone in the Jenkins family would cause Maggie, or anyone, harm, but right now he was speeding as if all three men had already been tried and convicted.

You're on a witch hunt, he told himself. This was the big build-up, two years of hating Barkley for what he did with Theresa. There was no reason to think Maggie was in any danger at all; he had just caught Teddy's panic.

Too many people, in the climate of fear and terror created by Greg Merrill's serial murders, were liable to react to anything. A pointed glance, an untoward word, an accidental touch . . . often John had defended clients who'd been wrongly accused, suspected of crimes for things having nothing to do with the case.

It was different, of course, when the case involved his own kids. He knew he wouldn't rest till he had Maggie safe at home. The Jenkins family, the East Wind Inn had nothing to do with it.

The cell phone rang. Praying it was Maggie, or someone at home saying she was safe, he fumbled the phone as he drove.

"Hello?" he asked.

"Hello, Mr. O'Rourke?" came a vaguely familiar voice.

"Yes?"

"This is Dr. Beckwith's assistant. . . ."

"Oh, hi," he said, bracing the phone, skidding around the corner.

"Dr. Beckwith just called in, said you were supposed to meet him over at the prison, and asked me to give you a call and see if there was a problem."

John couldn't think about this now. He'd forgotten all about his appointment with Merrill and Beckwith, their strategy session at Winterham.

"Sorry," John said, turning onto the East Wind drive. "Will you tell him I won't be able to make it today? Something important's come up. Bye."

Bouncing over ruts, the Volvo sped down the sandy lane. Pine branches interlocked overhead, forming a canopy. John looked left and right, between the tree trunks.

Mostly he heard wind in the boughs, waves breaking on the shore. But there, bass notes beneath the shore music, came the sound of power tools. Off to the left was the inn; to the right was the orchard, the brook, and the lighthouse.

He stopped the car in the pine grove, climbed out of his car, and strained to hear. From the right, definitely. The hammer blows were coming from the direction of the lighthouse, but not far away—just a short walk from the inn. Maybe Barkley was repairing the old barn—where, as kids, they'd all gone to drink beer. The memory was happy and wild; Theresa had been there.

In the declining light, as the wind picked up and began to howl, John began to run toward the barn.

Kate and Teddy stayed in Maggie's room. Teddy didn't seem to want to leave, as if being among her things would bring her home faster. The dogs, sensing that Kate and Teddy needed comfort, came upstairs to lie at their feet, furry guardian angels.

"I can't believe you gave Brainer another bath," Teddy said. "Thanks."

"You're welcome," Kate said. "Bonnie

needed one, too. She had this funny white dust all over her."

"Huh," Teddy said, drifting to the window, looking out into the dark.

"She'll come home," Kate said, sitting on the edge of Maggie's bed, chest tight with fear over the familiarity of the situation. She couldn't stop thinking of the first night she'd realized Willa wasn't where she was supposed to be. "Your father will find her."

"She's stubborn," Teddy said, forehead pressed against the glass. "She does what she's told, but she always finds a loophole. Like, she's grounded right now, but she probably found some way around it."

"Like what?"

"Well, say she has a homework assignment. If Gramps doesn't have the books she needs, she'll just ride her bike to the library."

"Do you think that's where she went?"

Teddy shook his head. "She'd be home by now. The librarian doesn't let kids there without their parents stay past four—to make sure they get home before dark. And besides, she and I had plans. We were going to make something."

"Like what?"

"Place cards," Teddy said, shrugging.

"Was that your idea?" Kate asked, smiling, already knowing the answer.

That made Teddy shrug and smile. "No," he said. "I was doing it for her."

"You're a good brother."

"I try to be. She misses our mother a lot. Dad tries, but he's busy so much. Maggie needs me."

"I know she does. Willa needed me, too."

"Your sister?"

"Yes," Kate said. "I tried to be like a mother to her. It wasn't easy, because I was young myself, and had to rearrange my schedule so much. My friends would be down on the beach, and I'd be taking Willa to the dentist."

"I never have to take Maggie to the dentist," Teddy said. "But I would. I will when I get my license."

"I bet you will."

"I change my schedule for her, though. I'm not complaining or anything. But like today—we had soccer practice, and afterward, the coach was going to take everyone for pizza. I came home instead, because I know Maggie needed me."

"Needed you?"

"Thanksgiving's coming," he explained.

"The holidays are the hardest," Kate said, agreeing. "It's when I missed my mother the most."

"Maggie comes to my soccer games, and I go to her school plays and concerts."

"I used to do that. Once I went to see Willa at a swim meet. Only, she had stubbed her toe on her way into the water, and she was crying so hard, she couldn't stay afloat. She lost by a mile, but I cheered like crazy the whole time."

They laughed, sharing stories of being the oldest sibling, caring for a younger sister. But suddenly Teddy's eyes flickered, and when he looked up at Kate, she saw him as a young boy, in his own right.

"I heard you cheering for me," Teddy said, clearing his voice.

"You did?"

"Yes. At my soccer game, when you were here in October."

"That was a great game," Kate said, remembering the brisk sunny day, Teddy's huge smile as he'd run over to say hello. "You were the star."

"I was really glad you were there," he said.

"So was I," she said.

"It mattered so much; I'm not even sure why."

"Everyone needs someone to cheer for them," Kate said softly.

They sat on the edge of Maggie's bed, smiling at each other as if this was the way it was supposed to be for both of them; easy, hanging out together in a cozy place with two dogs, talking about life.

"I just wish Maggie would get home," Teddy said, the worry returning to his face as he stared at the dark window.

"I know," Kate said, hugging the boy. "So do I."

Although it was dark now, the beam from the distant lighthouse flashed across the sky, helping John find his way.

Finally, just fifty yards ahead, John saw a light through the trees. Filtered through pine needles and the first fog rolling off the sea, the light glowed in the single window of a red barn. Getting closer, the louder the hammering sounded. Music played as well, as if a radio was turned up loud. Branches brushed his face and scratched his arms as he walked.

Dark red, hidden among scrub oaks and white pines, the barn had once housed the sheep that grazed all over these headlands. It had been common land, and some of the ship builders and whaling captains had let their livestock roam free. When John and Theresa had first bought their house, tilling the land for a garden, they had found a horseshoe. They had hung it over the kitchen door for luck.

Now, thinking of the luck it had brought them, he felt fury building. He remembered coming here with Theresa. They were in high school; their best friends were inside, waiting. Now she was gone, and he couldn't find their daughter. John didn't stop to knock, but shoved open the big rustic barn door and stepped inside, scanning the space for Maggie.

All the Jenkins men were there.

Not Maggie.

Barkley leaning over blueprints; Caleb on a ladder; Hunt, handing up a long board. John stood there, looking around. The barn's huge, open, rough interior had been broken up; they were framing rooms.

"Hey, John," Barkley, the senior family man, called over. "What brings you out our way?"

"Mr. O'Rourke, how're you doing?" Caleb asked, grinning down from the ladder. "We're building four new guest rooms, so we can outdo the Silver Bay Inn next summer."

"Where's Maggie?" John asked.

"Your daughter?" Barkley said, frowning. "We haven't seen her. Why would she come here? What's going on?"

John approached him. His eyes burned, staring at his old friend. They had been high school friends together; soccer teammates; lifelong buddies. And Barkley had taken John's wife away, been with her the night she had died, and returned home to live a normal life: Here he was with his son and brother.

Time was, John had wanted—needed—to rip Barkley's face off. But not now; Kate Harris had changed that, taken the old jealousy and thrown it into the wind. John only wanted to find Maggie, bring her home.

"Pretty cool place, huh?" Caleb called as John walked closer. He sounded a little worried. John had been his lawyer; perhaps he feared that there was trouble, the after-effects of his case, something to do with parole. "We're putting hot tubs in the bath-rooms. It's going to be—"

"Seen my daughter?" John asked, stand-ing at the foot of the ladder. Looking up, seeing Caleb's scared expression, feeling a rage beyond words building. He had gotten this kid off on a serious charge, and right now he didn't know where Maggie was, and he was fighting the urge to climb up and tear the boy apart.

"No, Mr. O'Rourke," Caleb Jenkins said, sounding frightened. "I haven't."

"Get down off that ladder and talk to me," John said. "You're scared of something, Caleb."

"No, I swear . . ."

"You look guilty, and you sound guilty, and I want to know why," John said, shak-ing the ladder so hard, he thought Caleb might tumble off. If he didn't, John was ready to climb right up and get him.

One foot on the second rung, John was on his way.

chapter 24

Kate and Teddy sat on the floor of Maggie's room, brushing the dogs. What else was there to do, waiting for someone—everyone—to get home? Teddy took handfuls of soft, white hair off Brainer's undercoat, while Kate had a hard time keeping Bonnie from rolling on her back, begging to have her tummy tickled.

Just then the front door slammed.

"I'm hooommme!" came Maggie's voice.

"Maggie!" Teddy bellowed.

"Coming!"

The dogs jumped up at the ruckus, and Maggie came pounding up the stairs. Both

Teddy and Kate scrambled to their feet, rushing to the bedroom door.

"Where were you, young lady?" the Judge called after her from his study. "We were just about to call out the National Guard!"

Maggie burst into her own room—red-cheeked, white scarf trailing, holding a huge tangled bouquet of dried flowers and beach grass, but at the sight of Kate she dropped it and ran into her arms.

"You're right here!" she cried out, squeezing Kate. "Not just in Silver Bay, but *here,* in our *house*!"

"I'm so glad to see you," Kate said, hugging her hard.

"I got your note, and I wanted to pick a Thanksgiving bouquet, and I rode over to the lighthouse on my bike, and the whole time I was thinking 'Kate's here, Kate's here . . .' Are you going to have Thanksgiving dinner with us?"

"Oh," Kate said, smiling. "I don't know about that . . ."

"Maggie, do you know how worried we were?" Teddy asked. "You were supposed to meet me after school."

"I know, Teddy, but I got home, and you

weren't here, and I got Kate's note and decided—"

"Dad's out looking for you!"

"He is? He's never usually even home by
now," she said, looking shocked and a little
afraid.

"Well, he was today."

"Sorry," Maggie said, gazing up at her
brother. "Can we call him on his cell phone
and tell him I'm home?"

"Yes," Teddy said, smiling with affection-
ate exasperation. "That's a very good idea."

"I'm just thinking of her," Caleb said, watching John come up the ladder at him. "With
that last girl in the breakwater, no wonder
you're worried. Watch out, Mr. O'Rourke—
I'm coming down. Okay?"

"Let him down," Barkley said, grabbing
John's shoulder.

"He's acting scared of something," John
said through clenched teeth. "And I can't
find Maggie . . ."

"That's not my fault," Caleb said, climb-
ing down. John grabbed his shoulder, and
Caleb's eyes flashed white, as if he feared
John might lose control. He was in his early

twenties, but he didn't look like a kid anymore: He had lines around his eyes from
working outside, and his hairline was just
starting to recede. But his body was rock
hard—John could feel the muscles under
his shirt, and he held on even harder.

"Did you know that girl at Point Heron,
Caleb?"

It wasn't his imagination: Caleb's face
turned bright red, and he looked up at the
ceiling, away from John.

"Answer him, Caleb," Barkley said. "Set
his mind at ease."

"Only from the papers," Caleb said. "She
looked really pretty. I felt bad about what
happened to her."

"Now, what the hell does it have to do
with us?" Barkley asked. "What brings you
over here like this so—your little girl not being home yet? We'll knock off work right
now and help you look for her."

John's phone was ringing; he could feel it
vibrating in his pants pocket. Hunt heard it
too; his eyes flicked downward. Looking
away from Barkley and Caleb, John flipped
open his cell phone.

"Hello?"

"Dad—she's home," Teddy said.

"She is?" John asked, his eyes locking with Caleb's. He saw the relief and vindication there—as if he knew he was off the hook—as he straightened himself out, shook his shoulder where John had been gripping him.

"Yeah. She was just out picking flowers. Believe it or not . . ."

"Right, I believe it," John said, swallowing, sensing three pairs of Jenkins eyes on him.

"See you later, okay, Dad?"

"Okay, Teddy."

When John hung up, he saw Barkley watching him. He took a deep breath. Until two years ago, he would have said Barkley Jenkins was one of the best friends he had.

"Your daughter okay?" Hunt asked now, from across the floor.

"Yeah. She made it home safe."

"That's good. I'm glad."

"We all are," Barkley said. "We're all very glad about that. Look, John—we know it's been rough."

"Don't, Bark," John said, his voice shaking.

"I've never told you how sorry—"

John felt his words like a punch in the

stomach. Nothing Barkley could ever say would explain his wife's betrayal, how she could have gone behind his back, put their whole family in jeopardy.

All he needed was to start down the road of Theresa, and he'd really lose it. He thought of Kate, hoped she was still at the house now that Maggie was safe. He remembered the way she'd felt in his arms, the whisper of her breath on his neck, their time by the west-running brook. And he wished more than anything that she wouldn't leave before he got home.

"Glad she's home, Mr. O'Rourke," Caleb said, and he laughed with clear relief. "You were really coming after me."

John glanced over at him. "You seemed guilty about something, Caleb," he said.

"No, not me. And nothing about your daughter," Caleb said, sounding uneasy again. "I was just talking about your house. That's what I thought you meant."

"My house?"

"The brick—you know," Caleb said, staring down at John.

John looked around; this was a construction site. Why wouldn't there be bricks somewhere on Jenkins property? His heart began to pound harder, remembering his children's cries of fear.

"Are you telling me you threw the brick?" John asked, the question exploding out of him.

"Hold it right there," came Barkley's voice, and John felt a hand on his shoulder and turned around.

Maggie sat on the edge of her bed, unable to stop smiling at Kate. Her blue eyes were bright, as if she couldn't believe Kate was really here. Kate felt the same way, seeing her. She couldn't wait for John to return, so he could see his daughter with his own eyes.

"Your brother and dad were pretty worried about you," she said.

"I'm sorry," Maggie said, her smile faltering slightly.

"Dad's not letting you out of his sight again till they catch the copycat guy," Teddy said. "You'd better face it."

"I had my scout knife!" Maggie said, drawing the red sheath from her pocket, handing it to Kate—as if wanting Kate to pronounce it adequate protection, congratulate her for carrying it.

"You shouldn't have gone," Teddy said kindly.

"I need freedom," Maggie said. "And I can't stand staying at Gramps's any longer. We have to go home—we have to! Kate . . ."

"Yes?" Kate asked, still holding the pocketknife, smiling at how shiny Maggie's eyes had just become, suspecting she knew what was coming next.

"Stay with us! Whyever you're here, for whatever reason you've come back . . . be our baby-sitter!"

"Yeah," Teddy said, nodding and walking closer. "That's a good idea."

"I wouldn't make a very good baby-sitter," Kate said.

"Why not? You were a good one with your sister," Teddy said. "You practically raised her, went to her swim meets . . ."

"That was different," Kate said, his words and their eagerness tugging her heart. If only she could. If only it were that simple; she'd just move in with this family she was growing to love, take them all under her wing, and everyone could be happy.

"Because she's your family?" Maggie asked.

"Well, partly."

"Why else?" Teddy asked.

"Well, I'm a marine biologist," she said. "I have a job already. Down in Washington."

"That's really cool," Teddy conceded. "I knew that . . ."

"Yes," Kate said. "You sent me that letter."

"I want to go to law school in Washington, like Dad," Teddy said.

"I'm going to be a pilot when I grow up," Maggie said. She touched the white scarf around her neck, as if to make sure Kate had noticed her wearing it.

Kate smiled, touching the fringe.

"Amelia." Maggie grinned.

"You'd make her proud . . ."

"You gave me the scarf; I want to give you my knife. Keep it—at least for a while. In return for the scarf . . ."

Not wanting to hurt Maggie's feelings, Kate smiled and put the red knife into her jeans pocket.

"I'm going to become an aviatrix when I grow up. And fly solo around the world!"

"A noble goal," Kate smiled, thinking of

the picture Willa had painted of her at the controls of her plane.

"In fact, I got a sign," Maggie confided breathlessly. "Something I thought you might have dropped on a walk with Bonnie. Want to see?"

"Sure," Kate said, watching Maggie reach into her back pocket. Her heart was filled with a sense of peace: Maggie was home safe, Teddy was calm again, John would be back soon . . .

"Here it is," Maggie said, her face glowing, pulling something from her pocket.

Kate smiled, looking down at the little girl's loose fist.

Her fingers opened, and Kate found herself staring at a tiny gold airplane with wings and a propeller that really turned.

"Oh," Kate cried, grabbing the charm, which still bore traces of white dust. "Where did you get this?"

"On the bluff," Maggie said, gaping at Kate's agitation. "Near the lighthouse . . . the clamshell road. Why, what's wrong?"

"It was Willa's," Kate said, her eyes filling with tears. "I gave it to my sister."

chapter 25

Kate didn't have a car with her. She had left hers at the East Wind Inn. Perhaps she could have waited for John. Or she could have borrowed Maggie's bike. But the little gold airplane charm was like a talisman burning a hole in her hand, forcing her to move *now*.

"Judge O'Rourke," she said, walking downstairs with the children right behind her.

"Yes, Kate?" he asked, looking up from the book he was reading to Maeve. They sat in a small study, fire crackling on the hearth as wind roared down the chimney. She lay on a sofa, under a plaid blanket, and he sat upright beside her, *Two Under the Indian Sun* open on his lap. They both smiled up at Kate.

"Judge O'Rourke," Kate repeated, tears pressing against her throat and eyes. She was so independent; she didn't like to ask for favors. But she held Willa's charm in her hand; it was covered with familiar white dust, and she knew where she had to go.

"What is it, dear?" he asked, frowning.

"She has a mission," Maeve said quietly, watching Kate's eyes.

"I do," Kate said, her voice cracking. "May I . . . I know you don't know me, but I have to ask . . . may I borrow your car?"

The Judge hesitated, listening to the storm rattle the windowpanes. But just then Maeve struggled upright to take his wrist, look him lovingly in the eye. "Kate and her sister were like Brigid and me," Maeve said gently, watching Kate with such sad eyes that Kate felt the tug of being understood by another woman who had lost her sister. "Let her use your car, Judge."

"It's raging out there," the Judge said. "And she's right. I don't know her . . ."

"Aye, but I do," Maeve said, nodding at Kate. "I know her."

"How?" the Judge asked.

"In the ways that are important," Maeve whispered. "Do you know what it's like to have a sister? To share the same parents, the same home, the same life . . ."

The Judge sighed, and Kate recognized the tremble of love and emotion that went through his body. He stared at Maeve, at the way tears formed in her eyes as her lips started to move, and Kate could feel him making up his mind.

Kate clenched her fists. Maggie had given her something to hold onto, the first real, solid clue she'd had about Willa since coming to Silver Bay.

"All right, then," the Judge said, staring into Maeve's watery old eyes. "It's the old Lincoln, in the garage out back. You have to pump the gas pedal a few times to get it started."

"Gramps, you're letting her take your car?" Teddy asked.

"It's his baby," Maggie said.

"Maeve asked me to," the Judge said solemnly.

"Thank you for that," Kate said.

"Well, I'm going with you," Teddy said.

"Me, too," Maggie said.

"And your father would have my head," the Judge said. "You two go, and all bets are off."

"Please stay," Kate said, turning to the kids, trying to smile at them. "You've done more for me than you can imagine . . . I want to go to where you found the charm, Maggie, and feel my sister. Do you know how long I've wondered? I've been here searching, and you've given me a place to . . . look for her. Maybe one last place." *Or maybe just a place to say good-bye,* Kate thought. Either way . . . "Willa was there . . . this charm tells me for sure."

"I can show you exactly," Maggie pleaded. "And it's scary there, by yourself."

"You shouldn't go alone," Teddy said sternly, hiding fear in his wide eyes. "Take us and Brainer with you."

But Kate shook her head. The charm was exerting a powerful, sorrowful magic on her, and she knew she had to do this by herself. Now that Kate had met the O'Rourkes, had started to feel the way she felt about John, she knew she couldn't go on unless she made peace with the past; with the betrayal she'd experienced at the hands of the person she loved most, with her own rage at her baby, her sister. What if Willa had left more traces behind? Kate had to find out.

The storm had brought it on: Even before she had become a scientist, Kate had learned that strong wind and waves could stir up the atmosphere, change conditions so completely that even human chemistry was affected. Full moons, sunspots, hurricanes, blizzards, and even good old northeasters could shake up the ions and make the world a whole new place.

Kate and Willa were storm children. Born and raised on a barrier island, a finger of sand standing strong against the powerful Atlantic, they had always loved storms. They'd rush across the dunes, day or night, and stand watching the waves batter the beach.

Tonight was the night. Kate felt grief building in her chest. Whatever had happened—whatever Willa had done, wherever she had gone—tonight Kate was going to learn everything she could.

Kate already knew that Willa would love the lighthouse. Perhaps she had walked out there, just as Kate had today. Maybe she'd been with Bonnie, stopping to notice the west-running brook. Kate felt a sob in her chest. The gold charm was so much more than a postcard, Willa's name on an inn register. This was something precious that had always symbolized the love between them, that Willa had worn against her skin.

Saying good-bye to the Judge and Maeve, Maggie and Teddy, telling them she'd be back soon, Kate bundled into her green wool coat and soft white beret. Then, head down against the growing wind, her heart filled with sorrow and a strange sort of hope for the future, she ran outside to start up the old Lincoln in the garage out back.

John and Barkley faced off. Here in the big barn, the great inn annex, John could feel the tension crackle between them. Maggie was safe, but they had some other unfinished business.

"Rough times, John," Barkley said. "I know you've been through a lot."

"Not for you to worry about—and besides the point right now. Did Caleb throw that brick through our window?"

"Now, relax. We all know about your big case, about you defending Greg Merrill. I got redneck kids working on my construction crew . . . they talk some shit about you trying to get a serial killer off death row. We know about the brick through your window because we know the plate-glass guy who fixed it—that's all."

"Caleb knows more than that," John said.

Barkley put his hands up. "He does not. Don't go making accusations you can't back up, John. I'm just telling you, for your own good—you're not very popular around town these days."

"It was a criminal act," John said harshly. "Whoever did it could have hurt my kids."

"Tell him, Dad," Caleb said.

"Shut up," Barkley said, his tone sharp.

"Okay," Caleb said, climbing down from the ladder. "Then I will! He deserves to know, Dad. He helped me win my case!"

"Don't shoot your mouth off about something you're not sure of."

"I'm sure," Caleb said. He stepped closer to John, his eyes nervous but friendly. He was a big puppy dog of a kid, who'd gotten in with a wrong crowd and done some stupid things that had led to trouble with the law. John's friendship with his father had changed with the betrayal, but John knew he would be wrong to hold Barkley's sins against the boy.

"Tell me, Caleb."

"I will, Mr. O'Rourke. It was Timmy Bean. He's a redneck."

"Caleb—Timmy's one of my best workers, and just because he opens his mouth doesn't mean he—"

"He threw it, Dad. I heard him say so."

"Kids brag," Barkley scowled. "About stuff they know nothing about."

"Thanks for telling me, Caleb," John said. "You did the right thing."

Caleb nodded, looking worriedly at his father, Adam's apple bobbing as he swallowed. He looked nervous, as if he feared what his father would say or do to him after John left.

"Merrill has the right to a lawyer, just like everyone else," John said.

"And you're a lawyer," Caleb said, smiling back.

"A good one, too," Barkley agreed reluctantly.

"We all feel that way," Hunt pitched in. "Regardless of how we personally feel about Merrill. Hell, I love kids. Teddy's one of my best players. I really hope there are no hard feelings . . . Maggie's safe, everyone's okay. Right?"

"Yeah," John said.

"So, we're square?" Barkley asked.

"I'm going to come talk to Bean—and bring Billy Manning with me."

Barkley shrugged. "Do what you have to do."

The men all stared at him, solemnly, as if they'd been afraid he would go ballistic and beat them up one at a time. John thought of Maggie, Teddy, and Kate safe at home, but for how long: There was still another killer working in Silver Bay.

"I will," John said, turning around and walking out of the barn, hurrying home to his family.

chapter 26

Kate drove past the East Wind Inn and parked the Judge's car by the chain stretched across the way. The wind was blowing so hard, she thought it might take her sailing right off the bluff, onto the rocks below. The beacon flashed overhead, telling her she'd come to the right place; that this was the end of the road.

Her throat caught; so many tears were trapped inside, and they had been for the better part of a year. She looked around for John, thinking maybe he'd come out here looking for Maggie. When she didn't see him, she walked toward the tower.

"Willa," she called out. "I'm here."

Voicing her sister's name filled her with tenderness and a sense of freedom. Wherever Willa was now, they were together on this stormy night. Kate knew it with everything she had. She held the airplane charm in her hand, feeling strength and love pour from the metal.

Elements rushing together, through the skin of her fingers, her palm, her bones and blood drawing strength from this little piece of gold. Kate had bought it for Willa so many years ago, given it to her with complete and utter love.

All those years, when Willa was a child and Kate was a new adult, wanting to protect her little sister, give her the tools and skills to make it in this world. How did parents know how to do it? Were they granted wisdom and grace upon the birth of their children? If so, Kate had missed out.

She had had to wing it. Do her best, with all the sisterly love at her command, with the help of her brother. Matt had always let her do most of it, but he had been there when she'd needed him. Two accidental parents with the child they adored.

Now, standing by the chain across the road, Kate rattled the lock. Willa's charm, according to Maggie, had been right here, on the clamshell-strewn path leading to the lighthouse. Willa must have come out here for a walk, when she was staying at the East Wind. It was a spot that would attract her— as it had Kate—for its wildness, beauty, majesty: The headland rose a hundred feet above the sea, and the lighthouse stood at least seven stories higher.

Holding the charm, Kate stepped over the chain. She started up the path, head down into the wind. Her ears ached in the cold. The night had grown dark, but periods of light flashed from the beacon. Storm clouds scudded through the sky, fitfully revealing the big moon. Kate had no problem finding her way.

Her heart was full. This was it. The night felt electric—she could feel her sister's presence as surely as if they were holding hands.

The night had begun with John's kiss, with Maggie's gift of this small gold charm, with the growing feeling that Kate had found a place—and a family—to love. A sob rose in her chest. She would never lose Willa now; her sister was with her forever.

She walked around the lighthouse once.

The white tower gleamed in a slice of moonlight. Her foot crunched on glass; looking up, she tried to see if one of the windows had broken. Waves rolling in from the open Atlantic smashed against the rocks below, sending spray skyward. Down the coast were the breakwaters, the rocky graves of girls who had died.

"I love you, Willa," Kate shouted out to sea, tears filling her eyes.

Had the wind lessened? Its roar no longer seemed so vicious; it whistled in Kate's ears, filled with music and whispers, alive with her sister's voice.

Kate's hand closed around the gold charm. Her plan was this: She'd wait for a perfect, white-topped wave, until its crest was knife sharp and ready to break—illuminated by the lighthouse beacon—and Kate would breathe in and feel the connection to Willa. And somehow—it had to happen—she would be given the answers about where to look next.

She watched carefully, seeing the wave build. Her eyes stung with wind and tears, but she focused her gaze and all her emotions: love, grief, the need to find her sister, to know at last where she was.

There it was; third wave out. The beam blinked, lighting it up.

"Where's my sister?" Kate cried.

The wind was so high and thin, it almost seemed to have a voice. "Katy," it called, reedy and distant. Kate froze, straining her ears.

The wind was dying; the third wave passed, crashing on the rocks. She remembered a time, twelve years ago, when she had been home and Willa had been stranded up in a tree down the beach. King, the most aggressive of the wild ponies, had charged Willa, sent her scrambling up a small scrub pine. She had stayed up there for hours, ten years old, crying for her sister. It had sounded just like this, like a message from the wind:

"Katy!"

Kate slowly turned her back to the sea. A step inland, away from the edge of the bluff. Another step, toward the lighthouse. Then a third step, a fourth, hearing her name again, hearing muffled sobs in the breaking waves. Was she hearing a ghost? Or was she being haunted by old memories, by her love? Was it what she had wished for on the wave—a connection, at last, to Willa?

Kate ran to the lighthouse door.

Looking straight up, she saw the white tower rise overhead. She thought of the little princes locked in the Tower of London. Fairy tales, where the wizard kept the girl hidden away, where the sorcerer trapped the princess, held her captive till all the roses withered and died.

"Willa?" she said, breathless. The lighthouse walls were thick white concrete blocks. No sound could possibly get through. But from up above—from the windows, the fine lens? That shattered window—

Kate had stepped on broken glass. The caretaker would have found it, if it had been broken for long. The storm must have knocked it out somehow. High winds had imploded the window, or blown debris into the glass.

The thin voice again: It might have been real, it might have been the wind playing with Kate's imagination. But she held the gold charm Maggie had found, and she was suddenly certain that her sister was there, inside. Kate knocked at the door, then threw herself into it, pounding harder and louder.

Kate felt all the sorrow and rage of the

past six months swelling up inside her. She shook the door, crashed into it with her shoulder, banged the latch. It was solid, locked tight, with steel plates—the lock and plates massive, industrial, impenetrable. Kate backed up, ran at the door with all her strength, felt the impact in her bones as she fell to her knees.

"I hear you, Willa," Kate yelled. "And I'm coming!"

She ran around the tower's base. Looking up the whole time, noticing one vertical row of windows rising up the east side, looking out to sea. The lowest window was a good fifteen feet off the ground—and yes! It was broken, a jagged star-shaped hole in the glass. But Kate could never reach it without a ladder.

A ladder . . . Backing off slightly, Kate pounded the surrounding bushes for anything the Jenkinses had left behind: planks, sawhorses, ladders . . . nothing. Stumbling in the darkness, she thought of leaving—she could run to the East Wind, get someone to help her. Or she could call John and the police . . .

But what if whoever had put Willa in the tower came back for her right now, took her away, hid her somewhere else? Or what if Kate was imagining it all, and Willa wasn't in the lighthouse at all? Kate let out a sob of frustration, running in the dark, back to the base of the lighthouse. The beam lit up the ground, she ran forward, the light flashed away, darkness returned, and Kate felt the ground disappear beneath her.

Falling, falling, into the darkness, into the earth, Willa's voice trailing into thin air above.

Heading west, toward his father's house in the center of town, John saw a big silver Mercedes sedan slow down to stop at a traffic light. Thinking he recognized the driver, he hit the brakes, and the yellow light of a streetlamp illuminated the other man's face.

What was Phil Beckwith doing in Silver Bay? Passing through, on his way from Winterham to the highway back to Providence, John realized—remembering with guilt that he had missed his appointment at the prison.

Merrill might have told Beckwith something that would help the police catch the new killer. John couldn't stand it if more girls died. The worry he'd felt for Maggie had finished it for him. The whole town was living on edge. They needed to make an end.

Looking in the rearview mirror, he saw Beckwith's brake lights at the stop sign. He watched the wide taillights swing around the corner onto the coast road. The highway was just half a mile away; if John did a U-turn, he could catch the doctor.

So he turned his car around in the IGA parking lot, pressing down on the gas. He gained quickly, and, as if Beckwith was watching in the rearview mirror, the Mercedes pulled over to the side of the road.

"Hello, John," Beckwith said, rolling down his window, a concerned look on his face. "Everything okay?"

"Sorry about missing the meeting," John said. "Something came up . . ."

"That's all right. Things happen."

"Are you on your way back home now?"

"Yes," the doctor said, looking tired. "It was a disturbing interview, but very productive; I have a long ride ahead of me, time to reflect on everything that was said and decide how to proceed."

"Proceed?"

"Yes—in relation to our case."

"I was thinking— Do you have a minute? I want to hear what happened—whether Merrill talked to you about the new killer working now. He did, didn't he? He trusts you. I'm a parent—I have kids on the streets of this town. We have to catch him, Doctor."

"You're very worried, aren't you, John?" the doctor asked, looking at him with great kindness and weary understanding.

"I am," John said.

"With good reason," Beckwith said gravely. He checked his watch, then gestured up ahead, toward a bend in the road. "The commuter parking lot's right there. I'll meet you."

Nodding his thanks, John followed Beckwith to the deserted lot. He pulled in beside Beckwith, and the doctor climbed out of his Mercedes and into John's Volvo.

"Excuse the mess," John said, glancing in back at one of Teddy's soccer balls, Brainer's car bed, and a few old newspapers.

"Quite all right," Beckwith said. "Now, to give you a report on what Merrill and I discussed tonight at the prison—"

Just then, John's cell phone rang again.

He thought about ignoring it—Beckwith was putting himself out by postponing his long drive home to Providence. But when he checked caller ID, he saw that the call was coming from his father's house.

Excusing himself, he answered. "Hello?"

"Dad," came Teddy's voice.

"Can I call you back, Ted? I'm with someone right now—"

"Is it Kate?" Teddy asked.

"Kate?" John asked, confused. "I thought she was there, with you and Maggie."

"She was, Dad, but Maggie showed her this airplane charm that belonged to her sister. She went out to the lighthouse—to look for clues or something, I guess. I thought maybe you'd want to know. To help her . . ."

"The lighthouse," John said, his pulse speeding up. "How long ago did she leave?"

"Um, maybe half an hour?"

"Thanks, Teddy. I'm glad you called."

As he disconnected, he looked over at Dr. Beckwith. The older man was sitting quietly beside him, seeing the worry in John's face.

"That was my son, calling to tell me that a friend of ours needs some help," John ex-

plained, trying to smile. "Her sister is missing."

"I heard you mention the lighthouse," the
doctor said, his eyes reflecting John's un-
ease. "She's on her way there?"

"Yes . . ."

John's stomach dropped at the sight of
Beckwith's expression. "What's wrong?"

Dr. Beckwith ran his right hand through
his white hair, eyes flicking around nervously, close to panic. "Merrill spoke of the
lighthouse to me tonight."

"What are you talking about?" John
asked, frowning.

"If what Greg told me is true, your friend
could be in danger, John."

"Kate?" John asked.

"Yes—would you like me to come with
you? I'd better come with you. I might be
able to talk to him, stop something before it
starts."

" 'Him'?" John asked as he threw his car
into gear, began speeding down the road.
He didn't even have to prod the doctor;
Beckwith just started talking.

"There's a man in town who's been fascinated with Merrill all along. Wrote to him in
prison, and Merrill wrote back. The two of

them—he and Greg—developed a sort of mentorship," the doctor said.

"What kind of person would want him as a mentor?"

Dr. Beckwith was silent, staring at his hands.

"You're talking about the other killer?" John asked, glancing across the front seat.

"It's possible."

"You knew about this all along?" John asked, shocked.

Beckwith shook his head. "I didn't know anything—even now, I'm not sure whether to believe him or not. He said his student became so intrigued, he decided he couldn't wait, had to try it himself . . ."

"Amanda Martin?"

"Yes. Greg claims his friend killed her."

"Based on details he picked up from Greg?" John asked, incredulous, remembering the way Greg had talked to him and Billy about the new killer's inferior understanding. . . .

"Yes," the doctor said, sitting calmly across the seat. "He was ranting about it tonight—very upset about the copycat. Infuriated because this other man is trespassing on his territory."

"But is it real or not? Does Greg really know him?"

"Is he delusional? Certainly. But tonight, regarding this particular instance, I feel there might be a germ of truth."

"Why?"

"Because, as you know, Greg's pride is his Achilles' heel. He enjoys his status . . . his notoriety. Even when he speaks of communicating with this other man in code, he says it's very elaborate, Byzantine."

John drove on; he could just imagine the stupid Mensa code Greg would come up with, that only someone as brilliant as he could understand.

"What makes you think it's real?" John pressed.

"Greg doesn't want to share the spotlight," Beckwith said. "And the story he told me tonight centers on the other man."

"What did he tell you?"

"Greg spied on a girl once," the doctor said. "In Fairhaven, Massachusetts. He said she was so young, so provocative, he was going to climb right through her window and kidnap her from her own bed . . ."

"But he couldn't get in," John interrupted impatiently. "I know."

The doctor nodded. "He told you that part. Perhaps he didn't tell you this. He revealed the girl's address to his correspondent—using that code I mentioned. Then one night, seven months ago, the protégé went to that Fairhaven parking lot—to try again. Something happened. The girl's lights were off, or the family wasn't home . . ."

"But someone else was there," John said, catching his breath.

Dr. Beckwith nodded. "Yes. A woman vacationing in New England. She'd been in New Bedford, touring the Whaling Museum. Her dog was in the car with her. The amazing part is that the protégé had seen the dog, knew the woman already. They'd been staying in his hometown—Silver Bay. At the inn . . ."

"Willa Harris," John said, his brain suddenly icy clear.

"Greg didn't tell me her name."

"And he killed her?" John asked.

"No," the doctor said. "According to Greg, he kidnapped her. Handcuffed her, set the dog loose somewhere in Rhode Island. Drove her back here to the lighthouse . . ."

"And then what?" John nearly shouted.

"From there we don't know. Except that . . ." the doctor trailed off, a look of torment in his eyes.

"What? Tell me!"

"He was a patient of mine," the doctor said, sounding anguished.

The Second Man

chapter 27

Kate fell into the hole and hit hard, flat on her back. Gasping in the dark, she swallowed water, and scrambled to her feet, trying to see, to get her bearings. She was at the bottom of what seemed to be a well.

Four inches of water rose around her ankles; in the pitch-blackness, with arms extended, she felt the stone sides, built in a tall circle against the lighthouse's north side—she couldn't see the top. The fall had bruised her back and legs, but nothing seemed to be broken. As she stumbled around the small, enclosed space, she tripped on a rock—stepping over it, walking in a tight circle, she searched for a way out.

Her head spun from hitting the ground. Reaching with her fingers, she tried to climb up the straight stone wall. Suddenly, about six inches overhead, she touched wood. Old and splintery, the plank came apart in her hands. Feeling around, she realized the wood had the dimensions of a door. What would a door be doing in a well? It would rot and decompose under water.

If she had something to stand on . . . it would be easier to work on opening the door. Crouching down, to feel underwater, she felt for the rock she'd tripped on. Instead, what she found was too round and perfect to be a rock—and it sat atop a pile of similar round objects.

Lifting the metal ball took all her might. Its weight pulled her shoulders down and forward, and when she dropped it again, it made a loud splash.

Cannonballs.

She must have fallen through a trapdoor into an old munitions depot. There were hundreds of them up and down the Atlantic coast, particularly in the thirteen original colonies: During the Revolutionary War, high bluffs and cliffs, lighthouse grounds, had been excellent spots for battlements. She,

Matt, and Willa had discovered a similar store in Chincoteague, where the dunes weren't so high but the view of the sea was as good as it got. Perhaps the lighthouse had been built around that time; hoping to combine protection with defense, the settlers had been ready for anything.

Now, excited, reaching overhead, she tried to crack the door.

The door wouldn't budge. Kate's fingers were bloodied, pricked with splinters, as she started to bang. She couldn't hear that voice anymore, that whistling, ghostly voice. And that nonhearing actually gave her hope—because if the voice had just been her imagination, wouldn't she still be imagining it from down here? But what if she couldn't climb out or get into the lighthouse?

And then she remembered: Maggie's knife.

Fumbling in her pocket, she took it out. Hand trembling with cold and tension, she dropped the knife into the water, heard it clank and skid, then had to feel around, locate it with freezing fingers.

"Oh, God," she cried, fitting the blade into

the space between the door and the stone wall. "Please, please work . . ."

The rusty latch popped.

Heaving with all her might, Kate scraped the door open inch by inch. She hauled and scrambled her way up the stone wall, pulled herself through the opening. Scraping her side on the rough edges, she climbed forward and stopped, catching her breath, waiting for her eyes to get used this new dark

There seemed to be no light whatsoever. She knelt on all fours, feeling in all directions. The space was narrow; by reaching from side to side, inching forward slowly, she realized she was in a tunnel, about six feet wide. A smell of damp mustiness choked her and grew stronger the farther she crawled from the well's entrance.

Her heart was pounding. She knew she was in the lighthouse, and she prayed— passionately—that Willa was in here too. She had to find her sister, but she had no idea where she was. In fact, she had lost her own bearings and wasn't sure whether she was moving toward or away from where she'd thought she'd heard Willa's voice.

The darkness was total. Advancing on

blind faith, she walked smack into another stone wall. She had come to the end of the tunnel. Now, still feeling her way, she realized that a set of rickety wrought-iron stairs stood to the right. Grabbing the handrail, she started up, and her foot smashed through the first rung as if it were lace.

Her jeans torn and shin bleeding, she ignored her leg and felt the stair rungs ahead of her, assessing their strength. These stairs were so old and unused; perhaps this basement had been long forgotten. In any case, the wrought iron's filigree had rusted through, become as fragile as paper. Knowing that the stairs' sides—where the connection would be strongest, the metal thickest—were her best bet, she began to move upward on all fours, staying toward the right, trying to balance her weight forward and backward.

Twenty steps up, she came to another door. Like the first it was locked, and like the other, she used Maggie's knife on the rusty hinge. This one, too, broke open. When Kate edged the big wooden door open, she found herself standing in a small anteroom. Light came in here: the bright occulting flash from the beacon. She checked her watch: eight-twenty. Barely fifteen minutes had passed since she'd heard Willa's voice on the wind.

And when Kate walked forward, opening the next, unlocked door, she stood right the middle of the large, open lighthouse. The column of windows rose on the left; a circular metal stairway wound like a helix up the cylindrical center. More glass from the broken window lay on the floor. Standing with her head thrown back, she could see all the way up to the Fresnel lens, to the beacon.

There was no sign of Willa.

Kate looked around, frantic. She had been almost sure—she'd heard her sister's voice. Just like that time on Chincoteague, carried by the wind, over dunes and trees and water. Kate, alone of everyone on the island, had heard her sister's voice then, and she would have *sworn* she'd heard it tonight, through the storm-smashed window.

She had just known, deep inside, that her sister had to be right here, inside the lighthouse. *Could* she have been imagining it? Could she be longing for her sister so terribly that she had conjured up her voice?

But Willa had been nearby . . . Kate had

her gold airplane to prove she had been here at some point.

Perhaps the strong wind had fooled Kate into thinking Willa's voice came from inside here—maybe she was somewhere else, close by the lighthouse, in a shed or barn that Kate had missed. Flying to the door, Kate began to shout.

"Willa? Willa, where are you?"

The cry came from the sky, filled with pure joy and disbelief.

"Katy?"

"Oh, honey, oh, Willa," Kate cried, a sob ripping out of her chest.

"You came, oh, you came! Here, Katy," came Willa's voice, still muffled but much clearer than before, drifting down from above. "I'm right here!"

"Where, Willa?"

"Up above," Willa said, her voice cracking with hysteria. "And hurry, Katy—before he gets back!"

Kate tipped her head back, looking. There was only one possible place: the lens. Running toward the narrow, sweeping stairs, Kate took them in long strides. Her leg was cut and bleeding, but she didn't even notice. The metal rungs clanged under her feet, and her heart was in her throat. The air was freezing cold, smelling of salt and rust.

When she'd gone six stories, she peered up the last two stories to see the round walkway circling the lens, but not Willa. She frowned—she should be able to spot her sister by now. The beacon's light flashed so brightly up above, scraping her eyes, and she had to shield them to see.

"Willa—where are you?" she asked now.

"Right here, Katy," her sister said, her voice so close.

Slowing down, her legs burning from the steep climb, Kate began to smell fresh wood. When she looked down, she saw clumps of old, wet sawdust on the stairs. And when she looked up . . . there, camouflaged against the narrow and shadowed section of the tower just below the lens, just one story above, was a wooden box.

Bolted into the lighthouse's impenetrable brick wall, bracketed to the walkway above and the staircase circling around, was a small structure the size of a garden shed. Painted white to blend in . . . As Kate approached from the stairs, she could see no possible way to enter.

"Willa," she said, touching the box. "Where's the entrance?"

"Are you here?" Willa asked, her voice breaking into a sob, knocking from inside. "Oh, Katy, get me out! Hurry, he's coming! There's no time . . ."

"Get you out how?" Kate said, touching the box, banging on the sides, trying to find the way. "Where's the door?"

"On top," Willa said. "From inside the light . . ."

Kate didn't waste a second. She ran up the last flight and a half, onto the walkway that encircled the lighthouse lens. It was a magnificent Fresnel crystal, brilliant and sparkling as it refracted light tossed by the beacon, splitting the beam into rainbows and throwing them out to sea. Kate hardly saw. Tearing around the mechanism, she came to a break in the metal walkway and looked down.

There was the trapdoor.

Cut into the top of the box, it had two metal hinges and one hasp held by a padlock. Hand around Maggie's knife, she could see that this was a different story from the locks she'd broken earlier: Both of them had been ancient, probably two hundred years old, rusted through. These hinges were new, solid, stainless steel.

Even so, she set to work with Maggie's pocketknife, digging into the wood. If that window hadn't been broken, no one would ever have heard Willa: Up close, she could see the brick and cast iron of the tower walls.

"Hold on, Willa," she said. "I'll be in there in just a minute. . . ."

"Hurry, Kate!"

The lock was unyielding. Once the knife slipped, gouging her hand; she shook it off. Willa was breathing hard—Kate could hear it through the wood, and the labored sound struck more fear into her.

"This isn't working," Kate said, giving up on the knife. If only she hadn't left her cell phone in her car, if only she could call John and get help. But she couldn't, so looking all around, she tried to see something that would work better than a small knife.

"Don't leave me!" Willa howled as Kate scrambled across the walkway toward the light itself.

"I won't—never," Kate promised.

The lighthouse lens was partially en-closed by a metal cage. The upper half was open, but the bottom half was fabricated from the same old iron as the stairs in the secret passageway. The light blinding her with each flash, Kate took hold of one of the half-round metal rungs. Woven almost like a basket, it had rusted to thinness in the middle, while holding strong at the bolted ends.

Cracking one rung in the middle, Kate pulled with all her might. She worked it back and forth, wearing it down at the bolt, pumping and pulling till an eighteen-inch length snapped off in her hands. Now, holding the rod, rushing back to the box, Kate wedged one thin end under the hasp.

It was a perfect pry bar, and as Kate put all her strength behind it, working it back and forth, she felt superhuman strength building inside her. Her sister was inside, and Kate was going to get her OUT. Gasping, screeching with exertion, she gave everything, and the lock and wooden door broke in one smashing blow.

Willa was crying, pushing from inside. Kate fumbled the lock, pulling it off the door, hinges and all, laying it beside her.

Yellow eyes in a dark space, an owl in a roost hole, a fox in a hollow lair. Shivering, she was dressed in rags. Oh, God: a prisoner in a cell.

At the sight of her sister, Kate's chest heaved and broke. The sob cracked in her ears as she looked down, as her eyes locked with Willa's. The questions came, but Kate ignored them. She reached down, inside the darkness, feeling Willa grasp at her arms, too weak to hold on. Kate did it all. Finding strength she didn't even know she had, tears pouring down her cheeks, she clasped her arms around her sister's thin upper body and pulled.

"I have you," Kate said. "Let's both hold on tight."

"Don't let go," Willa begged.

"No," Kate said, her voice hoarse with the knowledge that she had her sister in her arms.

Kate knew in that moment that she had never seen anything so beautiful, in her entire life, as her sister Willa, and she did what she'd promised: She held on tight, she didn't let go. Outside the lighthouse, the wind whistled, decreasing from its earlier roar, and waves smashed the beach. The sounds were loud enough to muffle, slightly, the sobs coming from both sisters as Kate led Willa to the relative safety of the walk-way.

"Can you make it down?" Kate asked, supporting Willa, feeling her thin arm around her neck, feeling her body heave with each breath, as if it caused wracking pain.

"My legs," Willa cried. "I haven't moved them in so long . . ."

Looking down, Kate could see Willa's legs, thin and spindly like a newborn colt's after so much time in the box. Choking with emotion, Kate took off her coat—wet from her fall into the well—and put it around her shoulders. Kneeling beside her, she began to massage Willa's legs and ankles. Willa cried out, cringing at each stroke.

"I can't make it down," Willa said.

"Yes," Kate said, rubbing steadily, trying to focus. Her mind was buzzing with what Willa had said before, "Hurry, he's coming . . ." She didn't know who or where or when, but she felt her sister's terror, and she knew it was real. "You can," Kate said.

"I want to, but I can't," Willa said, weak with frustration.

"I'll carry you," Kate said. "I did when you were little, and I'll do it now."

Both sisters looked down—eight stories on a winding, narrow staircase. Willa shook her head, letting out a sob. "You can't."

Kate didn't even reply. She just tucked the coat around her sister's body. The smells from the box were bad, but Kate had changed this baby's diapers. This was nothing.

Being careful, she stowed Maggie's knife in the front pocket of her jeans. Then, shoving the metal bar down the back of her pants, like a sword, she crouched beside her sister.

"Wrap your arms around my neck if you can," Kate said, lifting Willa against her chest.

Willa tried, but her arms were too weak and trembling. Kate knew it didn't matter. She had her sister in her arms, and she wasn't going to falter. She took the first step down, then the second. Her legs were powerful, her arms filled with energy. The electricity of love filled her, passing from her heart to Willa's and back again, forming a circuit that made her stronger with every step. She thought of Amelia, of John, Teddy, and Maggie, taking strength from all of them.

One story, two stories. She hurried down the steps, sure of foot, positive they were going to make it. Her mind raced, planning what to do next. She had her trusty pry bar. If the lighthouse door opened easily from the inside, Kate would take Willa out, put her in the Judge's car, drive her to the hospital.

If it didn't, she'd take her out through the secret passageway, into the well. Kate would find a way to climb out—she'd scale the walls if necessary.

"What time is it?" Willa asked, her voice weak and shaky.

"I can't see my watch," Kate said. "But about eight-forty-five, I think. Don't worry, we're almost down . . ."

"He comes at nine," Willa said, frantic. "He calls it *his* time, it's the secret hour . . ."

"The what?" Kate asked, her chest heaving with exertion.

"When he won't be missed; when no one will see him coming out here . . ."

Kate's feet moved faster. Willa shifted in her arms, crying out with pain. The unbalance nearly toppled them both. Steadying herself against the thin black rail, Kate happened to look up, toward the box.

She couldn't even see it from here. The cell was completely hidden in shadow and light, blending into the guts of the lens and light, camouflaged from sight. Her heart kicked over, knowing that it existed, that whether she could see it or not, danger was there.

"He built it," Willa said, following Kate's gaze, as if she could read her mind. "He built it to keep me in. . . ."

"What did . . ." Kate began, but she trailed off. There would be time to learn everything later. Right now, the clock was ticking, and she had to get Willa out.

Outside, she heard the waves breaking closer. The sound was deafening, as if the storm tide had risen way up the bluff, as if it was nearly dead-high. The association with Merrill caused a jolt of terror to shoot through her blood.

"Almost there," Kate said, carrying her sister down one more flight.

Just one and a half to go. Her arms were beginning to tingle, as if her body knew it was almost time to put Willa down. Her muscles ached and burned under the weight, and her lips felt numb, all the blood going to her arms and legs.

"I never thought I'd be rescued," Willa said, her voice breaking. "I thought I'd die in there."

"Never," Kate promised. "I'm getting you out of here."

Reaching the bottom flight, she bent over, to put her sister down. Wanting just to investigate, to try the door, Kate was nearly bowled over by Willa's clawing grip.

"Don't let me go!" she begged.

"Just for ten seconds," Kate said. "While I find our way out . . ."

Collapsing on the stairs, Willa was too weak to argue. Kate ran to the door, trying it. Three locks, including two deadbolts, ran up and down. None had a latch; keys were required to open each lock—from either inside or out—and the door itself was thick and new.

Removing the metal bar from the waistband of her pants, she wielded it with a flourish, giving Willa a huge smile.

"You make a good pirate," Willa croaked, smiling back.

"I'll get us out of here yet," Kate said, trying to fit the rod's flat end between the door and the jamb.

Just then, as if by magic, one lock turned.

Then the second—the noise rasping in her ears, metal on metal—being opened from outside. As she realized what was happening, that Willa's captor had returned, that it was nine o'clock and he was right on time, she turned toward her sister.

Willa was a ghost.

Pure white, all life gone from her eyes, she cowered on the wrought-iron stairs, clutching the railing and staring at the door. Kate wanted to grab her, hide her in the well, but it was too late. She heard the key in the last lock.

Putting her finger to her lips, to warn Willa not to make a sound, Kate knew the signal was useless. Her sister was frozen, waiting for him to come inside, afraid of what he'd do when he found her and Kate.

The door cracked open, letting in waves of cold, fresh air. Kate breathed deeply, feeling a new sharpness in her brain, standing behind the door. Her gaze was on Willa, and she saw her sister close her eyes in defeat.

The man stepped inside. He was six feet tall, lanky and athletic, with brown hair, less than two feet away from Kate. As he caught sight of Willa, he stood with one hand on the doorknob, shaking with rage.

"How did YOU get down here?" he yelled. Kate could almost imagine him running through his precautions, the fact that Willa couldn't possibly have gotten down here on her own. His shoulders seemed to expand as if inflated, and as he wheeled to look behind the door, Kate screamed and swung the rusty iron bar with everything she had.

Right in the face, right between the eyes, she connected with bone and tissue and blood—lots of blood. The man bellowed and staggered back, hands on his eyes, his blood and hands obliterating his face and identity, losing his balance and falling toward Willa when Kate struck again.

"You hurt my sister," she screamed, swinging the bar. "You took her and hurt her, and I'll KILL you for it!"

The metal rod connected again, then once more, and finally Willa's captor collapsed in a heap at Willa's feet like a slain dragon. Willa scuttled, crablike, away from him, and Kate stepped forward.

Her heart was pumping. Was he dead? She didn't know, and she almost didn't care. She knew one thing: She wasn't going to let him stand up and hurt Willa again. So she prodded him—first with her weapon, then with her foot. When he didn't move, she moved closer to peer into his face.

Caleb Jenkins.

Kate saw his chest rise and fall, heard blood bubbling from his mouth and nose. She had never before seen him up close, but Kate knew. He resembled his father, but so much younger—just twenty-something. Kate didn't stop for regrets or doubts. Lifting her sister from the floor, helping her to her feet, Kate gave her the chance to stand with her arm around Kate's neck.

"There are no more stairs," Kate said as the fresh sea wind blew through the open door, sharpening their senses. "Grab on, and I'll get you to the car."

"Maybe I can walk," Willa said.

"Later," Kate said, glancing back at the boy on the floor. "I want to get us out of here before he wakes up."

And so, lifting her sister once again—this time with her arms trembling and nearly breaking with effort—Kate held Willa close and ran down the sandy path toward the Judge's car.

The vehicle, gleaming white with each flash of the beacon passing overhead, and with moonlight—for during her time in the lighthouse, the clouds had blown away and apart, revealing a huge silver moon over the sea—was still parked at the base of the road. Slowing down now, passing across the rutted and rock-strewn precarious section of path, Kate carried her sister carefully.

When she reached the Judge's car, she glanced behind—no sign of Caleb Jenkins. Willa rested on her feet, taking her first painful steps in perhaps months, as Kate led her from the hood of the car to the passenger side. Opening the front door, Kate helped her sister inside. Then, running around the car, she began to climb in herself.

Just then, noticing Caleb's van parked off to the side, she calculated. What if he came to, ran to his van, caught her before she got past the East Wind to the main road? Taking a deep breath, she ran over to the white Chevy van, "Jenkins Construction" lettered on the side.

"Katy," she heard Willa cry. "Hurry—don't leave me alone in here! We have to get away!"

"I know," Kate flung back, opening the van door.

The keys were in the ignition. Palming

them, she backed away. But her attention was caught by two things lying on the front seat. A gold necklace, a locket with the initials "AM" entwined in script: Amanda Martin.

And a document, thick and official looking. Vellum bound, like one of Kate's Academy reports. Scientific, complete, expensive. Leaning over, to read the front title page, she saw:

ASSESSING VIOLENT PREDATORS
A Study of Gregory Merrill
By Dr. Philip A. Beckwith, M.D.

Wondering how Caleb had gotten hold of a psychiatrist's study, Kate grabbed it and jumped out of the van, keys in hand. Then, climbing into the Judge's car, Kate started the engine, threw her sister a wide smile, and backed out of the sandy parking area.

"We made it," Kate said. "I found you . . ."

"Faster, Kate," Willa screamed, weeping into her hands as if freedom hadn't yet hit her, as if she was trying to make herself compact because she wasn't used to all the space in the world. "The other one is coming!"

Kate drove, eyes in the rearview mirror to make sure Caleb wasn't following, shocked by her sister's words. "What other one?"

"That one back there . . ." she said. "He used to just feed me; bring my food . . . tell me the time. But it was the other one. . . . Oh, Kate, drive faster . . . he always comes at nine o'clock . . ."

chapter 28

John drove, as fast as he could, toward the lighthouse. Dr. Beckwith sat beside him, speaking in a shocked, bewildered voice—and John was just as shocked to hear the patient's name.

"Caleb Jenkins?" he repeated, to be sure.

"Yes. You see, Caleb presented with such mild symptoms of the disorder," Beckwith said, visibly distressed, "I completely missed it the first time."

"There was nothing about a sexual disorder," John said, recalling the defense he and Beckwith had developed.

"Nothing overt, early on. An addiction to the Internet disturbed his parents enough to ask me to recommend a therapist; I said I'd take him on myself. That's when we uncovered what was really there, underneath."

"He'd drive to Providence?"

"Yes. The longer we worked together, the more I realized that he had other . . . components to his addiction. A sort of comorbidity, if you will, of chat rooms and pornography."

"And he began writing to Merrill . . ."

"According to Greg," the doctor said. He checked his watch. "Faster, John—"

John tried to get his breathing under control, to listen and learn as much as he could so he could do whatever necessary to save Kate. He felt as if he and Beckwith were racing against a clock, trying to get to the East Wind Inn before Caleb Jenkins's path intersected with hers, on her way to the lighthouse.

"The Jenkinses sent their son all the way to Providence to see me, and this is the help I gave him. . . ."

"They kept in touch with you," John said, hitting the gas; the talking kept him from going crazy with worry for Kate.

"Yes. The family was not without its own rather serious problems by the time Caleb began acting out. Mrs. Jenkins was coping with depression. Her husband had been unfaithful. . . ."

John's stomach clenched with shame and fury, not wanting to hear that his colleague knew.

"I'm sorry, John," Beckwith said. "I do know about your wife and Barkley Jenkins."

"Felicity told you?"

"Yes. And, later, Caleb."

John was silent, concentrating on the road. They weren't far from where Theresa had hit the deer, on her way home from being with Barkley. But that meant they were getting closer to the lighthouse—closer to Kate.

"There's no need for you to feel ashamed," the doctor said. "It's nothing you did, and certainly, adultery is rampant in America. But his father's infidelity had a profound affect on Caleb—an unleashing, if you will, of a great store of rage. In turn, that reached back to his father—defending himself against his son's derision. Barkley Jenkins is a very angry man."

"Like father, like son."

"True. Felicity wanted Barkley to see me as well—a sort of family counseling, I guess. Barkley refused. He suffers, as does his son, from a sort of free-floating God complex. Thinks he can do just about anything and get away with it. What time is it, John?"

"Just past nine," John said as he veered onto Redcoat Road, the access road to the old munitions well where the colonists had hidden arms to fight against the British. It merged with the road to the lighthouse.

"Just in time," the doctor said. And when John turned to look, he saw Dr. Philip Beckwith holding a pistol pointed at him.

"What?" John asked, stunned.

"You'd have figured it out anyway," the doctor said as John drove into the unmarked sand road. "I knew you'd learned about Fairhaven, and from there it was just a matter of time until you made the connections between me and Caleb . . . and Merrill. They communicated through me, of course. I'd hoped to clean up before you did, but then tonight your friend decided to come out to the lighthouse. Perhaps she's with Willa now."

John didn't reply. *With Willa:* Was she still alive? The lighthouse beam was just over the rise, through the leafless trees. They were coming up fast on the bluff.

"Which was it?" John asked. "You getting tempted by the men you were treating, or you being just like them to begin with?"

"Shut up!" Dr. Beckwith roared, reaching across the seat to strike John in the face with barrel of his gun. John reeled from the impact, seeing stars. The car weaved down the road.

"You idiot. If you'd just stayed out of it. If you'd just defended your client, not gotten sidetracked by that woman. You're as weak as the rest—under the thumb of some woman. . . . She's steered you straight away from your duty, letting your client down, meddling where neither of you belong."

That's what the doctor thought of as weakness? Helping Kate? John had never felt so real or alive as he did right now, knowing that he had fallen in love with someone and that he'd die trying to save her life.

Knowing there was no way he'd drive this maniac even a foot closer to where Kate might be, John hit the gas as hard as he could and crashed his car straight into a tree.

The second Kate heard the crash and the car horn, she pulled off the sand road under the apple trees and doused the headlights. Willa was crying, begging her to get them away faster, but Kate motioned her to be quiet. Rolling down the window, she strained to listen.

The car horn blared. Then it stopped, and she heard the sounds of car doors being opened, a voice shouting for someone to get out. Peering through the darkness, she saw two men standing by a wrecked car.

"John!" she exclaimed, nearly flying out of the Lincoln. But just then the beam passed overhead and Willa caught her wrist, pulling her down in her seat.

"It's him," Willa breathed with terror. "The man with the white hair . . ."

He had a gun. Kate slid down fast, so that only her eyes were visible over the dash, and she caught a glimpse of John's bloody face, the shiny barrel pointed at his head, the white-haired man holding the gun as the lighthouse beam swept over.

The two sisters crouched low, watching the two men standing there. Hand on the door latch, Kate quietly popped it open and placed one foot on the ground.

"What are you doing?" Willa whispered frantically.

"That's John," Kate said. "If it wasn't for him, I wouldn't have come back to Silver Bay . . . I wouldn't have found you, Willa."

"When we get somewhere safe, you can call the police," Willa pleaded. "That other man—he's the one with Caleb!"

"The one who hurt you?" Kate asked, feeling the intense fury and hatred build.

"Yes . . . he came at nine. . . ." Her voice choked on tears. "What time is it now?"

"Nine-ten," Kate said, checking the clock on the dashboard. "He's late. And he has John."

"Don't go anywhere," Willa pleaded, tears running down her bruised and bloody face. "Don't leave me here alone."

Kate felt torn—her sister needed a hospital, and Kate could barely stand the thought of abandoning her even for a few minutes. But she couldn't leave John to face this danger alone. It wasn't that Kate was brave or courageous or intrepid inside. But her heart had changed since coming to Silver Bay, and she knew that had everything to do with John O'Rourke.

She had fallen in love with his daughter, his son, his father and his father's housekeeper, with his golden retriever, and most of all—and she knew this from the way her heart had started beating so fast, like a butterfly, in her throat and chest the split second she had seen his station wagon driving through the orchard and knew he had come for her—with the man himself.

"I won't leave you alone," Kate said to Willa, gathering up her knife and the rusty metal rod, giving her sister a quick kiss. "I'll be right back, but I have to help John. He needs me right now . . ."

Looking toward the lighthouse, John saw Caleb's van. Parked at an angle off to the side, it stood alone—no sign of Kate or another car anywhere. John breathed a little easier, thinking she wasn't there.

John's mind swam with all the times he had walked by here—on hikes with Maggie and Teddy, walks with Brainer. Was it possible—that for six months, Willa had been hidden here, under his nose? Kate had been right. Her sister was close by.

The automatic prodded his side, and John knew the doctor was going to kill him. Beckwith glanced at the lighthouse, then toward the East Wind—probably gauging whether anyone would hear the shot. John knew that if he stepped foot inside the light-house, he would die. Two against one: Caleb and the doctor. The beam mocked him, flashing overhead, warning mariners away from the rocky point. The most obvi-ous place on the shore, and John and the cops had missed it this whole time.

Kate . . .

He prayed she had already come and gone. She filled him with hope and tender-ness—for never giving up, for never ceasing to believe in her sister—and the feeling made him stand taller and face Beckwith without flinching.

"Okay," the psychiatrist said, staring John in the eye, pointing to the drop-off just past the lighthouse. "Walk over to the cliff."

John didn't want to do anything that might make it easier for Beckwith to shoot him, send his body into the sea, but he needed to buy time. The sandy path was rutted, tufted with dried grass. Beckwith must have hurt his leg in the crash, because he limped painfully over the field.

Suddenly, as John walked toward the lighthouse and bluff, the hair stood up on the back of his neck. He felt a chill run through his body, as if a cold front had just passed through, as if a ghost had just flown over.

It was uncanny, and he felt the way he had in Fairhaven, when he'd been parked on one side of the empty lot, looked across, and saw Kate Harris—where she shouldn't have been, where the chances were one in a million for them to meet.

Faraway places, two people in contact how? Through their hearts and souls, not through the spoken word. John had never had it with Theresa; he didn't even have it with his own kids. But he had it with Kate Harris, and knew—suddenly, with every nerve in his body—that she was here now.

Clouds raced across the moon; the light passed over. Darkness, light, darkness, light . . . the field was illuminated by the moon and beacon, then dark again. The path was empty, then a shadow appeared. Coming closer, footprints crunching on the broken clamshells, the shadow gained a face.

And a voice.

"Hello, John," she said, as if she hadn't seen the gun. And perhaps she hadn't . . .

Beckwith dropped his arm, hiding his weapon behind his right hip.

"Kate," John tried to say. He wanted to warn her, scream at her to run—but if he did, and she took off, Beckwith would shoot her.

"What a beautiful night," she said, her Virginia voice soft and melodic. "I just missed the dunes and waves of home so much, I swear, I hoped I'd just walk up to the lighthouse and see a pony. What brings you and your friend out here on this stormy night?"

"Same reason," Dr. Beckwith said, filled with charm and appreciation. "Hoping to see a filly. . . . John, don't be rude. Introduce me to your friend. Perhaps we can invite her inside, and—"

"Kate, get out of here," John said, the words ripping out.

Even as he spoke, Kate stepped between him and the doctor, laughter trilling from her lips, saying something about Yankees having no manners, bending slightly as if out of courtliness . . . John saw the metal rod protruding from the back of her pants.

Kate extended her hand, saying to Beckwith, "Hello, there. I'm Kate Harris."

"I know your sister," Beckwith said, bringing the gun up to her chest.

Kate ducked away as John swung. Smashing the rusty, blood-soaked metal bar down on the doctor's wrist, John heard the bone crack and the gun fire—both at the same time. The bullet hit the lighthouse, ricocheting straight into John's thigh.

He yowled in agony, the explosion searing flesh and bone. While Beckwith fumbled, trying to fire again, John charged straight at him. Kate had grabbed the doctor from behind, pulling his hair and trying to force him down. John was single-minded— had only one purpose in mind, on this earth, on this moonlit night—and that was to take Kate's sister's captor down. He pounded him with his fists, feeling the hot bursts of his own blood pour down his leg.

The men fought, Kate rolling out of the way, the gun clattering onto the shell-covered path. John clutched the doctor, rolling with him down the grassy bluff, feeling the east wind sweep up from the rocks, salty and wet.

"John, the edge," Kate cried.

Braking, trying to brace himself with his good leg, John stopped the roll three or four yards from the bluff's drop-off. He concentrated on battering Beckwith's face, hearing Kate shout, "He hurt my sister! He's had Willa this whole time."

"Hear that?" John asked, breathless, his leg burning, searing with pain. "She knows what you did. You put her through hell!"

"Make him tell you," Kate cried. "Make him tell you what he did to her!"

"I'm a doctor," Beckwith said, his cheekbone fractured and bleeding. "If it wasn't for me, she'd be dead! Caleb took her from that lot, and he would have killed her long ago. Young men can never wait. They don't have the patience!"

"Patience . . . this!" John shouted, smashing the doctor in the face.

"What did you do?" Kate screamed, coming over to the cliff's edge, grabbing at the doctor's face and clothes. "You could have helped my sister, saved her. But instead you . . ."

The doctor tried to breathe, wiping his

face on the grass, looking down. He ignored Kate completely, as if she wasn't even there—as if she hadn't even spoken. Instead, he looked down at John's leg.

"That's arterial blood," he said calmly.

John didn't speak. Teeth gritted, he felt the pulse in his femur, as his body pumped his blood out onto the ground.

"You'll bleed to death," Beckwith said, "if you don't get help right away, John."

Stars swam in John's vision, and he heard Kate gasp as she realized what John already knew—that the doctor was right.

"I'm a physician," he said. "I can help you. I need a tourniquet to start. Give me your shirt . . ."

Had he been talking to Kate or John? John wasn't sure, but suddenly he knew he had to do something, or he'd die and leave Kate alone with the monster. With caution, eyes never leaving Beckwith, he started to strip off his shirt—because he wouldn't, for anything, have Kate do that for him, in front of the psychiatrist—and while he was tangled in the fabric, he felt Beckwith's fist shoot out and jab him in the throat.

Choking and caught in his shirt, swearing at himself for being a fool and getting duped, he knew he'd die sending Beckwith to hell on the rocks below before he let him touch Kate. The moon and stars reeled overhead as he tried to get his balance.

But he was too late. Kate had reached into her pocket, pulled out a red knife— looking just like Maggie's—and with a raging sob, jammed it straight into Beckwith's neck.

The psychiatrist clutched his throat, staggered back, met John's eyes for one precarious second, and then tumbled backward off the bluff. John, reaching for Kate, pulled himself to the edge. They lay there together, holding each other, staring at Beckwith's inert body lying on the breakwater below. The lighthouse beam passed overhead, illuminating the cresting waves, revealing the tide: full high.

"Kate," he whispered.

"John," she cried, holding him, stroking his face. "Don't die, don't go. Stay with me! I'll go get help. Don't die now!"

John stared into her eyes. They were so beautiful, that odd color that had reminded him of river stones the first time he'd seen her. Of smooth round stones, their edges softened by the passage of water over them, through this century and the last, ancient stones polished by endless water. By that beautiful west-running brook, just across the orchard, where John wanted to spend all the time in the world with her. Eternal eyes . . .

"I love you, Kate," he whispered. He heard the sea in his ears, the salt-filled ocean rushing to take him away. Behind it a high call, a cry, a siren . . .

"I love you, too," Kate Harris cried, rocking him, holding him as if she didn't want to lose what she had just found. Because he felt the same way, just before the dark wave rose to take him away, he felt the tears rise in his throat, pumping out of his body along with his blood, into the cold ground.

epilogue

It was the day after Thanksgiving, and the morning of the first funeral.

All the Jenkinses had gathered at the Silver Bay Chapel, dressed in black and with heads down to avoid television cameras and news photographers. Their friends surrounded them in a cluster, helping them into their cars afterward.

Only Hunt Jenkins spoke to a news reporter, angrily stating that "My nephew didn't kill Amanda Martin, had nothing to do with Willa Harris's imprisonment. . . . He's a victim of Dr. Philip Beckwith, just like they were. . . . At most, he was hired to build the lighthouse room, but he never had any idea what it was for. . . ."

The second funeral, Dr. Philip Beckwith's, would be held at a later date, a private ceremony to be announced by his mother, his only surviving relative, of Boston, Massachusetts.

"What explanation can there be," the Judge asked, carving the turkey, "for a doctor who does that much harm?"

"I'm not sure we can explain any of it, Dad," John said, watching Kate across the table. She had her arm around Maggie, and she was staring back at John as if she never wanted to look away again.

"How come we get to eat Thanksgiving dinner with the TV on?" Maggie asked. "We never have before."

"We've never had it on Friday before, either," Maeve said, carrying the gravy over from the stove. "Or eaten in the kitchen . . ."

"Miracles sometimes take time," the Judge said solemnly. "And we can't rush them. Friday was our first available date."

"Daddy almost died," Teddy said.

"And so did Kate's sister," Maggie said, bending into Kate's body, closing her eyes as if she couldn't believe she had someone wonderful to sit next to, to lean against. "We couldn't have Thanksgiving until we knew they'd be okay."

"Will your sister be okay?" Teddy asked.

"Yes," Kate said, still staring at John so warmly, with so much love in those cool river eyes. "Yes, she will. After some time in the hospital . . ."

"I helped, right?" Maggie asked. "By telling you about the airplane pin, by loaning you my knife?"

"I wouldn't have known where she was without you, Maggie," Kate said, avoiding the question about the knife. Blinking, looking away—as if she could block out the fact that she had killed two men. John, sitting on the sofa in the family room part of the kitchen, leg extended, moved closer, wanting to reach for her across the table.

"Kate?" he said, stretching out his hand. "Come sit next to me."

She obliged, but Maggie came with her. As if joined at the hip, when Kate sat down beside John, Maggie plunked down beside Kate.

"Who wants white meat, who wants dark?" the Judge called over from the table.

"And who wants gravy?" Maeve said.

"Cranberry sauce, turnips . . . and don't the glasses sparkle? My sister and I washed them ourselves, every one."

"I know you did, Maeve, girl," the Judge said, blowing her a kiss. "You're quite a team, you and Brigid."

"Aye, we are," Maeve said, smiling quietly as she ladled gravy over the plate Teddy had fixed and handed to her.

The assembly line continued, and John sat with his arms around Kate. He felt her breath on his cheek, her heart beating through her skin. They were at his house— Maggie had begged to come home, to have Kate stay with them instead of at the Judge's—for as long as it took for her sister to recover enough to move back to Washington, and Kate had agreed.

Now, looking out the large windows at the sun shining on the silver sea, on the white lighthouse rising from the headland a half mile away, John saw nothing gothic, nothing frightening, nothing at all to show that lives had been lost there. He held Kate tighter, as if he could protect her from memories of what had happened.

"Daddy?" Maggie asked.

"What, Mags?"

"Are you Kate's lawyer now?"

"Not exactly," he replied.

"You advised me, though," Kate said, looking down into his eyes.

"Only because I wasn't sure what the police were thinking," John said. "When Billy came driving up, the cruisers right behind him . . ."

"Teddy called him," the Judge said. "He had a bad feeling when you didn't come right home . . . and with Kate on her way to the lighthouse on such a stormy night."

"I thought you both might be able to use some help," Teddy said with shy pride.

"Thank you, Teddy," Kate said, holding John's hand. "You saved your father's life. I was afraid . . ." She trailed off, not wanting to scare the kids by mentioning how close John had come to bleeding to death.

"Of the bad men?" Maggie asked, looking up into her face.

"No, Mags," Teddy said as he carried plates of turkey over to the sofa. "She'd already taken care of them. You're brave, Kate."

"I was defending people I love," she said.

"You love your sister," Maggie said, her eyes shining. "And who else?"

"Mags," John warned. "Be polite . . ."

"No—I want to know." Maggie asked, "Who else?"

John sat still, on the sunroom sofa, his leg, bandaged so clean and white, sticking straight out in front of him. He could feel his daughter smiling like sunshine, and he was almost afraid to look at Kate's face. What if she was embarrassed, or what if she wanted to dodge the question and move on—politely reply, give Maggie an answer she could live with, eat Thanksgiving dinner, and head over to the hospital to be with Willa?

Kate was smiling. That was the thing: John loved her smile. Even now, with Billy Manning wanting to question her again, with Willa hospitalized with more damage than they could even begin to imagine . . . even with all that, plus two kids watching her with huge eyes and the most obvious longing—as if she were Wendy and they were the lost boys and all they really wanted was for her to be their mother—even with all that, Kate just smiled and smiled.

"Am I being rude?" Maggie asked, and

Kate's grin grew wider. "By asking you who else?"

"Who else . . . what?" Kate asked, squeezing John's hand. "I forgot the question."

"Who else were you defending?" Maggie asked. "Who else do you love?"

And as Maeve began saying grace, thanking God and her sister and her four sons Matthew, Mark, Luke, and John, as Teddy and the Judge bowed their heads, John felt a huge shiver go through his body. Kate squeezed his hand, smiled a little wider, and turned to look at him with so much depth and love in her eyes that John thought he might go crazy waiting for her to speak again.

But she didn't, right away. She just stared at him, through and through, giving him the feeling that they were alone in the sunroom, that although the rest of the family were with them, they were also, somehow, all alone.

Just the two of them, man and woman, two friends, two strangers who'd happened to meet in a dark parking lot in Fairhaven, Massachusetts, and again at a lonely lighthouse in Silver Bay, Connecticut.

Two people, John and Kate, who couldn't manage to let go of each other's hand.

Of course Kate remembered Maggie's question.

It rang in her ear . . . and that took some doing. Kate's head had been filled with the sound of ringing for a few days now.

She heard the ringing of metal striking metal—Maggie's knife on the rusty hinge. And the sound of a revolutionary cannonball striking stone . . . and her feet clanging on the wrought-iron stairs . . . and the echo of Willa's voice, beseeching her to get her out of the nightmare box . . . and the sound of the bar hitting Caleb's skull . . . and the resonance of the Judge's tires on the clamshell drive . . . and the ringing of Beckwith's bullet hitting the lighthouse, ricocheting into John's bone . . . Maggie's knife stabbing the monster's neck . . .

Closing her eyes now, Kate gasped, taking it all in.

"Mags," she heard John say as he squeezed her hand. "You want to let it rest right now?"

"I didn't mean anything bad," Maggie said.

"That's okay, John," Kate said, her eyes flying open, not wanting any of them out of her sight for a moment.

"We haven't had a minute alone," John whispered. "There's so much I want to say to you."

"Me, too," she whispered back. Their faces nearly touching, she felt his breath on her forehead as his lips gently brushed her skin.

She shivered, unable to believe what had come to pass.

Willa was safe.

She was hurt, horribly traumatized, but alive. Matt—going against everything in him—was coming north to see his sisters. He would arrive late that night; his oyster boat pushed to the limit, it would arrive at Silver Bay marina around midnight, just after the tide change.

Kate's old family was going to be reunited for the first time in over six months. Last night, sitting by Willa's side, she had stayed in the hospital till long after visiting hours. Willa had sobbed quietly, telling Kate the story of what had happened.

"I was staying at the East Wind," she said. "It was so beautiful there, and I swear all I could think of was you coming up . . . me begging you to forgive me . . ."

"You wouldn't have had to beg," Kate whispered, although she wasn't sure that was true. So much had washed away these last six months; all the hurt and rage had leeched out, leaving nothing but love and forgiveness for her little sister.

"I would have anyway," Willa said stubbornly. "I would have taken you to lunch in Hawthorne, to see the American Impressionists in Black Hall . . . we would have walked together out to the lighthouse," she said, shuddering.

"Don't talk about it," Kate urged, stroking her hair.

"I want to," Willa said. "I sent you that postcard, and I felt so free. I didn't have the nerve to ask you outright . . . but I hoped. I thought . . . she'll come. I'll see her soon. And I checked out, thinking I'd just go to Newport for a few days. Bonnie and I would bide our time, wait for you to come north."

She had headed east, checked into the Seven Chimneys Inn, then driven up to New Bedford to the whaling museum.

"I remembered that time on Matt's boat," Willa said. "When we saw the mother whale."

"I thought you did," Kate said, knowing she had been right. She had smuggled Bonnie into the hospital, and the Scottie, over-joyed at seeing her mistress, lay blissfully across Willa's lap while the nurses all pre-tended not to see.

"The museum was great . . . spent hours there. Then I grabbed a bite to eat across the bridge."

"In Fairhaven."

"Yes. And I needed gas for the ride home. So I . . ."

"Went to the Texaco station."

"At the convenience store."

Willa nodded. "I saw a van drive out from behind the long building. I thought I recog-nized it, from Connecticut . . . the son of the people who owned the inn."

"Caleb."

"Yes. I didn't quite know his name, al-though we had waved to each other, and once . . ." she hesitated, reddening as if the memory still caused her shame. "Once I thought he was watching me in the shower. When I came out, he was pretending to replace a lightbulb. I should have told his mother. Or left right away . . ."

"But it might not have mattered anyway," Kate said soothingly, "because you met up with him again."

"Yes," Willa said, shivering. "Right there in Fairhaven."

"Fairhaven," Kate said, thinking it was such a pretty name for the place where such a terrible thing happened.

Caleb had told Willa he was having van trouble, asked her to follow him to the highway. He'd led her the back way, pulled over at a rest stop. When he'd gotten out of his van, she hadn't been upset or scared. But then he'd opened her door and let Bonnie loose—to run into the woods.

Willa had started to scream and run after the dog, but he'd forced her into his van.

"He had a knife, and he handcuffed me," she sobbed, bending down to bury her face in her dog's black fur. "I knew he could kill me, but all I could think of was Bonnie . . . of her thinking I'd abandoned her, wondering whether I was coming back. During that horrible time, when . . ." she trailed off, unable, yet, to talk about what had happened, "I never, never thought I'd see her again."

"I came looking for you," Kate said, touching her hand. "And I found her."

"Thank you . . . I never thought I'd see *you* again . . ."

"Oh, Willa," Kate whispered. "I'd never be able to let you go."

"I thought I had disappeared forever," Willa sobbed. "And I thought maybe you'd want me to."

"Because of you and Andrew," Kate had said, nodding. "For a while, I wanted you to. I was so angry with you, Willa. For falling for him—He should never have done what he did. You're my sister. He came between us."

"I let him! It wasn't all his fault."

"I know. And I was upset with you. But that's over now. Andrew is in the past. I love someone else now."

"I know," Willa had whispered. "And I know who it is . . ."

Now, sitting with John, Kate remembered Willa's words and felt a sharp chill run down her spine. Kate had strung the airplane charm onto a length of string, and she'd tied it around her neck to remind her of the people she loved, of how she had nearly lost both of them.

Brainer and Bonnie sat beneath the

Judge, hoping for scraps to fall from the carving platter. Outside, the sun began to set. It was just dark enough for the beacon to switch on, for the lighthouse beam to make its first sweep of the sky. Kate swallowed, feeling the chill in her bones and hands. Somehow she had found it in herself to wield two weapons and kill two men.

She had had nightmares since that night—woken up screaming, crying for help. Last night John, sleeping down the hall in his own bed, had rushed into the guest room, limping along on his bad leg, and sat beside Kate—holding her tight until she'd stopped crying and Caleb's and Beckwith's faces had faded.

He had touched her cheeks so softly, drying her tears.

"He called it 'the secret hour,'" she'd gasped. "That's what he told Willa."

"No, Kate," John had said. "It was just nine o'clock. That's all it was. The secret hour is ours . . . by the brook. Remember? The beautiful brook in the orchard."

"The west-running brook," Kate had whispered, feeling her heart begin to calm. "Where we stood with the dogs."

"Do you know how glad I am to have you

here?" he'd whispered. "How much I never want you to leave?"

She had nodded, touching his hand, feeling him kiss her lips, wanting more than anything to make love with him, to feel their bodies come together. "I want to stay," she had said in a low voice.

"You do? Even after everything—after me being Merrill's lawyer, bringing Beckwith into town . . ."

She had shaken her head, impatient, as if none of that mattered anymore. "Don't you understand?" she asked. "That wasn't you . . . you were just doing your job. Defending the principles you believe in. But we're meant to be together, John. Everything tells me that. We keep going against the grain."

"From that time in Fairhaven . . . and you showing up at the lighthouse to save my life."

"We're like your west-running brook," she'd said, clutching his hand. "Going against everything in nature, running from the sea . . ."

"To be together," he had said, taking her in his arms, kissing her deeply.

"Everyone have what they need?" the

Judge asked now, looking around the room and shaking Kate out of her memory of last night.

"We should all be at the same table," Maeve said, casting a disapproving glance at the sofa. It was her, Teddy, and the Judge at the kitchen table, Maggie, John, and Kate on the sofa.

"Dad has to keep his leg extended," Teddy explained gently.

"Christmas at the big table," the Judge promised. "All of us. Willa, too."

"Thanks," Kate said, smiling across the counter. The Judge nodded back, his eyes eloquent with emotion.

"You're welcome," he said, raising a glass in the air. "And here's to the young lady who saved my son's life."

"To Kate, to Kate," all the O'Rourkes and Maeve said, clinking glasses of cider and wine. Kate smiled and said, "And to all of you." Everyone nodded and drank.

"But wait," Maggie said, clunking her glass down and turning to look Kate sternly in the eyes.

"What, Maggie?" Kate asked.

"You STILL haven't finished answering my question," Maggie said reproachfully.

"I think she has," John said quickly.

"Remind me . . ." Kate said, smiling, to tease John.

"Okay. Who's the other person you loved enough to defend?" Maggie asked. "At the lighthouse?"

Kate just smiled. Maggie would have to wait a little longer for her to say the words out loud. Outside, the lighthouse beam flashed across the darkening sky, guiding sailors safely home from the sea. Matt was out there, and he'd follow the beacon straight to his two sisters.

Maggie's question hung in the air. Kate squeezed John's hand, and as their eyes met and held, she knew they had both learned a lot about finding what they'd thought they'd lost, about hearts that they had both sworn could never open again, about a time that was theirs alone.

It was the apogee. The tide was high, and Kate's heart was full.

The secret hour was here, right now.

about the author

Luanne Rice is the author of *The Secret Hour, True Blue, Summer Light, Safe Harbor, Firefly Beach, Dream Country, Follow the Stars Home, Cloud Nine, Home Fires, Secrets of Paris, Stone Heart, Angels All Over Town, Crazy In Love* (made into a TNT Network feature film), and *Blue Moon* (made into a CBS television film) She lives in New York City and Old Lyme, Connecticut.